THE DOLL FUNERAL

The Doll Funeral

KATE HAMER

FABER & FABER

First published in 2017
by Faber & Faber Ltd
Bloomsbury House
74–77 Great Russell Street
London WC1B 3DA

Typeset by Faber & Faber Ltd
Printed and bound by CPI Group (UK) Ltd, Croydon CR0 4YY

Epigraph: Sylvia Plath, 'Morning Song' from *Collected Poems* © the
Estate of Sylvia Plath, 1960, 1965, 1971, 1981, 1989.
Used by permission of Faber & Faber Ltd.

A CIP record for this book
is available from the British Library

ISBN 978–0–571–31385–3

FSC
www.fsc.org

MIX
Paper from
responsible sources
FSC® C020471

2 4 6 8 10 9 7 5 3 1

For Mark

... even through the hollow eyes of death
I spy life peering.

Shakespeare, *Richard II*, 2.1.270–1

Love set you going like a fat gold watch.

Sylvia Plath, 'Morning Song'

I

CAKE
20 *August 1983*

My thirteenth birthday and I became a hunter for souls.

I knew the moment that Mum called me something was going to happen. I heard it in her voice.

'Ruby . . .'

The open eye of the hall mirror watched as I came downstairs humming a nervous tune, my yolk yellow birthday blouse done right up to the neck and my brown cord skirt flicking against a knee scab.

The light from the open kitchen doorway, where my parents waited, puddled onto the dirty carpet in the hall.

On the Formica table was the birthday cake. It had white icing and Smarties. A big triangle wedge had been cut out and the sharp carving knife lay close by, pointing into the gap.

I blinked. I'd expected punishment for some minor crime committed, a cup broken or left unwashed. The back door left open or closed or whichever way my father currently ordained its status. But instead my mum and dad had turned into dolls or puppets, or so it seemed. Hard lines had appeared, running from their noses to their chins. Mum's cheeks were blotched with anxious red paint, corkscrew curls exploding from her head. Dad was strung stiffly behind her in his grey felt jacket. His arm came up and swiped at his nose. Mum jiggled, her shoes clacking menacingly on the lino.

Her jaw opened. 'Ruby. Now, we don't want you to create a scene or start trouble but it's time you knew.'

From behind her Dad said, in that furred-up voice of someone who's kept quiet for a bit, 'Yes. Thirteen is old enough.'

Between us the Smarties had started to leak sharp colours as if they'd flown and got trapped there and were now slowly bleeding to death.

'Ruby, there's something we've been keeping from you all these years,' Mum said. She paused then spoke in a rush. 'It's that you are not our natural child. We didn't give birth to you.'

'Which explains a lot—'

His voice got snapped off by my mother. 'Stop it, just for this once, Mick. Leave the girl alone.' She turned to me. 'Ruby, you were adopted when you were four months old. You are not our child – d'you hear me?' She turned. 'Honestly, Mick, I don't think she's taking it in.'

But I was.

I ran into the garden and sang for joy.

I burst out of the back door under a thunderous sky and air the colour of dark butter. Out, out into the waist-high grass. Beyond the garden, trees shaded the distance. This time, I ignored the Shadow sitting by the back door – and I launched off the step on tight sprung legs, running down the overgrown path with my hair flying in a wave behind and my arms outstretched to feel the feather tops of the grasses snaking under my palms. I glimpsed red, the corner of the toy ride-on plastic bus half embedded in the tangled growth, and the arm of a doll, its chubby fingers pointing straight up to a sky of seething grey scribble.

Tall spikes of evening primroses glowing the brightest yellow punched up from the grass as I waded to the middle where I stood and sniffed at the sweet dust of pollen on my hands. Then, arms raised, I started my song to the storm clouds.

'*There's a brown girl in the ring, tra-la-la-la-la. There's a brown girl in the ring, tra-LA-la-la-la-la.*'

And it must have been my tenth or maybe twelfth time, '*She looks like a sugar and a plum, plum, plum,*' when Mick's voice crackled a cold path out from the back door.

'Ruby. Stop that and get back in here, *now*.'

I dragged my feet all the way back up the path. Just inside the doorway his fist jumped out like a snake and cracked my head.

'Sit down,' he said.

I scuttled away and sat on the other side of the table, holding my head.

'Dear, dear,' Barbara muttered. She looked subdued, as if they'd been arguing while I'd been outside. 'Dear God.' She sat and folded her arms. 'Ruby, you were only a tiny baby when you came to us,' she said. 'It's hard to think of that now.'

'So, smaller than . . .'

'Yes,' she said quickly.

'But not *like* her,' said Mick.

Their daughter. Trudy. She died when she was three. Except Mick always called her 'sweet pea'. When he got drunk he cried for her – big drops of tears slid down his face and dripped on his jacket.

'No. You were small . . .' Mum said. 'But strong.'

'A whiner,' Dad interrupted. He was fiddling round with the gas stove now so he had his back to us. He struck a match to light the flame under the kettle and the sulphur smell took to the air. Three-quarters on from behind I could still see the quiff sticking out like a horn from his head. Now he was not so close I dared to release the protecting fingers laced around my skull although my temple still throbbed.

Mum's face looked strained under her mop of hair. So Trudy went and what she got was me, always falling down or causing trouble.

'Was I born here? Here in the forest, I mean?' The idea I could have come from anywhere else seemed strange and improbable.

The Forest of Dean. Here we lived in one of a row of small stone cottages with trees stretching over us like children doing ghost impressions with their hands, surrounded by closed coal mines slowly getting zipped back up into the earth.

Barbara screwed up her eyes as if she was looking, trying to see me being born in the distance. She nodded, like she'd caught a glimpse of it. 'Yes, you were.'

'What about my name?' I asked.

'Flood is ours but Ruby was the name you came with,' she said. 'When you were little you thought it was because of . . .'

Without thinking my hand flew to the birthmark covering the left side of my face.

'I know.'

4

Mick started picking Smarties off the cake so Mum snatched it up and carried it to the sink.

'Well, that's over,' she muttered, examining the pits the Smarties had left.

'But, but . . . nothing else?'

'No, not really.' She let out a breathy sigh and the cake wobbled in her hands. 'That's all.'

'Can I do my wish again?'

'Why, what was wrong with the last one?'

'I didn't say it properly,' I lied.

'Go on then. Mick, give her the matches.'

I arranged the yellow candles, their heads already bubbled from burning, and touched a match with its little ball of flame to each one and closed my eyes and wished and wished and wished. The twin stars of my real parents orbited my head, blinking on and off.

'Come and get me,' I whispered.

The Shadow from the back door had moved to the stairs now, his boy shape hunched over. He made way for me as I sat beside him and whispered, 'Guess what? Mick and Barbara are not my real mum and dad.' The curled bones of an ear brushed against my lips and I thought I felt him shiver in excitement.

Then I shut myself in the bathroom and ran the bath so hot it gauzed the walls in steam. I imagined my real parents appearing to me through the white clouds. My mother looked like me but with an arctic sparkle of glamour. My father had the same crow's wing hair as mine and a belted raincoat like the men wore in old films. I reached out to touch but my finger made them explode into a hundred droplets that fell in rain back into the bath, so I opened the tap to make more steam.

'Come and find me,' I begged again, hugging my wet knees to my chest.

'Ruby.' I wondered how long Mick had been behind the door, lurking. 'You seem to be using an awful lot of hot water. That sounded like a fiver's worth that just went in then.'

'Sorry, sorry,' I called, holding my cheeks so he couldn't hear my smile.

I'd always been a scavenger of small things. The glittering dust mote I reached up and tried to grab. The layers of shadow in the corner like piled clothes on a chair. Sliding my hands under rugs for what might be living there. Grubbing in the dirt for treasure.

But that night I became a proper hunter. Of true family. Of the threads that ghosts leave behind.

Of lost souls.

2

2 January 1970

Anna takes the turn up to the main road. It's a bright day and the sky appears eternally high as it always does in winter when it's clear and blue.

Fear quickens her step. There's been no period for – how long – she counts out loud – seven, eight weeks? Is it her imagination but does she feel a little swollen already; her flat stomach curving out slightly, visible from the side, like the bulbing of a convex mirror? She's convinced that she can feel something tiny but determined clamping onto her insides, sticking there, strong and hardy.

She shoves her hands deep in her pockets as she passes the telegraph pole and the shed by the side of the road. The copper beech is winter threadbare now. Old Turner used to be there every day with his fold-out chair and thermos. He'd built the shed himself – back in the day, back at the dawn of time. He puttered about on the common land, growing potatoes, swedes, cabbages, half of which he gave away. Nobody cared: things were freer like that when Anna was a child. Today there'd probably be a council eviction for building without planning. Now the structure looks ready to collapse so she sidesteps it in case it happens the moment she passes.

She walks faster, making her boots ring out on the road

7

and swinging her arms vigorously beside her. Perhaps she can break the thing loose, shake it out from its soft, pink nest. She starts trotting, purposely banging the soles of her feet onto the rough country road so the vibrations jar through her body; as the hill steepens she turns the trot into a run – a hobbled movement because of her skirt. At the top of the valley road she stops, cheeks flushed, out of breath, and looks out at the forest below. Bare branches bend and creak in the breeze. She checks her body again, exploring her stomach in its pencil skirt with her fingers. No, it's still there; she knows it'll take much more than a brisk run to break this loose. It's much stronger than she is.

3

MADE FLESH
23 August 1983

I felt sure, the more I thought of it (and that's about all I'd been thinking of since my birthday), that my real parents did not want to give me up. I expected that went double for my mother because mothers shouldn't want to give their children away. I refused to believe it could've been easy. There must have been a reason for it, something completely terrible. They'd chosen my name, Ruby, and – the way I saw it – why would you choose a name like that for a child you didn't want?

Three nights after my birthday the moon rose as fat as a peach. I watched it from my window turn the forest canopy into a shifting silver sea. Now I had a name for the big white emptiness burning like a desert inside. It was called 'Mum and Dad' and tonight it felt bad enough for my bones to crack.

Anything seemed possible in this light. My real parents, *my flesh and blood*, could be near, even living right here in the Forest of Dean. I just needed a way to find them.

I left the pillow bunched in my bed, took the pillowcase with me and crept through the moonlit spaces of the house. On the bookshelf were two books from my gran – an aged one that used to belong to her – *Pilgrim's Progress* – and the *Alice's Adventures in Wonderland* she'd given me for

9

my ninth birthday. I had the idea to open one on a chance page and see if somehow there might be a message from her there within the story. I hesitated, then picked *Alice* thinking even at that moment I'd probably chosen badly with these tales of disappearing cats and lizard gardeners. I put it in my pillowcase sack. I found the same sharp kitchen knife that had diced up my birthday cake and took it. As I left the house I used it to delicately fillet some ears of barley from the dusty flower display under the mirror in the hall and dropped them in the sack among the other things – a ball of red wool, some horse chestnuts, rags.

The flowers of the evening primroses were wide open and floated pale above the grasses. The back gate creaked on its hinges. It led directly into the trees. As I glided through the forest in my plain white nightie I thought, with my sack and this knife sticking out in front of me, if anyone sees me they'll think I'm a robber, and it made me brave, this looking-like-a-robber-girl and the belief that I could strike fear into the hearts of others.

Murderer, though. Murderer too, walking through the dark with a knife and sack. The badness in me rose up and made me think I could be a murderer. The knife began to bounce and wobble in my hand so I carefully dropped it into the pillowcase, hoping the blade wouldn't slice right through and cut my legs.

I walked deeper then stopped by a tree whose outline had something human about it – its slender trunk – and I put both hands there. I caressed the sandpapery bark; it felt like an ash – us foresters know how to tell trees so well I could do it even in this light. Despite the night the air was warm and soft. I sat cross-legged under the tree and unpacked my pillowcase among the saplings that grew haphazardly wherever seeds had landed: some forcing their way, springing up from the ground even where there was hardly any light at all. The forest was a strong body pushing out life wherever it could. I put everything out on the smooth white of the pillowcase one by one: the ears of barley; horse chestnuts from my bedside drawer; torn-up grass; cloth and red wool from Barbara's workbox.

When my gran was still alive she'd shown me things behind the others' backs. She'd drop a leaf into the stew when Grandad wasn't looking and wink – a quick sly movement. Girls came to see her sometimes, always when Grandad was out. For girls who wanted to catch pregnant she'd make miniature babies out of string and straw for them to drop in their pockets and keep there, secretly. That's what had given me the idea. She called it 'invoking' and said it had to be kept quiet because Grandad would disapprove. Everything you'd ever need was right here in the forest, she said – she'd never been away, not even as far as Gloucester. She died outside her cottage underneath the sycamore tree. They found her like a fallen doll against the trunk and said how sad it was she died alone. I think she'd decided it that way. There were sycamore keys in her hair. She had a lapful of them as if she might have to try a hundred different doors to find where to go next.

When I was little I used to copy her. I'd bunch leaves and herbs together and mutter over them. I'd put a stone by the door for evil wishers to stumble on. Then I was only playing, but tonight I felt life tingle in my fingertips as though if I stuck a branch in the ground it might spurt green leaves.

The knife winked as I lifted it up.

'This is the third time of asking.' I didn't like the way my voice sounded so small among the trees. I cleared my throat and started again, addressing the canopy and the moon's rays slanting through.

'This is the third time of asking. I'm here, now, invoking Ruby's real parents. After this, I'm not going to try again. After this, if you don't come for me I'll know I'm on my own for ever. Just a sign will do – something to show me you *might* come, not now but one day.'

The moon had risen so high and bright above the trees I could see everything clearly, better than day even; the moon was an x-ray that could show right through to the forest's bones. I started work: finding sticks from the ground and weaving them together with the red wool. Barley hands that looked like paddles on the ends of the four thin twig arms. I split horse chestnuts and popped out the gleaming conkers from inside for heads. Grass for hair. As I sewed the needle flashed quick and bright, in and out of the soft torn-up sheet I'd scavenged. I snipped and stitched into the night until I had two figures stuck into the ground on their single leg. Pegged out, they struck me more as crucifixes than dolls. The soft white rags meant to be clothes seemed to transform into limp white hanging bodies.

I leaned against the tree and opened *Alice in Wonderland* on my knees. There was Alice, falling head first down the hole. I frowned; what kind of sign was this? A horrible fall. I shut it quickly.

'For the last time. Come to me, Mum and Dad. You left me here with people who do not care for me. Well, Barbara is not so bad, I suppose, sometimes.'

I stopped, wondering what would happen if my parents really did come. I'd imagined a procession of birthday cakes, for all the years they'd missed: starting at age one – that would be small, pink and round – and ending at thirteen. The one with thirteen candles would be the most magnificent: gilded, topped with jewelled fruits in the glow of soft flame. But, for the first time I wondered about Barbara. Would I ever get to see her again?

I sighed. 'But she does what Mick says mostly.'

There was the rustling of the trees around me, the occasional scuffling of a small animal.

'These people are not my flesh. They are not my blood.'

I stopped and listened again. Everything seemed to have fallen silent.

'Rescue me,' I said, 'please rescue me. I don't know why you left me when I was a baby but I know it would have been a good reason. But now you have to come and get me back. You are my family.'

Finally, I leaned against the tree and felt the scratch of it on my face, and as the moonlight swelled, the two faces seemed to flash out at me, once, like in a horror film, before everything grew dark and shrank.

When I woke I stirred and flexed my shoulders, stiff from sleeping against the tree all night. A shower of leaves fell off my head.

Something yellow was flickering through the trees. It took a moment to recognise it as torchlight. I flattened myself against the tree trunk as I heard voices behind the lights – one was Mick's, I knew, and I almost stopped breathing for what seemed an age. By the time the torches were switched off the moon had gone and a thin, greenish light filtered down through the branches and fell on the tumbled objects in front of me. A breeze rifled the pages of the book and an insect that looked like a flea bounced across the paper with a pock pock sound.

Somehow it was worse without the torches. I could picture them stalking through the early light using their dark-adapted eyes to find me.

Something wound across at the corner of my eye, a slow worm, the early warmth rousing it. It crunched leaves as it moved and the crisped leaves rose in a tide either side of its thick grey body, then it curled in between the two stick figures making the man list to one side.

Then into the quiet, close by, came crashing, the sounds of bracken and fallen branches being climbed over or kicked aside.

'Oh, no,' I breathed, my heels pushing into the soft earth as I tried to flatten myself against the trunk.

Too late. Despite the dawn the beam got switched on again and pointed straight in my eyes. Behind it the outline of a tall man loomed. I recognised the lumpy shape of him. It was a neighbour who lived the other end of the row to us.

'Mick, I've found her. She's over here.' The torchlight wobbled away from my face as he turned to speak. He sounded eager, like he felt he'd done well.

'Mick. She's here, she's here,' the neighbour called again, shining the light straight into my face.

More crashing to my left. Then the walk slowed, became lighter, a confident step, a step of one who can relax now because the chase is over. The lights got switched off again. The morning struck harder through the ceiling of the forest, sickly pale but suddenly clean and clear on the rubbish of objects before me.

'A cheap trick.' Mick was panting slightly as he approached. The shape of him struck me as a giant who'd been made small. 'An old trick – a pillow in the bed. Why you thought that would work when you left the back gate swinging open I don't know.

'And there she is.' He slid his index fingers in the front pockets of his jeans and stuck out his hips. 'We thought we'd been turned over. We thought burglars might still be in the house, hiding.' He looked down. 'What's all this?'

He put out his toe and stirred everything on the ground in front of me. I saw them through his eyes. Something had happened to the figures overnight. I'd glimpsed their turning transformation before I'd gone to sleep and now it was complete. They had become hideous – their mouths grinning in their conker faces, their grass hair matted and wild. They looked like a species between apes and humans that hadn't been discovered yet. The hair of the man's head fell off like a miniature wig leaving his shiny conker skull exposed.

'What in God's name?' said Mick and an expression of disgust ate up all his features.

4

MONSTER
24 August 1983

As Mick marched me through the back garden his mood felt enough to make the shirts hanging on the line snap and clap their cuffs together.

Inside, his temper took the form of bees. Attack bees, buzzing at the bottom of the stairs. I could almost hear them from my bedroom. The magic of the night before: only a thin vapour trail of it remained, hovering above the ruin of the garden I could see from my window. It was early; the sun hadn't yet risen above the darkness of the trees opposite. When it did the vapour would burn away completely.

Out there, in the old days, Mick had grown sweet peas for his real daughter, for his little Trudy, or so I'd been told. Neighbours still gave him sweet peas in memory of her and sometimes he'd come home with one in his buttonhole. The white with a lip of palest green were his favourite. The sweet scent wafted through the house smelling of Trudy's ghost until I felt her frilled face, tinged with green, might show up in the hall. Like her, no trace of them remained. All submerged now under grasses and tall yellow weeds.

Downstairs, the attack bees were threatening to make their way up. I padded across the floor and cracked the door open.

'Hello,' I called, through the gap.

Sudden silence. Against the door my breath rasped against the wood. 'Barbara, are you there?' I could hear the tremor in my voice. 'I said . . .'

'Ruby, get down here now.'

That was him.

The two of them were dark shapes against the light that fell through the glass crescent of the door. One creature almost, one half of its head with curls exploding sideways.

The head divided. 'Look at you,' said Dad.

I looked down – there was mud across the front of my nightie and dirt wedged between my toes.

'Mikey, Mick, really . . .' Barbara pressed her fingers into her stomach, kneading the small pouch of her belly.

He put a foot on the bottom of the stairs. 'Shut the fuck up,' he said. Around his mouth and nose was mottling white and purple like cut raw beef, marbled with fat. I knew this look. When it came – slaps could too, like birds' wings flapping at my head.

Most children I knew got their backsides tanned once in a while. This was different. One day, I knew, it'd end up killing me. I walked with death shuffling in its strange boots alongside me. Sometimes it was far behind. Other times, like now, it was so close it looked out of Mick's raw beef face. It was saying in Mick's voice, 'So help me God. So help me God.'

'Mikey, calm yourself.' Barbara reached up her arms towards me like she was inviting me to run into them.

He turned and batted her outstretched hand away so it bounced against the banister.

'You leave her alone,' I said, but I only whispered it. He didn't hear.

17

'Tell me what you were doing out there.' He was yelling now. 'Go on tell me. Always running away.' He was on the third step now. 'Always Jesus bastard trouble.'

'Nothing.' I started to cry. 'Please, Dad. Don't. I wasn't doing anything.'

'A loony. It must be in the genes.' Sixth step. 'Go on, enlighten us, Ruby. Tell us what you were doing at four o'clock in the morning with one of your gran's shitty old books.'

'Nothing.'

'Was it voodoo?'

When he reached the seventh step I started crying harder. He paused. 'Shut up.'

'Please. Please be nice to me.'

He stopped as if in amazement. 'I am. It's you that's the problem, not me.'

'I want my real mum and dad to come and get me,' I sobbed through the snot. 'They must be better than you. I hate you. I hate you.' The words must have been heavy. Their weight fell down the stairs and banged into him. He staggered then righted himself.

The three of us seemed to freeze for a long moment and the peaceful sound of birdsong penetrated the hall.

'Did you hear that, Babs?' He turned his face to her, mock quizzical. 'What d'you think of that then, Babs? See. I told you. She's got a screw loose. Not right here.' He jabbed his finger into his forehead. A red mark stayed where his finger had been. 'Ungrateful cow.'

'Mick, stop it,' she warned, but he was coming faster now. I ran for my room, hearing his footsteps ring on the stairs behind me. I slammed the door in his face, some mad hope flashing that his nose might stick in there like an axe so he'd be pinioned, useless and swinging.

Instead the door opened and he stepped inside.

The colour in his face was darker. It frightened me. The bees must be inside him now. His body seemed to bulge outwards in places where they swarmed. I heard rapid footsteps and his quiff sticking out in a curled spike filled my vision. Over his shoulder I glimpsed Shadow in the corner jumping with fear, or excitement, as I fell backwards.

Downstairs I could hear Mum wailing, 'Oh Mick, Michael, be careful. Don't go too far now.'

She sounded far away. I must be falling down the rabbit hole, I thought, as I always knew I would one day, ever since I saw the picture. You're not falling, though, you're rising, Ruby. You've got it the wrong way round because, look – there's both of us from up above. Look, look how his fists are going in and out like little jackhammers working. See how his shirt has pulled out of his trousers with all the effort. See how Ruby's fingers are getting busted because she's covering up her head with them. Ruby's father, he intends to mash her into paste this time and smear her across the walls until she is no more. Maybe there'll be just an eye stuck to the wall watching him as he goes to bed tonight that he'll pluck off and lob out of the window like a golf ball. The eye will lie there looking upwards until it grows quite, quite dim and switches off . . .

I sat up with a gasp. At my bedroom window the net curtains, with a pattern of flowers, blew softly. The sun, above the trees now, speared beams through the lace spreading orange daisies across the room. My arms and legs weren't paste, at least. I could still move them although they felt hard and stiff.

The doorknob turned and I flattened myself against the wall.

Barbara poked her head inside. 'Christ, Ruby.' Her hands flew to her face and they looked like little kitten paws nuzzling each cheek. She bit at her lips, getting pink lipstick over her teeth. 'Christ, Christ. I . . .'

'My face is mashed. My face is mashed,' I shouted out of my lopsided mouth. 'And you just left me alone.' I staggered to the bed and crawled inside.

She sat on the bed, her bony knees pointing upwards. 'If I'd thought it was as bad as that I'd have . . .'

'Stop it.' I buried myself deep inside the covers. There was a long pause and then a click of the door shutting.

She came back with two bowls on a tray. One was warm water covered by a flannel, the other Heinz oxtail soup.

'Soup?' I lisped, pointing to my mouth. 'It'll all run out again if I try and eat that.'

She hesitated, balancing the tray in her hands. 'Yes, I see your point,' she said, setting the tray down on the bedside table, and something cracked a little inside me because I knew she was trying to do something kind, as best she could.

'Can I see my face?' I asked.

'I don't think it'll help.'

I sat up. 'Please. I need to check I've got all my teeth.'

Barbara took a gold compact from the pocket of her blue gingham house dress with collars the size of a baby elephant's ears. All her clothes were from the nineteen sixties. She'd never bought newer styles and when I'd once asked her why she said because they 'reminded her of better days'.

I hadn't seen the compact before. I studied the pink enamel flower on the top before opening it with a click and bringing it to my face. An eye – strangely folded in on itself so the lashes stuck straight out like a tiny broom had been embedded there. I snapped the compact shut.

'I'll not stand for it, Ruby. I've just told him that. Dear God, a slap is one thing. Everyone gets a slap from time to time – but he should see a doctor for doing this. Honest to God, damn him. Damn him.' She squeezed out the flannel in the warm water and handed it to me. 'Here, use this.'

Downstairs, the front door slammed and she forked her fingers in a V sign towards it.

Later, the pain kicked in as I knelt in front of the Sindy house. It comforted me still, sometimes, to play with them. A neighbour had given it to me whose daughter had grown too old for dolls. Sindy was jointed in sixteen places and had a boyfriend doll called Paul. I too had outgrown them because my play had changed. I now arranged for them to have little accidents about the house – a trip and a tumble down the stairs, or Sindy's head stuck in the oven while Paul stood outside and watched her through the window.

I opened the front door to the house and peered inside. Paul and Sindy were sitting at the table.

'Catastrophe,' I called through the door, and my voice vibrated the cardboard walls.

It felt like I'd been cracked open like an egg. I needed to do something. If I didn't this time, I knew somehow my cracks were never going to heal.

So I sat cross-legged and, with the dolls staring wide-eyed, began to think.

5

Anna's yellow patent shoe with its squared toe and chunky heel looks shiny and unnatural on the forest path.

She is alone.

Childhood stories have left her with a sense that every journey through the forest is an epic one, fraught with potential danger and adventure. She's never lost that feeling. She has it now even though she's only on her way to work.

Her job in the chemist's entails handing out bottles and packets of medication. Sweet-scented talcum powder in flowered tins. Bagging up Pears soap and cough drops and suggesting a bright pink ointment for a graze. It wasn't supposed to last for ever. It was for now until she'd decided. Perhaps she'd train to be a nurse? She even harboured a strong hankering to be the real pharmacist with her own room at the back of the shop, filling out all the prescriptions – although this would almost be putting herself on a par with a doctor and feels quite impossible.

All these options have melted away.

She looks into the shadowy depths of the trees. They'd done it out here too. They'd done it wherever they could find a place. The trees had kept their secret, though now that secret was growing day by day. Looking up once with him inside her the dizzying web of branches and leaves seemed to circle in joy like a carousel. Now they remind her of tall gallows.

She stops for a moment, transfixed, then shivers violently and hurries on.

6

THE SHIRT
31 August 1983

The idea came beautifully quickly. As all good ideas do.

By the stove was the matchbox and the little pink heads inside began calling to me as if they had tiny squeaky voices. Mick's favourite shirt was tangled with other clothes in the yellow plastic wash basket. I stuffed it up my jumper and left with the matches in my pocket just pausing to get paraffin from the shed.

In the safety of the forest the paraffin-soaked shirt lit quickly. Soon it was a burning man – a burning Mick – the arms lashing about on the bare earth as if in pain. It blackened and crumbled and fell away. I stood transfixed, the smoking match still in hand, until I noticed the holly bush to my side shaking.

'Who's there?'

A small figure in denim shorts wriggled out, yelping with pain from the prickles of the holly. It was Joe from three doors down, eight years old. I was the eldest of the children on the street. In the mornings a row of little eyes followed me as I went one way to big school and they went the other to their small one. Joe, like the others, looked like a forest child, with scratched legs and slightly greasy hair.

'A holly bush isn't a good place to hide,' I said.

He stood there chewing and the sweet smell of Bazooka bubble gum wafted over.

'What are you doing?' he asked finally.

'I'm burning my dad's shirt because I hate him, but you mustn't tell. Promise.'

He blew a large pink bubble and when it burst peeled it from his face and poked it back inside his mouth.

'I won't. My mam says it's criminal what he does to you.'

I shivered and pulled my sleeves further down in case any bruises were showing.

'Go on, get off home and don't forget to keep your mouth shut.' As he ran I stamped on the ashes and a wave of fear passed through me that almost knocked me over. I felt about five again hearing Mick's key rattling in the lock.

I fixed on the charred remains in front of me and breathed hard. This day will ever be known as 'the day of the burning shirt', I said to the trees. The plastic buttons were still there, but disfigured from the flame, and as I ground them into the earth with my foot I noticed the metal collar tips had survived the fire. They were still hot to the touch and burned my fingers as I put them in my pocket.

As I replaced the matches by the stove my skin rippled all over with what I'd done. It was so simple. Only one match gone and I'd witnessed the outline of Mick writhing on the ground. Despite the fear, it was beautiful.

That evening I saw a goddess on TV. Her face was carved like a mask, like a Japanese warrior's, and dark hair flashed from her armpits as she moved and sang. Her name was Siouxsie Sioux, the ticker tape across the screen told me.

I stood and stared. I could never copy the popular look at school: the bright white trainers with three perfect stripes, green or red; the thin plastic Adidas jacket done up to just the right point between the breasts; the love-heart necklace that you could wear as half a jagged heart, or with the organ intact depending on your current romantic status. These precious objects would never be mine. But Siouxsie looked like she'd run this all up herself from a pair of old curtains. This was achievable.

Once again I rifled Barbara's sewing box. I laid out all my clothes on the bed. I cut holes and stitched seams tight. Chopped collars. As I sewed my needle seemed to fly.

I backcombed my hair into a wide black crown, drew black lines on my eyes and made a dark red cupid bow for lips. When I stood back to see the whole effect in the mirror my breath stopped. My birthmark – it looked as if it was supposed to be there now. As if it was *meant*, like a mask that had been made especially for me.

I looked around for the Shadow Boy to show him, the one with darkness round his mouth. He sometimes made an appearance around this time, the time when blueness began to tinge the air and clouds of rooks shook themselves out from the trees and wheeled up into the sky. His shape would spring across the room and stop at the window, but he was nowhere to be seen tonight.

Downstairs Mick had come back from the pub and had made himself a sandwich. When he saw me the sandwich stopped on the way to his mouth and the bread flopped open to show the yellow cheese inside.

'My God, I've seen it all now. Is this fright night?' He

26

looked at his watch, pretend checking the date. 'Is it Hal-loween?'

I shrugged and sat opposite, at the same time reaching into my pocket and rubbing the collar tips together between finger and thumb. They were still warm, not from the fire this time, but from my body.

7

SHADOW

Ruby.

I see you.

I watch you play.

Your dark hair swinging about. Sometimes I long for you to come and join me, but then I think – you're not possessed of two arms and legs for a lot of time. You may as well hang onto them for as long as possible and run about. I try not to let the dread envy take hold.

Your poor limbs. The one that hurts them – they say he once loved flowers. Well, now it's the flowering season for bruises. They sprout all over you. Sometimes I kick his arse for that, though, of course, he can't feel it.

I was with you tonight. I saw you stitching. Because of the danger you are in day to day I thought 'shroud' at first. Then I could see it wasn't a death garment at all and you were making new arms and legs for yourself. You were so busy you didn't notice me. What a wonderful idea, I thought. Can I do that for myself?

I looked harder again and I saw it was just clothes, not a new body you were fashioning – though you were so intent it might as well have been. I tried not to feel dejected. Sometimes I took charge of the needle and helped stitch and the thread flew then. It was better that, than trying to talk. So often I get that wrong and my voice seems just a babble, like it's full of stones and water is running through.

The thing being, with each new beating I see how your eye gets cracked a little more, the hole that lets us in. Each time new Shadows slip inside, Shadows such as me. The crack becomes wider and wider as you grow. I'm afraid one day it will form such a chasm it will swallow the rest of you up. I'm frightened for you, Ruby. I've seen how close to death you have come. How it sniffs and stalks about you when the fists begin to fly. Then we come, the lost souls leaking into your eye, finding our way in, like rain into a building that isn't sound. We swarm in and out like ants.

Sometimes too, my longing to walk the earth once more becomes too strong.

I can't help myself. I eye you up and think how it would be if I could leap inside and shove you out. I covet. How I could feel the earth again, the wind on my cheek, the soft rain on my eyelids. I drum on your pillow in the night thinking to shock you into taking flight so I can crawl into the shell that's left. I want to grab it, the suit of flesh you wear, and have it for myself. Life. Life. Life. I crave.

Then I feel ashamed and creep away. I think about the time I did walk this earth wearing my own little suit of skin and bone and only jumbled fragments remain. I feel so lost. I try to remember more.

In the meantime I spy.

Ruby Flood. I see plenty in this house. I see there are flowers in the kitchen. They're buttercups you gathered for Barbara that she's put in a jam jar on the table. You don't see how she stops and touches them, and smiles. How they light her on her way to bed.

I watch you play for now. It's time to gather strength while you can. There are beings murmuring in the trees, readying themselves. They won't hold back for ever.

8

THE YELLOW DRESS
10 September 1983

When did Shadow arrive?

He'd always been there. Sometimes he was dense as a nut and moved swiftly. Other times he drifted. Often, I could whisper in his ear and he would listen. Then he'd disappear for long weeks and I'd almost forget about him. Sometimes I wondered if he'd been my twin – if he'd slipped out behind me from the womb like black afterbirth and nobody noticed. Yes, the Shadow had always been there. If he'd jumped into the womb with me he must have grown alongside. Perhaps we'd whispered secrets to each other as we'd lain in the darkness, jokes too, though when I tried to remember them I couldn't.

The darkness round his mouth I thought was dirt – or mud perhaps – I couldn't tell.

The first proper memory of him was when I was three. He was sitting on a shelf and watching me as I scribbled on the wall with fat wax crayons. Perhaps he knew better than me the pasting I'd get for that. Perhaps that's why he'd turned up that day.

He could be an irritant too. Like today.

Saturday, and Mick's brooding was filling up the house like gas. I'd missed the beginning of term – Barbara had kept me off until the bruises faded and now they mostly had, but this beating had skewed something deeper. Sometimes it felt that I walked ever afterwards slightly listing to the left like I was permanently being knocked that way, like I carried my very own North wind beside me.

I remembered *Pilgrim's Progress* and took it outside because I still believed that books could hold clues, secret messages in their text waiting to be unscrambled. Outside two small girls from our street, Libby and Jayne, sat chalking on the ground. A tendrilled multi-coloured tide of it spread over the pavement and dripped into the road. They both wore the same grubby pink hairbands, though they weren't sisters but lived next door to each other.

Libby looked up. 'Your hair looks lovely, Rubes.'

I patted it and it felt crisp and shell-like from hairspray. 'Ta.'

'Will you do the same for us?'

'Yeah, sometime. Not now, though.' I indicated to the book to show how I had more important things to do.

'Stay and chalk with us,' said Jayne, scrunching her eyes up against the sun. She had dirty sweatbands too, round her wrists, jogger-style.

I shook my head. 'I've got to go,' I said, and left them to it.

I walked a good half mile. This time it was clover glowing purple in the feathery grasses, not the yellows of our garden. The day was hot and the smell of river water was in the air.

There were fields among the trees, and a river that I knew would end its days down in the Severn, like all water did. As I walked I kicked up clouds of seeds. I hummed along to the juicy sound of the river, a mindless droning that matched the sound of the bees being swallowed into the open mouths of flowers. On the opposite bank I could see the Shadow keeping pace with me. Today he was fluid, light – he high-stepped along, skittishly lifting his feet and, I

32

imagined, tapping at balls of clover to feel the sensation of the spheres cupping in his palms.

I turned round to check there was no one about, as I always did before I spoke to Shadow. 'Hello,' I called. 'Hello, I see you there . . .' My voice bobbed out on the water.

Shadow stopped. I saw him flatten himself behind a young tree, an ash sapling.

'Oh, please yourself then,' I said crossly and turned to go, and as I did I caught the sticky threads of thought from across the water:

I hate this place. I'll throw that book in the water I will, I'll . . .

'You'll do nothing,' I grumbled and made a chopping motion with my hand by my right ear to sever the filaments.

I walked on and he continued alongside, a dark wind flowing through the tall grasses. The big book with its cracked leather binding was getting heavy in my hand. If the Shadow wanted to play silly beggars then I'd ignore him. He'd disappear soon enough. I was used to how he sometimes swarmed over walls or moved sharply from one end of the hallway to the other – almost in an instant. Here, there was plenty to keep him entertained – he could hop along the muddy riverbank. He could skim stones across the water. But when I looked up I could see him shrinking away until he was grey among distant, ragged weeds.

'Good thing too,' I muttered to myself and sat and opened the book.

The Pilgrim's Progress, From This World to That Which is to Come, Delivered Under the Similitude of a Dream.

The pages were pocked and mouldering and the smell of

damp flew up, making me do a messy sneeze over the grass.

I wiped my nose on my sleeve then studied the black and white picture opposite this title. A man with a curly moustache rested his hand on what looked like a hollowed-out tiny mountain. On the next page was a miniature lion with the same curly hair as the man. A skull and crossbones peered out of the picture to the left as if looking for escape. In the distance a man with a large rucksack was climbing up a hill to some gates where a sun's rays stuck out straight like it was a Christmas decoration. As I turned the page a dandelion clock exploded, mixing up seeds with words. The man, I read, meets Evangelist. Evangelist's command leapt out at me:

Flee from the wrath to come.

A sound buzzed in my ears. I looked up sharply. It struck me that every blade of grass and rock had been trembling and seething in secret and had stopped when I caught them at it. I kept an eye on them for a while, my black plimsolls rearing up over the top of my book appearing far away and disconnected from the rest of my body. All quiet. I read on, scanning for more clues.

Do you see yonder shining light? He said, I think I do. Then said Evangelist, Keep the light in your eye, and go up directly thereto: so shalt thou see the gate; at which, when thou knockest, it shall be told thee what thou shalt do.

A dandelion seed drifted by and I blew at it as it passed, sending it away with its tail skittering before going back to the book. Evangelist was running from his wife and children who were crying out for him to come back, but, I read,

34

'the man put his fingers in his ears, and ran on, crying, Life! Life! Eternal life!'

I rode with Pilgrim out of Calvary. I followed him up the craggy mountain.

Without looking I knew the grasses had begun their seething again. The day around me gathered and darkened like I'd been put in a drawstring bag. For the first time I noticed the bramble growing on my side of the river and how it coiled up towards my foot. The lines of the drawings in the book were fading, growing weak and ashy, falling back into the page. Maybe it's the sunlight, I thought: after sitting on that dark dank shelf for years and years they can't stand the glare of sun; the words too, they are shrinking from it.

At first I thought it was a plane, the distant hum in the background. I checked the sky – an empty clear pale blue.

I raised my eyes. Now every leaf, every blade of grass seemed to contain within it a vibration too, singing inside themselves, wanting to sway. The stand of trees on the opposite bank was joining in.

The car that jerked out of the horizon was dark and frantic like a crazed black beetle. It disappeared into the mouth of the trees. A crash came, unexpectedly small, far off, like a joke quarry boom in a cartoon.

I stood and the book fell, sending up a mushroom cloud of seeds. Hot air sucked at the grasses. The sky seemed to make a groaning sound, and lower itself a notch. I waded through the cold water on shaking legs, my feet slipping on the unseen rocks below, and scrabbled up the roots the other side then ran, scrambling through the buddleia on the bank.

At the scene the car was upside down and jammed into a tree. If it was a beetle it was one whose back had got cracked. There was a 'phut phut' of turning wheels slowly grinding to a stop. I could see the gouge it had made in the earth. The nose of the car wedged up against a tree that was half bent over from the impact so it pointed into the distance. Occasionally, there was the hiss of steam or a clunk of grating metal as the car lurched, settling into position. Inside I could see something, swaying, dark. A clawing sickness gathered in my throat and the sky swayed lower again.

Then silence. The wheels stopped turning. There was a smell, though – tough and acrid. It smelled of black things – grease and tyres, plastic bubbling. My feet tangled with each other as I approached, and I felt that North wind blowing, making me walk almost sideways in its teeth. Inside, a woman in a butter yellow dress hung upside down from the harness of the safety belt. A black stream of hair dangled, covering her face. The tips brushed the roof of the car.

A revulsion turned over in me. This thing was horrible with its bush of hair going the wrong way. I staggered, my foot catching on a knot of grass so I touched against the flank of the car, felt its hot metal against my side.

Death crawled out of her. I saw it happen. It came out of the window in its buttercup dress. It lay down on the ivy on the forest floor and fell into the ground. The shields of ivy leaves shone bright for a moment against the yellow.

The wind blew me like it would a leaf. It blew me past a tree and I reached out and encircled it with my arms and put my cheeks against its rough bark. Oak. I knew its roots were deep. The leaves reached over me, spreading, safe. I clung on.

Shadow pushed thought bubbles into my head.

There's nothing we can do.

We ought to go.

We mustn't tell.

9

SHADOW

See, I knew that they would come – the lost souls. They don't need much encouragement, I should know. That was the murmuring in the trees. 'I was here first,' I want to say, but they wouldn't take much notice of a little sprat like me.

She tried it first with me, you know.

Goodness, she gave me quite a fright. I turned around and there she was standing right next to me, barefoot and in a yellow dress. 'I'm Anna,' she said.

'Sweetheart,' she went on. 'Go and fetch Ruby for me, will you? There's things I need to tell her.'

I ran away.

It was the first time I'd seen anyone my side standing so close. It gave me quite a shock. I didn't know what she wanted either – to bring you over our way? Is that what she meant? 'Leave her alone to run about while she can,' I shouted back over my shoulder. As I ran I could hear her sobbing in the dark. But I didn't stop.

Though the way things turned out perhaps I should've stayed to listen.

What would I say to you if I could muster my thoughts properly? First, I'd try and convey to you what I remember from my own short days. There's the flare of candlelight against a glistening seam of coal. The plume of smoke

37

shooting from a pipe's bowl, the smoker behind it narrowing his eyes at me. Milk white feet, sore from walking, dipping into a soothing millpond. The moon through a window like an eye of death.

What would you make of my bag of remembered pictures from my life? What will yours be when your time comes? Are these jumbled glimpses all that's ever left? I jump high onto a tree branch and think about it. Slowly more and more of them come back. Stopping on a road to buy pancakes, small golden discs – the loveliest thing I'd ever tasted. Digging into the earth with bare hands. A small thing it seems, this bag of pictures, hardly worth paying heed to.

Until the pictures begin to fuse together like the rattling pieces are forming a spine.

I look down as you pass right beneath my roosting place. I see the top of your head. For a moment I think again of jumping right into your body from above and shoving you out. I'm sorry. I'm sorry. I'm sorry. I hate to see you like this really, your face downcast, your cheeks cupped in your hands. Sometimes I wish I could help but when I try I seem to get it no more right than the lady in the yellow dress. There's enough trouble heaped on your poor thin shoulders, Ruby. We should all leave you alone really.

10

THE WRATH TO COME
11 September 1983

Because the old cottage windows were thick and thin in different places, when the policemen came up the path the glass made them form and re-form – two blue figures crawling up the panes.

I'd spilled it out this morning. The car. The yellow dress. The upside-down woman. The secret was too big. It couldn't be contained.

'Why the hell didn't you mention it before? She might not have been dead at all when you saw her. She could have died in the night and it'll all be your fault,' Mick said, before calling the police.

'Ruby, I . . .' Barbara said over the whir of dialling, her face bleached white. 'Please.' She put her hand on her side and dragged herself into the hallway. I could see her shape there, bent over the stair post.

Now they were coming back to report on their findings.

The wind whipped their voices into the house. I couldn't tell what they were saying but when they all came through to the sitting room Mick's eyes had turned dull and slid towards me where I sat on the corner of the sofa.

'There she is,' he said and took a ready rolled-up cigarette out of his pocket and stuck it in his mouth.

The older policeman sat next to me on the sofa and

adjusted himself so his uniform puffed out the smell of out-side, of woods and rivers and soil where they'd just been. 'Now then, Ruby.' His voice seemed to waft, not speak. 'You know what telling a lie is, don't you? You know what the truth looks like. You know the difference, because you're a big girl now.'

In the corner of the room were Dad's dumbbells. I tried to focus on them.

I nodded. The policeman's eyes were blue water in his face. Whiskery stubble went right up to his cheekbones.

'Ruby . . .?'

'Yes,' I whispered. 'But I did see it. It wasn't just a shadow . . .'

'Shadows?' The blue water in his eyes was suddenly clearer, sharper. 'What are we talking about now? You think maybe it was just a shadow. Listen, love, we're really going to have to get this clear. We've searched where you told us. Now you're talking shadows.' He was getting annoyed now. I'd already heard goose chases mentioned and the section of river having to be checked that meant getting waders out of storage that were full of dust and right out of the ark. Not pleasant to put your feet in something like that, especially on a Sunday.

Mick was hovering near the doorway. He wasn't saying anything but I thought I could hear the buzzing again com-ing from inside him.

'In fact,' the policeman reached inside his jacket and slid out the book with its brown cover and cracked spine, 'this is all we found. Is it yours, Ruby?'

It was *Pilgrim's Progress* with the print of my shoe stamped on the cover. I must have stood on it. It looked ready to decay in his hands, turn to dust and a bundle of scraps of cloth and rotten leather. Long moments passed and it swam in and out of focus.

'I've had enough of this.' Mick snorted, stumping out, and I was left with Barbara and the two policemen.

'She's very imaginative.' Barbara's voice had taken on a different tone. Serious. Slightly hushed. That's because authority was here, I thought, puffing out its cheeks and sitting there as if it owned the place. I guessed how it would be as they left – Barbara forking up two fingers at their backs. I'd seen it so many times, her bony fingers raised in a V as Mick left on a night out, his little quiff extra high and perky over his shiny leather jacket and a cloud of aftershave left swirling in the hall.

Now, she walked them out and the door slammed and despite everything the thought of her flicking the Vs at policemen's backs meant I had to bend down my face to hide the smile.

Barbara came back into the sitting room and caught me. 'I saw that. You'll cop it now. I don't know what I can do to save you this time. I really don't.'

Outside the wind was picking up. I zigzagged across the garden and grabbed a windblown stick from the ground and as I ran began whipping at my own bare arms until red lines appeared. On the line were Mick's trousers and shirts flicking about. I stopped, biting my lip and thinking about the matches inside, their little pink heads asleep in the box. My fingers itched for the rasp of the sandpaper against my thumb. I remembered the 'day of the burning shirt' – how it had rippled with red and gold then turned in on itself. How I'd returned and the fact that everything in the kitchen was

41

the same seemed an amazement. The Saxa salt pot on the table. The red and brown of the sauce bottles behind the misty glass in the cabinets. How I'd sniffed the burn smell on my fingers and replaced the matches with just one pink head missing. How calm I'd felt the remainder of the day.

When I held the match to the hem of Mick's trousers on the line I was about to change my mind but the polyester lit first time. Flame licked upwards but it looked lopsided, just one leg being eaten away, so I struck another and held it to the other hem to make them even. The burning legs swung. I waited for the feeling – the calm – but it didn't come. I'd imagined everything on the line alight – the flame flashing across like an electric cable until there was a row of shirts crackling away too. But the trousers smouldered slowly and sent out clouds of smoke.

Rain began to fall, slapping hard against the fence. It fizzed and hissed into the flames, putting them out until there was a pair of severed legs in front of me – one gone to the knee and the other to the thigh. They smoked where they'd been cut. The energy ran out of my body like fat from meat. So he'd kill me now; I'd made that certain. I felt a kind of relief I'd soon be dead.

But he didn't do anything that day. He was biding his time. I wanted to flee from the wrath to come, but I didn't have the guts.

And I didn't yet know how.

I I

21 February 1970

Anna takes the slip of paper from the doctor and puts it in her handbag, snapping the clasp shut – the sound echoes round the room.

'Thank you,' she says, though she can't imagine what she's thanking him for. It's the same doctor that she's been too frightened to come to for a prescription of the pill.

'You'd better have a talk to the father. I'd advise the sooner the better.' The doctor turns away and begins flicking at his notes, scribbling at them with his fat fountain pen. The sound is scratchy and juicy at the same time. It's the ink flowing that makes the liquid sound. She stays seated even though the doctor has dismissed her with the turn of his shoulder.

'Anything more?' The doctor is turning back to her, because she hasn't moved. He's daring her to ask what she can do. What her way out is, the one they both know about. Doctors still have such power. They know all about silly young girls that get themselves knocked up. It sickens them.

'No, nothing.' Anna tries to sound dignified but her voice is far away to her own ears. She can't ask. He's daring her to so he can say no. Girls like her are a worm in the rose of their society. She knows he's religious. She's seen him go into the tall stone church in Cinderford, his hand resting

43

lightly on the base of his wife's back to guide her in. There are small children around them. His wife has the sort of figure where you can't forget about her body under her clothes, like a dancer's. One foot bends behind her in an elegant curve as she is swallowed up in the doorway. The children all vanish into the hole, one by one.

Even if he says yes he'll make it terrible for her, she knows that. He'll make her wait for weeks and weeks to try and effect a change of mind. He'll make sure her name will be called out in a hospital hallway – loud and clear. Nothing can be kept secret in the forest. She couldn't have possibly seen him with a borrowed wedding ring for a prescription of the pill like she'd heard of people doing. Information washes up and down the forest valley. It would have made its way to her parents' cottage, swirling through the door towards her father, usually so quiet and pious – until questions of sex came up. This wasn't the sort of place that Anna read about in magazines: Carnaby Street; the King's Road; swinging London. Here, things move as slowly as trees growing.

Anna stands and adjusts her coat. 'Thank you again, Doctor.' Her voice is crisp this time and his eyebrows – speckled with white – rise slightly. This is not the way he wants her to behave; brazen might be the word he'd use. She should be crying soft bitter tears; she knows that.

But outside the surgery she takes a sudden gasp of air and leans against the brass panel where his name – Dr Fennick, M.D. – is etched. Panic runs through her in waves.

You'll have to talk to the father. Oh God.

Anna tells her mother about the baby quickly. Once the

knowledge is in the room it can't be wrapped up and hidden away again. Suddenly it's everywhere, hanging in the air of the kitchen, escaping through the open window. The few pictures – framed religious tracts – stare down. Each missive has a bright flower winding through the lettering or a spray of red berries resting on top, like words are three-dimensional objects you can put things on.

Her mother nods. 'I wondered,' she said. She's making pastry at the kitchen table, sitting down to do it because it's been a tiring day. Anna watches the flour with bubbles of butter sifting, sifting through her mother's brown fingers – getting finer, as fine as breadcrumbs.

'Don't tell Dad,' says Anna quickly. He's the one who puts the tracts up on the wall.

Her mother looks up, sharp. 'He'll work it out soon enough. Like I said, I was beginning to wonder myself.'

Anna bows her head and cradles her stomach. 'How can that be? It's so soon; it must only be a speck at the moment. But Dad – he'll want to know who the father is. He'll try and make him do the "right thing".'

That was the next question.

'So who is he? Does he know?'

'I haven't told him anything yet. I . . . I can't.' Anna was starting to feel exhausted with all the confessing she was doing. Just the thought of more of it was enough to make her want to lie down and go to sleep.

'Married?' The sharp look again. She was no fool, Anna's mother, but this time she was barking up the wrong tree.

'No, not that.'

How could she explain? Lewis Black: he hadn't really wanted to go with a forest girl; she knew that. He had his

45

sights set higher than that. A forest girl would drag you down; she'd grab you by the ankle and jerk you back to where you didn't want to be. But when it came to it they couldn't help themselves: lips; limbs; sweat shining in a sheen across his back, she felt it on her fingertips when he was on top of her. She put her finger in her mouth where he couldn't see just to taste it.

He'd be worse than angry, she'd have to watch the waves of disappointment breaking over him as he took in the news. She'd have to watch him slump and see written all over his face: I knew this would happen if I went with her. Fool, fool.

She doesn't know why he hates it so much here. It's like the trees are grasping limbs that want to bind him in. Anna takes a moment and opens the front door to breathe in the winter air. Her parents live in a forester's cottage, alone in a valley. The name of it – Hollow Cottage – rang through her childhood as far back as she can remember.

There's balmier parts of the forest – summer takes an age to come here, creeping late and slow to spread its greenery. Spring turns up as a greenish icing over packed, cold earth. Even in summer the lush plants have a frostiness to them – things grown in the dark, cold dirt speckled in their hearts. But Anna loves it – the tang of river water in the air from the stream that flows at the bottom of the garden; the empty stone pigpen to one side; the smell of wood smoke in the air from their own chimney. She breathes it all in then turns back to the kitchen table and her mother.

'Well.' Her mother has been thinking while Anna was at the door, wondering the best way to react to the news. She's quickly dismissed the idea of feigning disapproval or anger.

46

What's the point in that? The mixture in the bowl is almost powder now. She resorts to the tried and tested. 'This is the way of things when people are young and the nights are long. I'll challenge anyone who says different.'

Her mother stands, walks round and puts a powdery hand on Anna's shoulder. 'Would you . . .?' She stops.

Anna isn't supposed to know what her mother does – sometimes – for girls who are desperate and frightened. She's not supposed to know about the hideously coloured pink tubing and the rubber bag to be filled with water, kept in a locked suitcase in her mother's wardrobe, to be squirted up into women's insides like they're bilges of a boat that need to be swilled clean. Anna has a certain curiosity – the kind that has got her into trouble now – she found the little bunch of keys years ago, thin and silvery, hidden in the bottom of a vase. She knew at once what they were for. The suitcase had been piquing her curiosity for a long time by then. Her father is chapel, this whole valley is. The squat grey stone building stands at the top of the valley like it's keeping an eye on them. There's an eye too, in the house. It's embroidered onto canvas and is behind glass, above the mantelpiece, with 'Thou God Seest Me' stitched underneath. Anna imagines when the girls come here it must drop its lid in a blink that hovers there, lasting until the girl has left, washed clean. Women here can carry on like that, under the cover of the forest. She knows obliquely there are many of them persisting with the old ways. The structure of men with the law and the chapel and rugby is the top layer, bolted on, and everything else happens underneath, close to the ground. Who knew what was out there, buried at the foot of trees, being covered year on year by another layer of leaves? When she was little her and her sister used to bury things there too, under the oak just over the stream at the bottom of the garden, or the beech just further on down the path. Little treasures or, once, a doll she'd thought'd been naughty. Though afterwards she could never find it. She went through the woods calling and scrabbled at the soil beneath all the trees around but the forest seemed to have sucked it in, right into the depths, and she never did unearth it. The forest ate it.

Anna shivers, even though it isn't cold in the kitchen. She shakes her head, slightly. They both understand what has been offered and refused. Anna can't countenance it – her mother picking her own grandchild out of Anna's body like a pomegranate seed on a pin.

Anna sits and rests her head on the table and covers it with her arms. She would be able to decide things easily if only she had more time. If only there wasn't the pressure of this thing inside, ripening away like something growing in the ground in summer; it seems to be happening in the blink of an eye.

I 2

THE DAY OF SUGAR
19 September 1983

My bruises almost disappointed me, fading and yellowing round the edges like old newspaper. Just a tiny cut on my knuckle remained. I hoped it would turn into a scar – otherwise it would be like nothing had really happened. Every time it healed over I peeled the scab away with my teeth. But I forgot it for a day or two and when I looked again my body had treacherously repaired itself and there was just clean pink wrinkled knuckle skin. There was always that North wind, though, should I forget, blowing unexpectedly and making me list to the side as if I was still being knocked that way.

While they were both at work I tried Mick's dumbbells. I had the idea to make myself as strong as him but I could hardly lift them to my shoulder let alone swing them above my head like he did. I kept trying, though, at hourly intervals.

Barbara told me it was time to go back to school as she was washing up after dinner, wearing bright pink rubber gloves. 'You've missed enough already,' she said.

I brushed off the crumbs from the table with a tea towel. 'What do I tell everyone why I've been away?'

She said, 'Honestly, the bits are all over the floor now. Go and get a dust pan and sweep them up.'

When I was under the table, sweeping, I heard her say, 'Yes, I've been thinking about that. What about telling them

49

you fell over and twisted your ankle?'

I jumped back up and stood with the brush in one hand and the pan in the other. We both went quiet for a while. She even clutched onto her side with the wet rubber gloves and squeezed there like the lying was causing her pain.

'I don't think that's very plausible.' And even though I said it quietly, in a very dignified manner, she went: 'Oh for Gawd's sakes, Ruby, I don't know where you get these words from. We all know what happened was wrong but I'm seeing to it it doesn't happen again, so you need to get on with it – and I do too.' And she stripped off her gloves and flung them in the scummy water and headed for the door.

'From a dictionary,' I said to her back as she exited the kitchen. Though I don't think she heard.

By morning she'd even persuaded Mick to take me in. Mick worked as a caretaker in my school. Sometimes our eyes met over his polishing machine – a whirring electric turtle he pushed along the corridors. Then he'd flick his eyes straight ahead again and move on, carving a clean shiny path. Usually, he avoided driving me to school like the plague, saying I didn't shut up in the car and that he needed to think that time in the day. I think it was nerves that made me talk like that. He liked to get in early so he could go to his cubbyhole and brew a cup of tea and have a bit of peace before he started work.

'Sit there.' He jerked his head towards the stairs. 'Be quiet. Be still, and wait.'

I sat and watched him while he got ready, combing his hair in the mirror. He took even longer than he usually did and I wondered if he was putting off going to school and answering awkward questions about why I'd been away.

I was so afraid of being in the car with him my insides turned to water.

'I can walk in to school still.' My voice sounded tiny in the stairwell.

He pointed his comb at me. 'You'll do as you're fucking well told,' he said and I could see those trousers were still alight in his memory. I thought of making a run for it but with his figure blocking the downstairs a feeling of weakness washed over me.

We rode to school in silence, even my usual chattering failed. I realised then he meant to make me afraid by making me do this. It worked. I clutched my school bag tight to my body all the way and hardly dared to breathe until we got there.

At school everything had changed. Before the summer holidays I'd been making good inroads on infiltrating Melissa and Nicola's little gang but being away at the start of term had put paid to that. Now they sat on a radiator with their arms around each other and Nicola said, 'Oh you, we thought you'd left you've been absent for so long.' They'd obviously been having discussions about how they thought I was weird and how they didn't like me. That my clothes were old. I could tell by their attitude. Since I'd decided to have a change and ape the goddess Siouxsie I'd stitched my school skirt tight across my knees and backcombed my hair so it stood out about a foot but Melissa just said, 'What on earth have you done to your hair?' And they kept asking why I'd been away and they knew I was lying because I kept going red or standing on one leg or trying to change the subject. Then they both stalked off with their arms around each other and their lovely shiny hair swinging down their backs – one blonde, one brown. They both used an apple shampoo that made it smell delicious.

So I walked off too and bumped into Mick who was standing on a chair replacing a light bulb. I stuck to the spot for one long minute as we looked at each other before I could peel my feet up off the floor and move away. I turned back and Sandra Crossley walked past and I spotted him trying to look down her top. She wore her collar wide and spread out across her shoulders so it was possible to see a fair amount. She seemed to sense something too because she looked up at him and gave him a big smile. I thought – why are you smiling like that if he was trying to look down your top?

That's when I started to smell it and at first I thought it was the apple shampoo wafting out behind Melissa and Nicola. Sweetness blew down the corridors, hanging over our heads like rain clouds ready to burst and cover us in sugar dust. Everyone put their noses in the air and sniffed, like on the Bisto ad.

'What is it?'

'It smells like toffee apple.'

'No, it's like candyfloss.'

'It's cook. She's making treacle tart and has burned three whole sacks of sugar. She's gone mad.'

We kept getting whiffs of it and people started licking their lips without even knowing.

After having to explain I didn't have a note I sat next to Ben. It was only as far as registration and already he had a big gob of spit gleaming in his hair. Because his hair was so black it shone out like cellophane. I whispered to him and he took his pencil case and started rubbing at the back of his head. But because the pencil case was plastic it didn't absorb and it just smeared it all around his head. It started making me feel quite sick, though that felt mean too – that his troubles were making me feel sick. The form teacher asked for a note and I had to promise to bring one in tomorrow. I think Barbara thought maybe because Mick was the caretaker they'd get away with it. Also I could tell Barbara hadn't really wanted to put lies down on paper, in real words. She kept saying she couldn't find a pencil. Then it was paper she couldn't find and then it was time for me to leave.

Later, at break time the smell was sending us mad, everybody couldn't stop talking about Crunchie bars and how they'd kill to lay their hands on one.

Science; second lesson. Mr Hart chose me when he realised he'd left the pipettes in the other science lab. I knew he thought he was being kind getting me to run the errands like that, that it got me more involved, but actually it just meant more being noticed. I had to walk past all the rows of benches to get out and there were Melissa and Nicola turning to stare at me. They had their white coats on already. The elastic on their goggles dented their shiny hair in and the plastic made their faces all froggy as they stared.

At first I couldn't find the pipettes and I thought I'd have to go all the way back with nothing while everyone looked on witnessing my dumbness. I discovered them in the end, behind the old plant whose leaves were burned in patches from the sun coming through the window. I wondered why nobody ever thought to move it. I hurried back because I'd taken so long.

That's when I caught his gleam from the corner of my eye. Can people gleam? He did. There was a bright flash of it and it startled me so much I jumped and some of the glass pipettes went shooting up from the box. They shattered on the floor into about a thousand pieces.

His dark brows looked shocking against his white-yellow hair, bleached and tied back into a ponytail. No school uniform but trousers that were too short and his feet in scuffed shoes with no socks so his ankles jutted bare and bony. His cheekbones were so sharp he put me in mind of a young Red Indian chief. It wouldn't have surprised me to see a feather sticking out of his hair, or his coat fall open to reveal a quiver full of arrows at his waist.

I bent over to inspect the mess – but really so he couldn't see my face. The glass looked sharp enough to cut my fingers to ribbons if I tried to pick it up. He leaned too and there were his eyes appearing, suddenly, like seeing the sea.

'What's all this? Do you need help there?'

There was nothing for it – I'd have to straighten up and show the damage. I thought – I may as well get it over with, the look in his eyes when he sees my birthmark. But it was as if nothing was wrong when he did get a proper look at my face. Later, he said this thing . . .

'Who are you? Where's your uniform?' I asked, just for something to say.

'Tom, and I haven't got one. I've just come in to take a look around to see if I might like it here.'

I gasped. 'What, you didn't ask anyone if you could come in? You can practically get arrested for that.'

He shrugged. 'I started worrying that I'm not getting educated and I'm only fifteen, but I've had a look around and I don't think I'll bother.'

'Who's that?' I asked, because another boy, similarly strangely dressed, had appeared down the end of the corridor, watching us. He slammed the door with his fist like he thought Tom was standing around too long, wasting his time with chat.

Tom turned his head but when I looked back the double doors had swung closed and the other boy had gone.

'What did he look like?'

'Long coat and leather boots with his trousers tucked in.'

Tom's eyebrows shot up and something passed across his face I couldn't read.

'Tell me exactly what you saw.'

'A boy. He looks like you but shorter. He's got a long coat with a rip down the side.'

'A rip? Which side?'

I thought for a moment. 'His left, my right.'

Tom's knuckles turned white as he balled his fists. 'Oh God, oh God no. That sounds like Crispin, my brother. Christ. Was he wearing a red and green tie with just a T-shirt?'

'Yes.'

'I can't believe it, he's here. I can't have him here. Crispin, piss off,' Tom shouted over his shoulder. I saw Crispin's face reappearing behind the window of the shut door, like a face underwater. He gave us both the finger through the glass then the window went empty.

He sucked in his breath and I noticed his hands shaking.

'He's gone,' I said.

He nodded. 'Thank God for that. Let me help you,' he said, as if he was glad to put his attention elsewhere, then he kicked the glass to one side like it was nothing and no trouble would be caused. I wondered what it would do to Mick's polishing machine – make it spit glass and choke to death perhaps.

'Now I'll walk you to wherever you're going.'

'OK,' I said. I'd never met anyone like him. He didn't seem worried that he was trespassing on school property without permission. Maybe we were being affected by the sweetness – like it really was a drug that had been released into the air and caused light-headedness. I certainly felt that way.

I asked, 'Where do you come from?' I expected any moment for Tom to go 'boom' and disappear.

'Not far.'

'I've never seen you around before. Do you live past Puzzlewood?'

'No, I live across on the blue hills.'

'The blue hills?'

'Yes, you sound like you've never heard of them. You can see them in loads of places from the forest – don't tell me you don't know them.'

I had seen them, shimmering in the distance, but I'd never thought of them as real.

'You must come and see me there one day, soon,' he said.

'Really?'

'Yes, of course. Promise me?'

Then he told me his name again – Tom, and about his sister Elizabeth and his brother Crispin, the nuisance one from earlier.

I thought, your hair is the palest yellow, like winter sun. He told me he lived in a huge house with eight windows at the front.

'A children's home,' I breathed. 'I've always wanted to live in one of those.'

'No. It's just a big house. It's got a face carved over the gate. It's an ancient symbol – a green man. He has leaves coming out of his mouth.' He spread his hands either side of his mouth to demonstrate. 'Like this.'

We stopped outside the classroom and there was a moment of awkwardness. Me with the box of pipettes – or what was left of them – and him looking up into the corner of the corridor. When I lifted my arms up to shift the box around to make it comfier my sleeves shot back. A few faded bruises were still there, yellow and ugly. I saw him looking at them and I felt ashamed.

'I like your hair,' he said.

'Thank you.'

There was silence again but he didn't mention what we'd both seen. I reached round the box and pulled my sleeves back down, one after the other. Finally he said, 'I'm going to hop off now, but tell me where you live so I can come one day and take you out. I have to see you again. I absolutely have to.'

I wondered if I was hearing things.

Then he said the thing and I thought I was going to fall down dead.

In my classes I had an attack of what I can only term as 'ecstatic shivering'. Nobody noticed and I sat there wondering if I'd just made him up.

When I got home I looked in the mirror. My hair was flat now because in domestic science Mrs Davis had given me a comb and told me to sort myself out.

'You have an uncommon beauty, Ruby,' I said. I studied my face. My left eye was a sharp blue-grey and always seemed brighter than my right because of being in the cradle of the birthmark that showed it up. The shape the mark took around my eye was of the eye socket on a skull. It made that eye look peering.

13

BRIGHT THINGS
10 October 1983

Thunder rumbled outside and every fibre of my being strained to hear Mick returning. I was on my own in the house, which always put me on high alert. I watched television with one ear cocked for his footsteps, or his car, knowing if I'd missed both it could be the rattle of his key in the lock next. He always seemed to open the door more loudly than anyone else and he had a habit of working the key noisily back and forth in the lock. It was an early warning sign and often gave me enough time to shoot out into the back garden or upstairs.

So when the front door opened with no scraping or rattling it sounded to me as loud as a pistol going off next to my ear. I jumped then crept over to the TV and switched it off, hoping against hope that I could remain in hiding.

'Ruby?' I could breathe again, it was Barbara. I poked my head out into the hallway. She was standing at the open front doorway with rain pouring behind her. Her face was in shadow and rain dripped off the bottom of her coat.

'You're getting the carpet all wet,' I said.

She roused herself. 'Am I? Oh dear.' She came in leaving a trail of water. I could see there was something wrong as soon as her face moved into the light of the hallway.

'Sometimes, Ruby . . .' She didn't finish, just stood there

twitching her fingers by her pockets.

'What's the matter?' I whispered, as if talking too loud could bring the furies down on us.

'Nothing. Be a love, make me a cup of tea.'

I went into the kitchen and filled the kettle. She joined me but she'd forgotten to take her coat off and it carried on dripping, this time onto the lino.

'Listen, I see that you've got interested in make-up. I've got you some proper stuff – not that war paint you've been going in for.'

She reached into her pocket and scooped out a fistful of eye shadows.

'I thought you could try these.' She dumped them on the table where they sounded like pebbles falling. She went for her other pocket and came out with three gold lipsticks.

'There, you can try different colours out, or we can together. Not now, though. I'm dog tired.' There were deep shadows under her eyes.

'Thank you,' I said. I unwound one of the lipsticks and sniffed it. It was a frosty pink colour. I couldn't imagine Siouxsie ever wearing anything like that. 'Where have you been? You're soaking. You're dripping everywhere.'

'Just walking out in the woods,' she said and went to hang her coat up in the hall. I knew she'd been out remembering Trudy. It's what she always did when the memories came crowding in too much for her to bear. I watched as her bent-over figure climbed up the stairs.

I took the make-up to my room and laid it out on the bed. I arranged and rearranged the tubes and eye shadows into patterns on the bedspread. The eye shadows were all the colours of the sea in different weathers – green, blue, purple. Each lipstick was in a tube of gold. I was grateful for the gifts, and they were beautiful in their shiny new packaging, but I didn't have the heart to try anything on.

14

25 April 1970

It's snowing when Anna and her mother come to the gates of the adoption agency. 'Late snow' her mother calls it, because spring came then went again and turned back to winter.

'You're more nervous than I am,' she says to her mother. Cynthia wanted to stop by the gate and smoke a cigarette before they walk up the long drive. She's taking short stabbing little puffs now, getting it in quickly before their appointment. The air around her is hazy with cold and thin drops of snow fall around her head. The holly bushes by the entrance have little spits of white on their leaves.

The smoke shoots out in a thin powerful jet and hangs there. 'Well, I've never done this before.'

Anna ignores the comment. She knows her mother disapproves of what she's doing – much more so than Anna getting pregnant in the first place. The light in Cynthia's eyes goes flat whenever it's mentioned. But she doesn't say. She's good like that. She told Anna's dad while Anna was away so he'd calmed down by the time Anna returned. Baleful stares from him are met by a sharp look from Cynthia so they are snipped off before they have time to gather. He's a good man, though, a good kind man and soon that overcomes everything else.

'Come on, let's get in there. We still have to walk up the drive, we'll be late.' The soles of Anna's feet are growing cold through her thin shoes. It must be the extra weight, pressing her feet into the ground.

'All right, all right.' Her mother takes a last extra deep puff and throws the cigarette on the snow. It sizzles, leaving a sooty black spot.

15

THE MILK MIRROR
1 November 1983

When Tom came to the house the mirror turned suddenly milky, spreading cloud to its centre like glaucoma. I'd never seen this before and it frightened me.

'I came when I could,' he said. 'Elizabeth is very hard to leave these days. She hates to be alone. My parents are away for a while.'

'What about your brother, Crispin?'

'Him? He doesn't really count. Always off, roaming. I thought I'd take the chance because Elizabeth found an old sleeping pill of my mother's – just one left in the bottom of the bottle and she looks like she'll sleep for a week. Listen, if I take you out d'you think your parents would mind?'

I thought of long summer evenings where I'd run away from Mick's fists and took shelter for hours under a pink arch of rhubarb in the allotments. I shook my head. 'I'm kind of a free agent,' I said at last, ignoring the fact that Barbara always said she'd been ragged with worry every time I ran off. 'Just let me go and change.'

On my way upstairs I checked the mirror. The milkiness had turned to gloom. The paleness coddled with something that looked like rot, or the white of an egg where its edges have turned bad.

My yellow checked birthday shirt looked childish already. Most of my sad old clothes had been converted with rips and seams to look like Siouxsie's. I'd even found some old coats of Grandad's under the stairs and had taken to wearing those, though Mick nearly choked when he first saw me – like the father-in-law that hadn't thought much of him, by all accounts, had come back in body to have a word.

I dressed in black and drew a red cupid bow on my lips. Downstairs, I noticed Tom still didn't seem to have acquired any socks and his ankles stood out even redder and more raw than last time like the chafing had got worse.

'What are those?' asked Tom, nodding at the open door of the living room.

'They're Dad's dumbbells. He lifts them two hundred times twice a day when he's trying to improve his physique.'

My own experiment with them hadn't come to much. I probed my biceps nightly with my fingers but they never seemed any harder or bigger.

'Really? I've seen them in pictures, let me have a go.'

'No, I . . .'

He was already at them, lifting them up and swinging them so wildly I thought they might fly off and crash into the TV.

'Look, look at me improving my physique.' He laughed and pumped them up and down high above his head.

'Don't,' I cried. 'Careful, please be careful.'

But he'd begun mimicking some ancient physical fitness routine, doing comic squats until the dumbbell in his left hand fell to the floor with a bang that seemed to crack through the walls.

'You've broken the house,' I gasped, covering my eyes.

'It's OK. Look, it's fine.' He'd managed to skip out of the way of it landing on his foot.

I uncovered my eyes.

'No harm,' he said. 'Let's leave this alone now and go. I've just thought too – I don't really like the idea of your father improving his physique.'

I pretended not to know what he was talking about and we left with me wondering if there might be a giant fissure running up the middle of the house. Part of me hoped there was.

His car was old. Mick's was old too but shiny and immaculately kept; this had mud on the back seat and smelled like dogs and cut wood. Tom seemed pleased when it started first time.

'Is fifteen old enough to drive?' I asked.

'I don't think so. It's quite easy, though, and I find you can do things in the country that you can't in town. You can get away with a lot more.'

It was true. People did all sorts of stuff here. They worked on the land when they were still kids. Drove tractors. Even drank in pubs in back rooms sometimes.

And we were off, with the forest sliding past the windows and rain forming in the corners of the windscreen. I spotted Shadow watching us behind the trees and my heart beat faster. I was glad to leave him behind in the misty patches gathering under branches.

Tom speeded up and we laughed when the car did kangaroo hops or went round corners too fast. We laughed at anything, even if it wasn't funny. On the way Tom told me his parents were in India. We laughed at that too.

*

65

Inside the club the air was swollen and heavy. Tom put a lemonade down in front of me, with a slice of lemon curling over the rim, clinging onto it like a yellow fish, half dried out and desperate to dive into the bubbles below.

'What have you got?' I nodded at his glass.

'Lager shandy.' He took a gulp. 'Try it?'

It tasted sweet and beery. I looked around. The room was so packed people swayed, locked together in an upright dance. Music started up and the surface of our drinks began imploding with tiny detonations. Girls, their bums barely covered by denim skirts and bare legs despite the drizzle outside. I noticed one with a festoon of fleabites round her ankles. Another had a dog lead crammed in her pocket and I remembered the dog with sorrowful eyes tied up outside with its paws planted in the wet. Boys with hair teased skywards squeezed around the jukebox and dropped coins into the slot, arguing about what to play, jabbing their fingers against the glass on the line-up of songs printed inside. There was a pause and Siouxsie and the Banshees' 'Dear Prudence' started up.

'Oh my God, this is my favourite song,' I said, smiling wide. 'It's not been out long.' He smiled back and we sat smiling at each other like loons.

He reached down and scrabbled in his pocket and drew out a piece of paper. 'Here,' he said, 'I found a poem in a book at home and wrote it out for you.'

I unfolded the piece of paper and read out loud.

This living hand, now warm and capable
Of earnest grasping, would, if it were cold
And in the icy silence of the tomb,

So haunt thy days and chill thy dreaming nights
That thou wouldst wish thine own heart dry of blood
So in my veins red life might stream again,
And thou be conscience-calmed – see here it is –
I hold it towards you.

'Why did you give me this?' I shivered. 'It's creepy.' I folded the paper and held it out to him. 'I don't like it.'

'No.' He reached across the table. 'It's romantic. It's very romantic – I think. It's about how you would give your life for someone else. Don't say it sounds silly, please. I'm holding out my hand to you. You've got to come.'

'Where?'

A sheen of sweat shone on the angles of his face. 'To my house. I really want you to. You've got to.' He drank deeply from his glass and wiped his mouth. 'You're the same as me,' he said suddenly.

'I know.' I was glad he'd taken the risk of saying it, not me. I would've messed it up.

I glanced up. In the mirror there was a pair of men's shoulders broad in a suit jacket. The dark hair on his muscular neck was shaved down to the white skin. I felt a sudden panicking fear that people would try and separate us and I dropped the poem in my pocket and reached across and grabbed his outstretched hand.

'Tell me in what way we're the same,' I said.

'You're like a Christmas cracker.'

'I don't know what you mean.'

'No, don't be offended. It's just like you have a weird toy inside.'

'Oh.'

'Don't worry. I've got one too.' He pressed both hands under his breastbone and looked down as if that was its exact location.

And as we left, the drizzle and darkness swirled around us. I saw a couple blow out of the mouth of the pub opposite on a fierce raft of beery breath. The man's shape I knew, inside out. The long jacket that made the legs look truncated in their narrow trousers. The wide-set legs, so they seemed to be attached on the corners of his body. The outline of the horn of hair jutting forward as he turned to the girl he had his arm around. She bent her neck to look at him and in the light of the street lamp I saw Sandra from school, her face tipping up like a dinner plate.

At home I crept up the stairs. I heard Barbara turn over in bed and mutter, 'Ruby?' as if half asleep. I didn't know if Mick was home or not. I lay in bed trembling in the dark. He saw me too I thought, we saw each other. The knowledge settled deep inside me and I tried to smother it because I knew as long as we could both pretend I might be able to keep safe.

16

WINTER
15 November 1983

The forest was heading for its small death, shedding its leaves for winter onto the roads and filling up ditches and streams making the water gurgle through the clots. The knowledge about Sandra and Mick made me quiet and watchful. When I left for school I walked alone and the russet leaves swirled around me in a pillar. Mick's red car passed me on the road every day, even though we were going to the same place. His raw meat look was back. It was on his face all the time now, as if it was an illness, a condition that wasn't ever going to get better. His face would mash up against the car window to look at me. Then he'd be gone around the corner, leaves twirling in his wake.

He was biding his time. Even Barbara was creeping round. Dragging herself from room to room.

At school, they sensed it, like the smell of blood – that I was a marked person. I saw Nicola and Melissa in the distance bobbing side by side. They looked so lovely sometimes there seemed to be a halo shining right around the outside of their joined-up figures. As I walked down school corridors people appeared to part before me.

A matter of time. It was nearly winter when it came. I'd been brushing my hair at the kitchen table, making it fall in a long gleaming dark wave over my shoulder, admiring the crow's wing shine of it, thinking about Tom and how it would look against his pale blond head.

I'd left the back door open to release the stuffed-up smell of the kitchen shut up all day.

The words came crawling round the door. 'Ruby, out here.'

I dropped the brush. I hadn't even heard Mick arrive home. He must have come in through the back gate.

'Come out here. I won't ask you again.' I wondered if he'd been outside looking into the lit-up room, watching me through the window. It was an eerie thought; being caught acting vain, whispering as I brushed, 'Tom, Tom – come back to me. Am I ever going to see you again?'

I spun it out as long as I could, putting my scarf and coat back on before I went outside.

He was standing on the garden path. It was turning night already, the dark iron of winter stiffening the trees and the thick tang of wood smoke in the air. The sky was clear, but darkening into a greenish hue with streaks of orange and yellow. He was a black outline against it, rearing up into the sky. I could see the silhouette of his quiff sticking out.

'Ruby, Ruby, I've been thinking about you, burning my clothes. Setting fire to my trousers. Good God, what a girl.' His voice was crooning, almost singsong. I caught a whiff of his smell, like the smell of a creature with fur. 'I've been doing a lot of thinking. About you, and your lies.'

I looked up into the sky. A lone star glittered there, Venus. It seemed like the coldest thing I'd ever seen.

'You've been upsetting your mum with them too.' I started; I'd never told Barbara about Sandra's high-pitched giggle, bubbling up out of the dark. She must have guessed herself and now Mick thought it was me who'd told her.

'She's known for ages,' I said, thinking of the forked fingers at his back.

'Right,' he shifted on his feet. 'Like there's anything to know,' he added hurriedly. 'You'd even lie to a policeman. You did lie to a policeman. There's documentation of it. I've seen it. They keep that in the records. They keep it for ever so don't think you can get away with it. There's proof.' He was clenching and unclenching his fists that hung below his waist, pumping them up. His belt buckle glittered in the light from the back door.

A long, low shudder went through me. 'I haven't told Barbara anything,' I said again, my voice sounding high and unnatural. 'She's worked it out for herself, though, hasn't she? That's why you're being like this. Taking it out on me.'

His head jerked back. 'Lies, Ruby. Shall I give you a medal for lying?'

Then I remembered seeing Sandra in the corridor that morning. She was walking along with a boy from sixth form. He had strong, dark stubble on his face. She was licking at her pearled lipstick with tiny dabs of her tongue.

Maybe Mick had seen them too.

'You leave me alone.' My voice sounded high-pitched.

'Should I? Should I do that? Leave you alone?' His hand went up to his belt buckle and he touched it lightly. Other stars had popped out now, as if the first one had told them all to come have a look – hey, Ruby is about to have another pasting. There was a whickering sound as leather shot through his belt loops.

I stiffened with fear. A low dark wind shuddered through me, that North wind. It lifted up my head.

'You'll never touch me again, you bloody bastard.'

71

He cracked the belt and it reared up like a dark serpent.

The wind flew out across the tall grass, flattening the tops. Strength surged through my muscles. Then the plank was in my hands, the one that had been leaning up against the fence for years, I could feel the splintery weight of it in my palms. The belt just missed me, but I'd felt its breath blowing on my face and its hiss in my ear.

'Ruby, what are you doing?'

'Ruby . . .' The plank wheeled through the air and smashed into the side of his head. There was a crack and his head wobbled. For a second I thought it was going to come off. What would I do with Mick's head then, I panicked, bury it in the forest? But his outline stayed where it was for a few long seconds. Then he folded sideways and there was a dense thud like a bag of blood hitting the ground.

The few streetlights at the front of the houses flickered on, orange. I leaned over, panting. In the dark the pool under Mick's head was black and shiny, like he was a car leaking its oil. The white of an eye gleamed. I held onto the plank in case he was awake and ready to rear up to me with a howl of outrage, but he was still, just one eye slitted open. With the toe of my boot I reached out and poked him and his body moved slackly against it. He was heavy and I had to push hard with my foot. I rolled him over onto his back and saw the black print of blood covering one side of his face. A wave of sickness passed through me.

'I've killed you,' I whispered, and the plank fell from my hands. 'Oh my God, I'm so sorry. I've killed you.'

Shadow bounced around the garden. Fence to back step. Back step to gate. *Oh, you've gone and done it now, Ruby. You've done it now. You've done it now.*

17

25 April 1970

The office in the adoption agency that Anna and her mother are ushered into is huge. Mrs Turner's desk looks marooned in it as if it could be carried out by the next tide. Oddly, it's in the middle of the room rather than being under the window. 'The winter strikes through the glass so and the walls just *radiate* cold,' she explains as she sits behind it and indicates the two chairs opposite.

'Lovely,' she beams, 'Mum's come too. That's always wonderful.' Like it's a christening or the choosing of a wedding dress she's talking about, not the giving away of a baby.

She's not that old, thinks Anna as she takes her seat, but she's made herself look old: the bouclé skirt she smooths over her hips before she sits; the pink twinset; the pearl earrings as big as buttons clipped to her lobes; the hair curled carefully close to her head, each curl standing out like a doorknob.

'Now,' she takes a blue and white packet off the desk, 'do you mind? I've just come out of a meeting and Mr Hamilton is a bit of a tartar about smoking.'

Anna and Cynthia shake their heads and Mrs Turner holds the packet towards Cynthia. 'I shouldn't offer you one, I suppose, dear?' she says, looking briefly at Anna.

Anna can see her mother wishing she hadn't rushed the

73

one outside but Cynthia changes her mind and takes another anyway; this could be a long haul. Mrs Turner lights both cigarettes with a small, clicking silver lighter that she drops into the top drawer of her desk.

'We'll go over today exactly what's going to happen. No surprises. Have either of you any questions first?'

'I've got one,' says Cynthia quickly. 'What if she changes her mind?'

'Mum.' Anna turns to her, shifting her weight in the hard, wooden chair.

Mrs Turner blows out a long raft of smoke. Anna is beginning to be wreathed in it. 'Well, there are measures in place . . .'

'I won't,' says Anna, 'change my mind.'

No, she won't. Telling Lewis was worse than she'd imagined. It was over coffee in the window seat of a pub, the light falling onto one side of his face and The Rose and Crown printed backwards because it was etched onto the outside of the glass. After she'd told him she saw the sick disappointment settling into the bones of his face, on the side that was in darkness too – that side was worse because it looked like he might be hiding something there. She felt sick too, a real nausea in her throat. The quiet chinks of glass from the lunchtime drinkers at the bar suddenly seemed very far away. Some tiny part of her had held onto the hope that his face would light up, that he'd reach out for her hand and say, 'Don't worry, love, we'll manage somehow.' But what had she really expected? She'd gone and done that thing that people said girls did to you.

'I remember the johnny splitting,' were his first words.

And somehow that'd been awful, him saying that, crude. And he made it sound like that split was something happening to himself; that she was splitting him apart.

'You could always . . . I'll pay,' he said. It seemed like everyone was offering her an abortion – her mother, Lewis, her friend Sonia who'd somehow procured one herself and was ready with advice – everyone except the one that should be offering, the good doctor.

'It's all right. I've decided.' She hadn't. It came to her right there, in the window of The Rose and Crown. 'I'm going to put it up for adoption.'

'I've made a firm decision,' she says now to Mrs Turner, again. 'My mind is made up.'

'Good.' Mrs Turner relaxes in her chair and stubs out her cigarette in the glass ashtray on the desk. 'Then we'll go over the procedure. Have you any questions about that?'

'Yes, can I name the baby?' She rubs the bulge.

Mrs Turner and Cynthia glance at each other. The smoking has made them conspiratorial; brought them to the same level – despite Mrs Turner's pearl earrings and the expensive-looking camel coat on a hanger behind the door.

'D'you think that's a good idea, dear?' asks Mrs Turner, mildly, and Cynthia makes a noise in her throat, agreeing.

'I'd like to if I can.' The baby is knitting together so quickly inside her. It's already taking on a personality of its own. And it's Ruby, Ruby, Ruby, Ruby.

'I'd like her to be called Ruby.'

'A gemstone, how lovely.' Mrs Turner is being kind; she actually thinks the name slightly vulgar, with a distinctly Semitic ring. Not really English at all. 'But of course. It might not be a girl. There's no way of telling.'

She peers at the pair in front of her – a little ragged round the edges. And the girl looks so young; she looks surreptitiously at her notes because she can't quite remember . . . seventeen, going on eighteen. Mrs Turner sighs, the situations people get themselves into, but she can't help but sympathise. She sees her job as a kind of midwife, delivering babies into lovely new homes, doting parents. Rescuing them out of the clutches of *what might have been*. These two don't look too bad, though. She's seen some shocking things: girls with slash marks still raw on their wrists where they'd tried to do away with the both of them; girls who'd stuck knitting needles right up their insides. It was amazing really, how life could cling on through all these things, despite being unwanted and attacked.

She gives a little shake of her head because she's realised something else has come up while she's been away in her reverie and the issue of naming Anna's baby gets skated over because something much, much more pressing is being announced.

'I want to keep the baby for at least five weeks, maybe more,' Anna says. 'I want to feed it myself.'

'Well, it is possible, anything's possible, but what we do find is there's less pain all round if it's quite immediate. Really, you'll be saving yourself, dear. The wrench can be difficult. It's only natural, after all. Are you sure your mind is quite made up?'

'Yes, of course.'

'Then wouldn't it be better—'

Anna interrupts. 'I want to keep her for a while. I want to be able to say goodbye.'

76

18

THE HOLLOW TREE
15 November 1983

The sound of my panting filled my bedroom. It's me that's killed Mick, I thought, not the other way round. I'm the one with blood on my hands. I spread them out. There was a dab of red near the centre of my palm.

Through the window I could see the dark stain of Mick's body on the ground. I could swear it was growing – its contents threatening to spill till it engulfed the house and washed me away in a tide of iron-smelling blood.

I crept downstairs and tiptoed past the body and the shadows around it. I thought I saw it twitch and I froze, my toe poised on the ground, but it was just the way the dark can make things bulge and move.

Then I ran for the forest that lapped at our feet, at the bottom of our gardens. 'The forest has everything you need, Ruby,' my gran used to say. But this wasn't her forest – the place of potions, of sweet nuts that could be gathered in handfuls from the floor, of wood that burned bright in the grate all winter. She was kind to me. It wasn't till she died I started feeling so alone. When I told her about the Wasp Lady I saw on the way to bed she'd said, 'Nothing but an old soul looking for succour. Tap her on the head once and she'll be on her way.' But as I climbed the stairs and the Wasp Lady swooped up from the void of the hall, her bottom half truncated and pointed like the insect's, when I tried to reach over the banister to administer the tap she'd fold herself sideways and disappear. And she didn't look like she needed succour. Her flat rubber-brown face was sly and her lips pursed coyly.

No, these weren't my gran's woods; this was a dark tangle, tree trunks wet to the touch as if covered in cold sweat. And it was Mick's young soul that scared me now, any minute he'd come roaring at me with rage at being newly dead. 'I didn't mean to do it,' I squeaked into the night because the shadows round Mick's body were probably following me now. Any minute I'd see they'd multiplied, fighting, swaggering, waiting ahead. They might have found a weapon, a sword, and be dancing around with it, jabbing. I ran, sobbing into the night. Branches slashed into my hair and poked me in the face and eyes. They struck like wet whips at my cheeks and I ran through it all, my arms stretched out as if I could push it all away.

When finally I stopped I realised I must be deep inside the trees by now. I sat against a tree in the dark until my breathing slowed. Something gnawed at me. It was the sound when I'd thumped against the tree. It had felt different. I peeled away the strands of ivy furling round the base of the trunk and my hands reached into nothingness. The tree had rotted out completely inside.

As I squeezed myself into its heart I thought perhaps the forest had given me what I needed after all and I wanted the tree to grow and seal me in so I could stay safe inside it for ever.

Everything had changed in the night. By morning every fallen leaf had a rim of white frost and they clattered against each other in the breeze. I looked round for Shadow. I peeped under brambles and around the trunks of trees. Mick and his weapons weren't there. I'd already made sure of that.

'There you are,' I said. Shadow was crouching behind a small shabby holly tree. I didn't have to worry about checking before speaking to him. I knew we were quite alone.

He stayed silent.

'Don't mess with me, not now. I'm in too much trouble and I'm really scared this time,' I pleaded as he stayed squat. I could see the indentations of both his feet pressing on the frosty leaves. 'So you can either come with me or not. It makes no odds to me.' That was the best way to treat him – pretend you didn't care and he'd soon be following after.

I turned to walk away and the cold struck me with full force through my thin coat for the first time. A bird lay stiff and immobile under an oak tree. It must have fallen out of its nest and frozen to death. That's what would have happened to me last night, I thought, without the hollow tree.

Out of the corner of my eye I could see Shadow following behind. Ignoring him had worked.

I don't think she knows where she's going. And you're hungry. You should go home.

'Of course I know where I'm going,' I lied, turning. 'Just follow me.'

I walked to warm up. As my brain unfroze, Mick's body kept coming back to me. Barbara must have found him by now, stiff and cold like that bird. There must be a search party out looking for me. Not just the neighbour this time. Not just that one policeman with the whiskery stubble. There'd be an army of them. They'd have sticks and shovels and maybe white hoods. I'd seen gangs like it on TV. My stomach squeezed hard, fear and hunger knitting together.

There's prisons for children.

'Shut up. I know,' I turned round. 'Can't you leave me alone if you're just going to frighten me?'

I can't help it. I . . .

But I'd spotted a cottage up ahead. 'Look. See that, in the trees. Let's have a look, there may be food we can steal.' A shot of saliva was in my mouth at just saying the word.

I don't know . . .

'Oh, come on.' I dropped down on my hands and knees. 'We'll do it like this.'

I slithered over the forest floor like a snake and peeped above the wall. A small boy looked out from the window, his eyes blank stones. I dropped quickly down again as the front door opened.

'What can you see?' I whispered to Shadow, the other side of the gate.

A witch.

I squinted through the gate. An old woman with grey hair came down the path muttering to herself. She had a cracked black plastic bucket in her hand. She turned the corner of the cottage and I could hear a door creaking open and chickens squawking.

'I know. We could sneak into the chicken run and take some of what they're having.' I remembered my gran's chickens got all sorts – stale bread and carrot tops. Right now it sounded like a feast.

No! She's a witch. She's got that little boy in there because she's going to cook him and eat him. She's . . .

I held my finger to my lips. I'd noticed that as I was getting older Shadow was sounding younger and younger.

'Don't be silly. It'll just be his gran looking after him. It's just an old lady.'

But Shadow panicked and darted across the gate towards me in a slick, black movement of a hare. From inside the house a child's scream pierced the air.

'You've got us caught,' I hissed. 'We have to run.'

After that it was all aloneness. Shadow was so spooked he left. Insects I couldn't see, only feel, had taken up residence in my hollow tree but I climbed in anyway and let them run all over me.

The hunger got worse and I found an icy quick-flowing stream and lowered my face into it and lapped there like a dog. It was so cold my lips burned. I found parts of the forest I'd never seen before. A dip so deep the dead leaves would go right over your head if you jumped in. I climbed down and lay under dry leaves. It felt dark and restful, the smell of earth in my nostrils.

After what seemed an endless time I emerged. It was evening. Using the lie of the land and the direction of the sun as it cast long shadows, I slowly made my way home. They could do to me what they liked. Being out here I'd surely die anyway.

As another night fell I found myself at the backs of our houses. There was a light on upstairs. From the edge of the forest I could see over the fence. There was a dark stain on the grey patio slabs where Mick's head had been. I curled under a tree and waited.

19

SHADOW

You stupid bitch.

You've really done it this time. You expect us to survive now?

If I could I'd put my hands around your neck until you were nearly gone then I'd creep into your body until I own it. How I long to taste the air again like you can.

I hate you sometimes.

20

SWEET PEA
17 November 1983

In the forest the seasons reverse. In summer the darkness is lush, the canopy taking the heat of the sun. In winter the light falls through the bare branches like light through bombed-out stained glass, just the lead work cutting into the sky. But even bare branches are a kind of shield and the naked sky made me blink. The dawn shone yellow, hurting my eyes. There was a smell of cold chimney smoke in the air.

Inside the gate the grasses waved at me. The doll's arm looked smaller than I remembered, though I knew this couldn't be the case. At the top of the path I saw it was more than a stain there; a crisp rind of blood had formed. I stuck my boot in it and my stomach turned over as the surface cracked.

Shivering broke out all over so violent it made me cry out. I thought of Barbara inside. She'd be weeping – first Trudy gone, now her husband. She'll point and scream. 'The only one bloody left,' she'll say, her finger reaching out like a bone. 'You're the only one I've bloody got left now. Just you.'

Poor Barbara. What had I done to her? I'd taken her husband. I'd replaced her beloved daughter. Somewhere it stirred in my mind – I'd murdered Trudy too. I could see it

– smashing her little flower face to bits until it was nothing but pulp. Stop it, Trudy died before you even came here. But something told me still it could be true. I'd wanted to perhaps, that was enough. I was a monster, my blood not rich red, but sludge, green and sickly. Trudy would have green blood too but being a flower hers would be thin and sweet-smelling like spring sap. That was the difference between us. I drew a hand across my eyes, trying to think properly.

Behind me I could sense Shadow hiding in the grass.

Ruby, come away. I've been thinking and I've decided it's dangerous.

I turned my head. His darkness made the air bulge.

'You again, you left me alone soon enough in those woods. Why should I talk to you now?'

I couldn't help it. The witch scared me so. Then I got angry.

The grasses rustled as he shifted in his hidey-hole; a puff of old seeds dislodged from the spot and drifted across the grass.

'You know how childish you sound? Like a baby.'

Silence for a moment. *I am a child.*

'Well, I can't be expected to look after you as well.' I looked down at my hands. My nails were filthy from being in the woods. 'I've come to give myself up.'

That's risky.

My throat hardened. 'I know that, stupid. What else can I do? I'll die in those woods all alone. What do you care any-way?' I stamped my foot. 'You ran off and left me. You—'

I had to, Ruby. That boy, he'll be eaten up by now. Or cooked at least.

'Stop it.'

It's true. He'll be in slices by now.

'Stop!'

Something white unravelled at the kitchen window and Mick's face reared up. Me and the Shadow screamed in unison. There was the sound of a door handle turning and he was there, filling the back door, holding a bandage to his head.

'Ho, ho. So she's come back again.' Mick stood in the hall at the mirror, trying to tie the bandage back on his head, his fingers tearing at the knots. 'I knew she would. It would only be a matter of time, I told Barbara.'

A fury was building in the mirror. I could see the edge of it at this angle, shining like teeth.

Mick turned. The bandage was back on his head, haphazard. His pyjamas were crumpled as if he'd been disturbed from bed and his bare feet looked white and bony on the dirty hall carpet. I couldn't tell if he was dead or not.

'Yes,' he went on, 'I said to her when she was wailing, "She'll be back soon enough. It's me you should be looking out for now, girl."' I could see he didn't believe himself to be passed, but that didn't mean anything. Was Barbara's wailing for me, or was it actually for him and he didn't realise?

I stood poised for flight in case he was alive and all this fumbling in the mirror was a prelude to being thrown against a wall. Then a dark red began blooming on the white gauze on his head, opening into a full red rose, and I cried out despite myself.

'Dad,' I cried out. 'Your head's bleeding.' My hands flew up and grabbed at my hair, hard.

85

'Damn thing.' He tore the bandage off. I could see the seeping slit spliced together with black stitches. It made me think of the dolls I'd made with their crude stitching, still out there somewhere in the woods. His head was shaved around it.

My arms jerked up as if on wires and I held them out towards him.

'Dad, I'm sorry.' I started crying. 'I'm so sorry.'

He didn't answer, just kept fiddling with the bandage in the mirror.

'Dad?' My voice cracked. A longing flowed through me harder and faster than I'd ever felt. The hunger and the tiredness had left a hollow for it. The longing wanted to fix on any breathing thing and wrap itself around it.

'Tell me you're alive.'

'What?'

'Please. Dad, please. Can't I be your Trudy? Your sweet pea? I truly, truly didn't mean to hurt you.'

'No.'

'Dad, please.'

He'd slumped against the wall. 'No. Don't talk about her. Don't say her name.'

'But, Dad. I could be.' I was sobbing hard now. 'I could change my ways. I could make myself how you'd want me.'

'No.' Slowly, slowly he sunk down until he was on his knees. 'Don't ever say her name,' he whispered.

'Dad?' He stayed still, his eyes raised to the ceiling. He reminded me of a picture of Jesus I'd seen, kneeling and with his eyes looking to heaven. Tears rolled down his face and splashed on his pyjama top making two dark patches on his chest. The falling tears were his only movement.

I nearly went to touch him to see if I felt flesh under my hand, but the thought he might rear up and put his hands around my throat stopped me in my tracks. Perhaps he was even meant to lure me closer with his stillness? It seemed like the sort of thing he'd do in life. I tiptoed away into the kitchen. At the sink I poured a glass of water and drank through the hiccoughs. After stream water it tasted warm and sultry.

When I went back into the hall he'd gone. Just the bandage was left, coiling white and red on the floor.

21

20 August 1970

Birth comes on quicker than she could ever imagine. At the hospital the pains are griping up and down her legs. Anna has a small suitcase packed. In it are only a few baby things, soft and fluffy like feathers. She hasn't gone to town – she won't need much before the adoption takes place. They've agreed for her to keep the baby for six weeks before it's taken so she can breastfeed. Sonia said it would be better to give it up straight away – almost as it was ripped from her womb, as Anna thought of it – but she stuck to her guns.

'In here,' the nurse says as she takes her through to a ward with four beds, but the only one being occupied is hers. She wonders briefly if she's being kept away from the married mothers. This is the forest – old ways are not challenged easily.

The pains gather in the base of her womb and she lets out a groan. 'Is it like bad period pain?' she'd asked her mother, who'd cackled, but not unkindly. 'No, love, if only it were. You're better off knowing now, though. I've known women so shocked by it they can't even push and the baby has to be pulled out with forceps. You don't want that if you can help it. Jim Fardine has still got the marks either side of his head and he's over thirty.'

Anna lets out a groan and steadies herself by holding

onto the bed rail. 'It hurts,' she beseeches the nurse.

The nurse's mouth is primping up like raw pastry. She pretends to smooth the bed, already as smooth and glacial as a frozen lake, and Anna hears her muttering something that sounds like, 'Well, you've had your pleasure.'

'What did you say?' The contraction has subsided now, leaving Anna amazingly pain free. She feels strong – ready to face this old nurse down with her uncooked pastry mouth. 'What did you just say?'

'Nothing.' The nurse's eyes are switching side to side. 'Get into bed. It'll only get worse and then it'll be harder to climb up.'

'It was a pleasure too.' She faces the nurse and says it before crawling into the cold sheets.

But the pain comes down, swirling in great torrents. It lifts her body up, arching, for it to be snapped back straight. It's not just in her womb; it seems to go right from the top of her skull down to her feet. It bounces her around – and the screams that she tried to hold back at first come thick and fast.

'Get it out. Get it ooouut.'

Not even her mother warned her properly about this. What was this conspiracy of silence among women when the subject came up? You knew by the way their eyes slid away from you there was something they weren't telling. Now Anna knows what it is, she's being initiated.

She grabs wildly at the younger nurse who's arrived with the first one. 'You've got to get it out,' Anna pants. 'You've got to help me.'

'Ssshh,' the younger nurse says, 'you'll be alarming the other mothers – the ones that haven't started yet.'

But they should be warned, thinks Anna, her body arching again, they need to know about this. Though her mind is too taken up to think what they might do about it at this late stage. There's a lull where she's so tired sleep overtakes her for a few seconds. She wakes with a start. The nice young nurse is holding her wrist, measuring her heartbeat against the little gold watch pinned to her white uniform.

'I'm so afraid for this baby,' says Anna from her pillow.

'Now then.' The nurse smiles down at her. 'Everyone feels the same at this stage, it'll all be over soon and everything will be right as rain.'

That's not what Anna meant. 'No, not the birth. That's not it at all. You've got it wrong – it's something else. Her life . . . or . . .' She's too far gone to articulate what she means properly. She hardly knows herself, just feels a dread that's been steadily creeping across the floor towards her bed.

'It's the adoption, that's all,' the nurse whispers to her. 'It's bound to be unsettling. Once baby's here you'll stop worrying so much, I'm sure.'

'Yes, yes. I suppose that must be it.'

Anna's body buckles and another scream rips through the room.

The young nurse goes out to find her colleague in the corridor. 'She'll be needing something to calm her down,' she says.

Soon there's a needle slipping into her vein. Then a funny distance to the bed and the woman lying there with her knees up in the air, so it's all still happening but somehow she's looking at it through a window.

*

Anna finally gets to leap back into her own body. She feels like she's sprung down from the top corner of the room. When she's reunited with her own flesh there's a baby in her arms.

The birth wasn't a blank. She saw the whole thing as if from afar: there was the journey down from the empty ward to the delivery room, the figure in the wheelchair looked huge – it didn't care how it wasn't holding its legs together despite the fact people were walking past – visitors with bunches of flowers and bottles of Lucozade in their arms. Then in the delivery room there was the pushing that went on for hours or maybe days.

As the baby is born the atmosphere in the room thickens, changes. Even the dark shadows seem to have colours in them, touches of deep blue, sulphurous yellow and red, as the child slithers out into the world. Despite how often they've seen birth, the staff always feel it, the crackle of electricity in the air at this moment. Then the little red thing is taken away and she is left on her own. Slowly, nurses gather around Anna. They begin stroking her hair and wiping and easing her out of her gown. They bear a pale blue nightie with flower sprigs towards her. It's neatly folded and taken from Anna's bag.

From her distance Anna can tell something is wrong. There's muttering from across the room. The nurses around her are trying to distract her, by telling her how well she's done.

'Where's my baby?' she keeps asking.

'Just five minutes, just being washed and weighed, just being checked over . . .'

Then the leap back into her body as the drugs wear out

of her system and the baby is in her arms.

'Rather a large mark,' the doctor is saying as he's wiping his hands on a towel. 'But nothing out of the ordinary, why my aunt she had a quite extraordinary birthmark – went right down her neck and shoulder—'

'Is that it?' Anna feels fierce with love for the creature and holds her tight.

'Is what it?'

'Is that why you kept me from Ruby?' She could just imagine what her own mother would have to say about *that*.

The doctor doesn't answer, just keeps wiping his hands. As a matter of fact he's not used to being spoken to quite so sharply and it's left him momentarily stunned.

Anna looks into her baby's face. The mark makes the eye on the left hand side seem extra bright.

'It's nothing that matters,' she says. 'It's absolutely nothing. She's beautiful. She's perfect.'

22

RETURN
17 November 1983

Into the silence of the house came the sound of the front door opening. This time I'd waited for hours for that noise.

'Barbara?' I called out cautiously, my head stuck in the fridge and a greasy chicken leg in my hand. I'd been chewing as quietly as I could, hunger overcoming everything. 'Barbara,' I called again, wiping my chin of slippery fat. 'Is that you?'

A rushing sound passed down the hall and I got thrust against a bony chest. Barbara's perfume filled my nostrils. For the first time I realised how unlike it was to anything else in the house. The scent was like a cool white flower rendered in abstract. It turned the air watery around her.

'My girl. My darling girl, you're back.'

'Oh Barbara.' I buried my face into the rough weave of her tapestry coat. 'I thought you'd hate me now for ever. Is he dead? Have I killed him?'

She took me by the shoulders so she could see me properly. There was a bruise under her eye that looked like a giant teardrop.

'No, of course not. Haven't you seen him?'

'Does it hurt?' I asked, my voice a whisper.

Barbara shook her head as if it didn't matter. 'I've been so worried about you. Mick said I was not to worry and you'd soon be back with your tail between your legs. But I couldn't

93

help it. He said you'd be out in the forest, like before, and I went and called and called but you never answered.'

'Really?'

'Yes. There were some nasty questions asked at the hospital. He kept his mouth shut and wouldn't say a word about it, though. He said he didn't want his family dragged through the mud and what happened was nobody's business but our own.'

We stayed silent for a moment.

'Oh Ruby,' she said, her eyes brimming with tears, and she hugged me again and I thought, she's doing this despite the fact I'm filthy with forest dirt. That my hair's matted and so full of leaves I must look like a walking bird's nest. She's doing it even though I probably smell terrible against her watery flower.

'Come on,' she said, and we crept upstairs and she ran me a bath and swirled her favourite strawberry bath crème into the water and the water foamed up pinkish. She fetched her best pale blue dressing gown with the fluffy fur around the collar and laid it out next to the bath.

'Come back downstairs,' she whispered, 'and I'll do your hair the way we used to do it when we were girls. None of that hedgehog stuff you've been going in for lately.'

Cleaned and dry the insect bites showed up round and hard on my face and arms. Barbara tutted and set me on a kitchen chair.

'There now, let me comb the tangles out first. You know, one woman I do cleaning for has her own hairdryer in her house with a leather chair and a big plastic dome that comes right over her head, just like at the hairdresser's. Lord, she looks funny staring through it and putting her cigarette up underneath so she can smoke at the same time.' She ratted at my hair with a pink plastic comb. 'The smoke gets all blown right back down so it looks like her head's taking off in a rocket.'

I felt warm and drowsy with her hands moving all over my head, combing, twisting, pinning. I remembered then how she'd been when my gran was alive. How they'd sit at the table shelling hazelnuts and if a specially large or sweet one got cracked, she'd call out to me, 'Sweets for the sweet, Ruby.' Though when I told Barbara the memory she sounded sad.

'Oh yes,' she said, as if she was remembering it too but the remembering wasn't a happy one.

I looked behind me and her face had gone tight and pinched above the big, flappy collar of her purple dress.

I tried to change the subject so her face would fill out again. 'I saw a fox in the woods when I was away, sniffing in the clearing. I went right up to it and it didn't mind at all or try to run away.'

'It probably thought you were another fox, Ruby,' she said. 'You were a bit whiffy.'

'I wish we could stay like this for ever,' I whispered into the darkening kitchen. We hadn't switched on the strip light and I knew it was because we wanted to stay feeling safe and warm and hidden like this.

'Be careful what you wish for, Ruby, it might come true,' she said. I wondered if she meant she'd wished for Mick, then got him. 'Besides,' she went on, 'nothing can stay the same for ever, that's what I need to talk to you about.'

Then she explained to me how I was to leave the house for good. It had all been planned out without me while I was away. There was nothing to be said and nothing to be done.

23

THIEF
17 November 1983

I jumped up and hairpins rattled at my neck. 'No,' I shouted. 'You can't make me go.'

The strip was on now in the kitchen and had spread its ugly light. Barbara looked small and crumpled in it. The long zip on her dress was askew and zigzagged down her front. She looked up, then instantly her eyes slid away like she couldn't bear the sight of me. I imagined my face, glowering, above the fluffy blue rim of the collar.

There were footsteps on the stairs: Mick, roused by the commotion. The wound on his head had dried up but it was a dull angry red that somehow looked even worse than fresh blood. Of course he's alive, I thought, alive and twice as ugly.

Barbara had already told me I was to be sent to Mick's sister in Coventry. Elaine's house was in a long street of brick houses where the only green was the odd weed growing between the paving stones. That street was the deadest thing I'd ever seen. There were so many pale kids in the house I remembered it as a nest of worms. She was a nurse, so fat and breathless that after work she'd sit on the sofa with her legs apart, showing her long old-fashioned knickers that came down to her knees, smoking until she recovered herself enough to heave up. Tim, her eldest, slapped me whenever he saw me and mimicked my accent, drawling – 'I'm Ruby, a retard from the country.'

Now I sat opposite Barbara and Mick and laid my hands flat on the table. 'Please,' I said, 'please, please don't send me away. Please let me stay.'

'It's been decided.' Mick flapped at the collar of his pyjamas like he couldn't get enough air.

'I can't leave the forest.' I lowered my head into my arms and began to sob.

'Perhaps . . .' began Barbara. 'I didn't think she'd take on so much, Mick.' Barbara's voice was hushed. 'Maybe we should . . .'

I could see the battle raging all over Barbara's face. It twitched and pulled the skin one way then another. She was trying to choose us both.

Mick wouldn't let her. 'No,' he said.

'We might be over the worst . . .'

'You know what we said.' His voice was firmer, threat creeping from the edges. 'You know what we discussed.'

I sat upright. 'See, Barbara does want me to stay. She'd like it.'

'Oh, Ruby.'

'You did, you just said it. That's what you meant.'

'It doesn't have to be for ever, perhaps,' said Barbara finally. 'And you could come back for Christmases.'

'I know what it'll be like,' I said. 'It'll be out of sight, out of mind. You'll forget I ever existed.'

She bit her lip. 'Listen, Mikey,' she said softly. 'Perhaps . . .' and her voice was so hushed and soft I wanted to climb on her lap, to take the zipper on her dress right down and crawl inside, like a baby, like a joey into its pouch.

'No, you both fucking listen.' Mick crashed his fist on the table. 'It has been decided. It'll help with the budget too after, you know . . .'

'Shut up, Mick,' said Barbara.

'I will not, you bloody silly woman.'

The bright red anxious paint was showing on her cheeks again.

'What?' I asked.

Mick stood up, dragged a plastic carrier bag out of a kitchen drawer and emptied the contents onto the table – the compact I'd seen before, with the pink enamel flower on the lid. There was a bottle of perfume with interlocking black Cs on the label and silver objects whose purpose I couldn't fathom.

'If you hadn't gone round nicking the contents of half the houses for a twenty-mile radius all these years you might still have a job. So *you* shut up.'

And I'd nearly been going to tell her about what I'd seen, about Sandra, but I couldn't. She sat opposite me with all the glinting silver and glass and tubes of lipstick on the table. She didn't look like a thief. She just looked like a sad, sad shopkeeper behind her counter. I remembered the make-up she'd scooped out of her pockets for me that rainy day.

'Things have been going missing round here too.' He stared at her accusingly.

Barbara sighed. 'I don't know anything about your stupid shirt, I told you.' She turned to me. 'Perhaps it's time you went to bed, Ruby.'

On the way upstairs I passed the mirror. My face was pocked with the bites I'd got out in the forest, now swelling red and blistering. I was still glowering; I was ugly with it.

I leaned over the banister. I could see their shapes through the ridged glass of the kitchen door. Mick standing. Barbara bent over the trinkets on the table. Already they looked distant, as if my real mum and dad, in all their gloriousness, might open the door of the living room and step right in front of me and Mick and Barbara would just be grey shapes behind them.

I thought about leaving this place and it felt unbelievable – that I wouldn't be there to witness all the white flowers that materialised on the forest floor in spring and the first flush of leaves as the forest simmered into life again. The summer sun warming even the darkest hidden places. Or gaze upon the wreath of honey fungus around a dying tree, as if the earth was trying to push out a sickness. Or even the yellow autumn leaves glittering against a cold autumn sky. I'd rather go out and die among the trees than that.

I stayed on the stairs because I wanted to catch Barbara and plead with her on her own. They talked for ages with Barbara's voice rising and falling. Then Mick came to bed. I squidged to one side so he could go past me on the stairs and we just looked at each other, me looking up, him looking down, then he was gone.

Barbara came out. I could hear her slowly dragging herself and it seemed to take an age for her to put one foot in front of the other. Despite everything my heart contracted for her. She didn't seem surprised to see me sitting on the bottom stair.

'What do you want, Ruby?' she asked.

I couldn't answer for a while because my throat seemed to have closed up so tight not even a squeak could get out. Finally I said, 'I want you to love me, that's what. If you could just love me, like I really was your daughter, then everything would be all right.'

'Oh, but I do,' she said in a flat voice.

24

THE LEAVING
20 November 1983

Three days later, I walked our street for the last time. I said goodbye to everything.

All the children of the street bunched together on the cracked pavement that bloomed with frost – Joe, the two girls Jayne and Libby, even the quiet redheaded boy who was so pale you could see the veins pulsing through him. They stood, a ragged band.

'Will you do our hair for us before you go?' asked Libby.

I nodded. 'I'll go and fetch the brush and hairspray.'

When I came back they'd stripped off their hairbands, which hung in dirty pink stripes on their wrists. 'Make it stand right out like yours,' said Libby.

When I was done they turned to each other and their backcombed hair buffeted behind their heads. They laughed, both mouths full of sharp little teeth.

'Here,' said Joe, reaching out his hand and showing me the tatty paper bag there. 'This is for you, from all of us to say goodbye.'

I looked inside. Cola cubes. The sugar shone like powdered glass in the winter sun.

'Thank you,' I said. 'Thank you.' I knew how much the gift meant. Sweets were treasure.

I left them there. As I passed, an overgrown garden rose

tipped its last few left-over red blooms on me. Flecks of crimson fell on my boots. The colour sang bright on the grey pavement and the temptation to mess with it was so strong I did a little dance. I looked down; now they were mashed into the ground in bloody splats, and I walked on with the unease of something having been spoiled.

A coincidence of course; that baptism of blood. The old green suitcase waited in the hall when I went outside to bid farewell to the grasses and the doll's arm. I waved to them and they waved back, as usual, not realising it was goodbye. The plank I'd hit Mick with had disappeared. No doubt hidden somewhere in case I gave in to violent urges again.

I hugged my belly. There was pain there. In an overgrown patch I hid and squatted, pulling my knickers down. In the T-bar of my pants was red the same size as one of the rose petals, but jellylike.

Barbara waved to me from the front garden using all her fingers. Her face looked like it was collapsing in on itself like her teeth had gone overnight. Her dress was cheery, though – lines of purple and orange daisies in rows of wide open eyes.

I poked my face out of the car window. A breeze shimmied at the tears on my cheeks so they changed direction and carved curves across my face. Mick was behind, shoving the case into the boot. I could hear him, grunting and swearing. The case was too big, and it was making him angry.

'Ruby, now.' She took a tissue from her pocket and pressed it to her mouth. 'I'm really going to miss you, you know. But for now, isn't it for the best?'

I closed my eyes. 'No.'

'You'll be able to forget about it all, everything that's happened, Ruby.' She leaned into the front hedge to whisper so her torso looked like it was growing out of green. 'I wish I could say the same – you'll forget once you're in a different place.'

Mick was in the driving seat now and the car was already sliding away.

'Ruby, Ruby,' Barbara was louder now, calling me back. 'Have you got – you know – enough?'

The pad crunching underneath me felt huge, like it was making me sit up high.

'I don't know,' I said, panicking. 'I don't know how many I'll need.'

Barbara tried to tell me something, her mouth working in frantic, black shapes. 'What was that?' I knelt up and leaned out of the moving car but I couldn't hear. Already she'd become a tiny waving figure, her hanky fluttering in her hand, then we turned the corner and she disappeared altogether.

'Goodbye, Barbara,' I yelled. 'Goodbye.'

25

BIRD
20 November 1983

Mick drove like we were late even though there was ages to the train. He slapped the horn hard and the driver in front of us veered and pulled in, letting us pass. After he'd overtaken he leaned back and turned the steering wheel with his fingertips. He'd been working out with his dumbbells like a madman in the last few weeks. His short-sleeved T-shirt showed his muscles off, the cuffs of the sleeves biting into the lumps on his arms they'd got so big. I guessed it must be because he found thirteen-year-old girls so scary. It was a shame the same hadn't happened to mine.

The silence pressed between us like shells were being held to my ears.

'What are you squirming about for?' he asked eventually.

I blurted before I could think. 'My first period began this morning.'

'Oh,' he said, and started driving faster, like he couldn't wait to get rid of me now he knew I was bleeding inside his car. For some reason I had the idea he might suddenly screech to a halt, drag me into the trees and beat me senseless for saying it too. I gripped the car seat either side and tried to focus through the windscreen to stop the picture of my body lying in the woods as stiff as the dead bird. The trees flashed past us making me dizzy. Each breath seemed to hurt.

'Don't bother giving me the silent treatment. It won't work,' he said finally in a voice humming with malice, although really it was terror gluing my tongue to the roof of my mouth. 'You. I don't know how you even thought you could carry on with us, going around setting fire to my clothing.' He gripped the steering wheel so hard the car bounced from side to side.

'Stop it, please. You're going to crash.'

'Plus there's this.' He jerked his finger up to the side of his head. 'This was the final fucking straw.'

I couldn't see the angry, purple ripple from this side. He'd tried to comb his hair to cover it; the cream he used made gaps in his hair the size of matchsticks, but the tail of the gash still showed like the end of a purple worm climbing up into his scalp. Several times he'd caught me staring at it and he shuffled back a step and instinctively put up his hand. It made me look at my own hands and ponder on how they were the very thing that had made that wound. They itched when I thought of it and I had to scratch them till they were red before they got comfortable again.

Now, I thought of opening the car door and throwing myself out but I noticed the trees had thinned as we approached town and then the traffic slowed us to a standstill. I felt glad to be among people.

Through the window I saw a little girl with her arm high up, holding her dad's hand. She said something to him and he stopped and took the sweet from her other hand and carefully unwrapped it. I had the strangest feeling that that little girl was me and that the man was my real father and there we both were as we should have been in some fork in the road that I might find if I looked hard enough. If I found that secret turning I'd be able to walk right into that little girl and hold my real dad's hand. My throat swelled. Then the car began moving and they both slid past the window. They made me think of Barbara too; she felt so distant now and I began to worry about leaving her – how would she survive?

We drove into the car park of the train station. I let myself out of the passenger side and gulped in the fresh air.

The shadows on the platform were black in the winter sun. We stood facing each other like a cowboy film where things were about to happen, where the train arrives and everything snaps into action. Mick's fingers tapped repeatedly at the seam of his jeans.

I felt safer out of the car despite the fact that the platform was deserted. I fiddled with the plastic handle of the suitcase. 'Is this because of Sandra?' I asked at last, throwing caution to the wind – a last-minute desperate bid. 'I won't tell Barbara, I promise,' even as I spoke I hated myself for being such a nasty little animal, trying to broker this deal, 'if it means I can come back.'

'No.'

I looked at the tracks and imagined my head coming off, sliced by the train that was coming to take me away. I remembered the girl who'd called for her real family in the woods one night and she seemed like a baby.

Mick eyed me up and down. 'Try to fit in with Elaine. Look at the way you're dressed, it doesn't exactly help. It's an embarrassment.'

I was wearing Grandad's coat that nearly came down to the ground and a bright pink scarf done up housewife style.

'I like it.'

'Fuck's sake.' He swung one leg round and began to hurry off.

'No, Mick. Dad, come back.'

He was already disappearing into the hole of the ticket office doorway. I heard the front door of it bang on the other side.

Left alone the sky felt huge above me.

'Look after Barbara,' I called after him, knowing it was futile, that he wouldn't hear.

The train arrived, spitting and whistling and a shaking broke out all over. Soon, Elaine would have enough of me too and it would be Social Services. The only way to be saved was to be with my real family. They were the only ones who'd ever care enough. If I didn't find them I'd be lost for ever.

The train was the kind with carriages, all lined up into little rooms. I took off my coat and folded it up on the seat next to me. The blue and red felt of the fabric stuck into the backs of my knees through my thin black leggings. The train throbbed, the engine idling while it waited for passengers, I could feel the vibrations through the floor. I held on to the plastic handle of the suitcase hoping that no one else would get in with me. They might try and talk to me. They might try and be kind and that would be the end of it, I'd crack open, spilling tears and runny snot all over the seats. They'd soon regret it.

I tried to fix on the tannoy above the door, forcing myself to notice the criss-crossed wire, the broken bit that stood out in a barb of metal, to keep from crying. Then with a certainty that flowed to the marrow of my bones I knew I was at a fork in the road that could determine things for ever. When I looked to where the train was heading it was all blackness, gloom. Outside the window was chaos and more uncertainty than I thought was possible. I had to choose.

'Come on, Pilgrim,' I whispered to myself as I picked up my suitcase and stepped off the train.

I watched the train getting smaller, the sun sparking off its back, until it got swallowed into the blue horizon. A sweat had broken out under my arms, down my back. What had I done? I shuffled the suitcase to the hedge that separated the platform from the car park. The leaves were large and speckled and hung down. Suddenly, I had the idea there could be eyes in there, peeping through, checking I'd gone.

'Mick,' I called through the leaves. I put my mouth close. 'Mick, are you there?' Something rustled and I jumped but I saw it was just a bird among the branches. Its yellow eye shone up at me from the darkness and it flittered against the foliage. I kept expecting to hear the rush as it escaped out from the other side and took to the air, but it just stayed there crashing about, flying from branch to branch like it didn't know there was an outside.

A hope occurred as I peered through those leaves – a strange hope given our history, some might think: I wanted Mick to be there waiting, smoking a roll-up cigarette and with one leg draped out of the open door of the car. In my hope he'd wordlessly flick his head to the passenger seat next to him and I'd get in and go back home. The hope flickered out. Deep within me I knew that was not safe, it was just familiar.

Outside the station was Shadow crouched in the blackness

underneath a coach in the car park. The engine of the coach was throbbing while the driver sat at the wheel and read a newspaper. I felt into my pocket for Tom's poem. I'd taken to carrying it around with me everywhere. I'd touched it so often the paper was becoming fragile. I took it out and began to read the words I already had by heart. Then the unfamiliar griping pain assaulted my belly and I had to hug myself.

What's wrong with you?

'It's my insides.'

You're lucky to have insides. Mine have long gone.

'Not when they hurt like this.'

Perhaps it's sorrow. Sorrow can feel like that.

I squinted at him and he moved aside, squeezing behind the tyre. I tucked the poem back into my pocket.

'Perhaps.' I dropped down. 'What do you want?' I whispered. 'You, that will leave me the moment my back is turned, or if the going gets tough.'

I heard a small cough pipe out from underneath the vehicle as if he could actually choke on the exhaust fumes.

I've been trying to think about what we should do next.

'Isn't that hard when you don't actually have a brain?' I asked. There was a small hurt silence and I called out, 'Sorry, sorry. I'm sorry.'

It didn't take long for him to reply; usually he'd punish me with silence or by vanishing altogether. But he was eager this time.

The answer came to me while I was waiting out here for you but now it's gone. If you'd let me tell you straight away I might still have it.

'That's it,' I said and a woman walking past wearing a jacket made of brown fur stared at me, alarmed. I smiled at her to show her that I wasn't just a mad person talking to myself.

I turned my back on him, and went to pick up my suitcase but as if he could sense me leaving he called out in a shrill voice, *I've got it, I remember, I remember – I might know where I can find some of your family, your real family, that is. The ones you've been looking for.*

I dropped the case and whirled round. 'What?' I said. 'What did you just say?' I checked the woman in the jacket had gone and crouched down again so I could hear him better. 'Why have you never told me this before?'

Because I've only just thought of it, or remembered, I'm not sure which. Besides I've been busy remembering other things of late. He coughed again. *It's not certain. Often I'm wrong or get things backwards, so I'm warning you about that.*

I realised my heart was pounding. My family, my own people.

Two girls, about the age of ten but with full make-up on their faces, walked past and pointed at me crouching by the bus, sniggering under their breaths. I grimaced at them and they scattered.

I thought how mean I'd been to Shadow recently for sounding so babyish, when in fact it wasn't him who'd changed but me. He'd remained the same since I first remember seeing him when I was three.

'Listen,' I said, 'even if there's just a chance, a tiny chance, then we must take it. But you have to tell me where to go and what to do because the way things are I don't know where to start. I'm as lost as it's possible to be.'

It's above us.

'What is?' I asked, looking at the sky.

No, no, the bus we need to get on. I purposely stuck here so I wouldn't forget to say.

Shadow climbed up before me and bounded down the aisle settling into one of the seats, bouncing and looking out the window like he was going on a school trip.

'Where to?' asked the driver.

'I'm not sure,' I said. 'I'll pay the fare till the end but I might have to get out before that.'

'Whatever,' he said, not interested.

26

21 August 1970

Despite her protestations in the delivery room at first it feels like a cruel joke: Ruby, the name Anna has kept like treasure all this time as the baby ripened inside her.

Anna sits up in her hospital bed and lifts the child out of the cot beside her, pulling the knitted yellow bonnet off the baby's head and examining the extent of it.

'What about Margaret? That's a lovely name.' The nurse bustles up to Anna's bedside: the nice one who never looks for the ring on anybody's finger. She's seen Anna examining the mark. You get to know the mother's thoughts when you've been doing this awhile, just by watching.

Anna smiles at her. 'Maybe.'

'Margaret also means daisy and she looks so fresh and clean, like a daisy. And such beautiful eyes. Not like some. I shouldn't say, but you see some horrors here.' She bites her lip; she hadn't meant to say that and runs on quickly to cover it over. 'Eyes like squashed currants. Not like your girl. Of course, you never say.'

Anna sighs. 'I don't know, Margaret's pretty, but it sounds old-fashioned.'

'Are we still going on the breast?' the nurse asks, wanting to change the subject.

Anna nods. 'Yes. She doesn't always latch on, though.

I think it might be because she's having a bottle at night. They say it has to be a bottle at night – so they can feed her in the nursery. I wouldn't mind feeding at night at all, though. They could come and get me.'

'Mother needs rest.' The nurse raps out the words automatically, even as she is reading a chart, running her fingers down the rows of numbers.

Anna doesn't tell the nurse that she gets up anyway sometimes. She puts on her dressing gown and slippers and limps down the hallway and peeps through the nursery window. The huge window makes everything inside look strange, like it's a zoo. The rows of babies are human exhibits. There's never any problem picking out her own, the red mark sees to that, it stands out bright against all the white and glass: white walls; white uniforms; see-through plastic cots; white bottles of milk. Seeing her own baby being fed by another woman is odd, like looking at a film. It makes Anna feel disconnected, as if all this might not really be happening. As if she could put on her shoes and coat and leave on her own with her new flat stomach and go back to her job in the chemist's as if nothing had happened.

'I've changed my mind about the adoption,' she says. She tells everyone, all the time, just to be sure.

The nurse smiles. 'Quite right too. Now, let's have another go on the breast.' She draws the curtains round the bed and takes the baby while Anna unbuttons herself. The nurse is practised; she has the knack of cradling the back of the baby's head and jerking it forward in one swift motion so the child grasps onto the nipple. Soon it's suckling away. It's Anna's left breast so the mark disappears beneath.

She looks down and runs through names in her mind: Vanessa; Angela; Christine; Diana. None of them fit.

No, it has to be Ruby. There's something so powerful and durable about the name. A red fire inside a stone.

Anna becomes aware out of the corner of her eye there's a flutter at the nurses' station outside the ward window. She turns and her heart thumps when she sees what's caused it, it's Lewis come to visit. The three nurses bend their heads, a flurry of pale fingers fly through the air to faces then down to the full white uniform skirts, smoothing. It's like a King or Emperor is paying a visit. Anna can't help but feel a lightness at the sight of him.

His tall dark figure – black-suited – is such a contrast to all the white. It makes him the bright one, somehow. He's carrying flag iris, loosely wrapped in pale green tissue paper. One nurse points through the window and he turns to look.

She smiles; she can't help it and, there, they are just the same.

He brings in with him the outside. Pockets of it are in the fabric of his suit: air that carries the threat of rain; car exhaust; wood smoke; fresh wind. The smells chase off the antiseptic tang of the hospital air and mingle with the faint cool perfume of the iris that reminds Anna of the graveside. He lays the flowers down on her bedside table and he stands over the cot, his head bent. Anna's heart compresses, nobody will have told him about the birthmark . . .

He picks his child up, easily, as if he's used to doing it and places a kiss, first on one cheek then the other, then slowly lowers her back down. A small fist appears over the edge of the cot as if Ruby has recognised her father.

'You came.' She can't help it, sounding so grateful and happy. She shouldn't, after he's left her on her own all this time.

'I'd heard it was a girl.'

'No one told you about the birthmark, though?'

'No, why should they? It doesn't matter. It doesn't matter at all. Don't you go thinking it does.'

She nods. It's the first time anyone has looked at Ruby without their eyes flicking sideways. Even the mother of one of the other women in the ward let out a small cry before scurrying off to her own unblemished granddaughter.

Lewis sits in the green plastic armchair next to the bed. 'I'm sorry, Anna. I've been a right bastard, haven't I? Young and stupid, I guess.'

She shifts; the tear that Ruby made as she fought her way out into the world is still sharp when she moves.

He takes her hand and the old familiar thrill goes through her. Again, she can't help it; it feels so natural. His fingernails are immaculately clean and his hand fits around hers perfectly.

'It'll be all right. We'll manage,' he says, the words she wanted to hear months ago. She's not sure if it might be too late for them now. Something has changed in her. Is this what she wants? She's not so certain any more.

'I can't decide anything yet, Lewis,' she says.

But he runs on – his plans, businesses, a ring, as if she's just agreed to his way of making everything all right. She realises the hospital smell has begun to exert its authority again. It's absorbed nearly all the scents he brought in with him. Just the cool graveside scent of the iris remains.

Gradually, he grows silent, like the river has run dry. She sees his eyes turn to the window that looks over the car park; she knows he's thinking of himself being outside already, striding briskly to his car. Though afterwards she tries to tell herself she imagined that.

27

RABBIT HOLE
20 November 1983

At the blue hills I watched as the bus disappeared, turning into a dot as it climbed the road, until it burned up in the sun that was falling hard towards the earth.

My heart began to race. It was so quiet here.

What had I done? What had I gone and done now? I nearly died last time and here I was again, running away. I could actually truly die this time and join Shadow for eternity.

Clouds raked fast-moving shadows that fell from the peaks, speeding away downwards before they dropped into the valley below. It made me dizzy. I hungered for the forest and the curling restful canopy of rustling leaves. This place looked shaved raw. The dizziness grew until I felt I could be tumbled down, down into nothingness. I sat, cupping my face in my hands, until the rocking subsided whispering, 'Fuck. Fuck. Fuck,' into my hands.

When finally I stood the pad felt full and heavy between my legs. In the suitcase, among all the folded clothes that me and Barbara had packed the day before, I found the fresh ones. I buried the used pad, clawing into the red dirt, although I hated leaving my blood inside the mountain. It felt too much like a sacrifice.

'Where do we go from here?' I asked, in case Shadow was still around.

All was quiet, just the wind blowing across the tops of the hills. I turned to see him streaking up a zigzagging path ahead.

'Wait for me,' I called. 'Wait for me.'

Further up I had to stop; my fingers ached with the weight of the suitcase. I unzipped the front panel and found some last gifts there: an apple and slices of seed cake – Barbara's favourite – wrapped in a napkin. Small offerings, but I was grateful for them and I ate the cake in tiny bites, breaking it off into pieces with my fingers. The seeds were small and dark like the cake had pips and I set them between my teeth and bit so the pungent, dry flavour flooded through my mouth.

As I was eating I noticed a dark patch concealed by a fringe of hanging grass. Carefully, I put my hand inside; it felt dark and cool and reminded me of the forest. I stood and waved my arms about to get Shadow's attention.

'Look, look – there's a rabbit hole.' I wiped my lips with the back of my hand. 'I can't go on lugging this case. It's too heavy. I'm going to put some stuff in there. How far have we got to go anyway?'

I looked around, emptiness and silence. I wanted to cry so hard it hurt but I wouldn't let myself, I decided suddenly, not here, not in this dreadful place. There would be no hope for me if I did.

I took out a pair of shoes and half the clothes and stuffed them in the rabbit hole. I marked it with a secret sign of crossed sticks, hoping my things weren't falling as I looked – deep down into the centre of the hill. I tried to remember Pilgrim as I set off back up the mountain, hoping I was on the right path, the one to my salvation. The certainty he felt, though, was not in my heart.

Streaks of orange and yellow unfurled across the sky by the time I stopped to rest nearly at the summit. There was a huge slab of stone. The back of it was chunked like a staircase so I climbed up to get a better view. Below me the drop was sheer and fell away into the approaching darkness. The sunset looked so different here. In the forest it was a slow end, light filtering and dividing and sub-dividing a hundred times as it was parted by the trees. Here, the sun felt like it might take you with it, burning up and dragging you downwards to the other side of the world. As the sun went down the real chill began to fall. I wrapped my arms around my knees and hugged them tight. I was all alone and night was falling. There wasn't even a hollow tree for shelter. Surely, I'd never find the warmth of real family in this harsh place as Shadow had said. There didn't seem a speck of it here.

'Stupid, stupid,' I said and slapped myself hard across the face like Mick would do. My cheek stung and the eye on that side began to leak.

Stop it. Stop it. Silly bitch. Why did you do that? Shadow was suddenly by my side, sounding frightened.

'Because I feel so stupid, dumb, running away like this. Don't call me a bitch. It's not fair – you sound like Mick. I could be at Elaine's now, eating her beans on toast, sitting in front of the TV with a plate on my lap with all the others. Instead I'll probably die of cold. Barbara told me I had to stop running away in case that happened, and now it will. At least at Elaine's we would've been warm.' I shivered and pulled my thin coat tight around my shoulders and hunched my knees further towards my chin. The heat of the day held in the stone beneath me was rapidly cooling.

She didn't want you there. There, that's the truth of it.

'How do you know that? She might have done.'

You told me yourself.

'Yes, I remember now. I did. But it would've been better than this and my real mum and dad aren't one bit closer at all. You've led me down the wrong path. I'm all alone now.'

No, you're not. I'm here.

'But you're not really, are you? Not like a person would be so it's not the same. You haven't got a stomach, you told me yourself. So you can't get hungry. You can't feel this cold.'

He didn't reply. At first I thought he was hurt, as he always was when I mentioned his lack of body parts, even though he sometimes talked of it himself. I sensed his shape being gathered into the falling night. Darker than that, though; a shadow even in the dark, if that was possible.

I turned my head. 'Well . . .?'

It was the clearest I'd ever seen him and he was smaller than I'd thought. For the first time I saw little grey tear lines in the dirt of his face. His hair was soft, fluffy – but not the healthy chick-like kind – this was scrubby in places and in others almost bare. The dark I'd glimpsed around his mouth *was* thick mud crusted there. His bare feet were hanging over the edge, the pale flats of them hanging in thin air.

He was shivering too. *I can. I'm feeling it now, right inside my bones. I can always feel the cold. It never goes away.*

I breathed out slowly. Then in and out until I slipped and stars exploded and a rushing in my ears sounded like the train that should have taken me away was now thundering past my head. I fell, that's certain, dropped off the high rock, soft and floppy like I was the dead thing. On the way down I woke again when I grazed my hand on a jagged piece of rock. Shadow had already made it to the bottom and waited for me in the grass. I lay for I don't know how long and the damp grass encircled me like a grave. When I came to, the sun had dipped below the earth and just the rim of it showed.

My suitcase was easy with two of us carrying it. It can't be that I'd just got stronger. We made light work of it together. When I put my hand into my coat pocket I found the cola cubes, the parting gift from the children on the street. I wedged one inside each cheek and set off again, sucking at the sweetness.

Soon, there were lights ahead. 'Look, look,' I cried, stumbling towards them. As I got closer I saw they were windows blazing out from a great box of a house, surrounded by a wall with a stone arch. I began to run and the suitcase banged against my thigh. I stopped by the arch.

Here, said Shadow.

In the twilight I saw the stone face carved into the apex of the arch. The leaves coming from his mouth looked like his entrails had been drawn up and laid across his cheeks. But there was no body underneath; just the empty open arch with metal posts either side where a gate had once been. I stood, puzzling, until I turned to the Shadow by my side.

'No, this can't be it. This is where Tom lives. He told me about that face, it's called a green man.'

Well, I don't know what that can mean. This is where I intended to come. Perhaps it was that poem you're always reading that confused me.

'Maybe I could stop awhile anyway. I can see him again.

He said for me to come and visit. I could just say hi, perhaps they'd let us stay the night.' I couldn't keep the excitement from my voice.

I turned but Shadow had gone. Was I really coming home? Perhaps, perhaps. But why am I listening to Shadow, I thought, he's an idiot, he's always muddling me up. All the same, the idea that Tom, or even my blood, might be within these walls sent excitement rippling through me. Whoever was inside, I had to take the risk of being turned away. I had to do it now. I dawdled for a moment then drew in my breath and passed beneath the green man's face. There was an ancient feel about it, like I'd been passing under that arch for ever, that I'd done it a million times already.

28

SHADOW

You escaped! I was overjoyed to see you hadn't been carried away in the insides of that train.

I've heard about people boarding trains and with the woohoo of the whistle being taken to their deaths. After my time, but I caught a glimpse of one once, a boy of my age pressed into the corner of a carriage. He was such a likeness of how I'd looked in life; I think that's how I came upon him. His freckles, the size of small pearls scattered across his nose, stood out dark against his pale, pale skin. Death was not at the end of that train for you but something else I could not quite see or understand. You would have become lost for many, many years, that's for certain. Though I'm not sure if this is any better. Your fate is unwinding too fast for me, Ruby.

There's ones this side waiting for you. Watching. Plotting. Longing to stick their fingers in and meddle. Just being dead doesn't stop them.

What d'you think happens to us when we die, Ruby? D'you think we just disappear? No. We are here. We are there. We become even tricksier than we were in life. Our vibrations snake through rooms and down hallways. Our tick sounds in the clock of your heart. We are like tender sunlight touching your hands and head. Like dirty air disappearing up your nose and choking you. We are there in the last kiss placed on the forehead. In the sound of a certain voice echoing down the years. We are in the tilt of your eyebrows. The way the corners of your mouth turn up even when you're not smiling. We're in the curl of your hair. In your eyeteeth.

We are not crumbling safely into dust, back into the earth. We are still raging. We do not die. We look out at you from likenesses that were made of our faces daring you to think that we are gone.

I fade back into my own story, of the times I walked the earth. I taste it. I feel it, but I do not know it fully yet. I hang back from you as you pass away under that arch. I've done my job and delivered you, though fret that it may all turn to bad and mayhem still. I shrink and remember. The rattling bag of pictures is back, getting tumbled so brand new ones rise to the surface.

There are two rivers, the first one bright and sparkling. It seems to me like moving jewels and I have to tighten my eyes against the brightness of it. I laugh with joy and the feeling of the laughter ripples down right to my toes. The second river moves wide and slow and this time my eyes hurt to look at it but I don't tighten them. There's raised voices in a place where day looks like night – two men, 'take your clobber and go,' says one to the other. Flares light up the horizon. There's a man's back ahead threading through trees.

I stop. My heart pounding.

And the taste of mud floods through my mouth.

29

GREEN MAN
20 November 1983

Outside Tom's house I looked up. A tattered peace sign hung in one of the windows.

Tall stalks of dried poppies stood like hollowed-out, thin people in the flowerbeds. I looked for Shadow among them but there was no sign of him. He'd vanished when I came under the arch.

Crispin came round the corner, whistling. I noticed how he was darker, the skin on his face thicker and tougher than Tom's, even though he looked younger. He had on the same coat as before with the rip on the chest. His eyes had a silvered-over quality, like an old mirror.

'What do you want?' His accent was what Barbara would term 'cultured'.

'I'm here to see Tom.'

'We don't have visitors here. It's not that sort of house. You should turn back right now and get yourself out of here smartish. Go on, piss off.' He disappeared soundlessly round the corner of the house. I followed him and peered but he'd gone.

Above the door the name *Hilltops* was chiselled into the stone. I banged on the front door with my fist so hard it hurt my hand. No answer. I banged and kicked the door again then sat on the cold stone doorstep with my arms wrapped tight around my body. I'd make a bed of the cold stone step if I had to. At least I'd be near humans.

I heard feet slapping behind the door and it opened a crack. It was Tom. I could see his gleam from behind the door, a slice of it anyway. My heart thudded. Maybe he'd forgotten about the night out and how he'd said we both had the same kind of toy inside. People are one thing one minute and the next something different. I knew that. It opened wider and Tom smiled down at me, his high cheekbones almost threatening to eclipse his eyes.

An arm reached out and pulled me in and my feet nearly left the ground with the force of it.

'I've been hoping and hoping you might come. I haven't been able to leave Elizabeth at all, and she won't go out any more. Come on, come on.' He hopped in a funny little dance as he spoke then reached out for my suitcase and dragged that in too.

Crispin must have come in through the back because he emerged from the depths of the cavernous hallway where black and white tiles covered the floor, making the three of us like pieces on a chessboard.

'You,' he said, 'I thought I'd already given you your marching orders.'

I pleated my coat between my fingers. 'I know you told me to go but Tom said I could stay. Didn't you?'

Tom stopped his hopping and turned very still. 'Yes,' he said quietly. 'Of course you will. You have to stay here, Ruby.'

Crispin tracked across the floor and for some reason it struck me as strange because his path was a diagonal one, like the movement of a spider. As he passed Tom barged at him and Crispin's sideways journey speeded up. It ended at a door that he slipped through. I tried to remember the chess piece that went sideways.

Without warning I gave in to the tears I'd held back earlier. Too much had happened. I was tired to the bone.

Tom looked just as I remembered him, the same broad forehead and high cheekbones, the same triangular blue eyes and the look of something of a young Indian in possession of a real horse and wigwam and it seemed wonderful that this should be so. Even his ankles were still bare, except now there was a rime of a scab on his heel where the back of his shoe had cut in.

A thought struck me. Shadow brought me to this place with tales of family. Could it be these people were my blood? Was Tom actually a brother? Was I about to meet my real sister for the first time?

'Sssh.' Tom put his arms around me and drew me close. I put my head on his shoulder and watched my tears disappear into the weave of his jacket. They absorbed quickly and I felt I could go on crying like that for ever. It felt good even, with him mopping it all up for me, the rough wool scratching pleasantly against my skin. His shoulder was heavy and angular and the side of my face slotted perfectly into the weight of it. I didn't want Tom to be my brother, however much I ached for family. Please, don't let him be my blood, I thought.

'I knew you'd come,' he said. 'I just felt it in my bones.'

The sharp prism of tears made everything in the hallway extra bright: the blue and white vase that was so big I could've hidden right inside it; the speckled mirror reflecting the stuffed animal sitting on the sideboard; the black and white creature shaped like a giant squirrel but with no fluffy red tail, instead a piece of bald leather stuck up stiffly from its behind.

Tom stood away from me and without his touch I felt panicky again. I could hear fierce whispering from behind the door and I knew it must be Crispin talking about me to Tom's sister.

'Your brother doesn't want me here.'

'He'll have to get used to it,' he said.

'What about your parents?'

'Still gone. Hang on here a sec.' He shut himself in with his brother and sister and I could hear his voice, sharp and insistent from inside.

Then the door opened and a tall girl came out. Her hair was ginger red and fell in a long wave down her back and her eyebrows were like red worms wriggling across her forehead. She wore a long green velvet skirt and matching waistcoat and a blouse with a ruffled piecrust collar that made her head look floating, like it was being carried on a dish.

She looked at me for a long minute before holding out her hand. 'You must be Ruby.' She had the strangest way of speaking, like a little girl pretending to be grown-up. 'Tom has told us all about you, dear,' she went on, 'and you've brought your case so you must be staying.'

Behind her, Crispin glowered, but remained silent, just kicked a boot silently at the doorframe where he was leaning.

I shook her hand, giddy with relief that I didn't have to go back out and stumble round in the darkness.

'Why don't you wash your hands in the lavatory there,' she nodded her head to a door behind me, 'and come in to dinner. I was just about to dish up.'

I turned and caught sight of myself in the silvered mirror above the heavy black-brown sideboard. The mirror also reflected the stuffed creature from the back and where there should have been his anus was just a neat row of stitching. I looked different and I wondered when the change had happened. With my long black hair hanging wild I seemed to have hardened round the edges, and become more distinct. In the toilet there were more stuffed animals, ranged around the pan and on the window ledge. A few were split with the stuffing leaking out. A weasel with a snake in its mouth stood behind the taps. Their beady eyes stared at me as I used the loo and then washed my hands.

'We try and make a point of sitting at the dinner table every night and being a family,' said Elizabeth, from her place at the head of the table. 'Do you do that at home?'

Again the strange way of speaking. I didn't mind much, though, everything here was strange.

'No, never,' I said, unable to compare this to the scratched red Formica table at home.

We were eating in the room that Crispin had shut himself into to whisper about me. The table was so large that Elizabeth looked tiny opposite me, and with her ruffled collar like she was on a stamp. Even her voice sounded small because of the distance. Crispin and Tom sat either side of us, Crispin hunched over his plate like an animal guarding its food. The table top was covered in stuff: jigsaw boxes and piles of magazines and a half empty open box of Black Magic chocolates. Each of our places was a square clearing in the junk. Elizabeth had cleared a new one for me before we sat down. The salt, pepper and jug of water were balanced on top of the flatter piles here and there. Three large purple candles were positioned down the middle of the table, each one in a saucer full of hard wax, and Elizabeth stood and touched a match to each candle and went to switch the harsh overhead light off. As the flames wobbled then flickered upright to a steady form I waited for the sight of fire to electrify and excite me, the feeling that was so close to fear and yet was singing joy. Nothing came, the flames just looked soft and benevolent.

'There, much more soothing,' Elizabeth said, although I knew what she really meant was that we didn't have to look at the mess any more. The piles had receded to soft dark shapes. 'And anyway,' she went on, 'that overhead light flickers terribly sometimes. It's quite beyond me how to fix it. I've been reading manuals, though, and trying to work it out. Peter, that's my father, said he'd fix it while he was here but of course it never happened. There's no point wishing for the moon, is there?'

I scrunched up my nose and rubbed it. It wasn't just the mess. There was a bad smell in the house too – sweetish with a slightly sickening edge.

Elizabeth must've noticed because she stood and held another match to a glass dish on the mantelpiece.

'There. Attar of roses. My mother's favourite – this is the last of it.'

An exquisite smell stole into the room and layered on top of all the bad ones.

'How long are your parents gone for?'

It was the first time I'd spoken in front of the three of them and I was aware of the burr of my forest vowels.

'See,' Crispin's voice slammed into the gloom, 'no one is supposed to know and *she* does. I told you, Elizabeth, this is the beginning of the end.' I jumped at his voice and the flames of the candles threaded narrow and then grew fat – writhing.

Elizabeth took a large gulp of whatever was in the cup next to her. At first I'd thought it must be blackcurrant juice because it left two smiley marks in the corners of her mouth, but then she'd said, 'Can I offer you some wine?' and I'd realised what it was. I'd never seen such a young girl drinking wine before and the sight of it and the long flow of ginger hair looped over one shoulder struck me as something out of a fairy story.

Even from this distance I could see as her eyes glazed from the alcohol. She took a deep breath. 'Both our parents are in India and they have been for some time and will be for some time.'

Then she forgot to talk in her adult way and her voice rose, breathy and childlike. 'Before they went, Roz – that's what my mum always says to call her – told me it was to "find themselves".' She stopped and gathered herself and her tone lowered again. 'Which as a notion is a little hackneyed, I think. Though when I told her such it didn't stop them leaving. I'm supposed to be keeping everything going while they're gone.' She took another deep pull from her glass.

So, she was trying to be a mother to the boys. That was why she had that funny way of talking.

'Fucking hippies. They'd find themselves if only they looked down the toilet,' mumbled Crispin. The other two ignored him. Tom carried on cramming food into his mouth and chewing noisily, his eyes darting between me and Elizabeth.

I peered at the plate, meat with a puddle of barely warm baked beans. I scooped some onto my fork and pushed them into my mouth. I was too tired to eat but felt I needed to, out of politeness. Everything seemed to pulse in and out. If these were my brothers and sisters could it mean that their parents were my parents too?

'Did they ever live in the forest?' I asked so suddenly everything went quiet and they stopped eating and turned to me.

'The Forest of Dean? Not as far as I know. And it would be the kind of thing they'd talk about. They'd probably stage a naked version of *Midsummer Night's Dream*,' said Elizabeth.

Crispin's silver eyes stayed on me as I ate.

'Are you enjoying the meat?' he asked, and somehow the question made my scalp prickle.

I peered down at it. 'Is it chicken?'

Crispin laughed all over his full plate. 'I fucking wish it was.'

'It's rabbit, Ruby,' said Elizabeth. 'It's very nutritious. And they run quite wild round here.'

I leaned over the plate. 'Poor rabbit.' It was a moment before I realised I'd spoken out loud.

There was silence around the table, until Crispin let out a crow and twirled his finger round and round by his temple.

Elizabeth saw me staring at the stuffed animal as she showed me the way to bed. 'You like our creature; I believe it's a racoon, though I can't be sure. There was all sorts of strange stuff left over from the last people when we first came here. A lot of it got broken, though.'

I followed her upstairs and her flowing green gown lipped along the dark red carpet like Christmas. I thought I might have fallen asleep for a moment while I was walking, then her head turned and I saw the white bone of her cheek and the red hair flowing against it and the sight woke me.

'I'll put you in the library. I can make up the couch for you in there. All the spare bedrooms leak.'

I had the sudden urge then to ask if she might be *my* real mother; the thought came to me quickly and felt so real. Then I remembered Tom telling me his sister was only seventeen and I scolded myself silently behind her.

30

15 September 1970

'He's here.'

Anna's dad continues stirring his tea at the kitchen table, but he's seen Lewis's car pull up outside. Now he's arranging his features to face the younger man.

'Still don't know why you won't marry him,' he mutters. 'Are you sure he's asked?' Anna's dad can't quite believe the possibility that a girl in his daughter's situation might turn an offer like that down.

'Dad, stop it. And try and be nice to him.'

Her dad has been banned from exacting any kind of revenge – or even giving Lewis a piece of his mind – by his wife and daughter, but he doesn't have to seem happy about it all. He doesn't have to go all soft and friendly with the man that's knocked up his girl.

Anna opens the door. The cottage is so small Lewis steps right into the room that they eat, cook and watch television in. He brings the day in with him, as he always seems to do. The outside is clinging to the folds of his long coat. He ducks his head and both women leap up, wanting this meeting to go smoothly, to make it, if not friendly, then without conflict.

'All right, lad?' Anna's dad doesn't smile.

'Aye, not bad,' says Lewis, and Anna and Cynthia relax.

'You all packed, love?' asks Lewis. He doesn't want to hang around.

'It's all in the parlour.' Her things have been waiting there overnight, becoming gradually chilled right through. The little room is only used at Christmas. When Anna arrives at the new flat her and Ruby's things take an age to thaw out. The cold's got right through to the middle of the suitcases.

Before they leave Cynthia insists on giving her daughter something. They have so little she's been puzzling what it could be. She's always worked hard – picking potatoes, child minding, even as a barmaid for a time, and her husband was a miner. But there seems not much to choose from. Finally, she decides on the green tea set that was her own mother's in the nineteen thirties. It's kept in a glass-fronted cabinet against the back wall.

'No, honestly, you can't.' Anna doesn't really want it. The cups are far too small for Lewis's hands. They'll never get used.

'Yes, yes, you must.' Cynthia is packing it up already, wrapping the cups and saucers in old tea towels to protect them. 'I need to give you something – for your new home. Look, there's a slop bowl,' she laughs. 'Who uses a slop bowl now? Never mind, best to keep the set together.' There's also a hot water jug with a chrome-plated cover and other surplus bits and pieces – a sugar bowl, a milk jug. Anna can't imagine what she's going to do with it all.

The boxed tea set means she has to squeeze her feet awkwardly to one side on the journey to Coleford and the flat that Lewis has leased along with the premises underneath it. Ruby lies in her carrycot on the back seat. When Anna checks over her shoulder she sees her gravely staring at the ceiling of the car.

'I won't carry you over the threshold.' Lewis says it mildly as he inserts the shiny new key in the door next to the shop-front window.

'You might drop us anyway,' Anna says, holding the baby higher up in her arms. She knows he was making a statement just then – *I offered to do the right thing. You wouldn't let me.* She doesn't want to try explaining to him – how time got slipped when 'We'll manage, everything will be all right' came at the end and not the beginning. It changed something in her, those months alone with Ruby growing inside. She loves her parents' cottage but she feels wrong there now, like she was an overgrown child that had done something bad. Her parents were the real grown-ups even though they couldn't do grown-up things any more – like making babies. Her stomach had waxed fatter than she'd ever imagined possible and she sat with her mother at the kitchen table at night planted on the chair, with the great stomach sticking right out in front of her and her arms hanging uselessly by her sides. It had all felt wrong, wrong, wrong.

Now Lewis pushes the door open on a musty staircase and a pile of unopened post on the floor. They turn to each other and laugh at the same time in a kind of delight because both feel they have escaped somehow when that door opened. He stoops and sweeps up the letters with one hand and chucks them on the sideboard.

'Come on, I'll show you around.'

Upstairs the big bed with the yellow tapestry cover in the

sunny front bedroom looks so inviting they soon fall into it leaving Ruby gurgling in her carrycot through the open door of the little room.

Later, Lewis shows her the premises downstairs. He's planning on opening a coffee bar now that he's decided to stay here and set up a life for her and Ruby.

'D'you like it?' he keeps asking. 'What d'you think?'

'It's wonderful, Lewis,' she smiles back. Secretly, she looks through the window and registers how it's one street back from the high street and wonders who'll find it.

'I'm going to put a sign down the end,' says Lewis, as if he's read her doubts. 'This'll be the first one. I want to have a whole string of them. They turn money over like nobody's business. No one wants fussy old tea shops any more.' Anna can see the money being landed in his eyes, whole golden gleaming shoals of it.

They've left Ruby asleep upstairs and Anna lifts her eyes to the ceiling. Her parents' cottage was so completely on its own and self-contained; a lone ship for them and their two daughters. This, with its shop and flats, is everyone fitting in among each other like a human jigsaw puzzle. It seems so funny to think of herself upstairs, walking about, while there's strangers below, drinking coffee and playing the jukebox that Lewis is planning on acquiring. It makes her want to giggle but she stops herself in time. She doesn't want to spoil anything for Lewis.

31

THE BAD FARMERS
21 November 1983

Dear Mick and Barbara.

It was Elizabeth who got me to write the letter.

'I feel so guilty about your mother,' she'd said softly in the morning. 'I know what it's like with Tom. When he's out of my sight I can dream up such terrible ideas about what might be happening to him. I can make myself almost demented with visions of it. You didn't tell your parents where you were going, though, did you, dear? I did hear that right last night? Because if that's not the case they might come after you and find us here and I'm not sure if that's a good idea.' She chewed her lip. 'What shall we do?' she whispered.

Then we'd agreed I'd write to tell them I was still alive and I'd privately vowed that the letter would never get posted.

I hadn't even thought of writing a real letter but once I'd written their names it was like I'd fetched Mick and Barbara into the house. They reared up off the page as loud as animals – scolding, shrieking, arguing.

Dear Mick and Barbara,
   You don't know where I am.

I looked out of the window in the direction of the forest. I thought of them, Barbara weeping, Mick crashing about and me high like a bird watching it all.

The ballpoint moved beautifully across the paper.

What's more you don't deserve to know. Well, maybe you do, Barbara, but the trouble is – you always do what he says, don't you? You let him smash me to a pulp and what did you do? Brought me a bowl of soup. Thanks a bunch.

The room I was in had a jar of dried honesty and Chinese lanterns in the window. They looked so old they might crumble any minute. Somehow I couldn't stand the idea of watching them flake apart. I sucked the top of the pen. I felt a compulsion to continue now I'd started – even though the letter wasn't ever going to be sent.

One day, I'm going to find my real parents, and Mick – my dad will be after you then. You'll find out what it feels like to be mashed against the floor. You'll know what it feels like to cry until your head's ringing. Plus . . .

I looked at the page.

. . . Plus Barbara, there's something you really fucking ought to know. I've not said anything before because a) I didn't want to upset you b) I might get mashed into the floor again. There's this girl at school – Sandra. She's only sixteen, Barbara, and d'you know what? I've seen Mick out, drinking with her. It makes me sick to my stomach. I really can't see what is in any way, shape or form attractive about him.

Then the old fear grabbed at my throat, the one that could drain the blood from my heart in an instant, as if writing to him had drawn Mick near. I scrawled random gibbering thoughts across the page.

I'm all right mostly, Barbara. Please don't worry.
I suppose sometimes I'm sorry I hit him with that plank. Not always, sometimes I'm glad.
I miss Gran.
I cried myself to sleep last night.

I stopped. I could feel myself getting worked up and tears brimming in my eyes. I doodled some flowers in the corner of the page.

I miss you too sometimes, Barbara. They're all so ladidah here. The house is full of stuff and I think, oooh Barbara would love that and then I realise you'll never see it. And maybe I'll never see you again either and when I think that I feel quite upset . . .

Elizabeth poked her head round the door. 'Finished?'

'I suppose.' I wiped my eyes, signed my name at the bottom and stuffed it into the envelope.

After I'd written the address she tucked the envelope inside her jacket.

'I can post it,' I said, panicking. 'If you give me a stamp.'

'That's quite all right,' she said in a firm voice. 'I'll post it myself.' Her quick green eyes were on my bare arms and I wondered if Tom might have told her about the shadows of the bruises he saw that day in school and that's why she let me stay. I didn't think I could curse him but I cursed him then.

'Come on, let's go outside. I'll show you everything.'

Elizabeth had exchanged her green skirt of last night for a man's tweed trousers and the bagginess of them showed up how thin her hips were. She carried a spade on her shoulder and left a vapour trail of breath that hung above the field. It looked like humanness written in the air, a thread she'd made of warmth just for me from right inside her body. I walked in its wake, sensing she was leaving me her trail to follow. It was a bright cold day and the earth felt hard with frost beneath my soles.

In the field were a couple of crumbling caravans hand-painted with looping flower designs and next to them the bare bones of a tepee without its canvas.

'People used to come and stay here to work the land with my parents,' Elizabeth explained in her grown-up voice. 'Of course we don't see hide nor hair of them now there's no free ride. There's only one from the old days who comes back sometimes to use the outhouses.' She glanced back. 'We'll have to find you some proper boots,' she said, nodding at mine that looked cheap and thin against the raw frozen red earth. 'There's all manner in the boot hole. I'm sure we'll find something that will do.' I thought about my things left in the other hole. They'd probably be rolling with rabbit droppings by now.

'Here.' She stopped where a row of bright green leaves looked ordered among the untidy weeds. 'I suppose we'll have parsnips with our dinner.' She started chopping haphazardly at the hard soil. Eventually the first one came out caked in wet mud. Its long end seemed to take for ever coming out of the ground like the root of a tooth. Elizabeth looked too thin for this kind of work. Her narrow hands were red from the cold.

'D'you want me to do that?' I asked.

'OK.'

I took the spade from her and she watched me work. She forgot her grown-up tone for the moment and spoke normally for once. 'My parents came here to be self-sufficient. They had the idea they wanted everything pure and natural. We've got three goats too, for milk. Sterling, Shona and Milk Bottle. Tom named Sterling, because she does sterling work. I chose Shona because it's my favourite name and Crispin named Milk Bottle, typical of that boy.' She gave a little smile, though, as if she was fond of his ways. 'There's some chickens too but there's never enough to eat. We rely on the cheques my parents send.'

'So why did they go away, if they planned it all like this?' I rested on the spade and blew a strand of hair out that had stuck to my cheek. I wanted to see the goats – I'd only ever seen pictures of them.

'My parents were bored of it by then. It was a kind of game to them. They are like two enormous children, Ruby, but ones with trust funds and bank accounts and who are allowed to drive cars and buy alcohol and set up "communes".' Her mouth turned bitterly around the word. 'It's quite dangerous because they're like grown-up babies. They were already talking about India, and they went once this had become boring to them. They said before they left – children are perfectly capable of looking after themselves; it's only society that ordains they can't. Society restricts our natural abilities for all sorts of things, they said, and this is one of them. You know, when we were little they wouldn't even take us to the doctor. They had some shady medic that would dish out the pills they wanted but that was it. Poor Crispin was always having earaches and he'd scream his head off but still they wouldn't go. Of course Roz and Peter never went either.' She looked up, her mouth twisted and her child voice broke through. 'But then those two losers didn't need to. They were as fit as apes.'

'I've never known people like that.' Suddenly the forest felt safe.

She shook her head rapidly. 'You're lucky. They haven't sent a cheque for a while but when we have them I go into town and get a shop to cash it for me. Not all of them will, though, and I always feel I have to buy something from the ones that do. I bought some wool because the nice lady in the wool shop cashed a cheque. I can't knit but I'm trying to teach myself from the chart she gave me.'

'Maybe they were right, about children looking after themselves,' I said, then felt silly for saying it.

'They also used to say "you can do anything you want to do", but when I asked if I could be an axe murderer they didn't have an answer for that. That's enough veg. We'll do the chickens now.'

We walked across the field together. The house stood squat and square looking out across the hills – not another house in sight. I stopped in my tracks. 'What's that?' At the horizon was a shimmer, sparkling and shifting. It gave me the sensation that the house was untethered, floating somehow.

Elizabeth wrinkled her forehead. 'That's a man-made lake, Peter – my father – told me. In medieval times people would have kept lakes stocked with fish. I thought I saw fish in there once,' she stopped and frowned, 'but I think I was mistaken. This lake would be later than that, though, and built for ornamental purposes. That's what Peter told me anyway.'

Our footsteps fell in time with each other, crackling across the hard ground. As we got closer I could see a small boat, with peeling blue paint, tied up to a post at the water's edge.

She carried on. 'In the old days everything had a system. The food scraps went to the chickens and the human waste was spread on the vegetable patch. It all went round and round – I've been reading about it in my father's self-sufficiency books. It's very interesting, everything feeding off everything else.'

'D'you know when your parents are coming back?' I asked as we drew up to the chicken run, the plastic bag of parsnips, with mud slimed inside, in hand.

She shrugged. 'Who knows?' She frowned. 'Look, there's another hole in the wire.' Her red fingers twisted at the chicken wire trying to weave it together again, although it kept springing back apart. It made me think of her trying to knit. She abandoned it and stood for a long moment with her eyes closed against the hole. I was almost at the point of shaking her by the shoulder when she opened them again. 'We've already lost so many to foxes. There were twenty at one point. Now we've only got five. Come on, you can help me see if there's any eggs today.'

Inside the hen shed we slid our hands into the warm straw where the chickens roosted. 'Nothing,' she sighed, and it struck me this was no game to her as it had been for her parents. I wondered how three children could survive like this. Where do you start farming eggs? Or farming any-thing? They weren't very good at it, that's for sure. Weeds were everywhere.

Then I remembered – how I'd got off that train and dis-appeared so easily. And I thought – it happens – children falling through gaps and getting forgotten and this time the idea gave me hope. If I can get forgotten by the ones who raised me, the mistaken life I was given, I have a chance with Elizabeth and Tom and Crispin for now, just to fill the space until I find my mum and dad. I rubbed at my eyes – if we didn't share parents of course.

There was a dead rabbit waiting on the kitchen table wrapped in gold velvet. It was bleeding onto the gold from its head and feet and I could see they'd never get the blood out of the beautiful material. It would break Barbara's heart to see.

'This'll be our dinner tonight,' said Elizabeth.

'It's still got all its fur.'

'Not for long,' she laughed, and stuck a knife in its stom-ach, neatly wicking it up the middle so shining spools of innards coiled across the table.

'That's gross.' I put my hand up to my mouth, sickness in my throat. The coils steamed slightly in the sun that fell across the table. Still warm.

'No, this is what has to be done. We'll skin it now. My parents didn't teach me much. They should've shown us how to do it all properly before they left. But Peter did show me how to do this, and Tom to milk the goats, so I suppose that's something,' she said, and I watched as her knife deli-cately peeled. The sickness went away and I crept closer

143

to the table. Her face was concentrated as she worked the blade, her sleeves rolled right up and a smear of red on the inside of her elbow. The outside of the rabbit seemed to fall away and it became a shiny bean. I was fascinated by the transformation, from furry creature to slick shining meat ready to be cooked. Elizabeth's hair was lit up by a shaft of sun coming through the dusty window.

'I'll learn to do that,' I said. 'Will you teach me?'

'Yes, I'll teach you,' she said. 'You need to know these things. These things aren't gross. They're survival.'

'Yes,' I said, the vestiges of dizziness fading, 'that's what I want to learn.'

32

WORM
30 November 1983

I watched the local news on their fuzzy black and white television in the same room I wrote the letter. I started thinking of it as my communications room to Barbara. I settled down, cross-legged on the floor. This is Ruby, calling Barbara. Ready to receive. I expected to see her, holding her tissue up to her mouth, her curls shaking: 'Ruby, we want you to know everything's all right. You can come home now. We're not angry but we need you home. We're worried sick.'

Nothing. The home sickness for her got worse as I guessed she'd decided to go Mick's way and that looking for me would be like looking for trouble because that was my middle name.

I turned. Crispin had appeared at the door and the sudden sight of him made me start. He'd been gone for days but nobody had commented. It was the way of things here.

'What use are you here, Ruby?'

'What do you mean?'

'I mean, what are your attributes? What can you do?'

Without thinking I whipped off my jacket and flexed my biceps. It looked pathetic. The dumbbells had done nothing and I stood there displaying my puny arm as if it meant something.

He raised an eyebrow. 'A muscleman? You need to be cleverer than that.'

Later, I asked Elizabeth if she'd ever posted my letter.

'Of course, dear,' she said. 'They would've had it ages ago.'

Hardly anyone came near. Only, once or twice from the house I saw the greenhouse at the back lit up, a blazing beacon in the dark. Or the sound of a car engine fading away.

'Who's that?' I asked Tom.

'Someone who knew my parents from the old days. Lived here for a bit, I think. He uses the greenhouses still. Ignore him. He won't breathe a word to anyone, I guarantee.'

Even the post got left in a special box down by the gate. I began to notice how they used things strangely. I found Tom using a silver jug to clean out the chicken run. The kitchen was filthy, with a cooker that sometimes worked and sometimes didn't. Occasionally Elizabeth said she was going to clear up but then she'd collapse on the sofa and say she'd changed her mind. That it was too much for her. Sometimes she'd start crying too and Tom would put his arms around her and say, 'There, there, old thing. It's all going to be all right.' And she'd say, 'How?' But he couldn't answer. He'd just shake his head and look frightened, which made Elizabeth cry even harder. There were empty tins and rubbish all over the kitchen floor and work surfaces but it never seemed a good time to do anything about it somehow and we ended up playing Scrabble or chopping wood to make a fire instead. There were even flies around although it was winter and they bashed against the window like they were desperate to get away.

I sneaked around and looked at everything. The smell was awful in places – like the overflowing bins – and it made me think how Barbara's house might be small and shabby, but at least she kept it clean. I even started thinking maybe they'd killed their parents and it was the bodies rotting somewhere that smelled. I realised how I wouldn't put anything past them.

I did start to clean up at one point. It was part of my new project – Project Worm My Way In – a bit like with Melissa and Nicola at school but not like it, because I'd realised they were never going to let me in their pathetic little gang. They were just toying with me. Once I started, though, I gave up almost straight away. First off Crispin sneered at me and said, 'Trying to impress Elizabeth, are you?' Then I started to understand how Elizabeth felt – how on earth do you keep a place this size clean and tidy? It was actually easier to ignore it.

I started snooping with purpose. If they were my family I wanted evidence. I rifled through drawers and boxes and black bags full of papers and old clothes. I found a box of photos in the carved wooden chest in the living room. I recognised the three of them in tiny form, lined up in front of their parents. Their mother looked like Tom, the same cheekbones that stood out like blades, but there was no child with a birthmark on her face in the photo.

I thought that Crispin and Elizabeth had decided – if not quite part of their family – then I was part of the furniture perhaps. I realised, though, as I walked through the hall, that they'd all shut themselves together in the big front room that had a marble fireplace so big three people could sit in it. The exclusion of it made me feel hot and sick so I crept up to the door and put my ear to the keyhole. I could just about hear what they were saying, especially Crispin.

'What's she even doing here?' he yelled.

Mumble, mumble – that was Tom and Elizabeth talking. Crispin carried on shouting right over them.

'Well, God knows what's going to happen,' said Crispin. 'Who's out looking for her. They could come here and next thing – bam, it'll be foster care for me and Tom before you know it. Or worse.'

I longed to burst into the room and put him straight on the idea I was being looked for.

Mumble, mumble.

Speak up, for God's sake, Tom, I thought – I can't hear you. I hoped he was defending me.

'Oh, it'll be all right for you, Elizabeth,' Crispin went on, 'you're nearly of age. Anyway, you shouldn't even be thinking of taking anyone else on. You can't care for anyone, can you? Or you, Tom. Not even yourselves. Well, you just be careful. I might decide to shoot her with my gun one day if I see her out while I'm rabbiting. There might be a little accident.'

I jumped up like I really had been shot, waiting until my breath calmed before putting my ear back to the keyhole – but everything had gone quiet.

I crept back up to the library where Elizabeth had made my bed on the leather couch and I remembered my idea I used to have, not so long ago in fact, of books holding clues about what to do in your life. I looked up; the books went right to the ceiling. The clues could run into the millions here. It would take an army of librarians to go through them. At home all the books were contained in one bookshelf, in dimensions that were three foot by four. I'd read them all: the row of *Reader's Digests*, even *The Guinness Book of Records*, dated from nineteen seventy-three. But in here I'd only drawn my finger along their spines because there were too many; it made me dizzy.

There were books on birds, books on bones, on *Myths and Lore of England*, on feathers and eggs and trees. Stories too – hundreds of them. I started looking for *Pilgrim's Progress* because I remembered how the story had turned out to be sort of information or advice – about Pilgrim rising and leaving and how it had helped me rise and leave that train. And now I needed some more advice of the right kind.

I took out one with *Tess of the D'Urbervilles* impressed into the cover in gold, and I opened the first page and started reading and forgot about looking for advice because it was like falling into the mud of someone else's life so it stoppered up my ears and eyes to anything else.

The nights grew ever darker. Sometimes it felt like the day barely lit up at all. Elizabeth went out early in the gloom and again in the afternoon, searching the post box twice a day.

'No cheque again,' she said. 'Nothing.'

'I'll dig the beds over for the spring,' Tom said. 'There's still seed left over.' He'd shown them to me, kept dry in their little greaseproof packets, curled up and ready.

Elizabeth didn't answer but I guessed she was thinking how far away the spring lay. Tom took me to milk the goats. His back was thin and stiff against the cold as we walked to where they were tethered across the field. The smallest had wound itself round and round the post it was tethered to. It bleated steadily and its breath came out as smoke.

'Trust you, Milk Bottle,' said Tom. 'Causing trouble, just like Crispin.' He carefully unwound the chain and we walked them back to their shed as the light was fading. The smell inside the shed was sharp. 'That's how goats smell,' said Tom. 'There's nothing else like it.' He settled them into their stalls and showed me how to milk them by gently pressing the teat with his fingers against the palm of his hand.

'They need to get to know a person first, they're very sensitive. They know me well, Elizabeth too . . . they'll know you in time.' And he closed his eyes and leaned against Sterling's rough white fur as he milked.

I helped Elizabeth too when I could. We cleaned out the chickens, stripping the straw away with tough bristled brooms to reveal the wriggling pink worms beneath that the hens pecked at hungrily.

'We shouldn't be living like this,' she said. Her cheekbones had started to stand out as much as Tom's, dark hollows underneath. 'Someone is bound to find out.'

I knew I must be parcelled up with her burden of worry, the runaway. 'It's all right,' she said, 'we won't send you back. You're one of us now.'

The new straw we laid smelled sweet and wisps of it stuck to the back of Elizabeth's jacket as we walked back.

'Shall we go that way?' I pointed to the stand of trees across the river. I had the urge to be underneath the spreading canopy.

Elizabeth shivered. 'No. It's dark in there. Let's go and check the post box again.' We skirted the house and looped round to where their post box stood by a bank just by the arch. I put my hand inside and felt cold metal.

'Nothing,' I said.

I watched the forest turn dark as the trees lost the last of their leaves. From a distance it looked like the decaying rabbit skin that Elizabeth had thrown out by the back door. She said it was a sacrifice to the foxes to keep them away from the chickens. Decaying is like movement. It marches along to its own beat like the forest. The rabbit skin first reared up and swelled before it flattened again and crumbled away. From up here I could see the forest doing the same: shrinking, turning black into the winter. Shadow hadn't been seen since that first night here. Sometimes I ached for him. It was the clearest he'd ever been to me that night we arrived – his hungry look, his small pale hands and feet. The sticky darkness around his lips and mouth. I wondered if he'd recognise me now, if any of them would recognise me. Elizabeth had taken one look at my tatty old man's coat with the rubbed elbows and said, 'This will never do,' and found me one from the back of the cupboard. It was thick navy wool with silver buttons that had anchors on them. It came nearly to the ground. She found some riding boots she said must have once belonged to a boy and as I put them on the leather of them seemed to web and grow around my feet like the skin was still alive. I tried to tell Elizabeth this and she said that's what expensive things were like. They were made to be like that. I let my hair go loose and rarely brushed it. It hung in thick black knots down my back. I found a cheap chain and attached Mick's collar tips to it with wire and wore them round my neck like a charm. I drew black kohl around my eyes every morning, sometimes powdering my face until Crispin told me I looked like a ghost.

Now I crouched on the front wall with my arms wrapped around my knees moving my head slowly from side to side like an owl. 'This is earth calling Barbara.' I didn't know which was worse: the fact that they were looking for me. Or that they weren't. 'Do you read me?'

Then one day I stopped calling for her because I knew the signal had gone dead.

In the morning there was no toilet paper left.

'What are we to do?' said Elizabeth. 'We're living like savages.'

'Is there any old newspaper?' I asked. 'And string?'

Tom fetched some for me and I showed them how to tear it into squares and hang it from a loop of string next to the toilet, just like in my gran's old privy at the bottom of the garden.

'That's so clever, Ruby. You're ingenious,' said Elizabeth. 'Fancy – problem solved like that.' She clicked her fingers.

I looked at them both and for the very first time began to question the wisdom of throwing in my lot with people who couldn't even wipe their own arses.

33

SECRETS
8 December 1983

'We're being watched,' said Elizabeth. 'I'm sure of it.'

I jumped up from the fire I'd been trying to light and cracked my head on the stone mantelpiece. 'Who? Who is it? It must be Mick. Did you see him?'

Tom said, 'Elizabeth's always thinking that, Ruby. She's jumpy. It was probably a bird or something.' It was true. She was often jumpy, this was just another outbreak.

He took my hand. 'My God. What's wrong with you? Sit down.'

But I couldn't. In one instant I was back in a prison with Mick's voice the jangling keys in my ear. The ground rocked. 'He's outside,' I babbled. 'He's come for me.'

'Look, Elizabeth, what you've done with your paranoia. She's white as a sheet.'

'I'm sorry. I'll try and calm down,' she said in a small voice, as I closed my eyes and thought of trees.

This trick I used when I was little, with Mick yelling in my face so close I could feel his hot breath on my eyelids. I'd make my feet tingle and on each sole little nubs would form. If I concentrated on growing them his voice became distant. The nubs would push out until they burst through the floor and became my roots, snaking downwards until deep set into the earth.

I felt them now, punching through the carpet, nudging aside earth and stone. Slowly, the rocking ceased. I felt Elizabeth take my other hand and the three of us stood interlinked. I began to sense their roots too, below me. I felt them twine with mine so we were bound together underground and we stood straight and strong.

Without opening my eyes I told them everything.

The bruising that drifted across my back like storm clouds. The hospital visit with the fractured bone being passed off as a fall downstairs. The look in Mick's eyes that was like trees lashing about in a gale. How I'd been adopted. Everything. When I opened my eyes they were staring at me, pale and quiet.

'Oh my God,' said Tom.

'Now, I want more than anything to find my real parents,' the nettle sting at the back of the eyes started up, 'to know who they are and for them to know me. I feel it's the only thing that will ever make me into something I can call a whole.' The film started up again, the one with me and my parents. This time we were in a triptych – three pictures in the same frame – with my mother in the middle and every one of us had the exact same mark on the left-hand side of our faces, like it was our own personal family coat of arms.

'I'll help you, Ruby,' said Tom. 'I'll do anything I can to help you.'

'How?'

'I can help you look.'

'That's the trouble. I don't know where to start.'

'Certificates. Everyone has certificates. Ones for birth – or you might have even had one to be adopted.'

154

'Yes, could be.'

'You need to look in the bottom of wardrobes. People always keep things in the bottom of wardrobes.'

I thought about it. He was right; it was possible. It occurred to me I might have been better off looking for paperwork than making dolls in the woods.

'I've told you everything,' I said. 'I've never told all this to a living soul before.' For wasn't that true, as the only being I'd ever confided in was Shadow?

They both nodded. 'Now you must tell me,' I said. 'Are you my blood? My brother and sister?'

Elizabeth let go of my hand. 'What makes you think that?'

I drew the photo I'd kept out of my pocket.

'I thought maybe you were my sister. I've been looking for myself in the photos.'

Elizabeth took it between her fingers. 'God, I'd almost forgotten what they look like.' I realised we were all whispering. She shook her head. 'I'd know. There's only ever been the three of us. You are *like* a sister, though.'

'I wish . . . I don't want any secrets between us. You need to tell me something now,' I whispered.

'What?'

'I don't mind, anything.'

Tom nodded, his face tight. 'I'll show you what's in that greenhouse if you like. That's a secret.'

Elizabeth caught my hand again and held it. We walked like that, crab-like, through the house then out.

Tom took a key from his inside pocket and unlocked the door.

We moved inside as one person and a sweetish smell hit

me. In the gloom I could see what looked like giant spiders nodding down.

'Cannabis,' he whispered into the dark. 'My parents began growing it with someone who could deal in London – the one you've seen driving away. It won't be long until this is ready and Mr Green Car said he'd still give us a cut when it is.'

'Mr Green Car?'

'That's the colour of the car he drives,' said Tom. 'I don't know his real name.'

'I'm glad you've told me about this,' I whispered. 'And even if you're not my real sister, Elizabeth, you seem like one.'

I saw her pale face turn away in the dimness. 'You wouldn't want to be a sister to a person like me.' I heard a sob beside me and I saw the slice of light at the doorway gape as she left.

'Leave her,' Tom said. 'She'll be praying. That's what she does when she gets like this. She prays for us all.' He looked down at his shoes and stayed silent for a long minute. 'Let's go outside. I hate being indoors sometimes and it's so stuffy in here. The heating has to be left on day and night. We can sit out front and watch the stars. It makes you forget your troubles, doing that.'

In the house Tom opened the door to below the stairs. 'I've seen a fur coat in here somewhere. I'll find it for you.'

For a moment he looked like he was wrestling a bear and then something slipped round my shoulders. I sneezed.

We settled on the step outside. The late afternoon was still, already beginning its slide into wintry blueness with a few stars popping out.

'It's hard to believe anything will live again,' I breathed and my words turned into tiny ice shards that hung in the air as if to demonstrate the truth of my words.

'That's what the green man's all about.'

I looked over to the archway. For the first time I noticed the back of his head was carved behind the arch, his curls clustered there like shrimps. I shuddered. 'I don't like him.'

'Why? He represents nature, that's all, nature in all of us. That life never ceases, it keeps on coming.'

'Why does it come out of his mouth? It looks like it's growing right through him.'

'I'm not sure.' Tom became quiet.

Inside the coat it was easier to let my passions at being so close to Tom run free, safer because of the layer of skin and fur between us. Now I knew he wasn't my brother in blood but I still couldn't imagine feeling any other way even if I'd found out he had been. I tingled all over, right down below between my legs.

'I'm so glad there's no secrets between us now,' I said, but he didn't reply. He was intent on gazing at the stars whirling above us.

34

5 October 1970

Anna cannot shake off the feeling that she and Lewis are play-acting.

In their new flat they're having a long elaborate game of mothers and fathers. It goes on and on and is exhausting. Every morning they get up and start the game over again. The tea set is part of it; the cups and saucers are so small it makes the flat seem like a doll's house. Snatches of nursery rhymes and stories even come back to Anna as she goes about things: Polly Put the Kettle On, One Two Buckle my Shoe – Lewis is like an elf from *The Elves and the Shoemaker*, that ultimate fairy tale of business. He wants this coffee shop to beget the next one, then the next until there are strings of them across the county and beyond.

Anna takes Ruby outside, the pram clonking down the stairs two wheels at a time. She pushes the pram through the high street and people stop to admire the baby, though Anna is convinced they only do this because of the birthmark and all their cooing and compliments are forced, false. It makes Anna want to kill them and to scoop Ruby out of her pram and run away with her, leaving the empty pram sliding backwards down the high street. Sometimes the buildings seem to rear over her even though there's nothing really very high in Coleford. On one of her walks she sees dandelions growing out of split concrete near a fence and she stops by them. They seem like the most important thing she's ever seen and she sits on the bench nearby and lingers for ages revelling in their yellowness; they are like falling suns blazing in the grey.

She takes fish and potatoes home and cooks them both nice suppers. But Lewis isn't cut out to run a coffee or a milk bar, that becomes clear. His clothes are too smart, he's too handsome. It's like he's front of house in Claridge's rather than behind the counter in some grotty little establishment in the forest. He puts the teenagers off who want to come and sit for hours over a single cup of coffee and chat to their mates or the opposite sex. Lewis's very presence dominates the room; he's more like their father even if he is only a few years older than them. Or, when in a gloomy mood, with his dark suit and carefully combed hair, you'd think this was a funeral parlour he was presiding over.

Still, there's a moment every night. Pure happiness. Anna has just put supper on the table and Lewis has locked up and come upstairs. The sun is just at the right angle to pierce into the room and across the table, the three of them frozen in a short blessing. Anna thinks of it lighting up the dandelions outside – making them fizz the brightest yellow possible.

Lewis and Anna take Ruby to see his father. Lewis takes longer to get ready than he used to on one of their dates. You'd think it was a state visit. His black suit is first brushed so every trace of lint in every seam is removed. He spends nearly an hour polishing his shoes. Anna wraps Ruby in a white shawl and kisses the soft skin on her forehead. The baby's eyes examine her carefully, as if she can read the thoughts in Anna's head.

Lewis's father is waiting for them on the crazy-paving path outside his bungalow. Hugh Black – he pushes his presence out beyond the limits of his physical body so all the spaces around are plugged with it. Anna has met him many times before but this is the first visit since Ruby came along.

'Lewis, Anna.' He nods to them formally and leads them through to the living room then goes to make tea.

'So, here she is,' he says when he's back and it's all poured, stirring his cup with a silver spoon. It's the first time he acknowledges the baby's presence.

Anna picks Ruby up and unwraps her. The mark on her face looks extra rosy against the white halo of the shawl and Anna notes Hugh Black silently assessing it. Anna's heart turns over for her daughter – if her own grandfather looks at her like that. Hugh Black nods and sips his tea. He's wearing a diamond tiepin, which winks when it catches the light. It looks to Anna like a tiny camera.

'So, how are the plans going?' There is a heavy accent of sarcasm on the word 'plans'.

'Good, Dad.' Lewis is eager to please. 'I've got ideas to open another place in Cinderford soon.' That's the first Anna's heard about it. 'We'll have coffee machines, shipped from Italy. The best there are.'

'I see. Coffee machines.'

This man hates his own son, thinks Anna. He looks at Lewis's face as if it's soft, as if it's made of silk or something he could never afford or want. He's always in competition with Lewis, Anna has noticed. Always wanting to take over or be first with everything. She can't talk about this with Lewis. The subject is too touchy. He defends his father at the same time as privately hating him. So privately he doesn't even know himself, though Anna realised some time ago.

The older man ignores the talk of coffee machines and looks over at Anna and the baby. 'I've heard there's research going on. That there may be an operation for that one day.' The diamond on the tiepin casts a speck of light on the shawl and flickers there. It's been doing the same on everything the old man looks at.

Anna waits for Lewis outside on the opposite side of the road to Hugh Black's bungalow with Ruby re-wrapped in her arms.

She'd needed fresh air; she couldn't breathe in that place. The atmosphere was always enough to choke you. Now, it's completely silent except for the hum of bees. The sky soars over her, pure and pale and blue.

Lewis comes bowling out of the front door at speed. Even from this distance she can see his fury. He walks so fast that his distant figure grows larger, quickly, and he's there beside her.

'I can't bloody stand it here any more, Anna, I just can't.' Seeing his father always gets to him like this.

'What was all that about Cinderford?' She lifts Ruby up and grazes her lips against her soft forehead.

'It's all balls, rubbish. I just won't have him looking at me that way, so superior. He can shove that bone china up his arse.' He flings out his arms. 'I've got to get away from here. I just have. All my plans, all—'

161

'I'm sorry.' It's her fault; she knows it. He would've been long gone if it wasn't for her.

'You could come with me – to London.'

'Where would we live? How could we afford to live?' She holds the baby a little more tightly. 'What about the milk bar and the flat? You've put the down payment on it already. The coffee machine is coming from Italy.'

He sweeps it all aside with one arm. 'I'll put someone in to look after it. That poxy place is never going to make my fortune, anyway. I was mad to take it on. It was just desperation, really.'

Now he's decided, his eyes turn beautifully clear. The sun strikes dark blue notes in his hair. Anna's gaze slips past his shoulder. Behind him the house sits burning in the sun. The windows seem alight with it.

Anna and Lewis pack the car to the hilt. She climbs into the front seat and Lewis hands the baby into her arms. There's a seatbelt and Anna winds it round so it's holding the two of them.

Lewis gets behind the wheel. 'Just have the seatbelt round you. If we had a bump it would cut her in half.'

'But if we had a bump wouldn't she just fly through the windscreen if she's not tied in?'

He shrugs: he's thinking ahead to the journey already, the road that ends with London, the city spread out and glittering.

Being chopped in half or smashing through the windscreen; it doesn't seem much of a choice. Anna unbuckles the belt and holds Ruby on her lap, tightly.

Lewis turns and grins. 'Here we go!'

35

SNOW
11 December 1983

It came as a light first before falling from the sky. The colour of the light was a piercing grey. It seemed to fill you up. Then the flakes began to fall. When I looked upwards I felt I was seeing the shifting particles that made up the world and they were falling down on me.

When the snow had come and lay in thick inches over everything, the white outside shone back at us through the windows, illuminating all the rooms. I could see Elizabeth's footsteps in it heading towards the chicken run through the diamond-patterned panes of the library window. Then I saw her returning in a man's long black coat, making another set of prints next to her first, and her back looked bent and hopeless.

'He didn't even eat them.' I heard her wailing from downstairs. 'He must just have enjoyed killing them all.'

Later Crispin caught me by the back door of the kitchen looking out at the white expanse.

'Put on your coat, we're going out,' he said.

His silvery eyes were dull today, more like pewter. The skin on his face was tougher than that of the other two, thicker than normal skin; like he spent a lot of time outside and the cold had made it quilt.

I thought of what I'd heard at the door. 'Why should I go anywhere with you? Especially on my own.'

Instead of answering he nodded towards the hunting rifle on the hooks on the wall and then I couldn't help myself, I gave a little shriek.

'Keep your hair on,' he laughed, and sat down on the bench where you sat to put your boots on before going outside. 'Just a small expedition. It'll do you good to get out. You look as white as a sheet, except for, you know . . .' And he fluttered his fingers at his face where my birthmark was. 'You're not going to come to any harm.' He grinned. 'You shouldn't believe everything you hear at keyholes.'

I flushed red and opened the door further to let the outside cool my cheeks.

'Besides,' he went on, 'I need help. I can't manage keeping us all stocked with protein. Tom milks the goats and organises stuff and digs. Elizabeth does what she does – it's time you paid your way here. You can be like my . . . apprentice.'

I reminded myself of 'Project Worm My Way In'. Surely, I told myself, if you can defend yourself against Mick, a grown man who has rages that could flatten trees, a fourteen-year-old boy shouldn't scare you.

Except he wasn't like any fourteen-year-old I'd ever known and I'd almost decided I was about to tell him I wasn't going anywhere with him, not with guns, but he nodded towards it again.

'Go on, you can be my wing man and carry it.'

I lifted it down and weighed it in my hands; it felt heavy and easy to wield at the same time. I remembered what I'd said to Elizabeth, about how I wanted to learn survival. I lifted it carefully over my shoulder.

'Good girl,' said Crispin.

'You'll teach me how to shoot rabbits?'

'Yes, that's the idea. Always catch on so quick, do you?'

We stepped out into the snow. 'Let's go and check all the chickens are really dead first,' I said.

I didn't feel so afraid of Crispin when I had the gun over my shoulder. It reminded me of the night I walked into the woods with the knife stuck out in front of me and how it had made me brave, until I'd thought the word 'murderer' and wrecked it all. I trembled then and it made the gun jerk on my shoulders.

'They are well and truly dead. Foxes don't muck about in my experience.'

'Well, there's no harm checking.' I wanted more than anything to find one alive so I could run back and tell Elizabeth about it. Since she'd seen them all with their throats bitten out this morning she hadn't said a word. She'd sat in the side room with the TV on the hard chair, with her knees pulled up to her chest and her hair covering half her face. I longed to give her some good news.

'This is loaded, isn't it?' I said.

'Of course. Why would you take an unloaded gun out? What would be the point of that?'

'Nobody at home carries guns about. They'd get arrested.'

Crispin's grey eyes had started looking like silver again out here in the white light as he turned to me. 'Well, we don't live by the rules, haven't you noticed that?'

'I suppose so.'

'You stick with me, kid. You'll be all right.'

'I thought you didn't want me here,' I said at last.

'Maybe I've changed my mind. You're skinny. Skinny

165

people are always useful. Much more than great fat lumps. I'll teach you to shoot. I've been thinking about it overnight, you can be the Artful Dodger to my Fagin. I'm finding it difficult to keep on top of everything at the moment.' For a second he looked perturbed then he gave a shake of his head. 'If I get you bringing the meat home I can concentrate on other enterprises. I see Tom doing it and it's not his thing. He's too soft to be really good. You need a hard streak – you'll be good at it.'

I thought of the bloody lumps brought into the house and shuddered. 'What if I can't nerve myself?'

'You eat them, don't you? If you can do that you need to be able to kill too.' He was right. I was as bad as the rest of them, chomping down on the flesh and sucking the meat off the legs like they were lollipops.

We were trudging side by side and the snow had started to fall again. Elizabeth's footprints from earlier were getting specked with more snow, starting to fill in. Flakes of it landed on Crispin's bare arms.

'You came out without a coat. Aren't you freezing?'

He stopped and shook his head. 'I can't feel a thing.'

The hens' cage loomed out of the snow and even though it was me who'd insisted on going I started to feel afraid of what we might find inside. I wasn't used to farm life. Even though I'd always lived in the country our meat still came out of the freezer, stiff and plucked, or in pies so it was hidden by pastry or potato. It stopped you thinking how it had come from warm animals with fur. Inside the run, I stood looking at the bright patches of blood and feathers against the ground – there was only snow around the edges where it had come in through the chicken wire because the hen run had a proper roof.

'Well?' Crispin had stayed outside. I could see him through the chicken wire and I had the funny feeling he might shut the door and bolt it from the outside. Maybe that had been his plan all along – it was the sort of thing he'd do and call a joke. I let myself out quickly before he had the chance.

As we were walking away I felt an unbearable sadness. 'Are we sure they're all really dead?'

'You're the one that looked,' he said.

I didn't explain to him how I couldn't stand to properly check every single nest. I just wanted to get out of there with its smell of iron and ripped feathers in the air and the stink of old fox. Now I'd started imagining one had actually still been alive and was cowering in the shed with its feathers fluffed up in fear, or crawling around with its throat half gone.

'If we see the fox we'll shoot it,' he said.

'That won't do any good now – the chickens are all gone.'

'Yes, but it'll be revenge. Don't underestimate revenge, Ruby. Often, it can be the right thing to do.' I thought of the plank crunching into Mick's head, of the elation and the fear afterwards, the sickening guilt, and I knew it wasn't as simple as Crispin was making out.

We trudged some more, Crispin scanning the horizon for the fox.

'I expect he knows we're after him,' I said at last. The cold was draining down the gap in my coat collar and all I wanted to do was go back inside now even if I didn't have a tale of live chickens to cheer Elizabeth up with. Then I saw something out of the corner of my eye, a dark shape against the white. The early darkness had already started to fall so the snow looked almost blue in places. The creature's movements were enlarged in the big blue shadow it cast. Its giant shadow form bobbed and twitched.

'Look,' I whispered.

Crispin's head turned slowly and his silver eyes narrowed, reminding me of bullets.

'It's a rabbit,' he whispered back. 'Good girl, good girl, Ruby. Now keep very quiet and still, don't do anything to startle it. It'll be your first kill. I'll teach you.'

Slowly, I raised the gun to my face. Below me I could see Crispin's boots shuffling in the snow to muffle the noise, as he inched behind. I felt his breath against my neck; already cold by the time it reached my skin.

'Now, keep it steady.' I could feel his breath in my ear now. 'Steady, steady. Don't try and do it with your eyes, do it with your feelings.'

I concentrated on the dark speck and I couldn't help it but a thrill ran through me, making a ripple pass over my skin, though afterwards I'd curse myself for that.

'Feel the bullet, Ruby, and squeeze, squeeze. Feel it enter the rabbit's head,' Crispin whispered in my ear, his voice resounding inside the hollow like he was speaking into a cave. I pressed and everything went black before the world jiggled and slanted and righted itself.

'Good girl, good girl,' Crispin crowed. I put the gun down and it sizzled and sent a puff of steam into the air. I looked into the shadows. They were still now and radiated a kind of deadness that pressed against me. 'Now, go and get it and we'll take it back to the house. It'll be on the plate before we know it. You're a better apprentice than

I imagined. You've made a very good start. I'm extremely pleased with you.'

My legs felt odd as I walked, like I was wearing the rockers of a wooden horse that lurched me back and forwards. Murderer, something whispered beside me from the gloom. I stopped and put my hands to my face, turning my head and forcing myself to look at the dark hump of the animal that lay on its side.

'Go on,' said Crispin, 'what are you waiting for?'

Up close I could see the rabbit's ears lying flat across his head and his back. The position made it seem like there was a moment when he knew what was happening to him. I couldn't see any blood. I stood, looking down at it and the day seemed to grow darker in an instant.

'How strange,' I cried out.

'What is?' Crispin was getting impatient now, hunching his shoulders against the cold and banging his hands together in their grey knitted gloves.

Slowly I sunk to my knees. 'One minute to be alive and the next dead.'

'What are you talking about?' His voice started to sound snappish.

'Where did it go?' I could feel tears gathering at the back of my eyes. 'What happens?'

'Nowhere of course, you silly girl. It's just a series of biological functions that cease to work all at the same time. It's the sort of thing I used to talk over with my father. Now, stop fucking about.'

I drooped forward and closed my eyes, holding my hands together, thinking I should say a prayer at least.

'Fuck's sake, Ruby. Get out of the snow. I'm beginning to

think I don't want you as an apprentice after all. You're too weird. What's the matter with you?'

'I don't know,' I whispered. I opened my eyes again and the sight seemed to fix me to the spot.

'Whenever you're ready,' he said. 'I thought you'd be glad, your first kill. You need to bring it back in, you know, because of it being your first. If you weren't being so freaky I'd blood you too if I could. Don't be too long about it either. And don't forget to bring the gun.' And he started walking away back towards the house.

When he was just a black dot in the distance I leaned over the rabbit. 'I'm sorry,' I said and bent to lift him by his ears. There was a scuffling in the dead bracken and brush next to me and I froze, my hand poised over the body.

'Who's there?'

It sounded bigger than a rabbit. Perhaps it was the fox. 'Clear off while you can,' I said in a fierce whisper, 'Crispin is out for revenge. He doesn't understand how it's just your nature.'

More scuffling that sounded bigger than a fox even. I fell on my knees pushing aside the frost stiff black bracken that cracked apart in my hands. 'Who's there?' I said again, even though I knew really, for hadn't I glimpsed the turning of a small pale cheek among the brush, seen it out of the corner of my eye like I had the rabbit?

'I thought you'd gone and left me for good.' I sat back in the snow.

I've been out here all the time. I didn't want to come any closer. The family in there aren't the good sort, I've realised that since. They're the bad sort so I decided to stay away.

'They're not my family. You led me up the garden path

yet again. You're always doing that. Why don't you come out? I've missed you really. You're so . . .' – I looked for the word and discounted 'dear' – ' . . . familiar to me.'

Why didn't you say dear?

I couldn't help smiling. 'All right, dear.'

There was a rustling and Shadow bulbed out from the undergrowth and walked towards me. He was more distinct again since the last time I saw him. I caught the gleam of muddy darkness on his bottom lip. It was thick and sticky at the centre of his lips and dried into a crust around the edges. His skin had an almost purple tone in the snowy half-light. On his feet were the ankle boots I'd left in the hole. He had them on back to front so his feet were pointing backwards. It was obvious he wasn't used to wearing shoes.

'My things. I was going to go back and try and find those. I'm wearing mostly their clothes.'

Too late. They have all been purloined. I was lucky to get these. It's all scattered to the winds and the fox you were seeking now wears your tartan scarf. He thinks it makes him a handsome fellow and has become quite boastful.

'Oh, you do talk rubbish sometimes.'

Yes, I know.

There was quiet for a bit and the wind picked up, shooting across the snow.

He shuffled closer. *What's that?*

'I've just killed something. It's a rabbit. I shouldn't have done it.' My face was in my hands now, the cold stinging against my eyelids.

That's not a rabbit, that's a hare.

I lifted my head up. 'A hare? No, it's not.'

I should know the difference between a hare and a rabbit and that's a hare, no mistake. You should be quite worried, it's supposed to be very bad luck. You should get back home to the forest.

'No, I won't. You're only saying that because you want me back. I like it here. We do what we want – there's no mothers or fathers.' I stood. 'I'm going back in. You can do what you want.'

No. I've realised you need to go home. The voice called out as I swung the animal up by its ears. All the blood was underneath, I could see that now. It looked black in the half-light against the snow. I swung it in my hand, it felt heavier than it should, and started walking back to the house with the rifle under my other arm. The ears felt slippery in my hand, like its body wanted to break away and bound across the field towards the woods.

You need to come home.

'Leave me alone,' I shouted over my shoulder.

His callings got smaller and smaller until the sound was just a breath of wind and the lights of the house blazed at me.

Elizabeth cradled the creature in her arms like it was a baby.

'It's a hare,' I said.

'Yes, I know. It's terribly unlucky, Ruby.' She looked up and her face was creased with worry. 'I can't have it in the house.'

She lifted the sash kitchen window and flung the creature out into the darkness. In flying it seemed alive again for a moment, as if it was leaping through the open window, but there was a dull thud as it landed below. Later I imagined

I could hear the fox, snickering under the kitchen window before carrying the hare away in his jaws, drops of blood falling on my scarf.

In the night I thought I heard him again but with the dead hare this time, crying out, chattering manically so the two formed a chorus. It woke me from a dream of Mick. He'd been standing outside watching for me with a weapon in his hand. In the dream I couldn't work out what the weapon was, though it resembled something like a club. I crept along the corridor until I was outside Tom's bedroom door.

'Tom.' I knocked softly. 'Tom, I'm scared.'

'Come in then.' He sounded sleepy.

I tiptoed in, suddenly conscious of the T-shirt I was wearing that came just to the top of my legs.

When I opened the door he was shoving a pillow into the middle of the bed.

'Bad dream?'

'Sort of.'

'You hop in that side,' he said. 'And don't be scared any more. Tom's here.'

He turned over so his back faced me.

'What did you dream about?'

'D'you remember the child catcher in *Chitty Chitty Bang Bang*?'

'Yes.'

'He frightened me more than anything. It was something about the way he moved.' How I'd hated him, his funny dancing walk, always towards the camera, never away. 'But I think we're too old now for the child catcher – well, you nearly are.'

'You're never too old for him.' Tom was starting to sound drowsy again.

'Mick and Barbara are child catchers.'

His voice tailed off into sleep. 'They're everywhere.'

From then on whenever I had a bad dream we slept side by side, the pillow wedged between us and Tom's back turned. Sometimes I tried to imagine what his face looked like sleeping. I imagined it to be beautiful.

36

COLD
18 December, 1983

There was no more wood to burn. The three of us sat in front of the fireplace looking at the sooty black hole. Three lots of frosty breath formed a cloud. I shivered violently and buttoned up the fur coat.

'We need to collect more firewood. Is there ash anywhere around here? Ash burns the brightest and you can burn it when it's green. Let's go and look in that wood by the lake.'

'No,' said Elizabeth. 'You can't go in there.'

'Why?'

'It's dangerous. There's old mine workings. Animal traps. All sorts.'

I shivered again. 'Well, I'll look elsewhere. I'm not sitting here until I freeze to death. Coming?'

No answer.

'You two get worse by the day. Honestly, I don't know what's wrong with you. Don't you want to survive?'

I slammed the door on the way out and went into the snow.

Outside everything shimmered white. Even the sky was the dense grey-white that promised another fall. It was the colour of a goose's wing. In the silence I could hear the roaring in my own ears. I glanced at the stand of trees in the distance. I didn't want to enter that quiet darkness all alone. I'd have to think of something else. I started walking, my hands deep inside the pockets of the fur coat. Opening up like a path in front of me were deep footsteps. I stopped and put my foot inside one. The foot that had made it was much bigger than mine. I huffed out icy breath wondering what to do then into the silence came a dragging noise, a tinkle of metal, a scrape. A man in a black coat came out of the greenhouse dragging something behind him. I turned to run and staggered, the snow binding my feet together so my hands plunged into the coldness and I fell on my knees.

'Hey,' he shouted. 'Hey there. Are you one of the kids from the commune?'

I stood and brushed the snow off my hands and looked up at him.

'Fuck,' he said, and his fists balled tight. I could see the blueness of his eyes and how under them his skin was pouched and ravaged. Lines decorated them like a child's criss-crosses.

'Fuck,' he said again. 'Tell me your name, who are you?'

I turned again. 'No, no,' he said, 'it's fine.' He unballed his fists and held up his hands. 'Don't be scared. I just came up to look at the plants in the greenhouse. I was worried about the snow. Don't go. Tell me your name.'

Then I remembered the man Tom and Elizabeth had told me about, Mr Green Car. The friend of their parents. The one that was going to give them a cut of his profits. I saw the object he'd been dragging out was a heater; its flex looked dirty coiling across the white ground.

'Ruby. My name's Ruby.'

His pupils contracted, like twin tiny cameras were taking a photograph of me.

He licked his lips. 'Ruby.'

'Yes.'

'What are you doing here?'

'I'm looking for wood. The firewood's all gone.'

Something moved across his face, under the skin. It travelled from one side to the other and out into the air. It looked like pain. His eyes defocused and stopped being cameras.

'What about that?' he said eventually.

He nodded towards the bare bones of the tepee sticking up into the sky. Where all the joists stuck together at the top there was a crown of snow.

'Too big.' I shrugged. I wanted to get away from him for a moment. Then the moment passed and the worry of no fuel filled the space.

'I've got an axe. It's in the car. Come with me and I'll fetch it.'

For the first time I noticed a battered green estate car parked by the side of the house.

'Why do I have to come with you?'

He smiled and shook himself. 'You're right. You don't. I'll fetch it now.'

While he went to get the axe I walked inside the shell of the tepee. I tried to imagine it with people living inside it as Tom said they once had – the painted caravans too – but it was impossible to think of them buzzing with life and children running in and out of the doorways in the sunshine. Before the snow had come desolation had been everywhere. Then the snow arrived and cancelled it all out. It had made everything blank and clean again.

He hurried back with the axe. I could see the metal head of it glinting by his side. I walked back out from the shell. It felt as if we were moving to meet each other but when we came face to face there didn't seem anything to say.

177

'Right.' He turned and with the same movement the axe swung into the air. The blade chopped down into one of the supporting legs and the force of the blow made the whole structure teeter. Then with two chops more it had lost a leg and it collapsed sideways, crashing down.

I stacked while he worked until the structure lay on the ground, half gone.

I heard Tom calling in the distance, the silent snowy air magnifying every sound. He was breathless by the time he reached us.

'What's going on?'

Mr Green Car stopped and leaned on the axe. He was drenched in sweat. It dripped off a lock of his black hair.

'It's firewood. Look.' I pointed to the stack I'd made. 'It'll keep us going for days.'

'I need to go.' Mr Green Car opened the top button of his shirt like it was strangling him. 'I have to go now. I only came to check the plants because of the snow and I found a heater broken. I need to take it away. You'll be warm now. I have to go,' he said again.

Tom shrugged. 'Do what you want,' he said.

When the engine of the car became a distant sound I leaned to pick up an armful of wood but the pain in my belly made me cry out. I felt something slide down my thigh.

'Oh my God.' The blood slid over my ankle and my boot and spattered on the snow.

'You go inside,' said Tom. He couldn't take his eyes off the bright red berries of blood.

'It's my period,' I said. I hugged my belly. 'It's my second one. D'you know what that means? It means I must've been here for one whole month.'

37

25 October 1970

London enchants Anna.

Everything: from the window boxes of winter pansies on the houses – all painted pinks, blues, yellows – to the way people hang out of their windows, lounging there and watching the passers-by. Even if they are at the 'bad' end of Notting Hill ('Not for long!' says Lewis).

She buys a doll – Ruby's first – from the market not far from her door. The market is a cornucopia spewing out pomegranates, potatoes, ancient fire fenders, brasses, even a horse's saddle she saw once with full riding kit included, the boots still with mud on them. The doll she chooses is on a stall writhing with dolls but this one catches her eye. Its soft fabric body in its red dress sits a little more than the length of her hand but the head, feet and hands are hard plastic. Her felt dress is scarlet and she has a white blouse underneath. The dark wool hair and face have something of an Eskimo look about her – even though there's no costume to go alongside it. It's something in her expression, her wide face and her red mouth on the verge of a smile and the strokes of her left eye puckering so they look like the beginnings of a wink. She gives the doll to Ruby who sucks on its left foot.

Sometimes they have a pub lunch, Ruby on her lap in

the smoky room and Lewis leaning back against the tapestry seat, laughing, cocking his new trilby hat at her with his index finger, happy to be here, happy to have finally, finally got away. Though some of London shocks her. Children play on the street with filthy faces and no shoes. In the boarding houses around some have 'No Blacks, no Dogs, no Irish' still taped to the doors. To her it just seems plain rude – she can't imagine a forester ever doing something like that, not through any great racial awareness, but because it would hurt feelings.

'This is Rose. What's your baby's name?' Their boarding house is not one of those with that sign taped to the door and Stella and Rose's skin is as dark as Anna has ever seen.

'Ruby.' Anna feels shy, standing there on the landing by the cubbyhole where they both cook.

'Ruby. It makes me think of Turkish delight, red and sweet.' Stella licks her lips – she obviously has a sweet tooth. 'Rose is such a good girl and sleeps like a dream every night.'

'Rose is a lovely name too.' Anna feels like she should offer some vivid comparison to the name, like Stella did, but all she can think is 'a rose, is a rose is a rose' – some quote from school.

She heaves Ruby up in her arms. 'But she doesn't sleep so well,' she frowns. 'She grumbles all night, it's like something is worrying her.'

'Then you need to rest,' says Stella, 'the baby feels what the mother is feeling.'

Was this true? Anna's been enjoying the experience of setting up a home here – even if it is one room – it all feels so different and new. She's scrubbed the bare floorboards until they're sweet and honey-coloured and bought a bright rag rug. She's hung yellow curtains at both of the sash windows that seem as big as the doorways of the tiny cottages of the forest. She cooks her and Lewis's meal every evening in the cubbyhole – chops or bacon, with tinned potatoes and peas heated up in the tin water in a saucepan. The smell of meat lingers in the hallway the next morning, the ghost of last night's meal. But lately she's been feeling strange; there's a pressure at the back of her head that she wonders if she should see the doctor about. The feeling of disconnection is back that she had on seeing Ruby being bottle fed by another woman in the hospital. It's more present than before. It crawls up the back of her neck and puckers her scalp.

Soon, she and Stella are bouncing their babies along side by side down Portobello Road in their second-hand Silver Crosses. Some of the older stallholders give Anna a look that she ignores. She knows disapproval when she sees it and has had enough of it in her short life to withstand.

'My husband works on the Underground,' says Stella, leaning forward to wipe a bubble of milk from the corner of Rose's mouth. 'He cleans the tunnels, they are full of human hair, he says.' She comes to a brief stop as if to pause at the wonder of tunnels of human hair. 'What does yours do?' Stella resolutely ignores the fact that Anna and Lewis aren't married.

Anna pauses too. How can she say: I don't know, I can't get to the bottom of it. 'Business,' she says, finally. Yes, business – it keeps him out half the night sometimes – whatever it is. When she asks him all he'll say is, 'It's a get rich quick scheme because I want to get us rich quick.'

Lewis also says, 'You shouldn't be hanging around with

that woman. You shouldn't be mixing our daughters.'

He's back early tonight and the chops in their grease-proof paper are still on the table, uncooked, between them.

'Oh, yes? And why would that be?'

'You just shouldn't. It should be enough that I say that.'

'Oh really?' Anna stands and holds onto the edge of the table. 'It's your father, isn't it? We might have come all this way to get away from him but you can't help it, can you, it's like hearing his voice coming out of your mouth.' It's true: Lewis's father constantly refers to the outrage of black faces on his telly, how he switches them straight off before they have a chance to start talking at him.

'Just be told,' says Lewis. And it's the way he relaxes back into the dining chair that really gets to Anna as if the whole debate has been drawn to its conclusion. Despite her father's religious pronouncements she's not used to men laying the law down. It's her mother that always really ruled the roost.

Lewis is wearing his good suit, made by 'a chap he knows', and his new trilby even though he's at the table, something her father would rather be dead than do. When the chops fly through the air one of them lands on his lapel and clings there greasily. He looks down with such horror on his face it's almost as if it's his own organs that have burst out. He takes it by finger and thumb at the skinny end and slowly peels it away. The greasy mark never comes out of the wool.

Anna starts to miss trees. She has the idea that the pressure at the back of her head would disappear if she could just stand under the cool autumn canopy of home for a while. She takes Ruby to Hyde Park on the tube – in her arms because the Silver Cross would be impossible with all the stairs – and shows her the trees. The plane trees cut into the pale autumn sky, their leaves are beautiful – reds and yellows – but they seem dizzyingly high. At home there are a million hiding places in the forest, here there are none. The spaces between the trees feel exposed.

'Look, Ruby.' Ruby's little face turns in the white wool blanket and she grizzles a little, but she goes quiet once her blue-grey eyes fix on the shifting leaves. Anna has the fancy that she's recognising her birthright.

'One day I'll take you home,' Anna whispers in her ear. 'I'll show you what a real forest looks like.'

38

THE HUNGER
21 December 1983

Me and Tom explored the pantry like animals.

'What about this?' I lifted a bag of rotting flour and the paper split down the seam. The flour inside had set like concrete.

'It's filthy,' said Tom.

'There's gravy browning,' I said, peering at the packet. 'But you need something for that to go with. I could try and hunt again, now Crispin's gone. He started teaching me. Then there'd be some meat to go with it.' As he was wont to do Crispin had left a couple of days ago and hadn't come back – I saw his figure trudging out of the gate in the starlight. I suspected he knew someone to stay with and was getting well fed. He didn't have that hollowed-out look the rest of us were acquiring. Knowing him, he wouldn't want to share.

'There's some rice,' said Tom. 'That'll be the last of the food then.' He went quiet for a while. 'I'm shitting myself,' he said eventually in a tiny voice. 'I really am now.'

I took the gun down from the wall and stared at it in my hands, nerving myself. I thought of Elizabeth's face when I presented her with a dead rabbit to give me courage.

Outside, the melt of snow had begun. There were sucking

sounds everywhere, small gurglings and the mushy noises of an ice-lolly breaking in half. The lake was a dull silver – the same colour as Crispin's eyes. I trod softly and kept the gun poised and ready but there was not a single other living thing about – not a rat or a bird, a worm, let alone a rabbit. Just the slide and drip of snow and ice turning itself back into liquid as if the whole world was on the move. It occurred to me it'd been as if the four of us had been frozen in ice too, still, and things would soon have to begin to churn and change again.

'Shadow,' I called softly but there was no reply.

He hated hunger, I remembered. If I left a mealtime too long he'd become anxious and persuade me to return home, to the table and the plate. Now my hunger stalked me like an animal on the periphery of my vision. If I ignored it it would stay away but give it too much attention and it came roaring all over me. I noticed a few blades of grass sticking green and strong through the snow and I squatted and picked a couple and the chewing helped. I plucked some more and put them in my pocket for Tom.

I lifted the gun again to try one last time and trudged on. As I passed the greenhouses a face swam into one of the panes and there was a splintering knock on the glass. I jumped and the gun swung wildly towards the sky.

'Hey,' called a voice muffled by glass. 'Hey, what are you doing?'

I looked again. It was Mr Green Car who'd chopped us the wood. I could see his dark hair and the paleness of his face. He disappeared from behind the glass and came out, breathing heavily.

'Christ's sake. What are you doing running around with

185

a gun? They're bloody dangerous, you know.'

I lowered it. 'Rabbiting.' I wasn't sure if I trusted this man.

He took out a red spotted hanky and mopped his face. 'Hunting rabbits? Are you lot that bloody desperate?'

I stood mute.

'If you are, perhaps I could help? You're as white as a sheet. You don't look well.' Neither did he. The skin was pinched underneath his eye sockets.

'How?'

He stared at me. 'I don't know. Give you an advance on what's due on this. Take you into town, whatever.'

'I don't know. I'll need to ask Tom. I don't know if he'll like it.'

He nodded. 'Go on then. I'll be here, waiting.'

Tom was by the boot store by the open back door. He was shivering in just his shirtsleeves, no coat or jumper. His feet were bare and I noticed for the first time how dirty they were. Wearing no socks had ground the dirt into them.

'I was looking out for you,' he said. 'I started worrying about you. I'm quite afraid of guns.'

'There's nothing out there, but there may be another way. That man, Mr Green Car, he's just offered to give you an advance. He says he'll take us into town.'

He searched around in his pocket and pulled out a pouch of tobacco.

'I've never seen you smoking before.'

He rolled a cigarette and a sleety rain began to blow into the doorway and made dark spots on the paper.

'Fuck, fuck, fuck,' he said, between puffs. 'Why should he do that? We've hardly had anything to do with him. I don't like this. He's up to something.'

'You're hungry, aren't you?' I didn't want to let on that I was scared of Mr Green Car too. Tom looked as if he was about to break apart.

'It'd have to be just us two. Elizabeth won't leave.' He took anxious puffs. 'I feel really peculiar at the thought of being away now.' He swiped a hand across his eyes. 'It's making me a bit dizzy.'

'It's just the smoking that's made you dizzy. You can't eat that tobacco, you know.'

We were quiet for a bit.

'I love you,' he cried out and his words shone through me like light had just entered my body.

Then over Tom's shoulder I glimpsed Shadow. He must have heard me call him. His eye glittered and the mud around his mouth looked fresh this time. He watched me from the shadows in the corner. His face was pin sharp in focus for the first time. His lips were black and glistening. His face was avid, with a pinched acquisitive stare. I pretended he wasn't there.

'I love you too,' I whispered.

Love. Once, I thought I'd have to pin someone down and half choke them before that word was ever uttered to me and now Tom just had.

I looked at him. He was in darkness except his face where the white bright light from outside caught at the angles of it. I would've thought a declaration of love would bring joy, but instead he looked more haunted than ever.

Christmas music jangled in the supermarket. We looked up at the spangle of decorations and held hands tightly.

'I'd forgotten it was nearly Christmas,' I said.

187

'Let's get some decorations,' burst out Tom. We wheeled the trolley over to the glittering pile. 'Do you think people are staring at us?' he whispered.

'No. We're miles from the forest. No one would recognise me in here.'

Then I caught my reflection in a silver bell and saw how we looked ragged and young like tiny tramps, like something people might stare at.

'Sssh, don't worry about it,' I whispered. 'We'll just try to look normal.'

We loaded the orange carrier bags in the boot in the car park outside then both climbed in the back seat. Tom pulled a mashed piece of paper out from his pocket.

'Will the advance cover this?' He grimaced. 'It's the electricity bill. We're on our last reminder.' It was the first time I'd seen it.

Mr Green Car took his wallet out of his pocket. 'How much?'

Rain, softer down here than the hard sleet of Hilltops, had begun to fall, running in rivulets down the windscreen.

'You stay here,' said Tom. 'I'll be two minutes. The place to pay is just round the corner.'

I watched as he walked away, his shoulders hunched against the rain, the blond tip of his ponytail pointing down, the wetness sharpening it to an arrow head.

There was silence inside the car for a moment then the man turned so I could see the speckling of white at his temple in his black hair.

'What are you doing with them?'

My stomach trembled. 'What do you mean?'

'What about your parents?'

'I haven't got any.'

A tapping filled the car. I realised it was his fingers on the steering wheel.

'You should be being looked after properly. Not attaching yourself to that rag bag lot. It's dangerous.'

'I'm searching for my real parents. They'll look after me properly. No one else ever has.'

The tapping had gone quiet. 'What makes you think they'll see you right?' he asked softly as the door opened and Tom climbed in next to me. 'Parents aren't all they're cracked up to be.'

'Mine will be different.'

He was silent. He'd turned his head again so I couldn't see his face and I started to feel afraid of him again.

I was so relieved to see Tom I squeezed his hand, then the engine started and the car swung away.

Tom lapsed into silence the closer we drove to the house as if he didn't want to go back there. I touched his ponytail and stole my hand over to his again, secretly in wonder that someone who loved me could be so perfectly made. I ached for him to turn to me and smile. For him to catch my eye just for a second so I could let the soft tenderness in my stomach blossom out until it was touching my sides.

He made no response and I took my hand away and I felt small and frightened just like the old days before anyone loved me.

39

30 October 1970

'Business' takes up more and more of Lewis's time. When he returns to his and Anna's room often it's with a group of men, two, three, four of them, sometimes more.

'Evening.' They tip their hats at Anna but the fact this one room is also the bedroom doesn't stop them staying half the night and dealing cards round her little dining table. 'How's the baby?' they ask. 'How's the little gem tonight?' But *that* doesn't stop them smoking their cigars and roll-up cigarettes in the room, the smoke wafting over the cot. Anna can't think it can be healthy and opens the sash window and a slash of cold London night air whisks into the room.

'Honestly, love,' says Lewis. 'It's freezing in here. Close that, will you?'

As winter nears it does get colder, open window or not, and Anna piles small blankets, woven honeycomb in pink, blue and biscuit brown, onto Ruby, then worries about her being suffocated and takes them off layer by layer. She's always testing it out: one off, two on. Two on, three off, trying to gauge the baby's temperature. The men stay later and later and she gets to know their names: Sydney, Terence, Michael, Vincent and Johnny. She sits on the bed, mutely; waiting for them to go so she can climb between the sheets. When they ignore her she starts lying down on the yellow

Jacquard cover and falling asleep anyway. Lewis rouses her later, in what seems to be the dead of night, with a shake on the shoulder. 'Come on, love, let's tuck you in.'

Then she begins to notice, or is it her imagination, when they arrive, clattering up the bare wooden stairs, do they tread heavier as they pass Stella and her husband Samuel's door? Do their voices become louder, heavily jocular? 'Bloody hell, Sydney, can't you go a bit quicker, old age creeping in, is it? Or do you just like, you know . . .' An explosion of laughter then, 'Oi, get off.' Mock scuffles right outside the door that stays resolutely shut.

'They're doing it on purpose,' Anna challenges Lewis one day as he puts his boots on, bleary from another late night out. 'It's because of who Stella and Samuel are, isn't it? You'd better tell them to cut it out.'

'I'm telling nobody to cut nothing out,' says Lewis with that heavy tone, implying he's keeping his temper. Her handsome passionate Lewis; Anna begins feeling she knows him less and less. His London is all night time – she's only ever out in the day. Her imagination works overtime thinking of the shadowy places he must inhabit – clubs, bars, places with girls. Girls without babies.

One night he comes back and she wakes up the instant the door opens. He brings something in with him – the cold night air, but something else too. She sits bolt upright in bed. 'What's the matter?' she asks, suddenly and instantly awake.

'Nothing, it's freezing out there.'

He stands, unusually unsure in the middle of the room, his hands in his raincoat pockets. She squints at the shadowy figure trying to work out what it is. She knows him so well she can see it even though there's barely any light in the room, it's like his *shape* has changed. Ruby stirs in her cot then quietens again.

'Get into bed,' she says, in her old voice, the one from the forest, the one that seems to have been fading in and out in the last few weeks. 'I'll warm you up.'

Lewis sheds his boots, his hat and coat, his suit, the night air and leaves them on a pile on the floor. He crawls in naked beside her and she puts her arms around him; he *is* freezing. The chill spreads through her but she wraps her arms around him anyway and tries to transmit her own warmth.

'Hold me,' he says. 'Please, hold me, hold me, hold me, hold me.'

40

BONFIRE

21 December 1983

The last of the light illuminated Hilltops. Long, whipped-out clouds tracked above the fields and the sky was a cool high blue. The ridges of earth stood out knobbly and cold-hardened. Mr Green Car let us out round the back. He rolled his window down.

'I'll be here again next week,' he said. 'Make a list of anything you need.'

I nodded and began trudging after Tom, both of us weighed down with carrier bags. The ground was soft and mushy underfoot from melt water.

'Hey,' he called out from the car. 'Ruby. Come here a minute.'

I paused and scanned Tom's retreating back. He hadn't heard and was walking with his head down back to the house. I could tell he was lost in thought.

'What is it?' I asked, not getting too close.

'Come here. There's something I want to ask you.'

I inched closer and water quickly seeped into the footprints I'd left.

'What?'

He was looking up at me from the open car window. The lines on his face were drawn tight to the bone, the blueness of his eyes arctic.

'Do you even know my name?'

I shrugged. 'We call you Mr Green Car.'

He smiled and looked down. 'My name's Lewis Black. Does that mean anything to you, Ruby? Have you heard of me?'

I took a step back and my bags swung. 'No – why should I? I need to get in now.' I glanced back, Tom was nearly in the house.

'No one's ever mentioned me?'

I was starting to get cold. I frowned. I could see that Tom had dropped all his shopping bags. 'No, why?'

'Right.' He took a deep breath then looked through the window and started the engine. I thought I caught the words 'no reason' as the car slid away. Then he was gone and all was quiet except for the sound of evening birdsong.

Tom had sunk down onto the wet grass by the back door. When I reached him I saw he was crying thick choking sobs.

'What's the matter? Look, look at all the food we've got. Things have got better.'

He shook his head and the tears dripped off his jaw. He shielded his face with his sleeves and suddenly he seemed about eight years old.

I knelt in front of him. With one hand I held his raw ankle. It felt cold and bony to the touch, the hairs standing bristly against my palm.

I looked around in case Shadow was loitering. Not that it was unusual for him to be gone, he was often off in a huff, or thinning himself out so finely he was as hard to find as dust. He'd be back, though, wasn't he always? I thought of the last time I saw him, how close he'd been, how distinct. How his craving greedy face had frightened me.

'Listen,' I said, cocking an ear.

'I can't hear anything,' Tom said in a tiny voice.

'Listen again.'

A faint thread of sound moved towards us across the earth. 'It's the goats, they haven't been milked,' he sniffled. I recognised it then: the high bleating cries guttering across from the shed. The bleats had a higher pitch than normal.

He stood and rubbed at his face. 'Shit. Why hasn't Elizabeth seen to them? We'll dump this stuff inside the back door and I'll take a look. Can you get the buckets? I'm really worried now – what's happened to Elizabeth?' He rubbed his eyes hard with his sleeves.

'I'll get the buckets and call her. You go to the goats, they sound like they're in pain.'

I came back, clanking buckets across the field. 'I called for Elizabeth everywhere but nobody answered. She must be out.' I was panting. Tom had already taken off his coat and rolled his sleeves up to his elbows.

He washed his hands in the sink in the outhouse. 'We'll have to make do with cold water today to wash their teats. We haven't got time to boil a kettle.' He seemed better now he had something to do. 'Let's get this done as quick as we can then go and look for Elizabeth. You've seen me do the milking, and had a go yourself. It's time to put it all into practice.'

He washed Sterling's pink bloated teats with a clean muslin square.

'Sterling's the biggest,' he said. 'I think she's having the worst time so I'll start with her. You can milk Shona.'

It took me a while to remember, a kind of muscle memory, the particular action of milking a goat. Teat has to sit flat against the palm and it's a squeeze, not a pull. Soon, both of us had thin streams of milk squirting onto the bottom of the metal buckets. The heat of the milk sent little jets of steam when it hit the cold enamel and perfumed the freezing evening air. Tom was quicker than me and I could see Sterling's teats already growing softer from the milking. When Tom stopped to go and drink straight from the tap above the stone sink she bleated softly for him, as if calling him back to finish. He slotted his cheek against her warm side, the pink flesh visible beneath the wiry white hair, and filled the pail before moving onto Milk Bottle.

When Shona's teats felt like empty balloons in my hands I waited for Tom, sitting on a hay bale, flexing my fingers. I still hadn't developed the muscles in them for milking and they ached. I watched Tom's face, his closed lids still red from crying, until he said, 'Stop watching me, Ruby, you're putting me off.'

'I wasn't,' I lied.

The house looked horribly disordered and filthy. I didn't know if it had got worse in our absence or if I was noticing it more after being away. The piercing winter light fell over everything exposing the ruin inside. We dumped our pails of milk on the kitchen table and covered them in muslin cloths so flies wouldn't fall in and drown.

Tom looked blankly at the stacks of greasy dishes in the sink, the stains of rabbit blood etched into the wooden tabletop and the dustbin with rubbish spewing down the side and overflowing in a tide around it. Down the front of the cooker was a long dried brown stain.

'Look.' I picked the saucepan off the top. 'Elizabeth

must've tried to make that gravy browning. It stinks in here.'

'I suppose it does. I ask myself at night, over and over, how are we ever going to get out of this?'

In the living room it looked like the ashes had been pulled out of the fire by a bird falling down the chimney – the grey dust, knobbly with bits of burnt wood, was spread across the Persian fire rug.

'Elizabeth.' Tom's voice bounced against the panelled walls on the stairs. 'Elizabeth, where are you?' He turned to me and his face hovered above me, pale. 'I don't even like to look. What if she's done away with herself? What if she's tried to end it all? I should never have left her alone like this. She's talked about it before you came – as a solution to our problems, you know that? That we should do it together. A kind of pact.' His voice began to take on a note of hysteria.

'No. That's stupid talk,' I said, with a conviction I didn't feel. 'Let's try upstairs.'

The house felt hollow without her, a hundred echoes of our voices bouncing off the walls. Her red lamp of hair, her swishing skirts and the laying of her long thin hand upon your shoulder as she asked 'How are you, dear?' had filled the place more than I realised. Despite the snow melt it was still cold like a blanket of freezing air had descended inside the house.

I tried to remember an instance when Elizabeth hadn't been there, or in the fields nearby at least.

'Elizabeth,' I shouted out in the hallway upstairs. The air there felt thick, the electric lights on even though it was broad daylight now. They flickered slightly. Prints of land-scapes hanging on the walls, or hunts spilling across fields

– the paper splodged with damp – floated past.

'Elizabeth!' Tom roared it now – his voice suddenly deep.

There was a slight scuffling from behind one of the doors and Tom flung it open. The curtains were drawn making the room dark and gloomy and Tom clicked on the light.

It was one of the bedrooms that was never used, that Elizabeth said leaked. A slab of cold fell across us at the doorway. The bed was covered in a fabric that looked like gold that had turned to rust. I imagined toads living, undisturbed, in the dark corners. A tangle of fabrics – I wasn't sure what – curtains, bedspreads? – lay in one corner. The room seemed silent and empty now. It must have been the dragging of a mouse or rat we'd heard that was here, somewhere, holding its breath and waiting for us to go away.

'No. Nothing,' he said, and switched off the light.

'Wait,' I said. I'd caught something. It was Shadow. His hand was reaching out to something red and the light had made him pull his hand back like it'd been burned.

'What?' The light clicked on again and spread its dimness.

I walked over to the tangle of fabric. 'Elizabeth?' I reached to touch the strands of red hair. There was movement and I caught a glimpse of her cheek, blotched and mottled with tears.

'Leave me alone.' Her voice was cold and flat, not like Elizabeth's at all.

'What on earth are you doing in this horrible room?' Tom said.

Her head stirred and poked up from the nest. I spotted flashes of her green gown mingled with all the split spoiled

198

fabrics. She sat up – her hand was gripping at something as if she wanted to squash it into nothingness.

'Tell us what's happened,' Tom said. 'We've milked the goats. They were bleating to be milked like it was hurting them.'

'Oh no, the goats. I didn't do it.' Elizabeth heaved herself up. Her green eyes were red rimmed. 'Are they all right?'

'They're fine,' I said.

'I can't believe I forgot them. It's this bloody letter.' She opened her hand and the white paper bloomed out of it. 'It's from Mum and Dad – Peter and Roz – Tom. The bastards.'

Tom crouched next to her. 'What do they say?'

She scrabbled at the pages, smoothing them out.

'They're heading to Sri Lanka. There's some kind of children's home there they've volunteered for. Oh, the irony of it.'

'Let's have a look.' Tom squinted at the letter over her shoulder.

'For a year, Tom. And look.' She picked up a ball of paper and uncrushed that too – it was an envelope. 'Look.' She opened the flap and jigged it up and down as if to magic something to fall from the inside. 'Nothing. No cheque again. No mention of a cheque either.' Her voice turned high-pitched. 'I cannot fucking deal with this any more. Everything's rotten and gone to bad. I can't stand it. Ruby, you need to get off home whatever your parents may be like. This is a sinking ship. We're all going to starve in this dump. It's not fair, Tom.' Her voice rose higher and higher. 'It's just not fair leaving us like this. They told me I could cope but I can't, it's all too much. I can't. I can't. I can't.' Her heels drummed on the floor in time.

'Elizabeth,' I said. 'Stop it. It's all right. There's food downstairs. Tons of it.'

In the morning we began to clean the house.

Tom filled sink after sink of boiling water and washed up – he emptied and filled the big stone sink five times while I swept up the rubbish overflowing from the bin.

Where's Crispin, I wanted to say, he never does his bit, but I restrained myself. I didn't want to spoil the good mood that spilled through the house. I bundled the gold material with the rabbit blood and put it in the rubbish bag alongside the empty tins and wrappers – that blood was never coming out.

I showed Elizabeth the crackers and tinsel in the carrier bags alongside the food and Tom lifted up his trouser leg and she laughed and clapped her hands together at the sight of the green and red striped socks he was showing her.

'So warm and comfy,' he said.

'Look, we got these too. We saw them marked down in the supermarket.' Tom drew out packs of sparklers. 'We forgot about Guy Fawkes Night so I thought perhaps we should have it tonight.'

He waved the sparklers in the air as if they were lit already.

As the bonfire crackled into life that night I felt only peace. Tom had worked hard all afternoon and through the twilight, building the bonfire out of fallen branches with the odd dining chair threaded between them. We've got too many anyway, he'd said. Who needs twenty-three fucking dining chairs in one house?

Darkness descended and I watched both their faces in the firelight. They might not be my blood but they were almost like it. Something deeper than blood maybe, if that was possible. I loved them both and the feeling of it made me shiver inside the fur coat, but it was a good shivering, a joyful one. Everything felt right. We ate smoky-tasting sausages between slices of bread right from our hands, ketchup dripping down our wrists.

'Watcha.' Crispin wandered into the lit circle. He must've been drawn by the fire in the darkness, like a moth.

'Hello, Crispin.' I knew my voice sounded flat. I didn't really want him there with his snide comments. He would spoil everything.

He seemed in reflective mood. He squatted by the fire and looked deep into the flames and gradually we fell into silence one by one. I watched Crispin, and his silvery eyes looked like mercury this time. Gradually, he became immobile, frozen in the squat he'd taken on the opposite side of the fire to me.

'Why isn't he moving?' I asked at last. 'He's not moving at all,' I said again, fear like a sudden cold rain on my back.

'He doesn't know,' whispered Tom beside me.

'Doesn't know what?'

'Ruby . . . please. We don't want to tell him,' Elizabeth pleaded. 'Later, I'll tell you everything later when he's gone. Please not now. It's not necessary.'

Of course, of course. I knew it then. How he disappeared for days at a time. All the fetching and carrying I'd done for him. He wanted me for his agent in the world because he wasn't ready to leave it yet. Like the woman in the car. Like Shadow. He was not of this world, not any more and hadn't been ever since I'd first seen him. Why didn't I know? Why hadn't I been able to tell?

I leapt up. 'So that's why you wanted me here. He's dead, isn't he?'

Elizabeth and Tom stood. Tom held his hands out, showing me the palms.

'It wasn't like that, I promise. Hush, please be quiet,' said Elizabeth.

'No. I will not hush for you,' I yelled. 'He's dead and gone and that's the only reason you wanted me here.' I slewed off the fur coat; it half fell into the fire and I sprung away into the darkness like one of Crispin's rabbits escaping from its own skin.

41

Lewis as Anna used to know him comes back to her after the night where he returned home freezing, in some kind of shock. It's like he's slowly thawing.

Anna knows better than to try and prise out of him what's happened; better she let him alone and he'll start confiding in her like he used to in the old days.

'I'll take you to this place,' Lewis says, 'you'll like it.' They start going out together and Anna realises how much of London he's got to know without her. The realisation makes her queasy for a moment, disconnected.

'There's this little place,' says Lewis, 'the other side of Notting Hill. Let's take a walk up there. A glass of wine and something to eat will do us the world of good. Blow the cobwebs away – living in one room, the three of us, we're bound to get a bit on top of each other.'

They step out into glorious late autumn sunshine with Lewis pushing the pram for once. They stroll side by side and she can't help but notice the eyes flickering over Lewis. God, he's so handsome in his long coat and trilby. Anna guesses seeing him pushing a pram like that makes him even more attractive to female eyes – the unobtainable. Anna looks down at her brown patent leather shoes with the buckles. She's wearing her new white plastic mac with a swinging skirt and a belt that does up with a squeak. She loves this coat, these shoes. She's aware of the figure they cut even though she'll never be Lewis's equal in the looks stakes. Lewis has even started teaching her to drive and they laugh each lesson as she kangaroo hops through Notting Hill. The car heater is broken and set to a permanent boiling temperature so they have to strip jumpers and ties and jackets each time and that makes them laugh too. It feels like a kind of seduction. London folds round her today, soft and gleaming, rather than she having to bend round it. Everything seems bright and modern.

Lewis pushes a glass door aside. 'Luca,' he says, 'how are you? I've brought my wife to meet you, I've brought our child.'

Luca greets them like old friends and spends a good five minutes leaning over Ruby's pram admiring her. Anna has started to divide the world up in two: those that flinch at the sight of Ruby's birthmark and those that don't. Luca is definitely in the latter camp. He settles them in a table in the corner and Anna starts feeling pleased that Ruby never really took to the breast properly and now just feeds from a bottle. This way she doesn't have to be running home every five minutes.

'I've never been anywhere like this,' she leans over and whispers to Lewis, because between the two of them they can still be forest people in awe of everything they see, holding hands and whispering about it.

'That's because it's continental,' says Lewis. 'I'll take you there too one day. It's only a hop over the Channel and we could be in Paris. Perhaps we should go soon.'

'Really?' This is enough for her for the moment. There

are jars of pickled vegetables for sale on the wooden shelves and long blue paper packets of spaghetti. Behind the counter Luca pours wine and Anna sees his arm raised in a triangle as he pours in the mirror there, she sees the shiny fabric on the back of his waistcoat and the white bow of his apron. Without asking, he brings them a glass of wine each and a plate of delicately curled meats and shavings of cheese.

Each thing seems to have its own distinct flavour and each one is as strong as the other in its own way. The wine is the most delicious thing Anna has ever drunk; she can hardly believe it exists.

She doesn't know why, but Anna starts buying a newspaper every day.

She unfolds it every day around ten o'clock and reads it at the table with Ruby in the crook of her arm. The dense type is hard to read with a baby jiggling about on your lap so Anna scans it. She knows she's searching for something but she hasn't a clue what for. Finally, she spots the head-line 'Bungled Robbery – Funds Recovered' and as she starts reading she knows she's found what she's been looking for all along. It was a mail van robbery, the same night Lewis came back and asked to be held. There's an almost jokey tone to it because one of the robbers had a gun and man-aged to shoot himself in the foot with it. He tried to limp off but a trail of blood was left – the police just sauntered after it and sat in wait in the house until the robber returned, that's the way that the article had been written anyway. But it was the names that caught her eye – Sydney the Knife, Vincent 'bookies job' Davis. Michael and John, who turn out to be brothers, are simply named as Donahue. All the names of the men whose murmuring voices she's heard so often in her and Lewis's room, playing cards and drinking as she fell asleep. There is no mention of Lewis in the article.

Anna thinks of her father – a good man, a patient man. One who wears his respectability in his heart – part of him, rather than as a costume. He'd rather rip that heart out than be mixed up in anything like this.

'How come you got away?' She asks it as soon as Lewis comes in an hour later. 'What happened that meant you were the one that got away? They'll be looking for you now. You know that, that's why you wanted to go to Paris, wasn't it?'

He sits down heavily and opens his mouth to answer but she never knows what the answer is, or even if there was one at all, because his face has turned into a hideous frightening mask.

42

THE CHRYSALIS
22 December 1983

I wished I could be dead like Crispin.

I locked myself in the library and Tom came and hammered on the door, calling, 'We're sorry, sorry, sorry. Please, please, we were just desperate. Forgive me, Ruby.'

'Stop it,' I yelled on the other side. 'If you don't shut up and go away I'm going to burn your fucking house down. You both lied to me all along. You've been keeping me here under false pretences. I hate you.'

He fell silent on the other side of the door but I could hear his ragged breathing.

'You bastards, you fucking bastards. I thought you were my family. You only let me stay because of this. You don't love me at all. You were just using me. You're as bad as Mick and Barbara.'

I curled up next to the door and put my hand flat on the wooden panel, as if I was silently, secretly reaching out, and started crying. 'That's why you wanted me here. All the time not telling me and it was your reason for looking after me. It's because I can see him and he's dead. No wonder you were surprised when I could see him that day in school. You're trying to keep him alive but it won't work. It'll make terrible things happen, you stupid idiot. Don't you realise that?' I banged my head, once, viciously against the door.

'You used me, you bastard.'

After a while the sound of his breathing quietened, a heavy silence fell and I realised he'd gone.

I left the light on all night, dozed and woke. In the morning there was more calling outside the library, Elizabeth this time. I'd switched off the lights now but the curtains were still drawn. I could just about see the gloomy outlines of furniture as it grew light outside. Elizabeth started up again, her voice like the bleating of the goats quivering through. Finally, I saw a note being pushed under the door.

Sister. Please come out. We love you.

I stared at the page until it blurred over. Wrapping a blanket around my shoulders first, I turned the key in the lock. The door opened with a click. In the strip of light let in she stood, her hair wild and springing away from her forehead.

'Do you want to see his grave?' she asked.

We walked in single file.

The sun was rising across on the other side of the field, a fiery ball that somehow only made the day more wintry. Its bloody colours flashed in the lake as we approached.

'Where are we going?' I asked.

Elizabeth turned. 'Not far.'

'You mean he's here somewhere?'

She nodded and resumed her plod.

I looked at both of them ahead of me. We all still wore the same clothes from yesterday morning. I noticed how the arm flapped nearly free from the body of the coat Tom was wearing and the white shirt beneath flashed bright every now and then, and it startled me in the same way that the glimpse of a bird's markings can. We're not some happy band of the free, we're just three sad stinking children, I thought. Lost and alone. Four, if you counted the one lying in a grave somewhere nearby being taken to the next world by worms. I'd been mistaken to think anything else. Led by Elizabeth our feet turned and tracked a path around the lake, the frost-hard grass crunching below.

'I've never been this far round,' I said.

Elizabeth nodded. 'We thought it safer for him to be far from the house but sometimes at night I long for him to be closer.' She spoke softly now, all trace of her grown-up voice gone. She seemed to have shrunk too and her tiny shoulder bones stuck out. All of a sudden she seemed the youngest one there.

Tom stayed silent, his head hung low. I still felt fury bubbling when I looked at him. The betrayal was worse with him, we'd declared our love for each other, sometimes slept like the effigies of stone Kings and Queens each night side by side – and he'd concealed all this, hidden it all from me.

'So all our secrets were shared, were they?'

His back stiffened. He knew what I meant.

As we walked into the stand of trees by the far side of the lake Elizabeth laid her long red hand on my arm.

'Here,' she said.

In between the trees the air felt softer, more sheltered, but because the sun had not penetrated like elsewhere there was still some snow around. Small chunks of it were dotted over the mossy mounds at our feet, like continents on a map. Next to us the lake churned slightly, as if it had its own tide.

I looked down. 'Where? Did you mark it?'

Pain flashed out of Tom's eyes. 'No, Ruby, not that. Look up.'

Slowly, my eyes tracked upwards. 'Oh my God,' I breathed. 'What have you done? What on earth have you two done?'

Hanging between two trees a white thing was strung like a monstrous chrysalis. It swayed slightly, heavily in the breeze.

Tom was holding himself, gripping his elbows. 'Elizabeth couldn't bear for him to be buried. I was all for nature taking its course but she couldn't bear it.'

'I hate nature,' said Elizabeth, her voice vicious.

I couldn't take my eyes off the thing. 'So . . .' The bundle turned a little, as if alive.

Tom cut in. 'I'd been reading about Egyptian mummies in the library. I started trying to do the . . . the . . .' He looked down, his body bent. '. . . the evisceration but I couldn't, I just couldn't. So I got the barrels of salt from the pantry. It's horrible, I know, to have thought like this but I knew it would work. Our parents had it because they had some idea to cure meat. It's a preserver. I poured salt on him then ripped up sheets and bound him up. When I finished – he was in the living room on the carpet – he looked like a, like an enormous grub lying there.'

Elizabeth laid her hand on his head. 'You were very brave,' she said in a small voice. Her thin shoulders drooped even further forward.

'I'd seen an old canvas hammock in one of the outhouses, that's what gave me the idea,' said Tom. 'But it was too rotten so I used the canvas off the tepee instead, and rope.'

'It was an accident. He had an accident with a gun,' said Elizabeth. 'I wanted him to be away from the dirty ground. The ground would just consume him.'

'Yes, I threw ropes over the branches and winched him up so he could be up in the sky, in the trees, with the birds. It happened in the spring,' said Tom. 'He was surrounded by leaves up there then, and all summer. I didn't think by winter it would all look so stark and dirty. Ever since the leaves have gone we've been worrying about him being seen. I suppose I should go up and cut him down but somehow . . . especially with everything with you, it seemed easier not to think about it, like it hadn't happened even.'

'You won't keep him alive like this, you know.' I stared at the swinging canvas, seeing now the streaks of grime the weather had put on it. Other stains too; I didn't want to imagine what they were. 'You can't encourage him. See, how this is, this sack of dead stuff? You must remember him as he was when he was alive.'

'But that's what you did, you helped him still to be real for us. You brought him back to us.'

'Stop it.' I was nearly shouting. 'You've got to stop this. Crispin is more alive than you two living like this.'

I stopped. Something deep was stirring in me, I sensed at that moment the demarcations between the dead and the living in a way that hadn't been so strong or clear before. I felt a hinterland, a place between sea and shore where the two mingled for a while before the dead embarked upon that voyage out to sea, out, out into the unknown, leaving their bodies far behind. I knew somehow I had my part to play in this. The hunter of souls. The divider of light and dark, righting the demarcations where they mingled dangerously.

The certainty flashed in me, then gradually sifted away leaving just the ones I knew who'd already reached that hinterland. Crispin, the boy with a mud-daubed mouth, the woman in the buttercup dress.

'He still leaves us rabbits.' Elizabeth was rubbing her sleeve between finger and thumb like the feeling of the green velvet gave her comfort. 'Always by the back door.' She paused. 'We tried to do the right thing. We thought of going to the authorities. But I was worried I might not be old enough to be left with minors at seventeen and Tom would be put away somewhere, or the both of us put away for doing this. But all the same we tried ringing Social Services, didn't we, Tom? – without saying who we were – to ask what age you have to be to be responsible. But they just kept saying, "Who is this?" "What's the number you are calling from?" until I just quietly put the phone down while they were still speaking. Then Tom told me that you could see Crispin. Up till then we'd only heard him. It started a couple of days after he died, we'd hear shots being fired outside, or a crashing in the hallway or all the ornaments getting toppled in the living room. We knew it was him almost straight away, he always was a crasher abouter. But you being able to see him plain as day meant it really was like having him around again, like this terrible thing hadn't really happened at all.'

'He's angry. He doesn't understand,' I said.

'Yes,' Elizabeth ran on, 'even I think I can see him too now sometimes, out of the corner of my vision. You helped this happen, Ruby. We couldn't bear for you to go. He might start *being* less and less again. Oh my God.' Elizabeth started crying, quietly. 'My sweet brother. What are we going to do?'

'You can't leave him there,' I said, looking up to the swinging bundle.

'I know,' she said. 'But I can't have him in the ground, I just can't.'

'I know a place,' I said.

They both looked up.

'Where?' Elizabeth breathed.

'It's a hollow tree.'

I walked back across the field with Tom. Elizabeth had already left us – worn out. The great red sun was higher in the sky by now. It was melting the very drops of snow that lay in the shade of the furze, the place where I'd seen Shadow wearing my boots back to front. The air felt powdery with it, making the sun appear a blurred red ball. Tom stood with his arms hanging by his sides.

'This must be where the hare died.' I crouched down and started parting the grass as if the blood might still be on the ground underneath. 'We should have done something else with it,' I was frantic suddenly, scraping at the ground, 'rather than just throw it out of the window like a piece of rubbish. Maybe it really does mean a curse. Maybe we're cursed for ever now.'

'Don't. It was just meat by then, Ruby.'

'Like Crispin.'

He held himself by the elbows again. 'Yes.'

Against the red sun he was a dark figure. He bent forward suddenly as if he was about to vomit. I left him be and gradually his body straightened up and his breathing calmed.

'I'm sorry, Ruby. I'm so sorry. It's not the only reason I

wanted you to stay, I promise.'

I nodded. 'It was part of it, though?'

He didn't answer but drew me up to my feet and kissed me on the mouth and the air grew red around us as the sun rose further and shone back at itself from the bowl of the lake so they looked like a lake and a sun on a different planet, or like it was the end of days.

On our way back we walked with his arm around me. Once, I thought, if this had happened, I would have felt I'd found the spell that made joy. Now, though, with the search for my real blood – my mum and dad – no closer, with that dead bag full of body swinging so close by, joy and fear felt entwined as closely as the vine to the flesh in that green man's mouth.

43

SANDPIT

23 December 1983

I waited for Tom and Elizabeth in the car. They were ready-ing themselves inside. Tom had already cut Crispin down and put him in the boot. I'd had to help him. I'd climbed the ladder and sat on a branch and cut at the ropes while Tom held onto the body. It nearly fell once but Tom managed to steady it at the last moment and carried it down slumped over his shoulder. From below Elizabeth watched with her hand over her mouth.

Perhaps it was being alone with the body in the car. Some-thing came that was more than a memory. A hole opened up. Time bent like cane. Somewhere in my skin there was a splice neatly being made and held apart. Inside was blood, dark and sticky. Inside were my workings.

Inside the dark hole, a small backlit memory: playing in the sandpit.

'Children, make your sandcastles neat now,' the teacher's voice is behind me and gets swept up in the breeze, 'like someone would actually want to live in there.'

I'm squatting down in the sand. When I shift my legs hurt. My back aches. Last night Mick sent me flying into a wall and I slid down it like a tangled puppet.

In front of me there's a girl, I know her name is Jessica. She's squatting down too with her knees wide open so everyone can see the crotch of her heart-patterned pants. Her long brown hair falls forward and snakes into the sand. She's concentrating hard on the sandcastle she's making, patting the top – pat, pat – with a red plastic spade. I want to pat like that too – it looks satisfying – so I approach. I shuffle over, even though it's painful, still squatting, so my knees poke out on either side.

'Can I help?' I'm looking at the top of her head that's leaning over her creation. The wavering white parting in her hair. She looks up and there's drops of sweat above her top lip. Her eyes squint in the sun.

'All right, you can. But you have to be very careful,' she warns.

I am. I've brought over a blue spade, just in case. Gently I pat the flat top of the sandcastle. I want to pat harder, to give it some shape of my own, to make some impression of mine. But I don't. It's Jessica's sandcastle and I have to be respectful of that. In a moment, I think, I'm going to make my own. Then I can shape it how I want and feel the satisfying slice of blade of spade through sand. But into that a voice is calling my name.

'Ruby. Ruby – have you gone deaf?' Not nasty, though, it's laughing a pretty laugh. It's the teacher again, Miss Plunkett. We all snigger at her name and say it so the plunk is loud and hard like something dropping down the toilet, but never in front of her. We like her. I like her especially of all the teachers. She wears short summer dresses with things like patterns of green leaves over or bright pink daisies. She smiles like she likes us. She does like us all: even the shy ones, the dirty, the snarly toothed, the scabbed, the slow.

She leans over me so she's a dazzling ball of sunlight. Sun striking off her yellow hair.

'Ruby, I want you to do me a favour. Run into the stockroom and get the tray of pencils and the sheets of paper. The ones on the bottom shelf. It's too nice to go in, we're going to have a lesson under the tree and write a poem. Quick now, before the bell goes so you won't get jammed up in the corridor.'

I hesitate. I really wanted to build that sandcastle. My fingers feel the itch for that crunch-through sound but I feel a swell of pride that she's chosen me for such an important errand. And a lesson under the tree sounds nice, instead of going back inside into the hot classroom, with a fly droning at the window. So I nod and make my way through the open back door of the school.

The building is old, red brick. At the front there are still girls' and boys' entrances – the words spelled out in brickwork over the arched doors. The back anyone can use, girl or boy, but today there's only me. Everyone else is outside. Either that or the teachers are in the staff room, desperately puffing on cigarettes in their break. That room, if you're ever called upon to deliver a message, is suffocating with the smell of sour milk and cigarette smoke.

The sounds today remind me of being inside a swimming pool. I walk through our empty classroom, weaving around the desks. It seems very dark in here after the sun. The stockroom is behind the teacher's desk, just off one side to the left. I turn the handle. Inside there's already someone there. There's a table with little children-sized chairs on either side. Sitting in one is a man, older, with a black suit. He has to pinch his knees together to sit on such a tiny chair.

I try to remember if the chair and table were there before, but I can't.

'Ah, there you are.' He shuffles the papers around that are in front of him. 'There you are at last. Now we can begin.'

I stand, uncertain. I don't know this man. But as a child the instinct is to obey. I know he must be some sort of teacher, even if unexpected, unscheduled. I take the chair opposite and he nods in approval.

'Very good, very good.'

He slides some of the papers over to me. 'Now take a look at this and make a start. Take your time, though, no rushing. I want neat work.'

I peer at the paper, torn, because I'm worried about Miss Plunkett. That she'll think I'm slow and dawdling. That I'll fail in the very important task she's given me. But on the other hand, this man is clearly a teacher, a senior one at that.

I look at the paper. It contains angry scribblings from a heavy pencil. The word 'fire' is written at the top then scrubbed out. My eye moves down – I read.

I AM LOST.

I'm confused. I look up. The man is engrossed with more scribblings and crossings out. His hair is cut neat and white. His gold-rimmed square glasses flash as he scans up and down the paper, looking for more things to cross out.

I feel a slipping sensation, as if the world is about to tip on its side and slide me off.

'I need to get some things for Miss.' My voice is tiny, barely a squeak.

He only half responds. 'Yes, yes . . .'

I stand up and tiptoe round him. I grab at the box of pencils, then any old stack of paper, not taking time to make sure I've got the one Miss Plunkett requested.

I run outside and all the time that strange slipping sensation, only this time like I could slip out of my own skin. Outside is bright, bright sunlight. I see Miss Plunkett and the other children, grouped round the sandpit. But they're far, far away. Like I'm looking at them through a telescope, but one that makes things further away rather than nearer.

It takes an age to reach them.

And later on in primary school, I remembered, like seeing excerpts from a film, looking at that door behind Miss Plunkett while chanting times tables or spellings and thinking . . . in there, in there, is he still in there, that man I saw that day? I remembered too then that I'd avoided the stockroom like the plague, always making an excuse or getting someone else to go.

And once being brave enough to look, because the rowdy class were behind me this time, waiting for the teacher. Being brave enough to look and he was . . . he was still there and scribbling and scrabbling at his papers. I fled just as he was looking up and the words forming on his lips that hadn't been spoken yet but I knew would be, 'Ah, you again. Sit down, sit down.'

I came to with a jerk, although I hadn't been asleep. I was sweating hard even though I could feel the cold in the car against the sweat. How many other things had I forgotten like this? There was the Wasp Lady but she'd almost come to be a picture in a book to me. Apart from Shadow

I'd always tried to push these things away. Shadow I could live with, he was almost like my twin. But now there was Crispin, and the lady in the buttercup yellow dress. There were more and more of them, crowding in. There they were coming towards me. Maybe this was my family – the dead. What was the difference between us after all? Maybe I was already one of them, not knowing, like Crispin. Perhaps Mick had really killed me. I shuddered. I knew at least the skin of this world was thinning hour by hour so you could look through it like the papery bit of an onion. I knew it and tried not to panic. I tasted metal in my mouth. I put my hand up and realised I'd bitten down so hard my bottom lip was dripping blood.

I looked in the car mirror to check the white bundle behind me was not moving.

44

BURIAL
23 December 1983

Death rode with us in the car.

It was with us the whole way. It was in the air, so we had to crank the windows down despite the blast of cold from outside. It was in the boot, wrapped in dirty canvas that moved slackly against the wheel arch every time we turned a corner. It was in the vapours coming up from the ground. It was in our hearts too. No one spoke. These people were not my family – my hunt for real family had not even begun. These people were just lost children. The dead were not my family either, I knew suddenly, certainly, I bleed, they can't.

Each of us had that journey to make – when you separated from the body you set sail in every day. I knew even as we were driving that each one of us thought about that at some point, the time when our own death wind would blow us right out of our bodies. The feeling came back I'd had when I'd seen Crispin's swinging chrysalis in the trees, the shape like he'd actually grown there and was about to hatch. The fleeting knowledge that I'd had of being a gatherer of lost souls. Who would I help and who would I turn away? What about Mick, when his time came and he saw his beloved – his dead sweet pea – his Trudy again for the first time? Would he have to explain to her what he'd done to me? Would she turn her little flower face away from him and would I have to be on hand to tell her how I'd survived? If I did survive without the family I was soul sick for. No, I knew then. I wouldn't have a choice. I'd have to be available for any stray soul that came to me. Their principal state is confusion. They wouldn't understand being turned away. They wouldn't take no for an answer.

I looked at Tom, at Elizabeth who had become so beloved to me and who'd betrayed me. They were doing what they did for each other, for their loved ones. I'd wanted to be a loved one too. I wondered if it was even possible.

We parked as close to the trees as we could, in a lay-by where the branches hung down and part hid the car. The day was the stillest I could ever remember. Not a sigh, not a breath of wind, so our noise seemed extra loud as we crunched through the trees. Tom tied a bright red cotton scarf around his face and carried Crispin in his arms. The bundle must've been heavy but the expression in Tom's eyes was set, like he'd carry it a hundred miles to find a decent resting place for his little brother.

I'd forgotten how secret and ancient the forest was. In my absence it seemed to have turned away from me, in on itself, so it was less familiar. The dark places were heavy with something I didn't understand, that could harm us if it chose to. I stopped, panicking. 'I think this is the way,' I said. I touched the trees and let them calm me. 'Yes, yes. This is the way.' I let my reason subside and my feet take over. There was Shadow, his hungry eye appearing through the tangle of branches. He whispered my name as I passed but I ignored him. That awful look, mad with want, was back. Thinner and thinner the skin. Deep behind the trees were others, their shadows the shape of sickles on the ground, they perfumed the air with the smell of below. I put my face forward and refused to look.

We walked deep so even with the lack of leaves it grew dark from the interlocking branches up above. Elizabeth carried a woven bag slung over her shoulder. She'd brought some of Crispin's things. Then there was the little clearing when it seemed everything would become denser and denser until we hit a solid wooden heart. There was the place where I'd seen the dead bird. I fell to my knees at the foot of the branchless tree.

'Here.' Carefully I peeled back the strands of ivy like veins on the doorway. 'This is the place. No one will ever find him here.'

'Oh, Ruby.' Elizabeth put her hands on the trunk. 'This is perfect for him. Absolutely perfect.' She moved her hands to her heart.

Tom laid his heavy burden on the thick carpet of leaves and took a moment to untie his mask and wipe the sweat from his face with it.

'You two move away for a while. Just sit over there until it's done and then I'll call you.'

Elizabeth nodded and rummaged in her bag. 'Here,' she said finally, drawing out a map and holding it with both hands. 'We'll leave this with him – his map of Africa. That's where he always wanted to go. He spent hours studying this, learning all the names. He would have got there too, I'm sure he would. He was determined.'

Tom nodded and me and Elizabeth turned to go, me leading her by the hand. 'One thing,' she said and turned back. 'Just one thing. Will you loosen the bundle so his head is open to the sky? D'you think that's possible?'

Tom nodded again and we threaded through the trees till we were out of sight and we stood and waited.

When he called us his voice was low. He sounded spent. When I saw his face again it carried the knowledge of things that would live with him for ever.

'Done,' he said.

'Did you loosen his head,' asked Elizabeth, 'so he might have a little glimpse of the sky?'

'Yes,' he said, and I could see how the act had cost him dear. That it was still happening for him so I could watch it in his eyes like they were two little television screens replaying the moment over and over again.

Elizabeth advanced on the tree and stretched out her hand. 'My darling boy,' she said and reached out and touched the quiff of dark golden hair that poked there. Among the ivy and the flakes of bark it was a small thing, only there if you knew what to look for.

'I feel like I should say some words but I don't know what they are,' she said.

'You need to tell him it's OK to go,' I said.

But she couldn't, she stood there mute, until Tom shouted, his face twisted with a kind of anger, 'Fly, brother. Fly.'

'How did it happen?' I asked. Me and Tom had walked off to sit on a fallen log. Elizabeth was still at the hollow tree. She couldn't seem to move away.

Tom shook his head. 'He'd been messing about with guns for a long time by then. We didn't take much notice any more. We didn't really need the rabbits then, we still had plenty of money left over and the warm summer was coming. I milked the goats every day and Elizabeth picked salad leaves that my parents planted before they went. It felt like everything was going to be safe, it was going to be like how Peter and Roz said it would – living off the land.'

He shook his head again, almost in bewilderment at the vision of their soft summer still unfurling its golden banner. 'But Crispin started getting good at hunting. He got right into it. One day he said he was going to fish . . .

'I came out to do the evening milking and saw something floating in the water. When I went close we realised it was him. He must've fallen over the side or gone after something he thought he saw. His leg was caught between two rocks at the bottom – I had to dive down to free him.

'Later, when we got his body to the shore we realised he must've shot himself, that's why there was blood in the water. It looks like the idiot was trying to shoot fish.'

I put my hand over his. 'You know I need to find my own family now. This has made it all start up again.' I turned my head as if I could almost smell them. 'And with Barbara and Mick's house being so close by I think I want to start today.'

'You know I said I'd help.'

'I've been thinking about it sitting here. It's the Friday before Christmas. There's a possibility the house might be empty. Mick will be at the school closing all the boilers down for the holidays. Barbara is often out shopping every weekday until Christmas Eve . . .' I paused, remembering the odd tide of stuff that always turned up at Christmas – little toy mice that wore Christmas coats and circles of cheeses with specks in them – pineapple, or onions. Was it really shopping Barbara did when she went into town every day the week before Christmas? The crowds would make it ideal for shoplifting.

'If I can get back into the house I can look round like you said, for documents that might give me clues.'

He nodded.

'Will you take me? We can keep watch on the house for a while and make sure it's empty. They never lock the back anyway.'

'Yes, I'll take you,' he said, 'of course I'll take you.'

Already, a prickling had started, tugging at my scalp like electricity. It was the thought of being back in that house again. Of being near Mick's presence. Of the possibility of finding something that would bring me closer, closer, closer to my real mum and dad.

45

Lewis has arranged it. He and Anna are to be married. Somehow Anna's resistance has been quite worn down. He insists
that it will mean a fresh start for the three of them. He seems
to think it will be the only way. He has even arranged that
they will have separate addresses on the marriage certificate
so it will ever after be buried that they had a time of living
in sin. Anna is to be registered at her mother's address in
the forest and Lewis here in Notting Hill. If she stopped to
ponder on it she might wonder about how he will always be
striving for something new and different – money one day,
marriage the next – and how everyone is pulled with him.
These days she feels more and more like a weak flapping fish
on a line with him sitting in a little boat and tugging.

'What if I regret it?' she asks from the cubbyhole with
the cooker. 'Do I know who I'll be marrying?' But her voice
sounds soft and yielding to her own ears.

He crowds into the tiny space and winds his arm around
her waist. Ruby is in her carrycot on the floor.

'That life is done with,' he says. 'We must think of Ruby
now. We don't want her growing up with a blight on her
name – not with everything else.'

Anna prods the tinned potatoes boiling in the saucepan.
'Who cares these days?'

'Plenty of people do; they're more old-fashioned than you might think.'

She looks down at Ruby's face and sighs. 'I suppose.'

Ever since that night Lewis came back he has changed. Now he seems determined to be a family man. He's found part-time work in a timber yard and has set his hopes on something in retail management. He talks excitedly about it – in fact, the only thing he won't talk about is that night. He manages to convey being on the outer periphery of any criminal action and Anna's head these days is too cloddish and thick to analyse things properly. When she thinks of his face and the mask that she saw in its place it frightens her. They've both dismissed this as 'a funny turn' – relieved by a sleep and a couple of Valium that Lewis produces. Sleep constantly eludes, though. It begins to feel like a distant country she'll never visit again.

Anna's wedding day is cold and bright. The clock from the church tower is chiming as she enters. It's an old tiny church down a side alley, as London places often seem to be. Lewis has let her have exactly what she wants: church after all, when it came to it; a pale powder-blue suit with oversized white buttons; a veil in the style known as 'bird-cage' because of its shape. Jackie Kennedy was in her mind when Anna devised the look. The veil bisects her face just above her top lip. There's lily-of-the-valley in her hands and at her breast; Samuel and Stella as witnesses; Ruby on Stella's lap in the front pew. Samuel holds his own daughter, cradling the back of her head in his large hand. Anna will send photos and a pressing of a stem of the lily-of-the-valley to her parents afterwards. It hasn't occurred to her to invite them. Imagining them in London would be as fantastical as seeing the trees marching on the city – an image retained from studying Shakespeare in school that she can imagine completely.

Lewis is already at the altar: black suit, black hair, white rose in his buttonhole. He is impossibly handsome like something out of a book of film stars or a black and white photo of Elvis she saw once. As Anna walks up the aisle she feels as if something is pressing her backwards and for a horrible moment that seems to go on for ever she doesn't seem to be getting nearer at all. Then she is beside him; there's no memory of passing Samuel, Stella and the two babies – she is standing so close she can see the weave of his wool suit.

The service starts, or she presumes it has because she can see the vicar's mouth moving but she can't process it, can hardly hear it. Lewis fills her vision. Everything about him is magnified. She feels his presence; his downcast eyes that make jagged shadows of lashes on his cheeks. The heavy musculature she can sense under the suit. She experiences his presence as something almost religious. He's a deity, a statue that has flown down from the walls of this church and somehow in its descent been animated. Surely, he is carved out of something that's not human. That hasn't even been invented yet.

46

RETURN
23 December 1983

We stood looking at the back of the old house from the edge of the forest. The darkness cast by the entangled branches overhead had lightened as we'd approached the clearing in the trees. It was wetter too, the rain fell more freely through this lighter canopy, and our feet were up to the ankles in soft mushy leaves. Elizabeth'd stayed in the car. She'd barely said a word since we'd left the hollow tree.

'It feels strange to be so close to where Barbara lives,' I said. 'It almost makes me want to see her again.'

Tom raised an eyebrow. 'Really?'

Then I remembered what'd happened after she'd done my hair that time: the packing, the train, my first period, and my heart turned against her again.

'It's probably because there's the hole of not knowing my real parents.' I realised I was whispering even though we were so far from the house no one would ever hear us or even see us; we'd be mistaken for shadows standing so far under the trees. I carried on whispering all the same. 'Sometimes it feels like my bottom layer is missing, Tom. Like I haven't got the soil to grow in. My real parents, they must be the soil. That's all I can think.'

'I can't even remember what my mum, Roz, looks like, let alone her funny ways. I can remember her voice, though.

That's about it. It was a high bright voice.'

I looked at the house again and remembered the Sindy dolls. I wondered if they were as I'd left them, tumbling down the stairs. 'I suppose it's now or never,' I said. 'It's probably better if I go in on my own. Less noise. Less chance of getting caught.'

Tom gripped my arm. 'Be careful. If you see *him*, just yell and I'll come.'

Dread began rising up in me at the mention of Mick. 'What is it I'm looking for again?'

'Documentation. A birth certificate or something. It might be rolled up and look like a scroll. Or have old-fashioned writing at least.'

I nodded. Behind us a mist had begun to wind its way around the trees. Tom dragged a fallen branch to sit on and leaned against a tree.

'Be careful,' he said again as I made to leave. His face was as pale as a skull's. The events seemed to have toppled him, like a game where the supports are removed and all the pieces come clattering down. A drop of water had gathered on his ear lobe and trembled there. His damp ponytail was splayed across his shoulder. I felt an infusion of tenderness at his broken state. I reached out and touched his arm in its damp sleeve. It took him a moment to shake out of his thoughts and smile at me.

'I'll be quick,' I said.

'Don't forget to look for the paperwork in the bottom of wardrobes,' he called after me.

When I turned back to look at him, sitting in the mist, I felt I was leaving him behind in the pages of a book or a film.

The doll's arm, the corner of the red bus, the tall grasses were all in the same places as they were, but yet they were not the same. It's like they'd been moving about all the time I'd been away and had just returned to their original positions as they heard me coming, playing a trick on me.

I turned the knob of the back door and it gave beneath my hand. Softly, I stepped into the kitchen. It was the smell that was most familiar, the faint whiff of gas and matches, an undertone of damp. Barbara's hairspray.

I stood and listened for a good ten minutes, attuning myself to the sounds of the house. I was used to doing this from the days of Mick and his rages, being hyper vigilant to what was what – a heavy breath full of suppressed fury, the creak as someone sat up from the bed as I came in, the particular motor of his car engine as it drew up outside. Sometimes I felt we spent weeks like that, listening to each other before the storm erupted. Now, not a breath seemed to be stirring. The house was swaddled in a heavy blanket of silence. I made for the stairs and my face appeared in the mirror like a dog jumping up.

'Ruby.'

Through the part-opened living-room door the figure looked tilted. A bundle of stick limbs and blankets. A shining brown eye roved then fixed on me.

'Who's that?' Pause. 'Ruby?'

Outside I didn't care who heard me now. 'Back to the car, drive, drive,' I shouted, waving my arms at Tom. He jumped up.

'What is it?'

'There's someone there. I'm not sure what it is.'

We ran back to the car and Elizabeth woke as we scrambled in.

'What's the matter?' Her voice was furred with sleep.

The car flopped back on the road.

'Christ, Christ.'

'Stop it, Ruby,' Tom yelled. 'We're going to crash if you carry on flipping out like that.'

As we drove, Joe from the street emerged from the forest wearing matching orange denim trousers and jacket. 'Ruby,' he shouted, 'you're back. You're back.'

Tom wound the window down and slowed. 'Ssshh, kid.'

'Ruby, Ruby.' Joe jogged alongside the car and threw his fistful of sweets through the window.

'Ow, shit, kid, what are you doing?' said Tom, rubbing at his temple.

'It's sweets,' I said. 'He's being nice.' I leaned across. 'Joe, go home and don't tell anyone you've seen me.'

Tom speeded up leaving the little orange figure standing alone and pale on the road.

'I saw something,' I said.

'What?'

I closed my eyes. The stick limbs and the brown eye rearranged and knitted together. A clump of curls appeared.

'I've got a horrible feeling it was Barbara,' I said. 'She looked terrible. She looked like a starved rat. I can't leave her like that. She looked half dead.'

In the living room the curtains were closed. It smelled slightly sweetish like she'd been in there for a long time. The corner where the green tinsel Christmas tree usually stood was bare.

She looked so worn and thin – I crouched next to her and put my hand on her arm. Her limbs felt brittle. It must have been me telling her about Sandra in the letter. It must've finished her.

'Mum, I'm so sorry. I'm so sorry,' I began to cry.

She struggled to half sit. 'What's happened? Has Elaine chucked you out? I thought that might happen. Did you upset them?'

'Oh Mum, the letter I wrote to you. I . . .'

Her face wrinkled up. 'You wrote to me? Well,' she sniffed, 'I never saw anything. Are you sure you put a stamp on the envelope?' She sat up. 'Bloody hell. What's Elaine dressing you in? You look like a tramp. You look worse even than before you went away.'

I saw it then. Mick leaning over the hallway mat. Slicing open the letter with his finger. Reading. Folding. Putting it in his pocket. I rocked back onto my heels and sat there and scrabbled at my wet eyes. 'Where is Mick?' I asked.

There was a murmur of voices from the kitchen.

Her head swivelled sharply. 'Who's that?'

'Nothing to worry about. Just some friends of mine,' I said gently. 'Just some good friends of mine.'

Tom and Elizabeth looked so strange in our tiny kitchen, Tom with his legs sprawling sideways on the chair and Elizabeth's hair a bright spot in the room.

'I don't think she's very well,' I said. 'And she's all on her own. She says Mick's been gone for days.'

The sun was setting in its winter way: early, low, the rays cold through the black trunks of naked trees. I felt then it had been tracking me all day, like a camera, or God's great

234

red eye, recording the day's events.

Sandra's parents' bungalow was three villages away. The front garden was wet. Water dripped off the beak of a plastic bird perched on top of a pole stuck into the front garden. The white plastic window frames loomed out at me and I had the idea the house was a giant head with its bottom half buried in the ground. Mick's car was parked round the side.

'Don't come with me,' I said. 'Wait here.'

'I'll stay where I can see you. If he tries to hurt you I'll tear him limb from limb,' said Tom.

I walked up the wet concrete path and something twitched and ruffled at the window, but when I rang the bell there was no answer. I knelt on the cold doorstep and pushed open the shiny plastic letterbox. A gust of warm air rushed up my nose; it smelled of cooking oil and meat. I stayed there for a long time thinking of what to say. The rain on the front step seeped into the knees of my jeans.

'You're disgusting,' I said at last.

The inside of the house was quiet. I could tell it was listening to me.

'You have a wife and she is called Barbara. You had a daughter and she was called Ruby. Except she's not your daughter any more because I hate you. But Barbara looks ill and you've gone off with a girl barely sixteen years of age.' I shouted the last bit.

There was a small scuffling sound inside.

'I can't believe her parents letting you stay with her here, what sort of people are they? I hope they heard that by the way.'

There was a rushing behind the door and it opened so I

235

nearly fell forward into the hallway. Sandra's mum stood there in blue slippers.

'I am a good mother,' she yelled. 'Don't you go telling me I'm not.'

Tom called out of the car window as I ran down the path. 'Come on, come on. I'm not going to tear *her* limb from limb.'

Later, I heard Tom's car start up outside Barbara's house and leave and a bleakness I'd never had before descended, not even the night I occupied the tree that Crispin's body stood in now. I left it for as long as I could to give him a chance to get home before I rang Tom's number, picturing the phone ringing in the vast echoing hall.

'Ruby.'

'Hi Tom.' I pressed the earpiece close.

'How is she?'

'I've just made a cup of tea for her but quite honestly I felt like throwing it over her when I took it in just now. Trust her to make herself look so ill I feel too guilty to leave. She keeps saying, "So you never were at Elaine's, even for a little bit?"'

'What's the matter with her?'

'I don't know. I keep saying we need to call a doctor but she won't. She says she's mortally afraid of doctors. I don't know what to do.'

'We're missing you here.'

'I know. Me too.'

'It's nearly Christmas, isn't it?'

'Yes, in two days. It doesn't feel like it, though, does it? D'you know what you'll do?'

'We'll cook something. Go for a walk. Remember. You?'

'I don't know. There's nothing here. Not even a string of tinsel on the mirror. I haven't told Barbara I know where Mick is. She's upset enough as it is. I've promised to go with Barbara to her new cleaning job tomorrow. The lady wants to get it all nice for her Christmas visitors and Barbara's worried about missing it because she's lost so many jobs already, but she seems so weak. What's it like there?'

'Quiet, quiet, quiet. Like the grave.'

I hated being back in my little bed. They say when you're away it's you that changes but it didn't feel like that. It was more like everything around me had subtly altered in a way that was hard to pin down. The jars in the cupboard were mostly the same ones that'd been there when I left – but they'd all been moved slightly. Some of the levels of jam and pickle had gone down and for some stupid reason I nearly drove myself mad trying to work out which ones. Did things look a bit older? The paint on the banister a little more chipped? Did the living-room carpet always have that stain under the TV stand? Certain things had disappeared completely – the blue and white mug I always used, for instance.

Sindy and Paul were still there in their house, though; I could see them from my bed. They were both at the bottom of the stairs so they must've fallen the full way while I was gone. For some reason I got it into my head they were the only ones who'd missed me. I could almost see them, sprawled across the floor, crawling from room to room and looking.

47

SLUT'S WOOL
24 December 1983

We travelled on the bus to her new job, me and Barbara.
No one else had been willing to turn out on Christmas Eve
apparently. There was winter sun again. It was low in the
sky and flickered through the bare dark trunks of trees as
we rode. Barbara seemed like a tiny ornament next to me,
diminished.

'So you saw him?' She kept turning from the window and
asking. 'You actually saw Mick?' She'd rooted it out of me.

'No, but I heard him.'

'What did he say?'

'Nothing, he was sort of scuffling about.'

'So maybe he wasn't there after all?' She sounded hopeful.

I sighed. 'Maybe, Barbara.'

She sniffed. 'You've taken to calling me Barbara all the
time now, haven't you?'

'What would you like me to call you?'

She sniffed again. 'I think Barbara's fine. On balance.'
The road cut into the forest before us and the trees rose up
in a crown around the scattering of houses.

'We need to get off here,' she said.

By the time we walked through the village the sun had disappeared and the sky had turned white with cloud. It was

the sort of day where the skin of the world is stretched out and thin. I looked round and caught the outline of Shadow bowling up the hill behind us, head down. A red dog was threading through the trees beside us. I stopped and narrowed my eyes in the distance. On days like this it was hard to know the true make-up of what I saw. There'd been something about the dog that jarred me, even though he'd been sniffing at the ground and wagging his tail in the way of a normal live dog. But I suspected it of being on a loop and if I came this way again tomorrow it would be doing the exact same thing. We passed by the village pub and reached a row of houses, all detached and set back from the road.

I looked at Shadow. His head was bent forward as he trotted along, his bare feet slapping on the cold pavement. There was a dull gleam in his eye. Something swayed between us like a chain, sparking gold and bright, then it turned thin and runny and dissolved. Somehow I couldn't fear him today. He was back to being my old familiar friend.

He was excited to be going somewhere new, I could tell. I hung behind. 'You behave yourself now,' I muttered out of the corner of my mouth.

Barbara turned to look at me and took a crumpled tissue from her pocket and wiped her nose, which looked red from cold. 'Mrs Theobold,' she said. 'This one.'

We turned into the drive and up the four wide front steps. The heavy carved front door reared up like an expensive coffin lid.

When Mrs Theobold opened the door she was already making a clucking sound through the gap before it was properly open. She had a hanky in her hand too, of soft cotton, and with it balled up in her fist she made the action of pushing her knuckles under her chin.

'You're late,' she said, then stared at us.

I saw us through her eyes. A woman with a garish purple and pink threadbare tapestry coat done right up to her chin, sweat-damp curls lying close to her skull. A skinny girl in a parka that came down to her knees, and a birthmark.

'I didn't know you were bringing anyone. Who's this?'

Barbara seemed to have sunk further down into her coat than ever. The bright red lipstick she'd applied before we left stood out shinily, stretching across her mouth.

'This is my daughter, Mrs Theobold.' Her voice had faded almost to nothing. 'School holidays, like.'

Mrs Theobold made her strange action again with her balled-up fist with the hanky under her chin, like she wanted to punch herself.

'All right, all right. You'll have to do your best to catch up. I've guests arriving later.' She looked at me doubtfully. 'She can accompany you as long as she sits still. I've got some very expensive pieces. Don't let her move about too much.'

Over her shoulder was an impression of Christmas lights reflected in polished wood and glass. In that, a movement, like the lazy flicking of a whale's tail. I looked down. Shadow was crouching underneath the brown dry heads of a hydrangea at the bottom of the steps. Just one cold grey foot was visible poking out from underneath the plant. His voice floated up to me, as light as a leaf blowing in the wind.

I'll not be joining you.

As Barbara started up the last step I caught her arm. 'Let's not go in,' I whispered.

Mrs Theobold had turned her back on us and was walking down the corridor and Barbara was saying after her, 'No, Good Lord. No, she'll be still as a statue.' She gave me a sharp poke between my shoulder blades. 'Go on,' she hissed.

Inside, a huge Christmas tree reached up towards the ceiling. It was spangled with little gold and white lights. A pile of green and red wrapped presents sat underneath. On a polished wood table was a glass globe, with a landscape of grasses inside. Dead butterflies hung there, to look like they were flying overhead. They must be on invisible wires, I thought, peering inside.

Mrs Theobold turned. 'That is one of the expensive pieces,' she said, as if I could crack it with my eyes.

I watched Mrs Theobold's tall back as she walked away. Halfway down the hall something stirred in the air as she approached, barely there, a jellyfish skein of grey and white, puffing in and out, as if it was breathing. As she walked through the skein in her smart black skirt and white silk blouse she became furred up, indistinct. Then out the other side she was clear again. The jellyfish puffed out like a giant pair of cheeks and submerged back into the air. I knew it, I told myself, with the day so still and quiet. With Shadow dogging my footsteps again then not wanting to come in. My eye was letting in more and more. I could no longer stop them. The skeins were nothing, though, just vestiges of God knows what. Whatever Shadow knew about, and I sensed, was elsewhere. I caught the faint humming of it like a queen bee at the centre of the hive.

Barbara walked on pins along the hall and I followed behind.

'You can start in here.' The woman opened a door with an ornate brass handle. 'I've to pop out for a little while but I'll be back to look over everything before you go.'

'Yes, Mrs Theobold.' Barbara's voice slid out in a whisper. I didn't recognise this woman, with the hushed voice and eyes that only looked at the floor.

Once Barbara had brought in her pail of cleaning stuff to the living room, the weight nearly doubling her over, and the door was shut, she started to return to herself. She collapsed on the leather sofa. 'You need to go across the hall and get the hoover,' she hissed. 'Cupboard under the stairs. Make sure she's gone first.'

I opened the door and peeked out. It wasn't Mrs Theobold that I was looking for, though; it was a skein of white ribbons, as slippery and falling as entrails, leaving its jellyfish trail, gently puffing and with the ability to turn itself inside out. There was nothing there. I nipped over and got out the vacuum and lugged it back.

'Plug's under the sideboard,' Barbara wheezed. 'Make sure you get the cobwebs in the corners.'

For twenty minutes I concentrated on sucking up dust. I noticed the beauty of the carpet. Not like our orange and brown swirls at home, with the edges sticking up, hard with dirt. This was silky grey, covered with delicate yellow and blue flowers with a thick fringe all around. As I worked I rearranged the fringing straight after it had been blasted with the hoover. As I clicked off the machine Barbara nodded her approval.

'Good. Now the polishing. Get the yellow duster and the tin of purple wax.'

I smoothed a layer of wax over the sideboard and the low

deep brown coffee table then buffed and polished. A little colour had crept back into Barbara's face.

'You're doing well, Ruby,' she whispered. 'Now the fireplace.'

The cloth was stiff with wax now. On either side of the fireplace a carved wooden shell tumbled out knobs of wooden pearls and brown trumpet-shaped flowers. I lifted off the Christmas cards and dusted underneath them one by one. 'To June and family,' inscribed inside them all below Christmas greetings and blood red clusters of holly berries.

'You have to polish the decoration on the sides. Don't get it in the black bits. She'll go mental.'

I looked harder to see what she meant. Two lozenges framed the fireplace, a wooden fretwork over a black background. I started carefully smearing wax over the top layer then moved to the other side.

'Good girl, Ruby. Good.'

I smiled then realised I had my back to her so she couldn't see. I was thinking of turning to her and smiling again when I stopped dead, my hand raised with the duster in it.

'Oh.'

'Get on with it, Ruby, she'll be in soon. Checking up on us. Running her finger over things.'

Inside the fretwork was a kind of hollowed-out place and there was shuffling, a movement there. My eyes adjusted to look beyond, to focus out the room and see . . . a creature there. No, a person. A felty coat pressed against the filigree. Scrunched up, folded into itself. My eyes travelled up. Grey flesh, a head, sideways on. No eyes, though, they were looking the other way, into the wall. It shifted again, as if trying to get comfortable in its confinement.

My throat turned tight and sick. If I disturbed it, it would know, it would turn and impregnate itself through the holes. It would cling onto me like a lover. Riding me all the way back to roll under my bed and make its home. Hurriedly I lightly flicked the duster to rub off the rest of the polish, to disturb it as little as possible.

Behind me Barbara was muttering, almost to herself, 'Running her finger over surfaces. Dragging her wrinkled old arse around looking for dust pockets. Easy life. Easy.' I could tell the fight was returning to her.

Her voice turned ruminative. 'Slut's wool we used to call it. Those clumps you get under the sofa, or under the bed. My mum used to say, "Barbara, I saw the biggest piece of slut's wool I've ever seen today. And in a Methodist's house too. So cleanliness isn't the thing next to Godliness like is said." My old mum, she was always saying things like that, she . . .'

I turned. 'Done.' My breath was coming now in little panicky gulps.

We repeated the operation in three of the bedrooms. In the final master bedroom Barbara even crept onto the shiny bedcover, the colour of a creamy orchid, to rest there. She watched as I dusted the red glass dressing-table set, my reflection thriced in the vanity mirror. It reminded me of the family I'd concocted: Mum, Dad and me, all with the same stamp on our face. When I got Barbara home I'd resolved to search the house. Any detail, I thought as I drew out Mrs Theobold's hairs from the kirby grips scattered on the glass dish, any detail might help.

'We've forgotten the back sitting room,' Barbara gasped, half sitting.

'I'll go, you finish up in here, then let's get out of here.'

She nodded. 'Downstairs, first door after the under-the-stairs. Watch out for you-know-who.'

At the back sitting room door I realised the humming was stronger. I touched my fingertips to the wood and felt the vibration of it and knew I'd reached the centre. Music drifted from underneath the door. It had a swaying quality; a band playing for couples dancing close. Slowly, I pushed the door a fraction. The strip of my view was bordered either side by the door and frame that made the scene inside like a long thin painting. A circular repetitive motion, I realised, was a record on an old-fashioned gramophone. The scene had a heaviness to it, like its paint had been thickly put on. Golden dust motes spun in the air like miniature planets. A tall woman with pinned-up hair stood looking through the window. The way it had been, the small routines upheld all vibrated through me. I even caught the smells of the daily food lingering – potatoes, cabbage, rhubarb. The air inside was brownish, the colour of the past. The woman's thoughts flitted brown too, like moths. Love, she was thinking, looking through the glass, I've given up on love, it was so nearly mine and I betrayed it. She turned a knife over and over in her hands. A noose formed and dangled in her mind. I thought I would find it over and over and the next time the circumstances would be suitable. And they were but the bright thing was not there this time. I had that bright thing and I turned away from it and now I might as well be dead . . .

Her head turned slightly. 'June?' she asked. 'June?'

I pulled the door closed.

Upstairs Barbara had fallen asleep on the satin bedcover.

She looked like a tiny brown spider at the corner of the bed. I shook her awake as I heard the front door open below.

'Come on. I'm done, and she's back – let's go.'

On the way out I glanced at the glass ball. Inside was Shadow shrunk to the size of a cotton reel. He was lying on the grassy plain inside, fast asleep. Butterflies swooped overhead.

He must have got lonely out there, frightened, and crept under the door and looked around for the safest place he could find. He looked so peaceful lying among the grass with the iridescent wings above him. In a kind of heaven. I wondered for a moment if I should leave him there. But the puffing violent cheeks would soon seek him out, I knew. They'd use their buds to find such a tasty little morsel and then he'd be gone, eaten up into God knows what.

Barbara was in the hallway, waiting for me. I tapped on the glass with my fingernail.

Mrs Theobold appeared from the depths of the house. 'What did you just do? Touching my things . . .'

Any colour left drained from Barbara's face.

Mrs Theobold had turned spitty. 'It could have broken quite in half. I knew I shouldn't allow it, a child like you. Touching. I'm going to get your money, Mrs Flood. Please wait on the doorstep for us, child.'

I stood on the doorstep and looked back in at Barbara waiting quietly in the hall. The moment seemed to go on an age.

'Steal something,' I mouthed at Barbara at last.

And by the way she tapped her pocket I knew she already had.

Halfway down the hill I looked behind and there was Shadow, lolloping behind us. I linked my arm through Barbara's to help her walk.

'Don't ever go back there,' I said.

As expected the red dog was there on the way back, exactly as it was before, snuffling along the same route. As far as I knew, he'd be doing that into eternity.

48

Somehow, Anna makes it back from her wedding to their room.

Lewis is to go away almost immediately, she knew that already. An opportunity had come up a few days before the wedding and it's too good to miss, he says. He's sorry, he'll make it up to her. Anna cannot argue. She watches London slide past the taxi window as Lewis describes the honeymoon he's going to take her on, on his return: Brighton, maybe. Margate. Or should it be Spain? There's these things called package holidays he's seen that take you there and organise everything. She laughs at the idea loudly and Lewis gives her a look that silences her. Then the places he's talked about begin to flash as bright as knives in Anna's mind. She longs for the coolness of the forest.

As soon as she's back in their airy room she strips off her gloves and lies down, Ruby at the foot of the bed in her carrycot. When she wakes she knows Lewis has gone because she can feel his kiss cooling on her forehead.

There's a sense of dread she's never experienced before.

She kneels up and Ruby's face hoves into view, awake, watchful. Anna looks round. Every object in the room seems to have taken on an unbearable significance. Their cups and plates on the table, left as they rushed out of the door to their wedding. Her gloves lying empty and wrinkled on the bare boards of the floor. Lewis's shaving brush, dried into a sideways clot in the mug at the sink. Even from this distance she can see a tiny drop of blood dried against the porcelain of the basin where they wash and brush their teeth – where Lewis stands to shave in his vest.

Her mind races with disordered images. Knives. Scissors. Knives. Then it stills and it comes to her with complete clarity. Lewis is poisoning her. He expects her to be lying stiff and dead on his return. She must get help before the poison finishes its work.

Has he poisoned the baby too? Ruby looks OK, if a little anxious, pinched around the nose and mouth. So is he planning on returning when Anna's dead to collect the baby? What's his plan? What's his plan? He's capable.

She picks Ruby up and creeps downstairs. Outside the heavy front door with its scarred black paintwork it's bright clear sunshine. People move up and down the street as if on wheels. She knows she doesn't have wheels like them so she's stuck there on the top step. She holds Ruby tighter until she hears a breath being squeezed from the tiny body, yet still the child doesn't cry. She merely looks up into Anna's face – her small blue-grey eyes questioning, the mark a red sickle moon on her face.

Around the corner comes an extraordinary creature, many-legged and with two bouncing heads on top. Anna freezes for a moment before loosening her grasp on the body in her arms slightly. It's help come for her – two policemen on horseback. The shadows that the horses cast are long and dark, stretching out before them. The creature passes her inexorably slowly; she calls out but its four heads are bending towards each other, talking. Anna calls out again – or has she? She's not sure if any sound has escaped her lips. She watches as the horses' rumps move away from her and disappear round the corner of the street.

Stella and Samuel. Anna remembers now. They were there with their baby Rose at the wedding this morning, marrying the man who is now trying to kill her. She creeps up the stairs, one arm round the baby and one hand steadying herself on the wooden banister. Outside Stella and Samuel's door she pauses on the landing, her hand raised to knock. She lays her ear to the door and she thinks she can hear noises inside, shuffling, whispering, but when she knocks there's no answer.

When she looks down there seems to be something strange pouring under the door, a yellow gas or an odd light that streams out. Anna flees back upstairs.

So this is what it feels like to die, thinks Anna.

The room seems to be pulsing, shock waves rippling through the window and up the walls. She can feel them through the thin soles of the pearly stilettos that she wore for her wedding. The bundle in her arms mewls a little and she lifts it up and places her cheek against the soft tiny one.

'Ruby, Ruby, Ruby, everything will be all right. Mummy *will* find help, she will.'

She just needs to find the courage to pass the seeping door, the people on wheels. She looks over to the table where the bread knife lies. The edges of it seem to gather and pool, blood forming on its surface. Is that blood dripping from the point too?

She lowers the bundle of Ruby down, feeling an over-whelming urge to hold the knife in her hand. But when she looks down Anna lets out a wrenching cry of fear. Where has Ruby gone? The face has altered. The red mark floats slightly above it like one of those tin masks her father told her about – that they fixed to the soldiers' faces coming back from the battlefields of the Somme where parts had been blown away. The little mouth is closed but Anna knows it's full of sharp teeth inside.

Anna cries out again and lets the baby slip from her arms. It falls with a soft thud on the floor. She can barely hear the cries as she grabs her bag and her coat, the bluebell blue swing coat she bought for her wedding. Each step towards the door feels like wading through glue but she knows she needs to get away from the knife before she grabs it.

At the last minute she notices the doll on the floor, the one with the Eskimo girl's face, dropped from the blanket that swaddled Ruby. Anna picks it up and stuffs it in her handbag before wrenching open the door.

The curtains move at the open window sending shadows rippling across the bare walls.

The fragile bowl of Ruby's head has landed on the quilted blanket that dropped with her on the floor. The rest of her body lies diagonally across bare boards. Crying has got her nowhere and gradually it tailed off like a plane disappear-ing in the distance. Her arms stick up and she paddles the air with her hands. Sounds from the street push through the open window. Shuffling, clanking, wheels trundling and voices:

'Sparky. All right, mate?'

'If you catch the number thirty-two and take it from there, don't get off at the stop by The Pen and Wig, though, not that stop.'

'Celia, look at this.'

It's all white noise to Ruby. There's only one voice that makes any sense to her and it's Anna's voice that says, 'Ruby, Ruby, Ruby, Ruby. My gem. My treasure trove.'

The light at the window begins to darken. Cold seeps in. Ruby's fingers become cold stiff sticks. She cries again but the sound is different. It's thin and feeble, barely penetrating the thick walls. Her lips have taken on a blue tinge and her stomach, under the little rack of ribs, hollows in and out with the cries. The sound fades until it's just a hum escaping from her lips.

It's not dark yet and the afternoon light casts long shadows across the room. But another shadow begins to take shape beside her, one that doesn't have a progenitor to cast it. It hunches over the prone body agitating. Ruby is leaving. She's hovering like a little cloud over her heaving belly. What to do? The Shadow knows how time can work, how it can fold over itself like unset seaside rock. How life can pinch out and what would be the future gets switched off. How, in the hollow that the life has left everything and everyone stirs and settles around it, filling in the gap. It happens before you know it.

The impulse to leap inside that little body is great. It would be like jumping into the still warm bed that's just been recently vacated.

49

THE EVIL BOOK
25 December 1983

When Barbara was taken by ambulance that night the
blue lights lit up the trees as we passed, turning them into
spectres.

The dawn crept up slowly on the ward. It picked out all
the Christmas decorations first: the red tinsel sellotaped to
the door frame, then the gold foil bells hanging from the
ceiling, but it couldn't have been less like Christmas if it
tried. The decorations just gave the hospital an extra sinis-
ter glitter.

The night before Barbara couldn't get up off the sofa to
go to bed. She kept saying, 'Give me a minute, Ruby. Give
me your arm, let's try again.' But every time she tried she
collapsed back down again white as a sheet and groaning.
The sound was terrible, like it wasn't even coming from her.

'I've left it too late,' she kept saying. I couldn't pretend I
didn't know what she meant.

'Sssh,' I said, like you would do to a child. I stroked her
curly hair. 'I won't leave you, I promise.'

She looked so ill, her jaw slack and her face grey and her
bouncy hair all limp. I cried properly then and the tears
splashed onto the arm of her best nightdress. I cried mainly
because I was frightened. I felt about five years old again.

'Oh Ruby,' she said, crying now herself, 'and I let you go

without a murmur to that awful fat sister of Mick's. A filthy house she keeps and not one of those children are quite right in the head.'

She still didn't seem to have really got that I never went there.

At the hospital they pushed her bed, with red tinsel wound round the iron railings at the bottom, into her own room and two more bits of bad news happened one after the other. A nurse popped her head inside the room.

'Your father has just telephoned. He's coming to get you.'

'I don't have a father,' I said.

'Well, he's coming to get you anyway,' she said and her head popped back out again.

'The jungle drums must've been going,' I said to Barbara. 'The neighbours probably heard the ambulance and called him. They'd love that – passing on juicy gossip about your own family.'

'Perhaps he'll come in to see me,' whispered Barbara, squeezing her damp hanky in a ball in her hand.

I sighed and that's when I noticed it. 'Oh no,' I said. 'I don't believe it.'

'What?'

'Look at that picture.'

She screwed her eyes up at the framed print of Alice playing croquet with a flamingo. 'She's got a lot of hair.'

'Talk about that book meaning bad luck,' I muttered. I remembered the night of the forest and the dolls I'd made, the picture of Alice falling down the hole. The beating. It all tied in together for me. Things from *Alice* began coming back to me, such as where she gets mistaken for a snake. I shuddered.

254

'It's only a story,' she said.

'No, it's not. Tonight I'm going to burn it. It is a truly evil book.'

'We can be mates now, Ruby,' Sandra said, standing in Barbara's house as if it was her own. 'I've come to cook Christmas dinner.' She was waiting in the hall while Mick fetched her suitcase from the car. I set my mouth at her in a thin line but she just took her coat off and hung it on the peg next to the door and looked around at the hallway as if what she saw didn't please her too much. I saw it through her eyes: the worn carpet and the dusty dried flower display under the mirror. The house felt full up with the two of them and their affair.

'School will go mental when they know,' I said.

'Oh, that's all right. I've left now – I can't see the point of exams anyway. I've got a little job lined up in a hairdresser's. I'm interested in beauty.'

Without her coat I could see the shape of her breasts under the thin shirt. Even though she was only sixteen they reminded me of older women's breasts, sort of heavy around the bottom part. It made me sick to think of Mick's hands all over them.

Sandra brushed past me on her way upstairs. I tried to catch her reflection in the mirror to see what it did to her but she was too quick, she went by in a blink. I could smell her perfume, though, and it smelled cheap and sweet. At least Barbara had the good taste to wear lovely perfume; I felt like telling her that, even if it was stolen.

Mick came in with a huge suitcase and jutted his jaw at me. 'Got something to say about it?'

I backed towards the open door of the kitchen. 'No.'

'I should fucking well think not. Especially after that let-ter you sent in your absence.'

'What did you do with it?'

'I ripped it up. I would've burned it too if I could've been arsed.' The raw meat look began to tinge his face. 'Just like you did with my trousers.' He shook his head and picked up Sandra's suitcase and started heaving it upstairs. I guessed I'd only escaped a belt because she was in the house. 'Mess-ing with Elaine like that. She thought she'd got the wrong day but when she phoned to say you hadn't turned up I guessed you'd pulled another stunt.'

'You didn't say anything to Barbara?' I felt safer with him halfway up the stairs.

'No, why should I? Didn't stay for long anyway myself and I can tell you I'm not happy to be back. It's your fault we're here. You caused a lot of trouble coming round and shouting the odds, silly bitch.' He pointed at me over the banister. 'One word and you're for it.' I noticed the purple mark on his head had nearly gone.

Later we sat round in silence picking at the Christmas din-ner Sandra had cooked. I guessed it'd been her dad the fall-ing out had been with because her mother had supplied the food, all wrapped in tin foil with instructions on how to cook it, and turkey ready-done in slices.

'Are you going to see Barbara and hear what the doctor's said?' I asked Mick.

'No,' said Mick. 'You can tell me all about it.'

I couldn't help but flick him a look over the table but he didn't even notice because he couldn't take his eyes off

Sandra as she sat there picking at her nails, her half-eaten dinner in front of her.

Later Sandra watched as me and Mick heaved the camp bed up the stairs.

'It looks like something out of the ark,' she said.

It looked like a strange animal set out next to my bed – all iron frame, great curling springs and a thin mattress. It looked like it might snap her up like a snack in the middle of the night and the way she was looking at it I could tell she was thinking the same thing.

'Just for now,' I heard Mick saying to her out on the landing. 'For decency's sake, until we can clear out of here for good. The neighbours . . .' I hardly recognised his voice. It sounded so soft and pleading. Sandra snorted, 'How would they know?' But as she unpacked her nightdress and laid it on the camp bed I could tell she was glad to be in with me, someone near her age. I wasn't, though, the last thing I wanted was to get friendly with Sandra. Mick would really have it in for me then. I guessed I should at least be pleased they wouldn't be rolling around in Mick's bed together for the time being. The thought of that, with all Barbara's sad worn-out clothes hanging in the wardrobe and her carrier bags of stolen things, made me want to cry.

Christmas afternoon felt like a month. Sandra kept sitting on the edge of her seat and fiddling with her charm bracelet. 'Come on, Ruby. Let me make you up. It would cheer me up no end to try out my beauty skills on you,' she said finally.

'I'd rather not,' I said, thinking again of how dangerous it could be to get on friendly terms.

'Oh, go on. Please, there's nothing else to do.' She went

257

on and on until I finally sighed and said yes. I couldn't help feeling a bit sorry for her. Her hair was bright strawberry blonde but her skin was doughy, and her nose. I could see that her little flush of young prettiness wasn't going to last long before it went the way of her breasts. She had beautiful hands, though, white and soft and tapering at the fingertips. I thought, as long as you wear rubber gloves before putting them in water nobody will be able to take those away from you.

She fetched her box that opened out with compartments on arms, each one crammed full of crayons and tubes. I couldn't help being a bit excited by the idea of having proper make-up so I sat there at the kitchen table with a tea towel tied round my neck to protect my jumper.

'Let me look,' I said while she was working on my eyes, putting glittery blue stuff from a pot on them.

'No, not yet. You need to wait until I've completely finished for you to appreciate the transformation.' I wondered if she'd talk to her customers like that – so stern – but I obeyed because I wanted to witness the transformation she talked about.

'There,' she said finally, pulling off the tea towel. 'You can look now.' And she held up a hand mirror with a pink plastic frame. When my face popped into it I couldn't help saying, 'Oh God.'

'Don't you like it?'

'It doesn't really look like me.' It was worse than that: she'd tried to cover up my mark. She'd put a thick layer of beige foundation over it but it still showed through, only now it was a faint bluey-purple colour and it looked like the left half of my face was in shadow. It made me realise something that startled me; I missed that mark now she'd made it fade. The blue eye shadow and bright pink lipstick seemed clownish.

'I'll wash it off now,' I said.

'No, don't do that, not with all the time I've taken. At least leave it on so your dad can see. You look like that girl from Abba, what's her name, or a model.' She sighed. 'I'd like to be a model,' she said, 'one day.'

I didn't know what to say; with her moony face I reckoned she had about as much chance of being a model as I did.

'What d'you think,' she asked, 'about me trying for a model?'

'Maybe you can be a hand model. There must be someone who does all those nail polish and hand cream adverts.'

'That's not what I meant at all,' she said, but as I left the kitchen I turned back and saw her holding up her hands in front of her face, studying them hard.

All Mick said when he saw my make-up was: 'What in fuck's name has she been doing to you?'

I carried *Alice in Wonderland* out the back.

'Goodbye,' I said, dropping it inside the tin drum that Mick used for burning rubbish. A smell rose up, of cold ashes. I paused and sniffed. The smell didn't seem dead to me, it was promising – the simple fact of ignition and everything would jump to life. I squirted paraffin from the bottle in the shed and dropped the match in after it. There was a ticking noise as the cold bin warmed and flames furled across the book, taking hold and licking up the sides of the bin until they were frilling the rim. I spotted *Alice in*

Wonderland at the heart of the fire, writhing in agony.

'Good riddance,' I said.

In the evening Sandra lounged all over the living room in her little stretchy mini skirt watching a Christmas special, her mouth making the shape of a horse's as she laughed. It seemed terrible with Barbara dying in hospital. So I decided to start searching for the documentation that might give me the clues to my real family right there and then. I tiptoed into Barbara and Mick's bedroom to look at the bottom of the wardrobe as Tom had suggested but there was only a jumble of shoes. I looked at all Barbara's old nineteen sixties clothes hanging there. The patterns and colours were all so bright it somehow made it worse, like they were mocking her. I put my head into them and tried to breathe in her perfume that clung to the fabrics.

I heard Mick and Sandra downstairs, having an argument. She yelled that she was bored and had been stuck in the whole day with me and it was driving her round the twist and she wanted to go to the pub. Then the front door slammed and I was alone in the house with my head stuck in a cupboard.

Christmas night and all the spirits of the forest were gathering outside. I phoned Tom from the hallway.

'Happy Christmas,' I said.

'Happy Christmas,' said Tom and we both stayed on the line for ages, listening to each other breathing.

Later, when they'd got back and we were both in bed Sandra tried to be friendly again.

'I bet you've never kissed anyone, have you, Ruby. I should give you pointers for when it happens.'

'Oh, do shut up,' I said. I was talking like Crispin, Elizabeth and Tom, as if their assurance had rubbed off on me.

There was a hurt silence. 'All right, you don't have to be so curt,' she said at last from down below.

I thought of Tom's kiss. How sweet and true it had felt. We didn't need any pointers; we kissed like we'd been doing it all our lives.

Sandra was making the springs creak as she turned over and over in bed, trying to get comfortable. 'Christ, this bed,' she muttered. I heard her head thumping down on the pillow. 'Still, I don't suppose it's for ever.'

'Barbara,' I said, very deliberately and slowly, 'is not dead yet.'

'I know,' she said in a small voice, then she became so quiet I thought she'd gone to sleep.

'Ruby,' she said, making me jump. 'Is it true what they said at school, you know, about your dad hitting you?' She sounded younger all of a sudden.

I stayed silent. The only people I'd ever confided in were Tom and Elizabeth. I hated people knowing. The thought that people talked about it in school made me shrink inside.

'If he ever tries to with me,' she said, 'I'll kill him.'

I turned over. 'Why are you even with him, Sandra?' I whispered urgently.

'Oh, he can be ever so romantic and he's said we can leave this dump.' Her voice became excited. 'I couldn't do it on my own but he's said we can move, maybe even to London.'

I slumped back down and listened to her breathing as it got deeper and deeper and I knew she was asleep. I imagined it to be Tom's breathing, and eventually the sound of it soothed me into sleep.

50

THE PROMISE
26 December 1983

By morning Sandra's talk was all about how she couldn't wait until she didn't have to be stuck here any more.

'I do feel sorry for you, Ruby,' Sandra said, 'being brought up like this. My mum and dad had everything so nice when I was growing up. Everything in Tupperware boxes. Central heating. A bathroom with hot water that doesn't run out halfway through your bath.'

'Why did you come here then?'

'Four's a crowd they say. Plus, you started trouble.' She stomped upstairs to get dressed.

Mick stood by the open back door, looking out. 'You know,' he said without turning, I could see his cheek moving up and down as he talked, 'all I'm after is a little bit of happiness for myself. It's not too much to ask for, is it? Just a little bit of happiness.' And he went outside to have a cigarette with his shoulders sloping downwards underneath his leather jacket.

Beyond him, I'd never seen the forest look dull before but it did that day, dripping and lifeless. The tired flatness of Boxing Day hung heavy in its branches. It seemed as if my time at Elizabeth and Tom's had been like an exciting book full of significant things – hares, goblets of bright wine, talk of scrolls, cut glass and snow. Now someone had snapped that book shut as I was reading it and forced me back to look at the things I didn't want to.

Barbara's head had turned into one of those meaningful objects, though. It lay upon the hospital pillow like a lamp, emitting pale frenzied light. Her eyes glowed bigger than I remembered them to be.

I leaned over and took one of her hands and it tremored with fear.

'Have they said what's wrong with you yet?' I asked.

She twisted her head back and forth. 'Grumbling appendix. I'm going under the knife.' She squeezed her eyes shut.

'It'll be . . .'

'The knife, Ruby,' she interrupted. 'I've always been in terror of the knife.' She looked up as if there was a real one hovering over her and waiting to fall and pierce her body. She grabbed at my hand.

Beyond the wall, breakfasts had finished and the hospital ticked back down to an almost unmoving pace.

'Ruby.' I leaned in close because she was speaking so softly. 'There's something I need to discuss with you.'

'Yes? What is it?'

'It's about what happens after. Just in case, you see. You never know what the outcome will be once they trap you in hospital and, well, the fact of the matter is, how can I explain?' She screwed then unscrewed her face. 'I don't want to be a ghost.'

I startled. 'Barbara . . .'

She interrupted. 'What I need to know is – and you're to tell me straight – how do you stop the afterlife? I need to know how to make it not happen.' Her hand moved to my wrist and grasped.

'I don't know, Barbara, please.'

'You do.' She squeezed my wrist tight. 'You do. I know about you. Remember the Wasp Lady?'

I thought she would've forgotten about the Wasp Lady. That was back in the days when I childishly chattered and confided in her. 'You won't be like the Wasp Lady. Ow, you're hurting my arm.' She let go and closed her eyes.

I shuddered even though I hadn't seen the Wasp Lady for years. How I hated the way she swooped up to me on my way to bed from the cavern of the hall below. How she pursed her lips and folded herself sideways like a fan.

'I thought you never believed me about her anyway. You were always telling me I was imagining things.'

'Accch.' An arm came up and batted the air, as if to brush something aside. 'I believed you but I thought you'd grow out of it all. It's often better to ignore things. That's what I've found.' It struck me then how many things were buried or obscured in our home, or seen dully as if kept in a dirty glass jar.

'It's nearly always family, you know, who are the ghosts.' She went on. 'That's what I've heard. They can't believe they're not part of everything any more so they hang around, making a nuisance of themselves. I've never doubted that they are real, my mum didn't either, but all the same being a ghost always seems like the most terrible thing I can think of. I mean, what does it feel like?' Her anguished eyes turned to me.

'Barbara, the Wasp Lady was never family.'

'Don't be too sure of that. The way you described her she well reminded me of an aunt of mine. It's just the sort of thing she'd do – taking up residence in other people's houses.'

We were silent for a while. 'If I do become a ghost will you know me, Ruby? Will you recognise me?'

I could almost see her already, dropping silvery trinkets from her sleeves. 'I expect so.'

'I'm going under the knife, Ruby. Maybe today. I'm going to say this quick because I want to get it over with.' I looked at her and somehow with her eyes wide open so suddenly fear tightened my throat.

She grabbed my arm again. 'You didn't recognise your mother, Ruby, but I did – from what you said. It was the yellow dress.'

I slid off the chair until my face was right by hers.

'What? You knew her? You knew that was her?'

She laughed, a single bitter snort. 'Oh, I knew her. You have to understand, it happened all the time in those days. Still does I'll bet, in the forest. Children who thought their own grandmothers were their mothers, all sorts. It wasn't so,' she paused to find the right word, 'segregated as it is now. I need to say this quick and be done with it. Me and your mother, we were sisters, Ruby.'

My bones felt as if they'd been turned to water. 'Sisters. You mean, you *are* my blood?'

'Yes. I knew it was her straight away, with her yellow dress. Oh, come back, have you? I thought. Can't you just stay away and let us try and get on with it? We were going to tell you all about it on your thirteenth birthday but then you ran off and sang and it all got wiped over again.'

'Why didn't you say later?' Every word seemed an effort to get out. 'You could've said later.'

'Mick said you didn't deserve to know, but you do, Ruby.

You do deserve to know. Your mother, we were never the best of friends, sisters, but not close.'

'But you were sisters?' I breathed.

A deep shudder seemed to go through her. 'Yes, and I made a commitment. I signed forms.' She turned her face away and closed her eyes, pain drawn into the lines around her mouth. 'I have not cared for you in the way that I should. I made a promise, a commitment. I thought feeding and clothing and putting a roof over your head was enough. But it wasn't, it was never enough.'

'Barbara, please tell me where she is. I have to find her.'

'You know, Ruby. You know where. You saw her.'

'Yes,' I whispered. 'I saw it. I saw death crawl out of her, didn't I?'

'I'm sorry, Ruby. I'm sorry that she's dead but it can't be helped. We never knew why she came back to the forest that day, but she did and that was the end of her, poor soul. That's the way of things. She crashed, just like you said. She came back and she crashed and that was the end of her. I'm exhausted to my bones. I need to see Mick. Please make him come here.' Then she turned over and great shaking sobs racked her tiny frame so hard she looked as though she'd break.

There was a singing in my ears. 'But what about my real dad?'

'God knows, dead too as far as I know. All wasted, dead and gone.'

Her face twisted up as she sobbed but she appeared to me a long way off. As if I was being drawn backwards into a tunnel and her bed was a light in the distance, hanging there in the dark like a bright white playing card.

51

4 December 1970

When Anna wakes there's a man standing over her bed. She knows he's a doctor.

The windows in the room are high up and bright light streams through them. The doctor smiles down at her.

'Good girl, come around at last.' He's young and it feels odd to have him right next to her bed with her hair all over the pillow and in a nightie she doesn't recognise. There's something incongruous about him too that she can't quite put her finger on. She shifts, trying to sit up. Her limbs seem to have become jellylike and her brain as dark and dense as the bottom of the ocean.

He has something in his hand she recognises. That's it – that's why he looks so incongruous, he's carrying a hand-bag.

'I thought I'd bring this along, might give us a few clues.'

Anna looks blankly at him. She has no idea what he's talking about. She seems to have entered some strange land where men carry handbags and are looking for clues.

He opens it up. 'Go on, have a look,' he urges.

Only when Anna takes the handbag does she realise it's actually hers. She hugs it to her belly because there's an empty ache there that needs comfort. 'What for?' she finally manages, her tongue feeling thick in her mouth.

'Identity. There was nothing in there we could find. No driving licence or letters. No chequebook.'

He frowns as if a person not carrying a chequebook must be some kind of criminal but then he sees her blank pained expression and kind creases appear under his brown eyes.

'Your name, dear. We were looking for your name.'

Anna sits up. What are they on about? She knows who she is, for goodness' sake. The memory of writing it in the church register – when? How long ago? – comes back to her. Written in thick black ink, nothing could be more definite. 'My name is Mrs Anna Black,' she says and for some reason this makes the doctor do a little laugh.

'Good girl, good girl.'

Her wedding, she looks down at her ring finger – it's bare.

'My ring,' she gasps, 'it's gone.'

'Don't worry.' The doctor takes a seat next to her. 'We have it for safe keeping while you're here.'

'But why do you need my ring?' She grasps the handbag tighter.

'You know, safety and all that.' The doctor doesn't want to talk about her ring, she can see that. He thinks it unimportant, but she doesn't. She needs to get to the bottom of it.

'Safety, what do you mean? How could a ring be unsafe?'

'Oh you know,' his eyes drift upwards, 'you might swallow it or something.'

'Swallow it? Why on earth would I swallow my ring?' She knows she won't be able to make this much sense for long. This is a valley where only a slender finger of light penetrates, dark on either side. She is criss-crossing constantly from the heavy drugs and this light patch is traversed infrequently.

'My dear.' His voice has taken on a more authoritative tone. He's fed up with all this talk of wedding rings. 'Do you realise quite how ill you were when you came in here? You were in a terrible way. Luckily, you were found by a medical professional who knew what to do. Anything could have happened. You've had some kind of psychotic episode, that much we know. We'll find the appropriate treatment, though, I can assure you. That's what we do here.'

She leans back. She has vague memories of cowering in doorways, trying to get on a bus, though she doesn't know where to. In her mind it was knives, knives, knives. She could think of nothing else. Then there were corridors branching off and it had seemed she was inside a heart because some of them seemed to be curving upwards. She started shouting, she was sure of that, then nothingness. She opens the big brass clasp that sits on the top of her handbag and peers inside. Everything is jumbled up; she would never have left it like that. They've shaken it around so much her lipstick is out of the soft suede pleat on the side and is poking out from underneath her purse, which has opened and disgorged loose change everywhere. A little face looks up at her from the depths. Gingerly she reaches in and takes the doll from the debris at the bottom. She brings it into the light. Its little Eskimo face purses its lips at her, ready to burst into a smile.

Anna starts wailing. 'My baby, my baby, my baby, my baby.'

The boy Shadow with his muddy mouth crouches next to Ruby. He can see life seeping, down, down between the cracks in the floorboards.

He rocks back and forth on his haunches wondering what to do. A chill is descending in the room enough to freeze his feet to the spot, if he had any. Ruby's mouth is pinched with thirst and her eyelids are fluttering. This night will see her off for sure. He thinks again of leaping into the shell she's leaving. The temptation is strong to borrow the clothes made of blood, flesh and bone to feel the world again, even if it's only for a short while. The wind on his face. The taste of butter. The sound of birds skimming overhead.

Ruby turns her head and fixes her eye on him as if she knows what he's planning and he hangs his head. He knows what it is to live through trouble.

He tries calling but no sound comes out. He blows across her face but his breath doesn't even have an ounce of the strength of the breeze blowing through the window. He gathers, denser, darker. Perhaps he'll regret it later. Perhaps he'll curse missing his chance but this small life will not end now; if there's anything he can do to save it he will. Denser still, all in the finger, the one pointing at Ruby. Into her ribs, jabbing hard enough to crack the little bones like sticks.

Ruby opens her tiny blue eyes, the mouth opens too and a roar of outrage lets rip. Waves of it. When it seems like subsiding he jabs again. It's using every last drop of her energy doing this. Finally, he's rewarded with a tap on the door, tentative at first then transforming into a steady thrumming. There's voices calling out. Then the knocking and the calls at the door fall silent. Come back, he says. Come back.

It does but this time it's not knocking but a chopping sound. Slicing, splintering wood. A blade glinting in the hole that's made. The blade withdraws; a hand fills its gap and wiggles round until it finds the Yale lock.

The door swings open and Ruby can only stare. Her saviour is a huge tall black man wearing a suit and holding an axe. Behind him a face peeps over his shoulder – his wife. It says, 'Child, child. Good gracious God.'

Stella runs in the room and scoops Ruby into her arms and holds her against her own beating heart. The child is like ice. Ignoring the small crowd that has begun to gather at the doorway, drawn by the commotion, she unbuttons her black dress and tucks Ruby next to her soft warm skin.

It's all happening so fast she hasn't got time to consider what she saw when Samuel first burst open the door – a little dark thing hunched over Ruby's chest that leapt back and faded into the corner of the room. That night, she tells Samuel about it when they're in bed. He tells her she's going soft.

52

THE HOUR OF THE WOLF
26 December 1983

Slap, slap, slap. The hardness of the road jolted through my feet as I ran. Each outward breath was a painful hum. The roads and the forest were deserted as if every person living there had melted away into the earth.

I'd called for my mum and she came for me. She came for me in a yellow dress and a pile of twisted metal. With her head upside down. She crossed the skin of this world and came for me and all that happened was that I was frightened, terrified by the sight of her.

Someone had looped red and silver tinsel inside one tree in the corner of the dirt track I knew so well. It flapped there, already looking tired from having been rained on and tossed about in the wind. I ran without stopping past the collapsed shed on its little ridge of land, the plasterboard and broken glass sheltered by the copper beech tree spread above it. I took the dirt track that always felt like a plunge down into darkness – into the shaded valley. The path was wet, as it nearly always was this time of year because the trees dripped continuously on it. The occasional rock stuck out like a bone. The forest opened out and there was my grandmother's cottage, Hollow Cottage, as it always was, in the clearing. In summer the light had a greenish tinge, the sun being filtered through a mass of leaves except for one half hour in the middle of the day when it would be directly overhead, pointing and burning into the hole and all the creatures and plants that were used to damp and dimness would recoil in shock, their little bodies drying out.

Now it was the tangle of bare branches shading the clearing.

I passed the pigpen to my left. Hung in the air was the smell of wood smoke, but dead, from fires burned many years ago. There was a sign sticking out at right angles to the front wall. It said, 'Acquired by A.J. Cooke, Property Developers.' There was the sycamore tree that my grandmother had been found under.

I looked through the window, through a film of dust. I wailed until the panes rattled. I wailed until I felt scooped out, hollow as the name of the cottage, until my breath itself was exhausted. When I felt almost turned inside out by the wailing I leaned my front against the wall and put my forehead against the glass and looked through the window.

Inside I could just see the shapes of the kitchen table and the chairs around it where I'd once sat with Barbara and my gran. 'Sweets for the sweet, Ruby,' Barbara would say as she shelled hazelnuts. But wasn't there always another one who wasn't there? Remember, remember, I told myself. So much from the years I'd filtered out, the beings that flitted about that had no earthly right to be there, and I'd been small, still the height when the adults seem to grow upwards into the sky. Remember, I told myself again. Yes – I saw her, or knew she was there, I'm not sure which. She moved among us with her long hair and her small round mouth. Had Barbara and Gran spoken of her and that's what gave me the sight of her? I pressed my cheek against the window and tried to think. No, they never talked of her, though they turned a little when she was in the room as if they could sense her too. They invited her without knowing by always leaving a gap at the table at dinner. So her name was Anna, I'd never known that.

There had been a day too where my grandmother held me and with tears falling down her cheeks said, 'It's her birth-day, it's her birthday,' and when I said to her, 'But Gran, no it's not, my birthday is the twentieth of August,' she laughed a little through her tears and held me tight again.

I stood back and the birds began to sing for the evening. I felt as if I'd been following something, a trail, a forest path, a treasure hunt, but all that was at the end was another hole. Only this one wasn't just for me; it had my mother in it too, she was already there, lying at the bottom, trapped in a filthy wonderland of twisted metal. I sat on the door-step, then curled up into a ball on the cold stone. Even then somehow waiting to be let in.

When I got home the house was empty and it was night. Mick and Sandra were out. I ran a bath and stripped off all my muddy clothes, then submerged myself in the water. I thought back to my thirteenth birthday and how I'd imagined my parents coming to me through the steam. I scrubbed my skin until it was red then tied my hair into two long plaits and dressed in jeans and a T-shirt.

In the hallway I phoned Tom.

'My mother's dead,' I said.

'Oh, Ruby.'

'Barbara is my blood. She's my aunt.'

'Isn't that good news?'

'I'm not sure. I don't think so.'

We listened to each other breathing for a long time.

'Tell me what it's like in Hilltops right now,' I said finally.

'Black's been here. He's coming every day, the harvest is nearly ready he says.'

'What then?'

'I don't know. I don't know how much longer I can keep things going here. Elizabeth gets worse. She cries every evening.'

We breathed together for a bit again.

'I went into the library today. I saw your book . . .'

'Which one? *Tess of the D'Urbervilles*?'

'Yes, I think so. It was lying open on the floor and the pages were flicking about in the breeze, there was a window open. I felt restless, I needed something to read, something to tell me what to do, advice.'

'I do that,' I sighed, bleakness settling round me like a blanket.

'I think about the future a lot and what I'd like to do but I'm not sure if I'll ever get there. I'd been thinking about being an archaeologist or a farmer. I wanted to feel real things under my hand but now I don't know. I'd like to study something that's not made of anything – philosophy or physics. So I went looking for information about that but I got distracted.'

'I used to have the idea that books hold directions, or clues for you to follow,' I said. 'I thought that about *Tess of the D'Urbervilles* but I couldn't find what it was trying to tell me. It just confused me, so I don't think I was right about all that. It was a silly idea.'

Tess was a murderer, though. She stabbed Alec dead with the letter knife in a boarding house full of chimes and glass.

The thought went through me like a jolt. Murderer, murderer.

'Maybe it was me that killed her.' My voice rose in a sob.

'Who?'

'My mother, maybe . . .'

'Sssh. You're imagining things now, how could you've done? Stop it, think of something else.'

Slowly, I calmed. 'Tell me about the book then, the one you found.'

'I found loads. Specially about history and folklore. There was one about how in the olden days they arrested people who tried to find out the secrets of the afterlife. They felt it should remain a secret, like they could be infected . . .'

His speech had become hectic, breathless.

'Tom. Are you afraid of me?'

'Sort of, I'm sorry. But I'm afraid of everything at the moment. I don't like being like this. I never used to be.'

'You won't always be.'

'I hope that.'

'Did you find anything else?'

'Yes, it was a book about old gods. The Romans and Greeks, you know. The Romans had something called "The Hour of the Wolf" – it was the time, at three or four in the morning, where spirits will get up out of their graves – like getting out of bed – and walk around.'

I thought about that. 'I'm not sure they need a special time,' I said finally.

'I can't stop thinking about it. It's an evil time too, chaos, and Ruby . . .'

'Yes?'

'I can't get it out of my head that this Hour of the Wolf is something that's going to happen to us. That it's nearly here.'

53

THE TREE OF LIFE
27 December 1983

5 a.m.

I woke. I sat and looked out of the window. I knew what I had to do. The certainty had been gathering overnight, crawling through me like a dense low fog crawls over the ground. Hunter. Gatherer, but not of mortal stuff or fleshy remains. There was hunting to be done now. The quarry was out there almost anxious to be found. I could feel it waiting, waiting, waiting for me. I'd heard its snappish voice calling my name from outside last night. 'Where are you?' it said. 'I've got a bone to pick with you.'

Sandra's pillow beside me was blank where her sleeping face should be. I dressed hurriedly, my fingers shaking as I did up the coat buttons with anchors patterned on them. I waited in the kitchen drinking tea until light came and then left the house to pay my third and final visit to the hollow tree.

'Wotcha,' Crispin said as he leaned against the tree that contained his rotting flesh. 'You took your time. I seem to have been here an age all alone. I don't know where everyone has gone.'

His metal-coloured eyes glinted at me as if he suspected it was my fault, which in a way I suppose it was. He reminded me of the drawing of the Little Prince, with his trousers tucked into his long boots and his coat and his languorous air. I forced myself to look at the heart of the hollow tree just to the right of Crispin's eyes.

'What are you looking at?' he said sharply.

'Nothing.' I shifted my gaze from the stubby tuft of hair that had sunk further since I'd been there last, down into the tree, and looked back to Crispin's face.

I was uncertain how to begin. 'Are you feeling tired?' I asked, rather like an elderly aunt enquiring after him. Clumsy, clumsy.

'Why should you say that? I'm seldom tired,' Crispin flashed back at me.

'I see.' I looked down and dug the toe of my boot into the thick cakey mixture of fallen leaves and soft loose soil. Already, I saw that the stems of trailing ivy were reattaching to the bark of the hollow tree, sealing it back up.

'Are you sure *you're* feeling quite well?' asked Crispin. 'You look rather peaky to me.' Despite his sarcastic tone his fingers had begun travelling nervously around the pockets of his coat. 'What are you looking at?' he said again and I dragged my eyes away from that tuft of gold hair sprinkled with bits of bark and soil and now with a dead brown leaf stuck on it.

'Crispin,' I said, struck with a sudden inspiration. 'Have you been to Africa yet? Elizabeth told me once that's where you wanted to go more than anything in the world.'

His look was shrewd, suspicious. The silver eyes flattening to dull metal again. 'Why? Are you trying to get rid of me?'

I flushed and shrugged my shoulders. 'Of course not. It's

just she told me once you had a map and that you looked at it all the time and learned all the names . . .'

His shoulders relaxed. 'Ah, yes. How strange. I'd almost forgotten about that. I'd give anything to see that map again. I can't seem to find anything these days. There's Botswana, isn't there, and I also fancied Swaziland. I'd like to meet shamans one day.'

I reached down into the undergrowth. 'It's here,' I said, showing it to him.

'How wonderful to see it again.' His eyes lit up then flattened again. 'Things have become rather difficult for me here. There was you to do things for me for quite a while but you seem to have gone off. It's not on, you know, when I made such efforts to get you.'

'What d'you mean? You never wanted me around. You're jealous of Elizabeth and Tom. You don't want anyone to share in them.'

He shrugged. 'Think what you like.' Then his eyes hollowed and he tilted his head to one side. 'What you don't know can't hurt you.'

Despite everything he could still annoy me. I felt the pricklings of it now on the back of my neck. 'You're playing tricks on me again. I bet you knew it was a hare that time, didn't you? I bet you made me kill it purposely because you thought it would be funny.'

He sighed and looked into the distance. There was a scuffling behind him of some small creature and he turned his head to listen. 'Maybe,' he said finally. 'I did always like a joke. Though . . . I didn't always play them so mean. I've been getting bored, though, and I don't really like the way things have been going lately. If I could see my way out of it

I would.' For the first time he looked really frightened.

I should not have asked. I should not. For didn't Tom tell me that once people were prosecuted for mining the secrets of the dead? That there are things we are not meant to know while living and breathing on this earth, but I had him there and couldn't help it. I wanted to peer inside that darkness of the tomb and see what was within.

'What's it like?' I whispered. 'For you?'

He stayed silent for a long time. 'Things weave in and out sometimes.' He looked perturbed. 'Time jumps about too. I can't seem to get a grip.'

'Apart from the usual things, what can you see?'

He looked up sharply. 'I've seen the woman in the yellow dress looking for you, if that's what you're asking.'

I stumbled backwards. 'Who? How do you know her? You're nothing to do with her.'

'That's what you think. Who is it then, your mother, is it?' He wiped his nose on the back of his sleeve.

'My mother? You've seen my mother?'

'Of course I have. It was her, wasn't it, who sent me to fetch you? She always arrives sitting in the back seat of Lewis Black's car, every single time.' He laughed. 'Though she dresses rather oddly, I've got to say. When she gets out of the car she's always wearing nothing but that summer dress in the middle of winter and her feet are quite bare on the cold ground. She'll catch her death if she's not careful. She needs to get some proper shoes on those feet.' He wiped his nose again, his eyes glinting up at me above his sleeve.

'Please tell me properly, Crispin, before you go. Why didn't she fetch me herself?'

'That's exactly what I said to her but she told me she'd

tried that and mucked it up like she always did in life.' He stopped and swallowed hard. 'Are you looking at that thing in the tree again? Why are you crying?'

'No, I promise I'm not looking, but you have to tell me. Is she still wanting to see me?'

'Oh, I don't know. I'm done running errands for her. It took enormous effort, you know, but I fancied an adventure. Those two – Tom and Elizabeth – had become very boring and mooned about all day by then. "Oh Tom, Tom. What is to be done?" That's all Elizabeth said. She always was quite annoying like that – acting as if she was our mother and now she went about wringing her hands together like the end of the world had come. So I did as the woman asked, for something to do. She was quite insistent too, which impressed me. I crept into Tom's room one night when he was fast asleep and went on and on that he go and fetch you from that school – and it worked. I was quite surprised because I wasn't sure if he'd taken it in, he was snoring and twitching so much in his sleep. It took ages but eventually you turned up – in fact I'd gone off the whole idea by the time you did – but in the end it was rather good because now *you* could run errands for me.'

'Tell me, tell me all about her before you go. I need to know everything. Crispin, I don't know who I am. Or where I'm meant to go or anything.'

'Stop shouting at me. I really don't like it. I'm going to Botswana now anyway so you'll have to sort yourself out from now on.'

Then as a bubble bursts the air was empty. I stumbled against the hollow tree then cried out to be so near the gold tuft of hair and I caught the smell of it too and gagged on that.

'Where have you gone?' I shouted out, but this leaving was complete and final. I could ask, Where? Where? Where? for ever, but all there would be of him was empty air and the stuff in the hollow tree sinking down, down further into the earth inch by inch. It was reaching back, longing to turn once again into the particles of which it was made. The urgency of my search struck me. Once I'd turned back into the infinitesimal rubble myself I could search until eternity and not find anything in that shifting anonymous soup. It would be like searching a desert whose sandy boundaries stretched into infinity.

'Come back,' I cried out. 'You went too soon. I need to know more about what you were telling me.' My cries disturbed the rooks above, dislodging them for a moment before they grumpily reinstated themselves on their branch. That's how much impact it had – a few birds fluttering off a tree. I could scream out for a year and he would not return and talk to me now. I was crying out into emptiness.

54

10 December 1970

Postpartum psychosis, says the doctor. Postpartum psychosis, says the nurse. Postpartum psychosis, says the lady . . .

Anna sits bolt upright in her bed. 'With the alligator purse,' she gasps, still in the depths of a kind of waking half-dream.

It's the verdict that's been delivered to her that morning. The doctor with eyes that drift upwards every time she tries to discuss something he doesn't want to talk about gave it to her. 'Quite uncommon,' he said, almost as if it were something Anna should be proud of and interested in.

The woman in the next bed to her regards her with stone eyes. Anna draws her knees up to her chin. The visions have retreated, chased away by the drugs that make her feel heavy all over, that set her hands trembling at a moment's notice. But there's a sense that they're still there just at the rim of things, gathering and waiting to return. Flashes of them break through, like the stone eyes.

'They found your baby?' asks stone eyes.

Anna hugs herself and nods. Somehow, after she'd run screaming after the doctor, 'My baby, my baby, my baby,' making him whirl round, with monumental force she'd managed to communicate that a baby was lying on the floor alone in a one-roomed flat in Notting Hill – a baby. 'Not a monster,' she'd said, confusing him. Then she allowed herself to give into the dark narcotic swirl of the drugs.

Lewis comes to see her. No flowers this time, she thinks to herself with dark humour. There's nighties and wash things and cardigans all packed up – enough so that it looks like she's going to be here an age.

'Stella is looking after Ruby for now,' says Lewis and a huge tide of relief floods through Anna's bones. He hasn't quite lost the otherworldly quality he took on in the church. Anna keeps blinking to try and make it go away.

She tied her hair back when she knew he was coming but the handbag has disappeared again so she can't put on any lipstick.

'You look pale,' he says.

He hates being here, she can see. It frightens him. 'The nurse had to unlock a door to let me in,' he says, wiping sweat from his brow as if he's going to be trapped in here with her. Trapped twice, once into fatherhood and now here.

'You should go,' she says coldly.

He kisses her tenderly on the forehead before making his escape.

'Look after Ruby,' she calls after him, 'kiss her from me.' But he's already gone, down the corridor that is full of whispers and the fluttering white of nurses' uniforms. Something at the end awaits her – some kind of dark angel that will block her path with heavy wings. The drugs mean there's only its trace left now, its distorted voice moving the stale air of the hospital around. But it could come back, Anna knows that, it could come back at any moment. The drugs come round with breakfast in small plastic dishes, then again with dinner like little coloured aperitifs.

'Let's go for a walk,' says stone eyes. 'We're allowed to walk to the coffee shop if we ask nicely. There's a garden you can look at through the window there. It's right in the centre of the hospital, though, so you can't get out.'

'Right or left?' asks Anna.

Stone eyes sits up in her blue nightie. 'What d'you mean?'

'Out of this door, right or left?' She doesn't want to risk bumping into the dark angel.

'Left. It's not far, just at the end of the corridor.'

'All right then.' Anna puts her feet into the pink slippers Lewis brought in for her. They're new – she didn't have any slippers at home – and a pink ball sits on the toes of each one like a fluffy cherry. They're too big and she slops along next to stone eyes. Anna wonders what's wrong with the woman – she doesn't seem so bad at all – but she doesn't like to ask. Besides, perhaps Anna doesn't look ill herself; it's all inside.

The coffee shop looks out onto a courtyard garden. The walls she can see zoom up so high there is only a square of sky at the top. There are a few blunted trees out there and dead leaves from them swirl up and down as if they're in a vortex.

Stone eyes goes up to the counter and asks the male nurse there for two teas. He serves them in baby blue plastic beakers with no handles.

'What's this?' she demands. 'Why can't we have china? We're not on the ward now.'

'Yes,' he says. 'You are.'

Grumbling under her breath stone eyes takes the teas to Anna who's sitting on the large old-fashioned radiator next to the window. The tea is tepid.

285

'Nothing is ever hot here,' mutters stone eyes. 'It's probably so we can't throw it at anyone.'

Anna wonders if this is true. They sit, propped on the radiator, drinking tea in silence for a while. Stone eyes has a lock of mouse-coloured hair hanging over her face that dips into her tea every time she bobs down for a sip.

Anna feels a terrible urge to unburden herself, to anyone, even to this funny woman with the lank lock of hair dripping with tea.

'I'm not a fit mother,' she says, tears gathering in the back of her eyes. 'I left my baby on the floor on her own. She could have died.' Anna struggles to think how long it must've been for – one night, two?

'Now then,' says stone eyes peering into her tea, 'don't take on.'

'It's true. I don't know if I'll ever be allowed near her again. I want to take care of her properly but every time I think about it I feel so ill. I feel—'

Stone eyes cuts her off, she's muttering under her breath again. She jumps off the radiator and slams the beaker down on the counter and the pale milky tea slops out of the sides.

'Not even a fucking,' she pushes the tea over and it spills across the white Formica, 'china cup.' She storms out of the room and Anna notices that she is barefoot. The soles of her feet flash up black and dirty red as she leaves. The man behind the counter sighs and starts mopping at it with a cloth.

Anna presses her face against the cool window so he can't see her tears. Outside she notices a flat concrete square dead centre of the courtyard standing proud of the gravel. She remembers dimly a story, from who knows where, about a

286

creature that occupies the centre of the earth – a Minotaur. He's under there, she can feel it, ready to crack the concrete and rise up. Only the concrete is too heavy for now, it's trapping him there. In between him here and the dark angel on the other side of the ward there are answers, both beings keep them ready to impart. For some reason they must never meet. The results will be catastrophic. It's only Anna's presence between that's keeping them separate. It takes a huge force of will.

'Postpartum psychosis,' says the nurse.

Anna wheels around. There are two of them there standing side by side like white twins.

'Come on, love,' the one on the left says. 'Let's get you back to bed. Your friend has got herself quite upset.'

Lewis brings Anna home. The hospital agreed she could come home if she has injections they say will help. In a brown paper bag on the back seat of the car is the medication they've given her.

'How are you feeling?' asks Lewis warily.

'Fine.' She knows that Ruby is being looked after by Lewis's father now, not Stella any more. She needs to devise a plan to get her away but her brain feels so clouded it's difficult to think.

'Maybe you should get straight into bed when we get back.'

'All right.' She'll agree with anything.

In bed she lies looking at the ceiling. When she finally turns she sees the letter on Lewis's bedside table. It's tucked between the pages of *Lady Chatterley's Lover* and she wouldn't have known it was even there if the white edge of the envelope wasn't sticking out.

She sits on the edge of the bed, forcing herself to focus every time her eyes threaten to slide down the page. Sometimes the letters spill apart and dance into hieroglyphs. When this happens she patiently stops and waits for them to re-form into English and carries on reading.

Dear Son,

I am very sorry to hear of your recent troubles. I, too, have had my burden of difficulties in this life and this is where fortitude has played its part. The same will go for you. I must say, I was a little surprised when I met Anna. I didn't comment – because the choice of wife is for each man to decide on his own. Your own dear mother was my blessing – and how she cared for you, didn't she, Lewis? I was surprised, because Anna didn't quite seem to add up to being a mother, Lewis. And from our conversation on the phone it seems you've possibly been having thoughts in the same direction. Well, when one reads between the lines. I don't give myself any particularly special powers of cognisance but I did divine something in her to that effect myself quite some time ago. There was a look in her eyes I didn't quite like or trust. I've seen it before and more often than not that person ends up in the care of a doctor. A breakage of the mind is a terrible thing and one, in my experience, that is never really mended.

Which brings me onto further matters and the purpose of this letter. An idea has recently come to mind that may be the solution to your current troubles. The child, Ruby – my grandchild – is in need of a home, and a home is something I'm in a position to offer. It would do me good too, to have the company here. This way, you'll be free to pursue your business interests and can come and visit her whenever you like. The mother, it may be that she'll never be well enough to take up that role again. It would be a blessing for her to know her daughter is in safe hands – it could even speed her recovery.

Do let me know your thoughts on this, son. I am quite taken with the idea and have already been looking at the bedrooms deciding which one she might have and how it could be decorated. Primrose yellow, I think. It's the sort of colour that a little girl would take to.

Yours sincerely,

Your loving Father.

Anna turns the letter over and over in her hand. A cold, cold man, Lewis's father. She remembers the light from the tiepin flickering on Ruby and she shudders at the memory. Hugh Black always wants anything Lewis has, she knows it, but Lewis hasn't been able to admit that to himself. When she thinks of the old man's grasping hands reaching out for her daughter she actually feels sick. Lewis has told her of the life he had, of the punishments, of being locked for nights under the stairs, the face always turning away so it was just an edge floating above like a cold sickle moon. Of his mother being derided if she ever tried to fuss over him. Sometimes he laughs it off and claims it was the making of him. Sometimes he broods on it, trying to square it with the exalted image he has of his father.

Anna knows one thing for sure. If she has anything to do with it at all Ruby will not end up with that horrible old man. She looks at the ceiling and tries to rally her strength.

55

THE HAND
29 December 1983

When I saw Barbara next she'd been moved to the main ward of the hospital. She was sitting up in bed and eating tinned grapefruit with a teaspoon. She smiled and waved as if she'd never delivered her portentous news or been under the knife.

'They've done it,' she beamed. 'I've had my operation. It went really well.'

The woman in the bed next to her was knitting. A red woollen hand was emerging from her needles. On the other side was a young woman who lay still and quiet with her eyes closed and her pale waxwork face turned up to the ceiling. The smell of disinfectant was strong in the air and all the Christmas decorations were gone.

I turned my back on her and sat on the plastic chair next to the bed. 'Trauma,' I said, and the word seemed to burst out of me.

'They said my appendix has been bad for ages. They said it could have blown at any time. I've been asleep almost ever since they did it. I can't believe how much better I'm feeling already.'

'No,' I turned. 'I mean me. I'm the one in trauma.' I was raising my voice now and the woman knitting clicked her tongue at me in time with her needles.

Barbara sighed and set her bowl down on the bedside cabinet.

'Why didn't you ever tell me about my mother?'

'She was not well, Ruby. It was . . . a certain illness. It's not something I like to talk about. It was shaming, I know, that's terrible, but it was.'

I stared at her and she crept a hand across the white candlewick bedspread towards my arm. 'I can tell you now,' she said, almost shyly.

I stayed silent, curiosity and fury fighting a battle inside. Her face was still pale under her curls. 'If you like,' I said finally.

'Come on, draw that curtain a little so we're private and sit next to me on the bed. You're not supposed to but it's quiet at the moment.'

So I unlaced my boots and climbed up to sit next to Barbara. She was so thin and light it was like lying next to a hollow bone. She stroked the hair back off my forehead as she told me her story.

Barbara has to get out of the house or she'll go crazy. Mick is brooding in the kitchen and mourning hangs over the whole household like black cloth. Trudy's death has hit him so hard he can barely stir, hasn't eaten for days. He was a wonderful father to her. She was the apple of his eye.

Outside the wind whips up. It's warm and sunny and the swaying trees hold a promise of spring despite the season. It doesn't seem right somehow. She takes the forest path to the valley where her parents used to live. Walking is the only thing that helps her.

Hollow Cottage looks so abandoned in the sun. The figures

of her parents and Anna, her sister, pop up at doorways and windows like ghosts in Barbara's mind. The empty stone pig-pen has weeds crawling up the walls inside. When they were little the pig had only just gone and the gate was still well-oiled and working. When Barbara was tiny Anna had shut her in there and told her that she had been turned into a pig now, there was nothing she could do about it. She'd howled for ages until her mother rescued her and told her sister off for being so cruel. Barbara half frowns, half smiles – the things you remember. It all goes so deep, deeper than you'd ever imagine. The 'cartoon sisters' people used to call them because Anna and Barbara sounded like Hanna-Barbera – that name that came on at the end of Saturday cartoons. Barbara didn't like it when kids called this out but as usual Anna seemed to drift above everything, too self-assured it seemed to even acknowledge her torturers. That was the way of things between them, it felt. Anna always going that one bit better. Even their daughters' names; Barbara always thought Ruby was a more refined, richer version of the name she'd chosen for her own daughter – Trudy. It'd felt deliber-ate, though of course it probably wasn't.

The smell of wood smoke that always hung about at Hollow Cottage is still there but there's a coldness to it now. Barbara shivers and hurries away back up the path to home.

As she opens the front door the phone in the hallway is ringing. Barbara can see Mick's outline slumped at the kitchen table like he's not moved the whole time she's been out. He's made no attempt to answer the phone. She picks up the receiver.

'Barbara, it's me.'

'Anna.' Funny, she'd been thinking of her sister ever since

she saw that pigpen. 'I've been at the old house today, d'you remember—'

'Listen.'

Barbara feels a prickling of the old annoyance – of course Anna's news would be more important than anything she might say.

'You've got to help me, Barbara.' Anna sounds odd. Calm, but her voice has no familiarity to it. Somewhere deep in Barbara's mind she puts that down to the fact that her sister's in London.

'I can't cope any more.'

'What d'you mean?'

'With being a mother, with Ruby. I just can't do it.'

Barbara sits down on the little spindly chair next to the hallway table and unties the headscarf.

'Anna, what's this all about?'

'I'm a terrible mother, Barbara. Terrible.'

Barbara frowns. Anna's baby is still alive and all she can do is complain.

'Why? What makes you say that?'

'I've been in hospital, Barbara.'

Barbara pinches the bridge of her nose and closes her eyes. 'What are you talking about? Why would you think you're a terrible mother? And what's been wrong with you?'

'I'm out now. Please God don't tell anyone but it was a . . . it was a certain type of hospital.'

'Type?'

'Yes, you know. For the mind.'

'Christ, Anna.'

'Please, please don't tell anyone. I couldn't stand anyone knowing. I wasn't even going to tell you but I need you to do something. For Ruby. Will you? Will you promise?'

'I don't know what I'm promising.'

'Please, just . . .' Anna begins to sound hysterical on the other end.

'All right, all right. I promise.'

'Lewis has given Ruby to his dad to care for her but . . .' Anna's voice becomes choked. 'I don't like that man. I don't trust him. He's creepy, Barbara. He says I'm unfit, I read it in a letter. He's too much of an influence on Lewis, even though Lewis doesn't really like him. He can't help it.' Anna goes silent for a minute. When she finally speaks her voice is tiny. 'It's true. I'm unfit. I'm so ashamed, Barbara. I left Ruby on her own. I can't bear the shame of it. If I only knew that Ruby was away from that man I'd start feeling better.'

'Then talk to your husband . . .'

'No, it's no good. He'll just say it's for the best. He looks at me like I'm a monster these days anyway. You've got to go and get her back. You've got to, promise me, Barbara,' Anna is sobbing down the phone, 'promise me to look after her until I can. If I ever can again. Please.'

Mick doesn't bother asking where she's going as Barbara reties her headscarf in the hall mirror, her mouth set in a determined line, and leaves the house.

The hospital room became silent. I leaned over the bundled figure next to me.

'Barbara?' I had the sudden piercing fear that she'd died in the bed right next to me and I'd never, ever get to hear the whole story. I gave her shoulder a shake.

'Ruby.' Her voice was thick with tiredness. 'Gawd's sake, let me sleep for half an hour. I'm exhausted.'

Relief flooded through me. 'It's all right,' I said, patting her over the blankets. 'You sleep, I'll go and walk around for a bit.'

Outside everything was snared inside the stillness of frost. I crunched over the grass and watched my icy breath shoot out into the air. I thrust my hands in my pockets and a terrible heaviness pooled inside me.

I tried to run over the definitions of 'abandoned' and 'unwanted' but they deserted me. I had to face it. My mother had given me up willingly. She couldn't cope with me either, even when I was a tiny baby. There never were any missing birthday cakes. There was never any missing anything. She'd given me up like a shabby parcel and now she was dead. If only she'd just tried a little bit harder she might've managed. How hard can it have been? I gulped in ice crystals and they trickled into my heart. 'I'm glad you're dead,' I said, hoping her spirit was there to hear me. 'I truly am. You're right – you were a terrible mother.'

Back in the hospital the curtains were drawn around Barbara's bed. I put my eye to the gap. Nurses surrounded Barbara.

'What's happened?'

Barbara's head popped out from behind one of their backs. 'There you are, don't panic. They're just making me comfortable. This is my daughter,' she said to the nurse by her head, 'her name's Ruby.'

'Lovely, we'll leave you two to it then.' They opened the curtains and glided away.

I climbed up on the bed again.

'It's the bloody indignity of it I can't stand,' Barbara was muttering. 'Blanket baths, bed pans . . . take your boots off,

Ruby – you'll get dirt all over the sheets.'

I toed my boots off and settled in beside her like a child getting their bedtime story.

'Now then, she muttered, 'I went to his house.'

Barbara takes the bus to the bungalow Anna's told her about on the other side of the forest.

I interrupted, 'I still can't believe you never told me all this.'

'D'you want to hear the rest?' Her eyes fluttered closed and she sighed deeply. 'You need to let me get on with it.'

I nodded. 'Go on.'

She stands on the crazy-paving path and the ugly gnome out on the grass is forbidding entry.

'Sod off,' she tells him ripely and bustles up to the front door. It'll take more than a plastic gargoyle to put her off rescuing her only niece.

The old man takes a long time to come to the door. He peers round it, not opening it properly, and Barbara sees what Anna means, this man *is* creepy – his skin too white, a little red vein threading through each eye.

Barbara smiles in what she hopes is a firm and slightly threatening manner.

'I've just spoken to Ruby's mother – my sister. She wants me to have care of the child. I can take her right away.'

Hugh Black affects amusement, amazement. 'Well, you can turn back right now. I have it on express authority. I'm to care for Ruby here. I mean, where she can have every advantage.' He reaches out his hand and holds onto the doorknob.

He eyes Barbara's clothes and she feels a small caving in – what kind of life would she be giving Ruby after taking her away from this neat prosperous house? She fixes on his hand holding the door cracked open, the black hairs standing out on the white of his fingers. It's the hand that gives her the courage to carry on; it's horrible. If he'd not put his hand on the doorknob like that where she could see its full horror so clearly she might've given in. She might have just crept away.

'Stealing children is a crime, you know.'

His grip tightens. 'What? What d'you mean? What are people saying?'

'That Anna isn't happy about what you've done. She's going to the law about it—'

'Goodbye,' he says and shuts the door – just like that – in Barbara's face. She stands on the step fuming.

She looks to either side, checking she's alone, and then creeps round the side of the house, putting toes down first so each footstep lands softly on the gravel. A ginger cat sleeping in the sun on top of the garden wall opens one eye and meows at her as if it knows she's intruding.

'Sssh now, moggy,' she whispers, more to steady herself than anything. Her heart is skittering. Each window she passes she peeps into. A thin cry penetrates the air. Barbara lifts her head, cocking her ear and following it with her eyes.

Ruby is alone, crying that thin cry – the kind that doesn't expect to be answered. She lies on the floor on a red cushion with gold tassels at each corner. Barbara tests the sash window with her fingertips. The bottom is already open a crack and it glides upwards smoothly, the mechanism must be well cared for and oiled . . .

*

I sat up. 'You stole me?' I clapped my hands. 'Barbara, you *stole* me.'

'Sssh, now . . .'

The window glides up smoothly; the mechanism must be well cared for and oiled. Barbara heaves her skirts up showing her pink knickers and one leg goes in after the other. Ruby stops crying at the sight of this woman appearing through the hole of the window. Her hands begin waving frantically and Barbara tiptoes towards her. Some glittering crystal bells on the mantelpiece that practically make her fingers itch momentarily distract her. She hesitates, they seem an age away across this room, he could come in at any minute. She lifts Ruby up.

'Hush, girl, hush,' she says.

It's the first time she's held a baby since her little Trudy died. The weight and feel of the child is unexpectedly familiar, piercing her through with longing.

'Everything will be fine now,' she whispers in the child's ear. She cradles Ruby firmly in the crook of her elbow.

Hugh Black is in the kitchen pouring milk that has been brought to boiling point then cooled into a baby's bottle.

He doesn't see the woman in the bright orange blouse with a baby under her arm taking off down the crazy-paved front path like a rocket.

'Maybe I should have left you there,' said Barbara. 'Maybe what you came into with me and Mick was worse. Perhaps you would have been better off without us.'

I took her hand. 'He sounds horrible, Barbara, with his creepy hands.'

'Yes, but what have I ever given you? Look at what you've had to suffer.' Her voice sounded worn out, sleepy.

'I had you, Barbara.'

'That's not much.'

I patted her hand. I wanted to tell her the thrill it gave me, that she'd cared enough to commit that daring act. That the vision of her racing down the path with me in her arms would stay with me for ever. That the very thought that people had once fought over me warmed every molecule of my being, but already Barbara was asleep. I sat up and carefully tucked the blankets round her shoulders. The hospital was heading for its evening routine, trolleys clanking across the floor outside and the smell of food wafting down the corridor. I sat with my head bowed next to the sleeping figure of Barbara. Outside the day was turning black.

I looked down at Barbara. 'Goodnight,' I whispered.

When I got back to our house Sandra was there. There was a smell of beer in the kitchen and she was painting her fingernails bright pink.

'Arggh, Pippi Longstocking,' she said, pointing to my plaits with one glistening fingernail.

'Where's Mick?'

'Getting more beer, he won't be a tick. What's the matter?' We heard the front door opening. 'That'll be him. No ruining things now, we've been having a lovely evening.' She bent her head back down over her nail painting.

Mick came into the kitchen carrying a Golden Wonder crisp box full of bottles of beer.

'Why didn't you tell me about my mum?' I yelled. 'Keeping secrets from me . . .'

Sandra looked up, the nail polish dripping from the brush in her hand.

'For fuck's sake,' he said. The beer bottles crashed as he dropped the box on the table.

Sandra jumped and she recapped her nail varnish. Her fingers looked shaky on the bottle and left pink smudges on the lid.

'Now, Mick,' said Sandra in a high strange voice. 'Remember what a lovely evening we were having.'

'Shut up,' he said. Sandra grabbed the side of the table as if she was about to get up, but stayed, half sitting, half standing.

The florid colour crept across Mick's face. He looked at me as if he wanted to crack my skull with his own. 'Can you never leave things alone?'

'Why should I leave it alone?' My fury felt like an armour. That any blow would bounce. 'I can't believe it – you knew. Both of you, all along. Barbara said she was going to tell me on my birthday and you stopped her.'

'Yes, I did.' Spittle landed on my face. He clenched and unclenched his fists.

'Go on, do something,' I yelled. 'You're dying to.'

There was a frozen moment before he turned and punched the kitchen door. I heard a tight gasp from Sandra. A large shard of glass crashed to the floor leaving a jagged hole in the door, and a long crack snaking to the bottom corner.

I backed round towards Sandra. Her face was white and the skin around her eyes tight. I collapsed on the chair next to her and a well of tears rose through me like a tide bursting.

'I can't believe this,' Sandra said shakily.

Mick was rubbing his knuckles. 'Love . . .'

She ignored him and put her arm round me. 'Sssh now. You've had a terrible shock.'

'I just want something, anything of hers so I can touch it,' I sobbed.

'Of course you do,' said Sandra. 'It's only natural.'

The feel of her turned a longing loose in me so strong it was physical pain. I buried my face into her shoulder and wailed, 'Anything.' The tears seemed to jump out of my eyes. 'A photo. A scarf. An earring. Just to show me she was real. I need to touch it.' My voice rose into a howl. 'I need to know she lived once and she loved me. I can't stand it otherwise.'

In the morning my throat and face were sore from crying. Mick and Sandra had already left the house. Outside my bedroom door was a cardboard box.

56

THE BIRDCAGE VEIL
2 January 1984

For two nights I slept with the box by my bed without opening it.

Sandra left. Off she went back home to her mum and the nice dinners and Tupperware saying she couldn't stand our house any more. Mick and I circled round each other. I stayed in my room as much as possible so we didn't have to cross paths. I put the box on the vacant pillow of the camp bed so I could keep reaching out and touching it through the night. I studied it to see if there were any clues as to what was inside, but it was just a plain brown cardboard box so old the corners were fraying. Without even any writing on it. Sindy and Paul both sat on the sofa in the doll's house with their legs crossed watching to see what I'd do.

Somehow I couldn't bring myself to take the plunge. What if there were actual photos of my mum inside? Would I be getting to see her for the very first time? What if there were love letters between my parents? Perhaps she was a diary keeper. I wanted to know so much I couldn't stand to know.

Night had fallen and I lay looking at the box by the weak light of the stars falling through the window. 'Go on,' I said out loud. 'Open it. Open it. Open it. Just do it now without thinking.'

I switched the light on and sat on the camp bed and opened the flap of the box. I reached in and took out each object one by one and laid them on my bed.

First. A baby's knitted pink jumper and matching trousers. There was a bonnet to go with it too with a satin bow. With a sharp intake of breath I realised I must've worn that once upon a time. I stood and laid it out on my blue bedspread and stepped back to regard the baby-shaped pinkness. I reached in again.

Next, a wedding veil, a delicate object that looked as if it might turn to dust at any moment. I balanced it on the flats of my hands. The material was ripped a little, near the bottom. It was so fragile I could see if I blew it would fly away like some large delicate insect.

'Mum,' I said, as if I was addressing her face and not a scrap of cloth.

I took it downstairs. I needed to see what the mirror would make of it. Carefully, I put it over my head and peered through. If I'd expected to see her, reflected back at me, I was disappointed. The thin net blurred my mark a little and my eyes blinked behind the curtain of it. I snatched it off and the fabric tore. Back upstairs I placed it beside the knitted suit.

Next were two green china cups, a green like bright jade. One of them had broken in half. I slotted the pieces together and placed them next to the veil.

I opened the flap on the other side and I startled as a tiny face stared up at me. I reached in and lifted out the doll. It fitted neatly into the flat of my hand. Her red felt dress looked brown and aged at the hem, as did the collars of her little white blouse. Her black wool hair tumbled over my fingertips and hung straight down. She had the loveliest expression, as if ready to burst into a smile, all expertly done in the brushstrokes of lips and eyebrows. I smiled at her. 'Hello,' I said. I placed her next to the cups.

The box was nearly empty and I felt a sense of panic. This was a mysterious patchwork I'd never be able to piece together. As I emptied the rest of the box disappointment clogged me up. This stuff was just junk. There were baby vests and ancient lipsticks, the gold tubes mottled and the stuff inside turned to hard orange paste.

When I saw the last object the box had to offer up, hope reignited. Perhaps finally I'd found what I'd been seeking. It had rolled into the corner. I was sure it was the scroll that Tom talked about. It existed after all. It was real. It wasn't tied with a red ribbon, as I'd pictured – a thick elastic band held it together. With trembling hands I unrolled it on my bedspread and started reading.

I saw him then, the one framed by the brightness of the snow outside Hilltops. He'd jumped at the sight of me and sworn. I could see it so clearly he flashed into the room right next to me and once again his pupil contracted like he was taking my photo.

There was no thunderstorm that night, but there might as well have been. It happened inside my room. When I read the words inside the scroll it was as if lightning rent the air. And rain ran down the wallpaper.

I pulled on my clothes and ran.

57

SHADOW

Yea, though I walk through the valley of the shadow of death ...
I forget the rest.

For what am I? A shadow walking in shadow. A mere peeling, a lick of darkness. Sometimes I go in search of my substance but not a hair of it exists. I visit the stone where I once carved my initials – JB – and I marvel that they can still be there when my body has dissolved back into the world.

Despite that, us, we, the shadows, we cannot help but haunt you. It's in our nature. I wish I could see my old mum again, you might say. Look in the mirror and you will. Or – thank God she's gone. Too bad, she's carved herself patterns all over you. My own particular contribution to you, Ruby. A birthmark, though mine was low upon my neck and could be easily hidden by a collar or a scarf.

They are all gathering round you now, Ruby. Well, you did go and call. You thought you'd be safer that way. Well, I can tell you it's not working because the things coming for you are nameless. Shadows.

But ... there comes a time when you have to move beyond the shadows. Out of them. Ruby, will you call for me now? My period of remembering is over. I long to be known to you. Call me, Ruby. Call me out of the darkness, the shadows. Let me move into the light. Let me speak with you and tell you everything for now I've remembered every little bit of it.

58

THE BURNING
4 January 1984

When I wake I don't recognise the room. There's no memory of getting there. It's night and moonlight streams through the window. It shines on the white bedcover where my feet make two lumps.

I can smell smoke.

I shift onto my side. Half hidden beneath the bed is Shadow.

'It's you,' I cry. 'Thank goodness. You've got to help me. I don't know where I am.'

Shadow shifts, doesn't answer. I begin to realise I have not said the words out loud.

'What happened?' I whisper. Again, it seems the words have not been said in the usual way, but all the same Shadow lifts his head a fraction, as if he's heard something.

'What's happened? What's happened?'

He sighs. *I'm not sure where to begin.* He shuffles out a little further from underneath the bed. *What do you last remember?*

I look up at the moonlit ceiling and try to think. 'There was a scroll. I unrolled it on the bed.'

Ah, yes. I saw that. I peeped over your shoulder at that point. It was your certificate of birth, I believe.

'What did you see?' My voice seems no more than a stirring of the air.

Squares.

'Squares?'

Yes, the kind of squares with important writing in. The first, your mother's name, Anna, with her address – 'Hollow Cottage'. You read it out loud – I myself have never read words.

'I knew about that already. It was the other square . . .?'

That's the one that led to all the trouble.

'I thought so.'

Well, I suppose I'd better tell you all but don't interrupt too much or I'll forget.

'All right, I'll promise.'

In that square was written the name 'Lewis Black'. His address was 12D Mansion Gardens, Notting Hill, London, WII. At first, you did not quite seem to understand the importance of this. But very quickly, because you can be quick sometimes, Ruby, you remembered.

'Yes, I remembered.'

You did. You thought of the man you'd met at Hilltops who saw you and jumped away like a scalded cat then swore. You remembered how his pupil went small and, at the time, you thought of it as if he were taking a photograph of you.

'But not because he wanted something to keep.'

No. Not that.

'I've just thought. You said there was someone of my blood in that house and you told me they might be bad.' Thinking makes my head hurt. 'So what happened next?'

Something jumped up straight away in your mind.

'Fire.'

Yes, of course fire. I travelled with you on that bus. In your bag was the bottle of paraffin used to destroy the dark book. In your bag also were the matches kept by the cooker in the kitchen. Both of these things.

'I had the means.'

Yes, and you used the means too. When you arrived you stopped at the green man and it nearly made you think of Tom, but the fire was already leaping up too brightly in your mind by now and was much stronger than him. You could almost smell the flames. You could hear the crackle. Lewis Black's vehicle was outside, as you knew it would be as you'd been told this was harvest time.

'I saw him there, didn't I, Lewis Black?' It started to come back to me. How I'd marched right up to him in the greenhouse. 'You're my father,' I'd said. 'You're my fucking father and not a word you said when you realised this.'

'He tried to explain himself, didn't he? Of course he did. How pathetic. How terrible.'

Yes. 'Oh Ruby,' he said. 'Don't think I haven't been in anguish, in agony. Your darling mother and what happened. And you. I didn't deserve you, Ruby. Only trouble I ever caused.' But, I would say this. You did not listen. 'It's too late,' you said, 'it's too late for all that.' You took your bottle of paraffin and sent the liquid out in a spray all over the hothouse and the plants inside. The lit match went after it.

'What happened then, Shadow? What happened? Did I kill him? Am I a murderer really now?'

Ah, but at that point I hotfooted it. Literally, because it was becoming rather warm in there and I have the memory of that if not the skin for burning. I went to the outside

308

where I could see the fire at every window taking hold and lighting up the night. Lewis Black, I saw stumble from the front door. Yes, I can recall that. But there was another one came running. He didn't see Lewis Black stumbling round in the dark and he ran inside . . .

'Who was it?'

You know.

'No. No. Not Tom. Please, not Tom.' I pushed my face in the pillow. 'Tom.'

Yes, that was the name I was trying to think of.

'Have I killed him? Is he dead? Please tell me.'

But on this point Shadow was silent as he often was when he became frightened. He scuttled underneath the bed and wouldn't come back out.

59

CAT TONGUE
5 January 1984

Shadow melts away eventually. The moonlight dims.

I open my eyes to a man leaning over and staring down at my face. 'Ruby,' he says.

He straightens up. 'I'm Dr Brannon. You're in Lydney Hospital.' He smiles. 'Why don't you try sitting up?'

I shuffle up the bed. I want to ask, 'How do you know my name?' I want to ask, 'Is Tom dead?' and, 'How come I'm here?' When I try, all that happens is a grumbling noise in my throat.

He smiles again. He looks young for a doctor and has chestnut-coloured hair that stands up on end. It makes me like him straight away. He could almost pass for a member of Siouxsie's band.

'What's the matter? Cat got your tongue?' He has an Irish accent.

I push the hair off my face and nod and he looks at me again, deeper this time.

'All right. I'm going to examine you now. Nurse, give me a hand.'

I hadn't noticed the woman by the door. Together they go over me inch by inch. Dr Brannon produces a little hammer and tells me to sit on the edge of the bed and taps on both my knees. They laugh when my foot goes kicking up in the air each time. He gets me to hitch up the nightie I've been put in, and runs his fingers down my spine feeling each knob. He listens to my heart with his eyes closed and looks into my mouth.

'Well, there's definitely a tongue there. D'you want to try using it again?'

The growling noise again.

'Never mind, don't force it. Perhaps you'd like to write down your name and address because when you were found wandering last night, you didn't seem to know.'

I wonder about the wisdom of doing this. I think of the police turning up and arresting me. Without warning, hot tears fall down my cheeks. I try to say Tom's name but it just sounds like gears being changed in my throat. In the end I write my name and Barbara's address down on the piece of paper they gave me. I'm too tired to think of what else to do. When I lie back down I fall into a deep tumbling sleep.

Barbara doesn't turn up but other things do. She sends a neatly packed bag that comes in a taxi and a note.

Seems we have swapped places. What are you doing . . .? Never mind. At home convalescing. I'll get there as soon as I can but Mick won't be driving me because he scarpered as soon as he knew I was coming home. Keep your chin up, much love Barbara.

Dr Brannon tells me I should try and walk about, that lying in bed all day will do me no good at all. He tells me he would like to talk to me properly. He'll soon have me chattering away nineteen to the dozen. I put on my dressing gown and slippers and walk down the corridor. It's an old building with window bays to sit in. I sit in one and let the light fall over me. The bottom half of the window has glass that's bubbled, opaque, to preserve the privacy of those inside. I watch the comings and goings through the bubbles. It causes the people walking past outside to move in a strange way, making them do sudden leaps across the window. When a ripple of ginger red passes it takes my fuddled brain a long time to figure out. It sits atop a familiar shade of green, not quite apple, nor sage but between the two. An hour later I'm still there and it passes the other way like a flaming torch being carried. By then I've realised what it was. It's Elizabeth coming to inform on me.

This is it, I realise. I really am a murderer now. Elizabeth must be telling Dr Brannon everything.

60

THE OTHERS
7 January 1984

Dr Brannon wants to see me this morning. I'm going to ask him if he's heard anything about Hilltops. I've decided. I need to know what's happened to Tom more than I need to save my own skin. Well, when I say 'ask' I mean 'write' because my voice is still nowhere to be found. And anyway Elizabeth has probably told him everything already. Unless, it's just possible she hasn't, that she's trying to save me. Not that I want to be saved, if it's true that Tom is dead by my own hand. I always knew I was destined to be a murderer.

Maybe, the thought gives me hope, she was here to see me. Yes, yes, she came to see me and was turned away and her and Tom are fine and waiting for me somewhere.

I've been scribbling in the notebook Dr Brannon's given me all evening and morning. I can't face writing about the fire and Tom just yet. Every time I think of it I panic and shy away. Instead, I'm trying to lead up to it gently by writing about bits of my life. Weirdly, I seem to be writing about Melissa and Nicola a lot. Bitching about them or sounding so wistful I sicken even myself. Now I'm rereading it I'm wishing I hadn't started it at all because something completely unexpected has happened. The page I'm reading begins normally enough:

At school that day Melissa and Nicola let me sit with them at lunchtime. We talked about make-up and stuff and I thought it'd gone really well, but afterwards . . .

Then the breaking through happens, even the writing looks different.

And the gold knitted top that'll go beautifully with the black tapered trousers and the patent court shoes. Trust him to spoil it, though. I had it all laid out on the bed with the patent clutch and he comes bowling in. You, you, running up tick all over the place and the next week it'll be in the jumble then all the neighbours walking about in clothes that we're still paying for on credit. Oh but you know, I wanted to say, I'm a sucker for anything with Paris in the label. Well, if you come from a place like this you need a bit of sparkle, a little bit of glamour. Just so you can go to the club in something nice of a Saturday night and have a gin. Not much to ask but when you come home there's Ted with his head in his hands going: 'Rita, Rita, it's got to stop . . .'

I carry on flicking through until the change in writing catches my eye, thin and spidery, almost as if the person didn't have the strength to press the pen to the paper.

One year and five days since I came here . . .

And another one in bold ink.

Today on my walk I passed the fallen tree that has become quite rotten. I stayed for hours, watching. It's as if the tree

has become the environs of a city so much life is held within.
I made many drawings and notes in my new notebook.
When I got home father laughed and said perhaps I would
be a naturalist when I grow to be a man. Mother just
pulled a horrid face and told me to stay away from it. She
said there was all manner of diseases to be caught from
such things. I shan't take any notice of her of course.

I sit back on the bed. Even here the others have been
leaping in and taking over. That's it; I've decided I'm going
to tell Dr Brannon everything. I need to unburden myself. I
need to unburden my soul.

I slop along the corridor in my slippers. He's told me where
his office is – right at the end of the hospital. It's dark and
gloomy down in this bit, endless corridors with doors off
them. Finally I find the door with his name on and then a
load of letters after it. I knock but there's no answer so I just
wait around. It feels pretty weird waiting in my slippers and
dressing gown, a condemned person, contemplating things
like murder and arson while wearing pyjamas with love
hearts on them. Then he comes rushing down the corridor
in his white coat, his stethoscope flying and papers under
his arms.

'Sorry, sorry,' he says, 'got caught up. I'll just put these
away, I won't be a jiff.'

When he finally calls out he's ready and I go inside he's
got rid of most of the papers, they've joined the rest shoved
haphazardly in files. He's sitting behind a big wooden desk
and he's taken off his white coat and his stethoscope and
dumped them in an open drawer of the desk. At the window

an old lady looks in. I know she's passed. I can tell it's his mother because she smiles across at him as if he's the brightest gift she's ever seen.

I tighten the dressing-gown belt around me.

'Sit down, Ruby. Let's try to get to the bottom of this now.' He lines up paper and pen in front of me. 'Now, you tell me what you think the trouble is.'

I stare at the blank paper. It's hard to know where to start. In the end I pick up the pen and write, *I think I might have killed my mother.*

When he turns the paper around and reads it his chestnut-coloured eyebrows shoot right up.

'Ruby, I read in your notes that you were adopted when you were only a few months old. Why on earth would you think you killed her?'

Of course the tears start welling up then and I drag them off my face with my towelling sleeve. *I just do,* I write. *Ever since I was little I've thought I've killed someone, I just get mixed up who it might be.* And then because his 'Oh, Ruby' is so soft and gentle, I can't help it, I take the notebook out of my pocket and show him what I'd found this morning. I've never had more of an urge to unburden myself.

'What do you think this is?' he asks.

The passed, I write. *They won't leave me alone. I can't stand it any more.*

He pauses, licks his lips a little, trying to figure out what to say next.

'And who are they?'

It's an interesting question. Not one I've ever properly addressed. I think for a minute and then shrug to show him I'm not sure.

316

'Ruby,' he says, his eyes still on the note, 'I'm going to arrange for you to stay here for a few days. Just for a rest and so I can keep an eye on you. Physically you are fit and well but we can't let you go out into the world without a voice now, can we?' He smiles at me and it's such a lovely kind smile it makes me want to weep even more. The lady at the window points at him, looking at me, as if to say 'see, see, what a marvel he is. What a fine young man he's turned out.' She's practically bursting with pride.

'I'll see you again tomorrow,' he says. 'Same time.'

I trudge back to my room knowing I have put off once again asking about Tom because a part of me never wants to know what's happened in case the news is bad. When I go back Shadow is waiting for me there.

61

MUD MOUTH
7 January 1984

Because Shadow has always been there, in a way, he hasn't given me cause for wonder. He is part of me like my hand or foot. Sometimes he frightened me, I know, but even then I knew I would be unable to separate from him.

Dr Brannon has got me thinking, though. And seeing Shadow waiting, at the foot of the bed, it's almost like seeing him for the first time.

'Shadow,' I say, finding again I can just about whisper hoarsely to him. 'Shadow, who are you?'

I thought you'd never ask.

He sounds a little hurt like he often can. 'Well, I'm sorry.' I sit down on the bed with a thump. 'You could tell me now?'

Perhaps.

'I'd like you to, I really would.' I decide to try a little flattery. 'You've been alongside me always, Shadow. You've been my most faithful friend.' I realise this is not flattery, it's actually true.

Only if you will truly listen. I need to make sure that you won't become bored or wander off because I can only tell you this once. If you do not listen now then my story will be lost for ever.

'I promise, I'll listen.'

Then it's Alice's rabbit hole again – but the sides, when my fingertips catch at them, are dry and dusty. The air is full of dust too so it's difficult to breath. I flail my arms but the fall is a slithering relentless one. Even when I stop falling, I'm not sure if I've come to the bottom. There's a high voice there, among the dust, fluting in my ear.

My name is Joshua. Joshua Black, lie still.

The fight leaves my body. I listen.

Ruby, these things have only just been remembered by myself. I have spent these times past recalling them although it's very hard to know how long it took because we really have no idea of things like that. I have waited to tell you and this has not been related to any human alive or dead for you were always chopping them off or telling me to go away. When that happened I'd creep away for a while – remember? I'd weep for minutes or months, then I'd creep back and sit and spy on you, peeping out from tall grasses or from behind outhouses. You looked so bright, the way you flashed about, playing – your long hair like the wind behind you, the pretty colour on your face.

I coveted.

Often. I wished to wear your little suit of skin and bone so once more I could feel the wind on my cheek. But no more. I have remembered all now. Once I saw the whole of my life whilst on this earth, I saw it was an egg that I'd never get back inside.

Ruby. My name is Joshua Black. I am the only son of Patrick Black. We are both ancestors of yours but from a long, long time back. No one alive remembers us at all. No one knows we even existed. There was a daughter, later, long after I was gone but I don't know her very well. Patrick

Black was an agitator, a man of large hands and black moustaches. Together we worked in deep pits. You'll never know how dark it is in the middle of the earth, Ruby, or how hot. Candlelight flickered in the hallways of coal there and when they made me squeeze through narrow gaps I never knew if I'd be able to get out again.

But an agitator he was and always running things on the side – selling things he got from who knew where – meat mainly. When he was receiving a dressing down from the foreman for his slipshod manners Patrick coughed right in the man's face, his gusty breath blasting up his nose, and we received our marching orders.

'I've heard of opportunities,' said old Black, 'in a forest not so far from here. Men are able to mine their own seams – if they can discover one. They can keep them for themselves. They have names that are delightful: New Fancy, Gain All, Gentlemen Colliers, Pluck Penny. If I should discover one I'd name it Mary after your mother.'

So we started our long walk. At first it seemed like we'd walked out of hell and straight into paradise. The black slag heaps receded. The clouds of dust and steam and dirt in the air began to part like curtains. We came across sights I never knew possible: a clear stream tinkling over stones where fish leapt into the air, country lanes hedged with cow parsley humming with bees and where everything seemed to shimmer. I've always loved bright things.

When we reached Monmouth I wanted to linger because I'd never seen buildings like it but Patrick soon hurried me over the little bridge that led to the forest and everything went dark.

Try as he might Patrick could not discover a seam of his

own – New Fancy, Pluck Penny, Mary. Our shoes became broken down. I could feel the forest floor on the ball of my foot. Already, I was beginning to know you. At times of hunger there was a sphere of red light among the trees and I knew its name to be Ruby.

One day we were arrested for vagrancy and taken to a stone place that was a jail called Littledean. The warder had moustaches that were so black they frightened me, even blacker than Patrick's. At night it was colder than it had ever been outside. The moon poured over me on the stone bench that I slept on and I felt then, how it was the reverse of the sun, its cold face. I thought I would be killed by its light that night.

We survived long enough to be let out and Patrick told them we would make our way to Liverpool where he had a sister, which turns out was a lie. There was another lie too, the lie when he said 'we'.

'We'll part ways here,' he said at the edge of the forest and I saw in his eyes that his brain had become dead to me.

'Don't leave me,' I pleaded. 'Let me come with you. I will sleep under your bed and eat only what's left on your plate. Your sister won't even know I am there.'

He told me then it was not his sister he was visiting but a woman who used to have feelings for him that he hoped to reignite because she had a snug little house there. I knew at that point all hope was lost – a motherless son would not be a welcome addition if he hoped to smarten himself up and go courting – though it did not stop me from following him along the winding road that led down the hill. Ahead the River Severn shone like a great gleaming snake that was twisted in on itself. From time to time my father would turn and see me still there and make a batting movement with his hand, like he was trying to shoo away a horsefly. His large back in its black coat, which always seemed like a square, began to be farther and farther away in the distance. I could not keep up. When his back was just a tiny little black square I could see I was never going to catch him up, he was so determined to get rid of me, and I sunk down on the roadside amongst the grasses and the nettles.

Truly, I was alone. My worst fear was that the warder with the black moustaches would catch me again and I'd be put in that stone cell to be killed with moonlight. So I kept to margins – of the forest, of fields, of scrubland. I caught rabbits by staying so still that they came close, nibbling on the grass. I'd jump out and grab them round the necks, though often they were too fast for me and I would land flat on my front. If I did catch one I'd skin it and roast it on a fire made with rubbing two sticks together. I left the hares, though, because as you well know killing a hare brings bad luck. I also stole potatoes from fields. But winter was arriving. I woke up one morning and my clothes and hair were white and crackling with frost. Everything was too cold and damp to make fire. I became slow and stumbling – even to catch a rabbit. My hunger was like an insanity. The river flashed at me cold and bright and I had the idea I could catch a fish.

When I arrived by the shoreline I was amazed at how wide the river was, as wide as a great grand road. I saw the impossibility of catching fish there. They were all contained in the great moving mass and I didn't have a hook or even a piece of string to try and get one out with. I realised that thinking that I could meant I was somehow not in my right *mind. The mud on the side was soft and oozed into the holes in my boots. I felt strange, as if the world was turning very slow and that I could feel its turning and that I might drop off it at any moment.*

I lay down to stop the feeling and the mud rose up around my sides to greet me. I turned my head. The mud looked thick and glistening. I imagined it filling my stomach and the thought made me want to eat it. All I could think was how it would feel to have my stomach full again. So I turned my head and sucked. I'm eating the stuff the world is made of, I thought.

Later, when I could see my dead body I became frightened. I roamed around my body trying to gain access to it again. I crouched by it, mourning myself. Then I was above it. It swelled like a great grey pod and every day the tide gently tugged at it. Water washed over it but as the tide receded there it still was, stuck in its bed of mud. As it swelled I felt glad for some time because it looked like there was once again flesh on my bones. But then I grew afraid of it and it seemed once you are afraid of the arms and legs and head that once carried you around then all is lost.

One day the tide grew to a big brown swell and tickled it out of its resting place. The waters shrunk and it was gone. I forgot about it for a long time. You were ahead by then, far away, like my father had been when he left me. Unlike him, though, you were shining bright. I walked for many years trying to catch up with you. The place I walked through was grey and the walls disappeared when I touched them. There were corners too so sometimes I would lose sight of you entirely and I would lose all hope. Sometimes I would turn a corner and there you'd be again, gleaming, and such joy would flood through me I felt the need to sing. You were elusive, sometimes far away and sometimes almost near enough for me to reach out and touch you.

Then, one day, you were there right in front of me. You were lying on the floor and your eyes were misting over. The window was open even though the night was chilly, and the sounds of the street came through it. Soon you would be outside yourself as I once was. I took a chain from my pocket and fixed it onto both our wrists so I would not lose you again. I crouched by and waited.

62

COIN
8 January 1984

By the time Shadow has finished his story it's nearly morning. It's so early the breakfast trollies haven't even been around yet. Shadow retreats and becomes part of the corner. I take my clothes out of the locker and they stink of paraffin and smoke – I've decided to smuggle them into the loo and get changed. I've run away before. I can do it again.

I no longer care what I do.

The pillow trick didn't work last time but maybe this time it will. I bunch it under the thin hospital sheets and hug the bundle of clothes to my chest to hide them, but I shouldn't have bothered. Nobody notices me. It's like I've been painted all over with invisibility paint.

I peer through the glass at the woman in the room next to me; she has hair the colour of wet sand, and the rest of her is the colour of dry sand. I get the idea that if there was a wind in this hospital ward she'd blow away particle by particle until there's nothing left. I see her when I pass and every time she's looking out of the window like she's wondering if spring will ever come.

Beyond the big arched stone doorway there's an early morning mist outside. It floats above the grass that's stiff with frost.

Outside it looks like everything will be dead for ever. The

hedges are bare and black and the sky looks like a thin grey skin. My boots shuffling over the grass leave two long lines through the frost like I've been skiing. Mud and rot and wetness everywhere. It'll never recover. Spring will never come, that's what it feels like.

I stand in the front garden trying to make a plan but when I do all I see is a row of rabbit holes ahead of me and I wonder which one I'm going to fall into next. There's no one to catch me now; I'll be going down them head first. I'm still on alert for the police to come for me, for murder, or arson. Or possibly both. Perhaps I should just run for it before they do.

The grounds are big so I carry on walking trying to think how to run away with no money and just the clothes I stand up in. I'm biting at my lip and kick at some fungus that's sprouted up through the grass and the white pieces of it shoot out across the lawn in a spray.

I turn the corner. That's when I see you, Tom. You're in the distance. It's quiet here, a square quiet garden with high green hedges all around it. We are the only ones in it.

I know you're dead. I know because the afterlife has put a mark on your face like mine. It stands out bright through the mist. The afterlife has also turned your hair a white gold again and it shines out like a coin. The afterlife has not stopped you gleaming. You gleam brighter than ever. You have your back to me but are half turned. You don't see me. I wonder what it is you do see. Clouds. God. A shifting vortex whirling around you. You stumble a little, then with a sideways movement you disappear in a gap in the hedge right opposite.

I slowly sink to my knees. The cold of the wet mud strikes through my jeans.

326

'Love,' I cry out. 'Love.'

Seeing you has given me my voice back and I use it. I scream into the void with my eyes closed and my fingers digging into the ground.

Into that, a pounding of the earth, a whoosh and I lift up into the air.

I open my eyes. You are there. You are real. You are not dead. I'm in your arms looking up at you. The life, it shines out of you like a lamp.

'What's that on your face?' I ask. 'Oh my God. Is it . . . is it a burn?'

63

CHAPEL
9 January 1984

When I see Dr Brannon again I surprise him by opening my mouth and saying, 'Hello.'

'How lovely to meet you properly,' he says, smiling like he really means it. He's putting all his papers away and flinging his white coat on the armchair in the corner. Things fall out of the pockets as he does.

'Now then, it would be lovely to hear what you think has given you your voice back,' he says as he sits down.

I think back to yesterday. It'd started raining, icy sheets across the grass. Me and Tom walked back into the hospital and I realised he was wearing his coat over stripy pyjamas. He had his big boots on, unlaced so the tongues were flapping about, instead of slippers.

I smiled at the doctor. 'Maybe I'm seeing light at the top of the hole.'

'You mean at the end of the tunnel?'

'I suppose so.'

'Listen, Ruby. I've been thinking about you, your condition. What you showed me in your pages.'

'Oh yes?' I'm instantly alert. He's got the same look in his eyes that doctors always get when they spy my mark, like they're just itching to get their fingers on it and do something.

'I've also been doing a bit of reading. I may be a general hospital doctor but I've always retained an interest in the mind. Tell me, Ruby, do you ever feel your limbs have gone numb? Gone to sleep.'

I think about it for a minute. 'Not that I recall.'

But he's up and taking a book from the shelves and flicking through it. 'I've come across this thing called Cotard's syndrome.'

'Oh yes?' My wariness has just increased about tenfold.

He sits back down in front of the open book and puts his palms together and props his chin up with his fingers. 'It's fascinating. It's where the subject believes themselves to be dead. It's often after some kind of trauma or shock. Sometimes they have limbs that feel numb and useless . . .'

'I've never felt that.'

'Oh.' He looks disappointed but all the same I resist the temptation to tell him, yes, I often think I'm dead, it happens frequently, just to make him happy. I think doing that may lead to trouble.

'What about your notebook? The things you showed me?'

That was them that's dead, I want to shout at him, I told you that. Instead, I suck in a deep breath and take the easy way out. 'They were just stories.'

'Stories?'

'Yes, stories. I made it up. My adopted mother has always told me I was very imaginative.'

'Oh.'

'Sorry.'

'Yes, well.' He's a bit embarrassed now, I can tell. He knows he got carried away. He starts tidying things on his desk, only it's a lot less like tidying and more like relentlessly moving them about for no purpose.

'I'm probably deluded, sorry.'

He looks up sharply. 'That's a very grown-up word.'

'Yes, I've always liked words.'

He relaxes back a little and smiles. 'Never mind. You look so much better today, a different person almost.'

Yesterday, as me and Tom sheltered from the rain in the hospital doorway, a feeling shivered over me and it hasn't stopped since. We needed somewhere to go, somewhere private. He spotted the hospital chapel and that was perfect. Who prays at seven thirty in the morning? It didn't smell of hospital inside, it smelled of wax and coolness. There was a modern stained-glass window set high up and it shone its red light over everything.

'It's my fault, your burn,' I cried out.

'Well . . .'

'It is. I hate myself.'

'Don't hate yourself. D'you want to know how I survived? Lewis Black came in and dragged me out. This is the first morning I've been up. Smoke inhalation.'

'Oh my God.' I covered my eyes. 'How are you feeling?'

'Better today. It's all right about the burn. It's not so bad, the doctors have said. It'll hardly show. Where did you go?'

'I'm not sure. Here, I think. It's very fuzzy after the fire. Tom, I'm so sorry. Elizabeth, she must've been so worried. I guess she hates me now.'

'She came to look at you but you were sleeping and she crept away again. I don't think Elizabeth could really hate anyone. She came back in and brought stuff to bleach my hair again. I didn't really want it done but I think it made her feel better, feeling she was doing something for me. The nurse went mental when she saw what we were doing.'

I smiled. 'It makes you look so bright,' I said.

And he put his forehead to mine and said again how we were the same and always would be. That in this chapel we were having a sort of marriage that would last for ever, a pledge. Then we were both quiet for a long time.

I've zoned out of what Dr Brannon is saying. 'Pardon?' I ask.

'I said, I have a theory.'

'Oh yes? About what?'

'About ghosts.'

'Yes?'

'Well, when you think about it, it's about the generations.' He's getting excited again. 'I mean, I don't know who my great-grandfather was, or my great-great-grandfather, same with my female ancestors, but when you think about it they are all still exerting their influence.'

I frown. 'How do you mean?'

'By the way they were, the way my great-grandfather was with his son forged him and that in turn forged my father and then me in turn. So, all these ancestors are still working away, flexing their power. Even though mostly we haven't a clue who they were. There's no spectres, or apparitions.' He smiles at me again, pleased with his theory. 'The real ghosts are just family.'

'I see what you mean, I suppose.' His mum has appeared at the window again and is pointing and smiling. He's half there with his idea, I guess. His mother is practically bursting with love for him, still exerting her influence.

He shakes his head and focuses back on me and I can see he thinks he's been talking over my head and getting carried away. He sees a child again in front of him.

'Now then, you might be getting a visitor. Your adopted father has called asking when would be convenient to come. What's wrong?'

I'm bowing my head in despair.

He reaches over and takes my hand, which I'm not sure doctors are supposed to do, but I'm grateful anyway. 'You don't have to see anyone you don't want, Ruby,' he says softly.

64

CHRISTMAS ROSE
11 January 1984

Mick's come to see me.

He sits on a bench in the grounds bent over and looking at his shoes. I can see something colourful in his hand. I stand a hundred yards away from him. 'I don't have to see you if I don't want,' I shout.

He squints up out of the corner of his eyes, like it's a sunny day, and says, 'I know.'

I stand for a while, trailing my toe in the dirt on the path, before I go and sit next to him.

The colourful things in his hand are flowers: pink, white and red, tiny rose bushes planted in one pot. 'Christmas roses,' he says and hands them over.

'Thanks?'

'That's OK.' He obviously hadn't noticed the sarcasm in my voice, but all the same I can't resist lifting them to my face and breathing in their smell. It's not sweet but cold and clean.

'Not sweet peas,' he says. 'I can't even look at them these days. I've been doing a lot of thinking lately. I think I've been going a little crazy. Sandra's helping me, though. Sandra's changed things for me.'

'I'm not afraid of you any more.'

'I think perhaps it was the wrong thing to do. Thinking

we could look after you as our own. I'm sorry,' he mumbles.

'That's not much of an apology. You're a grown man. You work out with dumbbells.'

He twists his head away as if he doesn't want to hear it. 'Listen,' he shoves his hands into the pockets of his leather jacket and adjusts his hunch, 'me and Sandra, we're moving on. We're getting a flat in Bristol. If you like you could come with us. Sandra said she'd love to have a little friend around and it would be great to practise all her hairstyles on you. She's not a one to bear grudges.'

I shudder at the thought of being Sandra's plastic manne-quin head. 'I don't know. I can't think about it now.' I pause. 'I quite fancy a children's home again actually.'

'What, not with family at all?'

'Family has been one long disappointment.' As I say it I realise it's mostly true – a year ago I would have sold my soul to go and live with my real father. My bones ached for it. Now, the children's home idea really appeals to me. I called for my real parents and they came. How they came. Now I'm wishing I'd never bothered. There were never any birthday cakes – pink or covered with candles and fruit. They were both just as bad as everyone else. You have to be careful who you call for. I called for my dad and he came, Black came like the night. He didn't even want to let on he'd recognised me. That's how much I've meant to him – his only daughter.

'Just keep your head down and you'll be all right. It's something you need to learn, Ruby, keeping your head down. It's a lesson that comes to us all sooner or later.' Mick gets up and I can see he's relieved I haven't jumped at going to live with him and Sandra. I can't even be bothered to tell

334

him it's obvious she's never going to stay with him in the long run. He's just her way of getting out of the forest.

Mick glances over and nods. He's becoming cold and bored now, I can see. He wants to go home so him and Sandra can carry on with their plans, sweeping the past away.

'Oh, Barbara says to tell you she'll take you to her grave.'

'Whose?'

'Your mum's.'

'You mean my mother is buried here, in the forest?'

I'm shouting again, clutching the pot of Christmas roses to my chest. First her things in the box, now this. All the time she was lying close by.

'Calm down. She said she'll come and get you the same time tomorrow if you like.'

'Tell her to bring the doll in,' I say suddenly. 'When she comes, tell her to bring that doll that Anna had in her stuff.'

'Why?'

'I don't know. I just feel I want to look at it again.'

'I suppose. I have to go round there to pick the last of my things up this afternoon. I'll tell her then.'

I see Mick startling and then staring at me. I look down and realise he's just glimpsed his collar tips hanging round my neck.

As he walks off I call after him, 'What was my mother like?' but he doesn't hear, just carries on his wide-legged walk across the wet grass.

I sit for a long time holding the Christmas roses. A small grey shape appears by the flowerbeds. Bowed stunted legs propel a tiny figure across the grass, diagonal to the tracks that Mick has made in the wet.

Shadow climbs up next to me on the bench and I put the pot of flowers next to him. He sits looking at it as if it's the most wondrous sight he's ever witnessed. The flowers are so bright they look like colour film superimposed on the black and white of him.

65

FIRE
12 January 1984

I called for my mum and dad and it seems their ripples are
still arriving at my feet. My father, Lewis Black, his arrives
by letter. It comes in a crisp bulging white envelope. When
I open it a small black box falls out onto the white hospital
bedspread. I read the letter first.

Dear Ruby,

*How strange it is to be writing to you now, after all
these years. I thought I needed to. I have the notion that if
I don't communicate with you to tell you to do otherwise
you will carry on looking for me for the rest of your life.
I want to explain how this will be a fruitless search. How
strange that we met without you actually knowing that I
was your dad, and that our brief time together ended in
fire. I would like to tell you that I always meant to get
you back over the years but both of us know that would
be bullshit. If nothing else in my life I've gradually tried
to attain a kind of honesty. You might find that hard to
believe given everything that's happened but I don't guess
at what other people think or don't think any more – they
will decide what they want and it's no business of mine.*

*The most I can say is that perhaps I had some dim idea
that once my life was successful, on the up, I would come*

and find you. In truth, I never even neared that point, there was always striving, things going from bad to worse and little rays of light shining through now and then, businesses and failure and failure and failure, then a small success that would keep me going that little bit longer. Maybe I should have tried for steadiness, for a job – any job – that would keep me on an even keel, but I'm simply not the type and people would look at me and know that. They know it in one glance.

Ruby, I will be away for good now. Arson is a serious offence and one that the authorities will not let me go for lightly. I think you understand what I mean when I say this. I've done so little for you but this is one thing I can do – allow me. I'm telling you all this to make it clear, Ruby, to save you. You will not see me again. This thing I can do for you is purposeful and real, not some chocolate-box declaration, I hope you feel that – I do. Understand me and act accordingly.

What I want you to know, Ruby, is that at the time of your birth your mother was hardly eighteen and I was nineteen. An excuse? Perhaps. I truly at that time thought you'd have a better life with her family. And the truth is, after she died I found it hard to look at you without my heart feeling it was going to burst with guilt and shame. Both of us so young and unprepared, but I wish you could have seen your mum as I did, sitting up in the maternity ward with you in her arms and looking so proud and defiant. It made me love her over again, seeing her like that. I'd only come to see her out of duty – to tell her I'd try and help financially as best I could but then I fell in love again and everything else that happened, happened. Your mother tried – but she became ill. Don't judge her harshly for becoming ill. I should have stayed with her instead of making off for some promise of money on our wedding day. I knew that really, even then. She tried her best but I didn't really try so much, I can say that now. We were a young joke really. Don't let the laugh be on you.

I can't get away from the feeling that we were at the bottom of a spiral then. The spiral was already built and we had no choice but be pushed around and around the form of it. She died alone; no one even knew what she was doing back in the forest when she crashed that car, or what her intentions were. She was not in her right state of mind, Ruby. Know that.

Recent events at Hilltops House began in this distant time, the harvest that you know of was meant to cover promises made years ago. These promises were about to come to fruition, and reparations due to a group of men who helped me out by staying silent were coming up shortly. The fire put paid to that. The fact that they were not fulfilled is another reason I must not return.

I also want you to know not to overestimate what family is. My own father disliked me. I didn't realise at the time, not fully. There was only a prickling discomfort deep within me whenever we were together. I knew and didn't know. It was only years later I fully realised and the knowledge came to me one night walking along a dark road on the way home. All those years later the knowledge made me sink to my knees right there and then on the road – that was the power of it.

I tell you this so you have the chance of following another path and don't spend your life jerking like a puppet on a string by the hands that made you, without even realising you are being moved about in such a way. Be your own person, Ruby. Make your way, girl. Throw off our shackles – because that's what they are – and soar free.

I send you what I have left of your mother, my darling Anna, my forest girl. It's our wedding ring. I'm not sure quite what I mean by this gesture but I thought you might like to have it.

I would sign this letter off by something like, 'your ever loving father' but that would only be a bitter joke to you, I'm sure. Instead I'll say,
Be brave,
Lewis Black.

I open the black box; its velvet is worn down to the skin in places. The ring gleams in its black velvet nest and I go to find Tom, to show him.

66

THE DOLL FUNERAL
15 January 1984

Dr Brannon says there's nothing to keep me at the hospital any more. He's discharging me tomorrow. I think the staff have got fed up with us. Tom's in my room nearly all day because he's on the male ward and there's no privacy there. We go for long walks and trail mud back into the hospital. We spread magazines and sweets and newspapers across the bed and munch on toffees. The smell of disinfectant is getting up my nose now anyway. Tom has to stay in a little longer – at least until the dressings on his chest are removed. I still haven't seen Elizabeth. I pretend to be asleep when I know she's coming. I can't face her yet. Not with what I did.

Barbara arrives in a car to take me to the cemetery. I've never seen her driving before.

'Well, I'm going to have to get used to doing things on my own,' she says. 'What do you think of the Mini? I bought it for a hundred and fifty quid.' She loves it, I can tell.

There's lilies on the back seat and they perfume the whole car. I'm surprised at the tastefulness of these, the coolness and elegance of them – Barbara has always loved showy bright things – but then I remember they're funeral flowers.

We drive out; the cemetery itself is overflow from the little graveyard belonging to the stone church next to it. The graves in the churchyard are all ancient and they get newer and newer as they flow into the cemetery. It's like an encroaching tide that reaches halfway across the field now. The church and the cemetery are at the heart of the forest and a ring of trees surrounds everything.

The day is soft, cool, wet. The trees circle us in a dark guard. They're nowhere near pushing out their spring greenness yet. The smell of wood smoke is in the air from some distant chimney. That smell can travel for miles.

'Show me,' I say, but the moment I say it I don't want to see. 'No. Let's go.'

'We've come all this way now. You may as well see.'

I'm covering my hands with my eyes. 'No, no. I don't want to any more.' It feels too much like this is the end.

'Come on. It's time you did. We should've brought you here when you were little. Let you put bunches of snowdrops or primroses on it. Let you talk to her. We did it all wrong.'

'It doesn't matter,' I said. 'OK, I'll look from a way away then. Just for a moment.' I feel for the doll inside my pocket.

Barbara points out the grave. My mum is three rows back. She's with all the others from the nineteen seventies.

'I'll wait in the car,' she says, after laying the flowers at the foot of the grave, even now putting distance between her and her sister.

The grave looks like a bed from this far off. Like my mother might just be having a good sleep there and she'll rise up out of it in her buttercup dress, stretching her arms and yawning. It's grey, and the top of the headstone ends in a point.

I feel for the doll in my pocket and I think of a funeral on a miniature scale. Imagine it, a doll's funeral, laying her in a little box made of plywood, fastened by a miniature gilt latch and furnished inside with a scrap of pale blue satin. She'd only need a tiny plot. One shovelful of earth would cover her. At the wake plastic tears would fall and a tray of little plaster currant buns would be passed around.

I shake the vision from my head.

The air goes soft.

'Mum,' I call across, half expecting her to walk towards me, her feet bare on the grass and her buttercup dress shining out in the grey day.

Nothing. Just the sound of nature around me – rustling, cheeping, carrying on as ever. I try not to think of her body down there with nature doing what it does.

Time parts like a pair of stage curtains. I see it all.

It's a misty day, proper funeral weather. The grave is black, wide open. Look, there's Mick. He's wearing a cheap black suit and a tie so wide it almost fills the gap between his lapels. Barbara's face is pale and her lips move – could it be, could she possibly be praying? Trudy's death is still raw upon them; this is all bringing it back.

Where's Lewis Black? I scan the people grouped round the grave. He's not there. Typical.

The service hasn't started yet. People are milling, stamping their feet, wiping their eyes. I walk among them, threading through, until I'm by the graveside. The coffin rests on the freshly dug earth. The pale wood is thickly varnished so it shines; it looks new and trashy against the crumbled earth. A yellow rose stem lies across the etched metal plate screwed to the lid. The colour is so bright it's like a small sun about to be swallowed inside the earth.

It's then I notice a figure at the rim of the trees. Lewis,

343

my father, young and handsome. I recognise the bulk of his shoulders straight away. He's smoking a cigarette and the smoke reaches up above him and joins the mist. Even from this distance I can see a deadness settling round his head. He's trying to decide whether to come out or watch from there among the trees. The look on his face is so broken and terrible my heart does a little crack and the contents flow out towards him. Daddy, Daddy, Daddy, I cry, but of course he can't hear me. Didn't I really know all the time – from the very first time of seeing him – that he was my father? When he'd leaned over to look at me I saw my mud. I knew it in his shape and eyes. I turn back and take the dolly from my pocket. I drop it into the grave and it lands on the lid with a tiny thwack and lies, spread and smiling.

I stumble and look down. The doll lies on the moss and bare earth of the filled-in grave next to a clump of snow-drops. Someone must've planted those and they've spread. Maybe it was Barbara.

I stoop to pick the doll up and sit it so she's resting her back against the headstone like it's a comfy chair she's sitting in. As I walk away her arm sticks straight up, she's waving to me.

67

AFTERLIFE
15 January 1984

I wake in the middle of the night and Mum is standing at the bottom of my bed.

I'm not dreaming and I know it's her straight away.

I recognise the wedding veil she's wearing, birdcage style. She's wearing a suit – I can't see what colour it is because of the light – and there are pale gloves on her hands. A long deep feeling floods through me. It pushes to every part of my body, even right into the hairs that are standing up on my arms.

'Mum?' I struggle to sit, as the thin blankets have wound round me in the night. 'Mum, it's you, isn't it?' I speak softly. I can't bear the thought of someone coming into the room and scaring her away.

She puts her gloved finger to her lips. 'Ssssh,' she says.

She reaches up to take her veil off. 'Don't,' I say in an urgent whisper. I'm worried what I'll see there and for a moment I have the crazy idea that she could even have a bird's head instead of a human one. Stop it, I tell myself.

She lays the veil on the bottom of my bed and it retains its head shape. The veil glows white like a skull. It has knitted itself back together and become miraculously repaired. As fresh as the day it must've fluttered into her hands in the shop.

'Look,' she says.

Her face has that newsprint look that darkness gives but I can still see – she's not striking or glamorous like I imagined. She's almost on the plain side: a small mouth and nose. But her big luminous eyes and the loose hair flowing down over her shoulders make her pretty.

'I wanted to show you my wedding outfit,' she says.

'It's lovely,' I say although it looks quite ordinary to me, just an old-fashioned suit with a spray of flowers tucked into the collar between her breasts.

'I wanted to come looking my best,' she says. 'These are lily-of-the-valley.' She touches the flowers lightly and they resemble skulls too – a row of tiny trembling ones.

I nod. 'I've seen you before,' I say.

'Ah, yes.'

'I saw you in the forest, there was a car . . .' I stop, because a big sob has just racked my body. I sit up and squeeze my arms around my knees.

'Yes, I was coming for you, Ruby. That's the way it is, I'm always coming for you.'

She touches the veil lightly with her finger and thumb. It's so light it does a little jump on the bottom of the bed, springing on the honeycomb blanket like it's alive. Then she tells me all about it. She tells me how it happened.

Anna and Lewis drive back to London in silence after they've left Ruby with Mick and Barbara. It's been agreed that Barbara will take care of her for now and they've been taking most of the last of her little things down. Secretly, Anna has hung onto a few of them. She's pushed them under her jumpers in the chest of drawers so Lewis won't see.

346

Now Anna keeps her eyes on the road but all she sees is a grey blur. The clouds swirl overhead as if animated, as if stirred by restless hands. London has lost its dazzle. It looks flat as a picture postcard to Anna as the car noses into Chiswick. The buildings are filthy, grimed over by bygone peasoupers. Why has she never noticed this before?

Back inside their room Lewis fusses over her.

'You rest,' he says, 'I'll go out and get something for dinner.'

'All right,' she says dully and sits without taking off her coat.

When he returns he has small packets of food wrapped in greaseproof paper and a bottle of red wine. He's been to the deli that they had lunch in that time. The paper crackles as he unwraps cheese and great discs of pinky brown salami. The food that once seemed so exotic to Anna turns her stomach over now. The smells are too penetrating and pungent. She craves invalid fare – blancmange, mashed potato, ice cream. White food.

'It feels like we're celebrating. What are we celebrating, Lewis?' she asks, something twisting at the corners of her mouth.

Lewis is in his waistcoat and shirt, the sleeves rolled up above his elbows. He looks like a fish porter, thinks Anna, or a greengrocer – for once his attraction transmogrifying into something completely ordinary and slightly ridiculous.

'Of course we're not,' he says, keeping his voice smooth. 'We need to build you up is all. And anyway,' a slight temper ruffles the smoothness, 'why shouldn't we enjoy being quiet, just the two of us for a little while? We can concentrate on you getting better.'

He doesn't say it but he felt relief seeing Ruby handed over like that. It felt like he'd stood up straight for the first time in months and a building he'd been carrying on his back slipped away and fell in a landslide of dust and masonry on Barbara's living-room carpet.

'Better?' Anna says in a small voice.

She puts the wine to her mouth but just lets the liquid wet her lips.

'Better?' she echoes.

There are words forming in Lewis's mouth. I never wanted to be a father, he wants to scream. I never asked you for a child. But one came along and time changed. It began to flicker faster so all those things I thought I had a lifetime to achieve had to be done instantly. It all had to be done in a twinkling of an eye and it was too much for me. He bites the words back. 'Take off your coat,' he says, 'and have a glass of wine. Yes, you'll be like new soon, you'll see.'

Better and like new seem far off to Anna, a distant glittering city. Her mind feels fugged over by confusion and pills. She's like one of those houses she saw coming into London. The choking black fog might disintegrate and fall away but she knows it'll leave its mark behind, great dark shapes up the sides of buildings, soot clustered in the corners of windowsills.

In the night Lewis snores gently next to her as she lies wide awake looking at the ceiling. It seems no time at all when morning comes and he gets up for work. He seems to have got another job since she's been away, driving vans for a friend of his.

'You sure you'll be all right?' he asks before he leaves, yesterday's cheeses and salamis made up into doorstep sandwiches of white bread.

She wants to say, no, please don't leave me on my own.

'Yes,' she says.

Once he's gone the room takes on an eerie aspect. It's so quiet. The absence of Ruby is like a wound inside her. She can actually put her hands on the place it hurts – right in her solar plexus, like the baby has been ripped out through her stomach. When she looks down she's amazed to see her skin still intact in her trim yellow dress.

She keeps seeing her brother-in-law Mick's face, in her mind. His eyes dulled over with grief still at the loss of his darling daughter. He was a light switched off. He didn't reach out for Ruby. He barely said a word, sitting back in his chair with those dulled eyes sliding over the baby in Barbara's lap. Outside, weeds had begun to climb over the flowerbeds that were once so neatly kept. Too soon for them both to be doing this, Anna had thought. She's thinking it again now but with a deep certainty in her bones, it's too soon, too soon, too soon.

She needs to go back to the forest. Back to her baby. Her Ruby. She needs to hold her again and not let her go this time. She needs to be rid of this fug so she can do it. She stands abruptly and takes all the bottles of pills to the open window and they fall in shiny plastic rain to the street below.

Without pausing, she takes the car keys off the paint-encrusted hook on the back of the door. She pauses, then turns back. The suitcase is gone, it held Ruby's things in it and all she can find is a cardboard box. She throws everything she can find of hers in there, and a last few things of Ruby's that she's kept – the pink knitted suit, a

349

vest. There's such a sense of urgency she leaves most of her own clothes behind. She's not thinking straight at all. At the last minute she even throws what she can find of the green tea set in there, not wanting to leave behind what her mother had inherited. Her wedding veil and gloves tangle with sweaters and shoes inside the half-empty box as she runs down the stairs.

She tries to remember starting the car exactly as Lewis taught her, the sequence of the pedals. The car does a kangaroo hop and she turns the ignition off, removes her shoes with the sharp pointed heels and starts again. She drives so slowly out of London that cars beep behind her and every time it makes her jump. The heater is still broken so she has to strip jackets and cardigans off as she drives. She stops at one point and takes her tights off too so it's just the thin yellow dress she's wearing.

'Keep driving,' she says to herself as she starts the car up again, clutching the steering wheel. 'Just keep driving. You know how, Lewis taught you. Make your body part of the machine, he said, don't even think about it.' She forgets how she hated him the night before and longs for his solid presence beside her now.

These incantations work until she gets to the recently built motorway. She has to circle the roundabout three times before she can gather the courage to take the slip road. Driving in London is so slow – you may as well be in a horse-drawn carriage. This speed feels terrifying; entering the motorway is like taking a plunge into deep water. She's too scared to stop for a while in case she never regains the courage to carry on. 'Keep going,' she tells herself, 'just keep going. Find your child.'

350

After what seems like an eternity she pulls off and the roads begin to thread narrower and narrower. Then the sight of the forest, standing tall and black ahead, is nearly enough to make her weep. She laughs out loud at the sight of it. The tops of the trees seem like wings ready to swoop down and gather her up. The pain in her solar plexus begins to ease now she can feel Ruby's presence getting ever nearer and nearer. The thought of having left her at all seems ridiculous, preposterous. She takes the curving road up the hill and the River Severn, sparkling in the light, jack-knifes below her in the distance. It's so familiar and quiet now, the driving seems less terrifying so she pulls up and gets out to look, to breathe in the familiar air that contains trace elements of salt and wood smoke and earth. It's beginning to get dark and she shivers, suddenly feeling very alone. She looks down and sees her feet bare on the road. She imagines the London room, the scraps of cheese in greaseproof paper on the table, the unmade bed, the window clotted with dust on the outside. Lewis won't even be home just yet. The forest entrance beckons her, yet also seems to swell as dusk thickens, into the form of a mouth. The back of her head begins to crawl. It looks like the sort of place a Minotaur could live. Of course, she realises suddenly, that creature is not pinned to one place but can bound through tunnels underground. It must have a whole network of them. The dark angel also, whose transport may be above the trees but in the same way is not tethered. Anna jerks open the car door and flings herself inside knowing she must find Ruby before the two finally meet and the earth will open in a giant rent. It's not possible to keep them apart any longer, she doesn't have the strength.

The road enters the forest and there's a sudden move from light to darkness. It's the dark angel's wing unfurling across the road. It was already here, waiting for her all along. The scaled tip of the wing opens further and brushes the trees opposite and she swerves to avoid it. The car begins juddering beneath her hands, out of control. Anna stamps on the pedals, her feet slipping and sliding across the metal and the car swerves. The black leaves of the wing smother over the windscreen just before she hits the tree.

All Anna feels is a turning, a curve downwards into nothingness. It's the last thing. She'll be turning and turning for ever now but the thought remains like a single note hanging in the air for eternity. Find your baby. Find Ruby.

When my mum leaves the room, when the very last of her story has been told, the air remains charged with her presence, as if there are hundreds of tiny crystals dancing there. They've passed right through me too, stroking me a different way like the nap on velvet. I'll always be pointing that way from now.

68

ELIZABETH
16 January 1984

Dr Brannon comes round for the last time in the morning.

'You look different,' he says. 'Older all of a sudden.'

I nod. I know what he means. I can feel it too.

Barbara has arranged for a taxi to pick me up later and my things are packed already. They have been since six o'clock this morning.

Dr Brannon gives me his number. He says he never does that normally but he can sense maybe I might have need of him at some point. That he's liked spending time with me and thinks I've got a lot to offer in life.

No one has ever said anything remotely like this before.

'Thank you,' I say, tucking the card he's given me carefully in the pocket of my jeans.

'And if you ever think you might want to do something about the birthmark when you're older,' he's got that look in his eyes again, the one where it's like his fingers are itching to experiment, 'then get in contact. There are all sorts of techniques being developed as we speak.'

'No.' I smile, then to soften the word because it's come out a bit sharp I say, 'Thank you.'

'Well . . .' He shakes my hand.

When he leaves I fidget for a bit then they come in and strip the bed and tell me I have to go and wait in the day room. I wander in there with my bag but it stinks because that's where people go to smoke.

In the end I walk down the corridor and sit in one of the bay windows. Yesterday I promised Tom I'd come and see Elizabeth before I left when she came in to visit him. I agreed, but now I'm longing for and dreading that glimpse of her flaming head of hair, bright in the distance. I keep jumping up and peering through the top window – it's clear above so it's easier to see. But then I realise I actually feel better being concealed by the opaque glass on the bottom half of the window. I pull my knees up and circle them with my arms and wait for the red and green figure to kangaroo hop across the glass.

In the end I never get to see it, though. It's one of those days when the sun is setting impossibly early, there hardly feels like there's been a scrap of day. Tom comes to find me, wearing his ragged coat over his striped pyjamas and his boots just half done up. It strikes me as a kind of battledress – like he's climbed out from the trenches in the middle of the night during some terrible war.

'Come.' He holds out his hand to me. 'My parents are on their way back, I've heard. Soon they'll know about everything. Let's just the three of us be together before that happens.'

I blink up at him, clutching onto the handle of my bag like it's the only thing left. He says, 'Elizabeth is waiting for us.'

And there she is in the canteen. It's long after lunch so it's near deserted, just a few early guests sipping tea from WRVS mugs. The hushed clink of china and the smell of old food ingrained into the very floor. She's not wearing green; it's a dress that looks like it's made out of tapestry, little flowers embroidered over the cream puffed sleeves. Her coat is in her lap. We look at each other.

'I'm sorry I set fire to your place,' I say at last.

'Oh, Ruby,' she says, half standing. 'Ruby.'

She reaches over the table and pulls me to her and my face goes into her hair and everything turns tangerine.

We sit down and Tom goes to buy tea. The woman behind the counter smiles at him. She's seen his gleam too, just like I can. It has an effect on people for the good. It makes them feel natural and healthy and the way they should feel all the time if the world wasn't so harsh to live in. He comes back slopping tea onto a tray.

'Look,' says Elizabeth. 'I've brought a cake. I'm eighteen soon, I'll be of age. I thought we could celebrate now. I made it myself. There's a proper electric oven in the flat I'm staying in.'

She opens the box and lifts it out so carefully it could be a baby. It's beautiful, shining with hundreds of silver balls on pale green icing, with eighteen pink candles stuck in holders around the rim, that I don't even pause for a moment to feel sad that she's had to make her own birthday cake. She's just ecstatic she's got an oven that switches on as and when you want it.

'Oh,' she frowns, 'I forgot to bring matches.' My heart starts beating a little faster then, but only because I'm expecting them both to look at me when the word 'matches' is said. But they don't, Elizabeth just goes to the counter and asks if she can borrow some and the woman there gives her a lighter out of her handbag.

Elizabeth clicks the lighter, turning the cake around by its silver board as she goes so she doesn't burn her hand. The fire glows on her chin and travels up her face until her green eyes are full of tiny lights. We sing happy birthday and clap and the woman behind the counter joins in. Then Elizabeth blows out all the candles and closes her eyes to wish before she slices into the cake with a knife that she brought with her in the box. The lady comes to collect her lighter back, saying she needs it because she's going for a smoke now, and Elizabeth gives her a piece for later.

The very last of the sun slants in through the windows and makes everything warm. I glance around – there's an old man in a wheelchair dozing in the sun across the room and the woman drinking tea that keeps stealing looks at us out of the corner of her eyes. I imagine how the three of us must appear and the thought gives me a knot of excitement in my belly because I realise, without a shadow of a doubt, that we must be interesting and beautiful.

We talk about everything. We remember Elizabeth teaching me how to gut a rabbit. We talk about Crispin, remember him. We talk about the day I first arrived with my suitcase. We hold hands, the three of us, then stop to shove cake into our mouths and the tea grows cold but we drink it anyway.

We are what our families have made us. But sometimes you can escape that. You can close a door on it and walk into another room. This room is furnished differently. It's all things you chose yourself. My room is furnished with Elizabeth and Tom. The light illuminates them through the window. They glow as brightly as the setting sun.

69

THE BROKEN EYE
1 August 1984

When I run through the forest the trees flicker by so fast I'm like a girl running inside a magic lantern.

I'm running to Tom and Elizabeth's where I am to be found most days. They live in an old forester's cottage, not Hollow Cottage, but like it.

I was a scavenger for family and what I found was love and souls.

I still live with Barbara for the moment, but we live as aunt and niece and it's better that way. We gossip and cook and polish like we're friends. We *are* friends.

But, we are here, we are here, we are here. The departed still come and tell me their stories as if they can hardly believe them themselves. Mum arrives, sits by the fire and waves at us all. I should get her to leave, really, but I'm being selfish and want to hang onto her just a little longer.

I know about my broken eye now. I tend it so it doesn't become any bigger. I'm sorting out what seeps in.

Crispin's long gone.

His parents are also long gone, not dead but gone: accused of neglect and stood trial. Neglect – funny, I would never have used that word to describe the way they were, in that huge house. Tom's parents were lucky to escape prison, we heard. Shadow mutters that they've escaped justice. Crispin's body has been moved and now lies in a churchyard and his mother goes and weeps every day over his bones, so that doesn't sound much like an escape to me.

When Mum comes, she carries the doll I left on her grave that time. Sometimes it's another doll too I don't recognise – one that she said she lost a long time ago and that it was all her fault. She's happy now she's found them both. She lays them carefully on the hearth for them to warm their feet. I tell her how everything's all right, that it turned out all right, and she nods and smiles, though always with an anxious little bob of her head like she can't quite believe me. I don't think she is ready to leave yet either. I guess this world is harder to depart when you've left a child behind in it.

Shadow – Joshua – comes all the time; of course he does, for he is almost myself. We fall in and out of each other and I feel his particles move through mine a hundred times a day. He knows he loves me now, he's told me. He says he's sorry for his covetous ways and that they're long gone.

In the old days I never thought about what it had been like for my parents. My longing was too great. Its hungry mouth ate everything until there was nothing left but its gaping hole. Now, I think about it a lot. They have become real to me now I know their stories. And after all, I called for them and they came. My father and my mother came. My father sent me the only thing left from between them – their wedding ring. I wear it on a chain around my neck – replacing the collar tips – and think of him, as he was, young, proud, handsome.

My mother came. I tell myself now she might have died because of having me, but that's not the same as being responsible for her death. It gives me a lightness of feeling knowing that and knowing how she loved me as best she could.

358

After all, she came back for me, even though she was ill and young, even though she was drugged and desperate. She still came for me, even though she was dead.

Acknowledgements

Thank you to Louisa Joyner for your impeccable editing and for generally being such a damn nice person.

Alice Lutyens for being a superstar agent.

Sophie Portas for your absolutely tireless and brilliant publicity work.

Charlotte Robertson and the sales team. You are all so passionate and a lovely bunch to boot.

Katie Hall for the wonderfully inspired marketing.

Rebecca Ritchie for looking after me so well while Alice was away. Melissa Pimental for your fantastic work in the Curtis Brown foreign rights department. Lily Williams for the sterling work in the film department.

Donna Payne for the haunting and beautiful cover.

Samantha Matthews for the way you project managed the whole book so magnificently.

Tamsin Shelton for your astute copyediting.

James Hannah who took the time from his own brilliant writing (check out *The A to Z of You and Me*) to read the manuscript and give intelligent and incredibly perceptive advice.

Anna Davis and all my fellow Curtis Brown Creative writers.

Sarah Savitt and Hannah Griffiths for finding me.

Faber & Faber for being such a creative and inspirational home.

To my family.

To Mark. For everything. You know.